D1343030

Love Walked
Right In

Pam's saga novels, *There's Always Tomorrow*, *Better Days Will Come*, *Pack Up Your Troubles*, *For Better For Worse* and *Blue Moon*, and her ebook novella *Emily's Christmas Wish*, are set in Worthing during the austerity years. Pam's inspiration comes from her love of people and their stories, as well as her passion for the town of Worthing. With the sea on one side and the Downs on the other, Worthing has a scattering of small villages within its urban sprawl, and in some cases tight-knit communities, making it an ideal setting for the modern saga.

Also by Pam Weaver

Novels

There's Always Tomorrow
Better Days Will Come
Pack Up Your Troubles
For Better For Worse
Blue Moon

Featured Short Story

Christmas Fireside Stories

eNovella

Emily's Christmas Wish

Love Walked Right In

PAM WEAVER

PAN BOOKS

First published 2016 by Pan Books
an imprint of Pan Macmillan
20 New Wharf Road, London N1 9RR
Associated companies throughout the world
www.panmacmillan.com

ISBN 978-1-5098-9556-4

1 3 5 7 9 8 6 4 2

A CIP catalogue record for this book is available from the British Library.

Typeset by Palimpsest Book Production Ltd, Falkirk, Stirlingshire
Printed and bound by CPI Group (UK) Ltd, Croydon, CR0 4YY

Visit **www.panmacmillan.com** to read more about all our books
and to buy them. You will also find features, author interviews and
news of any author events, and you can sign up for e-newsletters
so that you're always first to hear about our new releases.

This book is dedicated to the memory of Jane Pinfield-Wells who, as a child, graciously shared her mother with me and many other foster children during their time of need. Thank you, Jane. R.I.P.

CHAPTER 1

March 1937

'Roo-by!'

Ruby Searle rubbed her floury hands on her apron and put the mixing bowl into the stone sink. Ignoring her husband's call, she glanced up at the clock and smiled to herself. She had made good time. The casserole was already in the oven and the suet dumplings were ready to drop into the dish twenty or thirty minutes before serving. All that remained was the washing up and the laying of the table.

'Ruby . . .' Jim, her husband, sounded agitated, but Ruby knew only too well that he often made something sound desperate when it wasn't desperate at all. Their lives had changed dramatically since Jim fell down some steps some three years before and permanently damaged his legs. When he'd first come out of hospital he'd run rings around her, until her mother pointed out that rushing to do his bidding the second he called did neither of them any good. Still, she wouldn't keep him waiting too long. She filled the mixing bowl with cold water. If she left it for any length of time, any suet stuck on the side would dry hard and make it difficult to wash up quickly.

'Ruby, where are you?'

'Coming,' she called. Ruby was an attractive girl with big sultry eyes, and she wore her dark hair in a short bob, rather like the style of the American film star Louise Brooks.

She'd left her husband outside in the garden and she supposed he was ready to come back inside. He was perfectly capable of getting himself indoors, but because his injury made it an effort, he preferred to get Ruby to help him.

Their house in Heene Road, Worthing, had been unexpectedly inherited from a family friend. It was only a short distance from the sea, although the road and a high shingle bank hid the beach from view. Even though it wasn't strictly true, Ruby and Jim kept its old name, Sea View. The house was light and airy, with the sun on the front in the morning and a sunny aspect in the garden throughout the afternoon.

'Ruby, it's important.' Jim sounded impatient.

She washed her hands, hung up her apron and smoothed down her dress. She loved the feel of the material. She had made it herself from an 'easy-to-make' pattern and she was rather proud of her efforts. The material was red with white spots. It had a scoop neckline with long raglan sleeves coming from a yoke in a contrasting colour, and she had spent several happy evenings with the treadle sewing machine to get it ready for today.

The past few years, and more, had been difficult for both of them. Ever since Jim had fallen on the pavilion steps back in 1934 and been crushed under a weight of bodies, there was an ever-present fear that he might never walk again. While he spent months and months in hospital, 'Magic Memories' – the photography business he'd founded, his pride and joy – had been put on hold. A year after the accident Ruby had had high hopes that things would at last get back to normal when, on her birthday and after weeks of practice, the whole family had met in the newly refurbished Southern Pavilion on Worthing pier and Jim had struggled towards her on two sticks. Sadly, her happiness was short-lived. A bad infection followed and, when he recovered, the discomfort in his hips meant that Jim couldn't stand for any length of time, so going back to wedding photography and taking holiday snaps was out of the question.

Ruby had been devastated. 'It's not fair,' she'd told Bea.

'Life's not fair,' her mother had said philosophically. 'We all have to make the best of what we have. He needs you to be the strong one now.'

At first Ruby had been angry with her mother, but as time went on, she began to see the wisdom of her words and adjusted to the changes in their lives. As it turned out, it wasn't all doom and gloom. When they had been lucky enough to move into Linton Carver's old house, Ruby turned it into a guest house and became the main

3

breadwinner. It was a lot of hard work, but she had never been afraid of that. She had kept reminding her husband that they would be all right, but Jim wasn't all that happy about it.

'A man should support his wife,' he'd said mournfully, 'not the other way around.'

Ruby had sat on the arm of the chair next to him and put her arms around his shoulders. 'I still have you, and that's all that matters,' she'd assured him with kisses. 'Anyway, I'm not doing this on my own. We're a team. We'll do it together.'

But as far as Jim was concerned, the life they'd once dreamed of was slipping away for good, and he made it clear he couldn't see himself playing the role of *bon ami* to the guests.

'Ruby!'

Ruby opened the back door and almost tripped over next door's cat. 'No, no, you can't come in now. Off you go, Biscuit,' she said crossly. 'Shoo.' Biscuit mewed and stepped back, his tail in the air. Ruby closed the door firmly behind her. She didn't want the cat in her kitchen.

Jim was near the hedge at the bottom of the garden and seemed to be hunched over. As she hurried towards him, her heart almost stopped. Had he slipped out of the chair? She should have come at once. Maybe he had been taken ill with some sort of attack? Oh God . . . was he all right?

'Jim, what's happened?'

He turned his head as she came down the garden

and beamed. 'The trap worked, Ruby. Look, I've caught the little beggar!' And Ruby found herself staring into the frightened face of a little grey monkey.

For the whole of the previous week Worthing had been on tenterhooks because an escaped monkey was running up and down the roofs in Rowlands Road. As it darted from one hiding place to another, people tried to be helpful to those aiming to catch it by waving bananas, but the animal's fear of being caught was stronger than its hunger and it remained at large. When the story reached the front page of the *Worthing Herald*, visitors to the town flocked past the Lido and turned inland, craning their necks skywards in the hope of seeing it. Newspaper photographers tried in vain to get that elusive picture. The hunt was also on for the owner of the monkey, but no one seemed to know who it belonged to. Some said it came from the circus in Victoria Park; some believed it belonged to a rich entrepreneur who lived in one of the big houses along Shelley Road; while others thought it had been in the town as part of an exhibition on India and had escaped out of a window. The exhibition had moved to another town, with no mention of a lost monkey, and no one had laid claim to the animal. It was a complete mystery. Once the weekend was over and everybody had gone back to work, the whole thing was treated as little more than a nine-day wonder.

Then, a few days ago, the monkey had come into their garden and Jim had set himself the task of catching it. Ruby wasn't very keen, but it was the first time in weeks that her husband had shown any interest in anything, so she kept quiet. He had shut himself in the shed for a day or two and emerged with a home-made wire trap. Ruby had raised a questioning eyebrow, but he'd left it on the top of a cold frame and had put 'bait' – bits of fruit – all around it. Inside the cage was a large grape, speared on a piece of wire.

Now that Ruby was face-to-face with the monkey, it was obvious what had happened. The little creature had obviously spent some time walking around the cage, eating the food on the outside and, confident that he was safe, had finally been tempted by the grape inside the cage. But as soon as he'd made a grab for it, the wire triggered a spring and the door snapped shut behind him. Despite his frantic screams, the little monkey was trapped.

'Oh, Jim,' cried Ruby, 'poor little thing. What are we going to do?'

'Help me into the bath chair,' said Jim, 'and we'll take it back to the circus.'

Ruby's jaw dropped. 'What – now?' She was horrified at the thought.

'We have to,' said Jim. 'You know they're leaving today. Come on, there's not a moment to lose.'

'But it might not belong to them.'

'Well, we'll soon find out, won't we?' said Jim.

'It looks too small to be in the circus,' Ruby insisted. 'Don't they use chimpanzees?'

'If you've got a better idea, Ruby,' Jim challenged her, 'fire away.'

The monkey regarded her carefully. It was grey, with a black face and ears, and it had a long S-shaped tail. As Jim talked soothingly to it, the little chap sat on its haunches and tackled the grape hungrily.

Ruby's heart sank. The last thing she wanted to do was rush up to Victoria Park. It wasn't far, but it was far enough – probably a good mile and a half inland. 'We can't take it now,' she protested. 'The family will be here soon. Percy and Rachel will be here at noon, and Mother, my father and May are walking over at half-past. We can't be out when they come.'

Jim looked at his watch. 'There's a good hour and a half before they get here. Plenty of time to get to Victoria Park and back again.'

Ruby opened her mouth to say something, but the expression on his face told her arguing would be a waste of time. With a resigned sigh, she trudged wearily back towards the house.

Once Jim was sitting in the bath chair with the cage on his lap, Ruby pulled on her coat and hat. She turned her back so that he wouldn't see her blinking back her tears. Jim could be so infuriating at times. This wasn't meant to happen. By the time they got back, she'd be hot and out of breath from pushing him all the way to the park and back. It was hardly the best way to greet her relatives, but it seemed as if the monkey sensed her irritation more than her husband did.

Normally Ruby enjoyed walking down Heene Road, a road that was cut in two by the road leading to Goring and beyond. Once part of the village of Heene, which

7

had been swallowed up by the ever-growing popularity of Worthing during the Victorian era, the southern end of Heene Road consisted mostly of large houses with big gardens, while the northern end was flanked by more modest terraced houses. The Great War had put an end to the upper-middle-class households with live-in servants, leaving behind a genteel poverty and live-in lodgers.

The old-fashioned bath chair – the only contraption Ruby could afford – was unwieldy, and Jim was no light weight. In 1935 someone had lent them a wheelchair for a while, but it had to go back for a relative, and being inactive for so long meant that Jim's weight had ballooned. Ruby covered the monkey's cage with a piece of blanket and, once it was in the dark, the monkey became less agitated. As she pushed the chair, Ruby almost envied it. If only she could cover herself with a blanket and find a bit of peace and calm.

Right now, she felt cross. Cross with herself, and cross with Jim. She should have dug her heels in and refused to go, but if she had, Jim would only have sulked. This was spoiling what had promised to be a happy occasion with the family. Thank goodness she had got everything ready for them. But just in case finding the monkey's owners took longer than Jim thought, she'd left a note on the kitchen table to say where they were. She had thought of popping next door to ask Mrs McCoody to look out for Percy's car, but she knew how much her neighbour liked to talk. If she stopped to explain what had happened – and, knowing

Mrs McCoody, she would have to share every little detail – the whole trip would take twice as long.

Biscuit followed her down the road, mewing. Ruby shooed him away again. 'I don't understand what's wrong with that stupid cat today.'

It was hard work pushing the bath chair. Jim wasn't very good at steering the front wheel at the best of times and, with the monkey's cage on his lap, he was easily distracted. At the end of the road they hit a stone on the pavement and the chair jolted sharply forwards. The cage slid dangerously near the ground.

'Look out!' Jim snapped. 'You nearly had both of us on the ground.'

Ruby's face flushed with anger. 'You're the one steering,' she said tetchily. 'I'm doing my best.'

Jim was immediately contrite. 'Sorry, love.'

While he heaved himself back into the seat, Ruby gripped the wire to put the cage back onto his lap. At the same time she felt a sharp set of teeth on her fingers. 'Ouch – the little beggar bit me!'

'For God's sake, Ruby, be careful,' Jim said. 'Did it break the skin?'

Ruby examined her fingers. 'No.'

'You could have ended up with blood poisoning,' Jim went on. 'There's no telling what an animal like that has been eating. Use a bit of common sense!'

Fuming, Ruby held her tongue and pushed onwards, but as they turned into Cowper Road, Jim said, 'Oh, bugger! I think it's just peed on me.'

With an exaggerated sigh, Ruby stopped the bath

9

chair and rearranged the cage, this time on top of the blanket, but too late to prevent the wet patch on Jim's best trousers.

'What's the time?'

'Five past eleven.'

This was going to take a lot longer than they'd both thought. Ruby pursed her lips and set off for a third time.

Victoria Park, a large area of green sandwiched between terraced houses and a school, was almost empty. The big top and the animals were gone, although there were a few circus people milling around, clearing up the rubbish. A couple of children played outside a caravan. Eventually Ruby caught up with one man and they showed him the monkey.

''Taint ours,' he declared firmly, as he sniffed back the dewdrop on the end of his nose and wiped it with the back of his hand.

'He must be,' said Jim. 'Who else would have a monkey?'

'Sorry, mate,' said the man, shaking his head and walking away.

'Well, we can't keep him,' Ruby called after him desperately. 'I run a guest house near the sea. The guests won't take kindly to a monkey running around the place. Isn't it possible you can give him a home?' The man hesitated, and Ruby crossed her fingers behind her back. 'He's very tame.'

'Sorry, darlin',' said the man. 'Wrong sort. That's a grey langur. Comes from India. Got any organ-grinders

10

left in Worthing?' He chortled, revealing a line of brown and broken teeth. 'Them's the sort they use.'

There was nothing left for it but to trudge all the way back home with the wretched thing. Ruby and Jim didn't speak, but the atmosphere between them was very tense. They arrived back at Sea View just as her brother Percy and her sister-in-law, Rachel, pulled up in the car. For Ruby, coping with a lost monkey was overtaken by the thrill of seeing her four-month-old niece again.

'Hello . . . hello, sweetheart. How are you both? Hasn't she grown . . . Oh, you're beautiful. Come in, come in.'

Jim struggled out of the bath chair and, using his two sticks, wobbled towards the back door. Biscuit was back again, mewing and threading himself around people's legs. 'Damned cat,' murmured Jim as he pushed it away with his foot.

'Hang on a minute, mate.' Percy was unloading gifts from the boot of the car: flowers, some fresh eggs and a couple of bottles of beer. 'I've got something here that might help you.'

Inside the house, Ruby and Rachel hugged each other, then Rachel held her at arm's length. 'New dress?'

Ruby nodded. 'I made it myself,' she said, giving a twirl.

'It's gorgeous,' said Rachel, 'and red really suits you, with your dark hair.'

'You look amazing as well!' Her sister-in-law was looking particularly lovely in a green silk blouse with a fan-tail at the back of the waist. Her black pencil skirt complemented it perfectly.

Rachel stooped to take Alma out of her Moses basket and put her into Ruby's arms. The two of them looked at each other. Alma was a pretty child with thick, dark hair like her mother, and she had her father's merry eyes. She was awake and regarded Ruby with a curious stare, her mouth poised in an 'oooh' shape. Ruby's heart melted as she smiled and talked softly to her niece.

Percy pushed the door wide open and Jim crashed inside.

'Look what he's brought me, Ruby,' said Jim. He was walking behind a brand-new upright wheelchair. Ruby gasped with delight. 'It's the very latest model. Isn't it terrific?'

It certainly was. She'd seen a chair just like that in a magazine. It was very expensive, an Allwin Ensign with padded armrests, a sturdy canvas seat and a back that could be placed in two separate positions. The frame was metal, and the sloping handlebars made it look a lot easier to push than the bath chair. It had a footrest for Jim's feet as well. 'It can be folded away,' said Percy, demonstrating, 'so it won't take up too much room.'

'Percy, it's amazing,' said Ruby, giving her brother a kiss on the cheek. She could hardly take it in. 'It must have cost a fortune. You shouldn't have done it.'

'Why not?' Percy shrugged. 'We're family.'

The two men took themselves off to the sitting room with the beer bottles and a couple of glasses, while Ruby handed the baby back to her mother.

'What's that?' asked Rachel, jerking her head towards the monkey cage, which had been left on the floor by the back door. Ruby pulled back the blanket and her sister-in-law exclaimed, 'Good Lord!'

'We'd better keep it well away from the baby,' said Ruby, lifting the cage onto the very top of the dresser. 'And you be careful, too. It bit my fingers when I put my hand on the wire.' The monkey hopped from one side to the other, but there wasn't much room for it to move.

'What in heaven's name are you going to do with it?' asked Rachel. 'And where on earth did it come from?'

Ruby explained what had happened. 'I've no idea who it belongs to, but it obviously can't stay in that thing very long. It's far too small.'

'Are you going to keep it?'

'Absolutely not,' said Ruby. 'I don't want a thing like that running around the house.'

'If you can't find the owner,' said Rachel, 'it's probably better to let it go again.'

'I already suggested that, but Jim won't hear of it,' replied Ruby, pushing a piece of banana in between the bars. 'And another thing: what do we feed it on? I'm sure it needs more than just bananas.'

The animal settled down to eat again, and Ruby put an eggcup full of water into the cage with it. After washing her hands, her thoughts turned towards her guests. Before long, the kettle was on for a cup of tea.

Rachel glanced towards the sitting-room door. 'How is Jim these days?' she asked in a low tone.

Ruby sighed. 'I don't know how to answer that,' she began. 'Miserable, grumpy, difficult . . .' Her voice trailed off. Rachel reached out and gave her arm a sympathetic squeeze. 'I know what happened to him was awful,' Ruby went on, 'but it's like he's given up trying, and I don't know what to do.'

'Oh, Ruby,' said Rachel sympathetically.

Things had changed so much that it was hard to remember the carefree man who had wooed her and won her heart only a few years before. Ruby sighed. When they had married, she had loved Jim to bits and had been happy to give up all her dreams of foreign places and travel. She had promised to love him in sickness and in health, but as it turned out, they had only had a few short weeks of young love before everything changed. Although she knew she would keep her marriage vows, sometimes she felt old before her time. She was not yet twenty-one – good gracious, she wasn't even old enough to vote under the Equal Franchise Act – and yet she was having to deal with some very difficult issues. And then there was the question of babies . . .

She shivered and forced herself to think of better things. She was lucky, she told herself. She had a loving family and good friends. She had a roof over her head and people who genuinely loved her. She glanced at Rachel again. Rachel had known heartache too. She had miscarried her first baby in 1935. Alma had been born the following year in December.

With the men out of the room, Rachel unbuttoned

her pretty green blouse and little Alma sucked at her mother's breast contentedly. But although she smiled, Ruby felt the ache in her heart grow with every passing minute. No, she mustn't keep thinking about it. No good ever came of longing for something that might never be.

'Any chance of something to eat?' Jim called from the other room. 'Only my stomach thinks my throat is cut.'

Ruby gave her sister-in-law a quick smile. 'Not long now,' she called cheerfully. 'Just waiting for the spuds to boil.'

'In that case, bring us both another beer,' said Jim, and Ruby rose to do his bidding.

'So tell me,' she said, returning to the kitchen. Her sister-in-law had leaned back in her chair and put Alma onto her shoulder. 'What have you two been doing with yourselves?'

'Percy's business is going from strength to strength,' said Rachel, patting Alma's back. 'And most of my days are taken up with looking after the baby.'

Ruby was glad for them. Neither of them had had an easy start to life. As a child, and through no fault of his own, Percy had suffered for years under Nelson's harsh regime. His father had always resented the boy, and there were times when her half-brother had suffered more than one tanning in a day. Their relationship was never that good and so eventually, when he was old enough, Percy stood up to his father. Things had changed from that moment on. He'd left home and joined Oswald

Mosley's Blackshirts, just to spite Nelson. Although he had learned new skills whilst he was with them (skills that had been very useful after he'd left), he'd never really embraced their ideology. The one good thing that had come out of that whole episode was meeting Rachel. Percy was smitten from the moment he saw her.

Her sister-in-law had been a Jewish refugee who had escaped the tyranny of Nazi Germany in 1934. She had come to England after her own sister and nephew had been murdered; but, rather than nurse her grief, Rachel had attended British Union of Fascists rallies as a heckler, determined that people should know what Fascism really meant. She was a tough woman, but she had a gentle and loving spirit. Their baby was her pride and joy, and Rachel was a good mother.

'Percy is branching out again.' Rachel was putting a blanket on the floor and she placed the baby on top. Alma kicked her legs happily. 'He's going into long-distance haulage.' Having learned to drive, Ruby's brother Percy had begun working for a small business delivering perishable goods from Covent Garden to upmarket restaurants in London. He did well, and before long he was driving his own vans. 'We're looking for a place with some land. I'm trying to persuade him to come in this direction.'

'Good-o,' said Ruby, genuinely pleased. 'Sounds just like our Percy. Always looking ahead.'

Rachel smiled. 'He's not the only one, you know,' she said teasingly. Ruby put the cloth on the table and laid the knives and forks on the top. 'I've just joined a

committee trying to get Jewish people out of Europe.'
Rachel began to set the table.

'Why?' asked Ruby.

'I know what they're going through,' said Rachel,
'and I have to do something. They can't work. Their
houses are confiscated. They're not allowed to mix with
other people, and prices are so high that all their money
is being used up. We have to help these people before
it's too late.'

'We?'

'Mrs Whichelow and I work for the Deborah
Committee,' said Rachel. 'We have pledged ourselves to
help single Jewish women get out of Germany while
we still can. Other committees work for families, but
what happens to single unmarried girls on their own?'

'Britain is only a small island. Where will they all
go?'

'They can stay in this country, if they can get work.'
She hesitated. 'Ruby, I wanted to ask you something.'

'Fire away.'

'Would you consider taking some of our girls in?
We are looking for good, clean accommodation. These
people have absolutely nothing and many of them are
traumatized by the time they arrive here. I know you
would be an ideal person to help them.'

Ruby cast her mind back to Isaac Kaufman, a German
escapee who had been in the same digs as Jim before
they got married. His landlady had thrown him out
when her Blackshirt lodger objected to living under the

17

same roof as a Jew. Ruby chewed her bottom lip anxiously. 'Oh, Rachel,' she began apologetically.

Her sister-in-law's face coloured. 'No, no, don't worry,' she cut in. 'It's all right. Forget I asked.'

'It's not that I don't want to help,' Ruby explained. She lowered herself onto a chair. 'It's just that this guest house is the only way I can make a living. The house at Newlands Road, where Mum and I lived, is empty at the moment; and, with Jim as he is, I can't leave him to go out to work. The guests are my only source of income.'

'We can pay you!' said Rachel. 'We are a charity, but we ask people to sponsor them. I promise you, if you agree to have them, your income would be guaranteed.'

Now Ruby felt embarrassed. 'I wouldn't want you to think . . .'

'Ruby darling,' said Rachel, 'I know what you and Jim – and your mother, for that matter – did for Isaac. I would never expect you to make yourselves destitute by trying to help a fellow human being. The way it works is that the charity pays for their board and lodging and, as soon as their papers come through, they move on.'

'In that case,' said Ruby, 'we'd be delighted to have them.'

'Don't you need to discuss it with Jim?' asked Rachel.

Ruby shook her head. Jim took little interest in the guest house. 'It'll be fine,' she said.

'Do you know anyone else?' asked Rachel. 'I mean, could you recommend another guest house?'

'Mrs McCoody next door,' replied Ruby. 'I don't know her well, but she keeps a clean house and she's often sent her people to me, if she's already full.'

'I'll pop round and see her sometime,' said Rachel.

There was a soft knock on the back door and Bea called, 'Anyone at home?' as she walked into the kitchen, with Biscuit hard on her heels.

'Mum!' cried Ruby, running to hug her. 'Lovely to see you.'

Clutching the bottle of beer that Ruby had pushed into his hand, Rex Quinn joined the other male members of the family. The house had two reception rooms down-stairs: one at the front of the house, which was used as a dining room for Ruby's guests, while the room Rex had entered was for the family. It was comfortably furnished with plenty of sofas and a bookcase in the corner. French doors led out into the garden, with a small vegetable patch to one side, which Ruby did her best to keep neat and tidy. From the sitting room, they could see across the grass to a tall hedge at the bottom of the garden, which hid the washing line and the compost heap from view.

'They're still clucking over the baby then?' said Jim.

Rex smiled. 'That's about the sum of it,' he said. He glanced towards Percy. 'Can't say I blame them. She's a pretty little thing.'

Percy grinned proudly.

'Good trip?' asked Rex as they all sat down. Jim

handed him the bottle-opener and he tackled the cap with a seasoned hand.

'Not too bad,' said Percy. 'We did it in under two hours today. There wasn't a lot of traffic.'

Rex poured his drink into a glass and all three men sipped their beers.

'You and Mum completely settled here now?' asked Percy.

Bea and Ruby's father had relocated to the other end of Heene Road, where Rex, a GP, had a good practice and was popular with his patients. They had lived in Hastings when they first married, taking Ruby's younger half-sister May with them; but as soon as the full extent of Jim's injuries became apparent, they had returned to Worthing to help out.

'I think so.' Rex nodded. 'This is quite a nice road. Not as quiet as the bungalow in Hastings, but the practice is growing all the time.'

'That's good,' said Percy.

As if synchronized, they all raised their glasses and sipped more beer. After a short pause, Rex said, 'I saw the wheelchair you brought for Jim. Rather splendid, isn't it?'

'Much better than that old bath chair,' Jim agreed. 'Ruby is useless at pushing.'

'I noticed,' said Percy with a laugh. 'When we arrived, you and Ruby had only just come back from somewhere.'

Jim explained about the monkey.

'I'd take it to the vet's,' said Percy, rearranging the

cushion at his back. 'You can't keep it here, can you? Ruby's got enough on her plate.'

'If I take it to the vet's,' said Jim, 'he's just as likely to put it down.'

The other two nodded sagely.

'No, I've decided I'm going to make a bigger cage,' said Jim. 'We'll keep him here. He shouldn't be too much trouble.'

They drank more beer, each lost in his own thoughts.

Rex turned to his son-in-law. 'Have you been back to the swimming pool, Jim?' When he and Bea first came back to Worthing, Rex had taken him to the municipal swimming baths across the road every Saturday, but lately Jim had made excuses, complaining that the water was too cold or the pool was too crowded.

Jim shook his head. 'I reckon it's not doing me much good,' he said glumly.

'Shame,' said Percy.

'There's not much point,' said Jim, 'seeing as how I'm going to be like this for the rest of my life.'

'Chin up, old chap,' said Percy.

'You should try to keep moving,' said Rex, absent-mindedly running his finger along the rim of his glass. 'Remember the old adage: *If you don't use it, you'll lose it.*'

The three of them raised their glasses again.

'I was talking to a mate of mine the other day,' Percy said, after a quiet burp. 'He's a watchmaker. He tells me he's looking for someone to do watch repairs.'

'That might be something you could do, Jim,' said Rex enthusiastically. 'You could sit down to do that.'

'I don't know anything about watches,' replied Jim.

'He said he'd be willing to teach you,' said Percy.

Jim frowned. 'I hope you haven't been going around telling all and sundry my business,' he said crossly.

'Of course not,' said Percy. 'He happened to ask me if I knew anyone who was willing to learn, and I told him about you – that's all.'

The atmosphere had chilled, but they still drank in unison.

'What about some other interest?' asked Rex. While they were on the subject, he didn't want to let it go until they'd made some sensible suggestions. 'What do you enjoy, apart from photography?'

'Nothing,' said Jim.

'How about writing an article on photography?' Rex suggested. 'There are plenty of magazines out there that are willing to buy something from an expert.'

'Or maybe you should think about teaching people about photography?' Percy added.

'I don't know why the both of you are so preoccupied with me and my life,' said Jim tetchily.

'No offence,' replied Rex quickly.

'Sorry,' said Percy, and they lapsed into another awkward silence as they concentrated on what was left of their drinks.

'Nice drop of beer that,' said Percy, draining his glass. 'Bright Star of Sussex – it's brewed near Lewes.'

The other two smiled appreciatively, and all three of them wished the dinner would hurry up.

The women had spent their time in the kitchen. Ruby saw her mother two or three times a week, but she was still delighted to have the whole family together. As soon as she'd come in, May, looking particularly pretty in a cream dress with a blue sash, had gone straight to the dresser and looked up at the monkey. She begged her sister to get it down, so that she could have a closer look, but Ruby refused.

'Sorry, darling, it's not safe. It's a wild animal and it may bite.'

'But I know how to look after animals,' May protested. 'I've got my pets' badge at Brownies.'

'May,' Bea sighed. 'Please don't argue with your sister.'

'You can play with Alma, if you like,' said Rachel, and a second or two later May was sitting on the floor beside Alma, the monkey quite forgotten.

Ruby smiled. Her younger sister was doing well at school and was all set to go to Worthing High School for Girls by the time she reached eleven later that year. An accomplished reader, she was good at sports and enjoyed drawing and painting as well. Any fears the family might have had about her not coping with her father Nelson's death were short-lived, once her mother and Rex had married. The stability that Rex had brought into their lives seemed to make May flourish.

When Ruby finally called the men, everybody came together in the kitchen.

'We were beginning to think you'd forgotten all about us,' Percy teased.

'All that clucking over the baby,' said Rex.

'I imagine you were doing your fair share in the sitting room,' said Bea.

'Absolutely not,' replied Rex, pulling his chair out and sitting down. 'Men don't cluck. We were having a proper conversation.'

'Time to eat now, May,' said Ruby.

'Up to the table now, darling,' said Bea, and her younger daughter got up reluctantly. Ruby smiled sympathetically.

At long last everybody was ready. She had put Jim at the other end of the table, with Rex next to him, then Rachel. Ruby sat at the top of the long table, next to Percy, May and Bea. It was lovely having them all together again, and she couldn't help thinking how well everybody looked.

As for Bea herself, the transformation in her life was amazing. The gaunt face and bad chests that had put her in her bed for the greater part of the winter were long gone. These days Bea was the picture of good health and looked younger than ever. Although she was still wheezy at times, she had lost the worry lines from her face and, best of all, she laughed a lot. Today her mother wore a smart yellow jacket with a matching half-pleated skirt. The jacket had a pocket at the shoulder with a blue handkerchief in it. The colour matched the buttons on the jacket and a small blue belt at her waist. Her hair was cut short and she had a permanent wave.

Ruby smiled at her mother admiringly. Bea had always had flair when it came to clothes. It was clear that Rex adored her and did his best to make her happy. She herself loved having a father to hug. Although Nelson had always found time for May, he had never shown her any affection. On the other hand, Rex – her real father – was a good man, and Ruby was so glad that he'd come back into their lives. Since the accident, Rex had also spent a lot of time with Jim, encouraging him to persevere with his walking, although just lately she had noted that Jim was becoming less and less inclined to try.

Inevitably the conversation drifted towards the unsettling news coming out of Germany. 'Do you reckon we'll go to war, Rex?' asked Percy.

'If we do,' said Jim, 'they say the civilian population will be in as much danger as the front-line soldier.'

'You may be right there,' Rex sighed. 'I've just been sent a government memorandum about these new air-raid precautions.'

Ruby shivered. 'Oh, please let's not talk about war on a day like today. I've so been looking forward to being with you all.'

Her father reached across the table and grasped her hand. 'And we love being with you too, my dear.'

'How's the guest house?' her mother asked. 'Are you getting many bookings?'

'It's a bit slow at the moment,' Ruby admitted, 'but

in the summer months we've got a full house. I've even had to turn some people away.'

'That's a shame,' Rex observed.

'They'll only be next door,' Ruby laughed. 'I've sent them to Mrs McCoody's. She'll look after them, I'm sure.'

Rachel came back from the scullery, where she'd been changing the baby's nappy, and they watched her putting little Alma back in her carrycot. May covered her up adoringly.

'Did May tell you she's enrolled in a ballet class?' said Bea, suddenly breaking the spell.

'Ballet!' cried Ruby. 'I didn't know you liked dancing.'

'Oh, but I do,' said May. 'And Miss Beech says I'm not too bad.'

Ruby suppressed a smile. Whatever would Nelson have made of this? His little princess doing ballet.

'Do you have to wear proper ballet shoes?' asked Rachel.

May nodded. 'And a tutu.'

'Can we come and watch you?' asked Ruby.

'They'll be doing a show at the end of the summer term,' said Bea. 'I'll make sure you get an invitation. It's to raise funds for the sick and destitute.'

'A worthy cause,' said Percy, lighting up a cigarette. He took a long drag. 'I don't know about you, but I could do with a brisk walk along the sea front, to blow the cobwebs away. Anybody feel like coming?'

The idea was greeted with great enthusiasm. 'We'll

help Ruby stack the dishes first,' said Bea. 'It's not fair to leave her with all the work.'

Ruby protested, but her mother waved her away. The three women made light work of clearing the table and putting the leftover food in the meat safe and the pantry. Rachel emptied the teapot into the slop bucket under the sink, while Ruby rinsed an empty milk bottle and opened the back door to put it on the step for the milkman to take, when he called in the morning. As she put it down, she heard the sound of falling bottles and looked up sharply. The back doors of the two neighbouring houses faced each other, and Biscuit had knocked over all the milk bottles on Mrs McCoody's doorstep. The brown cardboard tops had come off and the little cat was greedily lapping the milk, which had run all along the path. Suddenly Ruby froze.

'What's the matter?' said Rachel, coming up behind her.

'Oh, dear God!' said Ruby, her voice breathy and anxious.

Bea had come to join them too.

'The cat has knocked over the milk,' said Rachel with a chuckle. 'So what?'

'Not just one bottle,' said Bea. 'It looks like she's knocked over all of them.' She put her hand to her mouth as realization dawned. 'Oh dear . . .'

'What?' said Rachel.

'Mrs McCoody has a pint of milk a day,' said Ruby quietly. The colour had drained from her face.

'Well, there's four there now, and all the tops have

come off,' said Bea. 'One has spilled all over the drive, but the other two—'

'Are completely solid,' said Ruby. She looked at her sister-in-law. 'If this was summer, you would expect milk left outside in the heat to turn fairly quickly, but it's March. It's not even warm.'

The three women looked at each other as a feeling of dread washed over them all.

'Now that I come to think about it,' said Ruby, 'that cat has been a pain for days. He's been outside the kitchen meowing all the time, trying to get into the house, following me down the road.' She paused. 'Oh, Mum . . . Are you thinking what I'm thinking?'

'May, you stay here and keep an eye on Alma, will you, dear?' said Rachel.

'Rex,' Bea called over her shoulder. 'Can you come here a minute, darling. I think we might need you.'

By now Ruby was halfway down the drive, with Rachel hard on her heels. 'Is Mrs McCoody very old?'

Ruby shook her head. 'Not really. She's forty . . . forty-five. She runs Sunny Beaches on her own. Like I said, we sometimes recommend each other, if we're already booked up and other trippers arrive.'

By the time they reached the back door, Biscuit had fled and Bea and Rex were tearing down the driveway. Ruby knocked on the door, but there was no answer. Rachel peered through the kitchen window, but could see nothing. Several large flies crawled along the inside of the glass. Ruby tried the handle, but the door was locked.

'Do you have a key?' asked Bea, coming up behind them.

Ruby felt sick. She should have thought about this before. Why hadn't she put two and two together? Mrs McCoody was devoted to her cat. She would never have left Biscuit outside to fend for himself. If only she had been paying attention, she might have realized there was a problem sooner. She could only hope that she wasn't too late. She lifted a flower pot by the step and they found the key underneath. It didn't take a second to get the door open.

'Let me go first, Ruby,' said Rex, as the rank smell of something putrid drifted towards them. 'Stay here.'

He crossed the kitchen in four strides and disappeared down the hallway. Ruby couldn't wait. Despite her mother's protestations, she followed her father.

The cloying smell was even sharper in the dark hall. It went into her mouth and stuck in her throat. Ruby pulled her cardigan sleeve over her hand and clamped it to her mouth as she went forward, but she couldn't stop herself from gagging. The sound of buzzing filled the air as her head was bombarded by flies. A second later her father came out of the sitting room.

'I think this is a job for the police,' he said, taking Ruby's arm and propelling her back towards the kitchen. 'I'm afraid there's nothing we can do. She's been dead for some time.'

CHAPTER 2

'So, when did you last see Mrs McCoody?'

Ruby stared into the middle distance as she stirred her tea and tried to collect her thoughts. Finding her neighbour dead had been the most awful shock. Her father hadn't allowed her to see the body, so perhaps that was why everything seemed so unreal. Ruby felt as if she was in some sort of ghastly nightmare. In a moment she would wake up and everything would be back to normal. She wasn't close to Mrs McCoody, but she was appalled that her neighbour had been dead for so long before she'd realized anything was wrong.

'Mrs Searle?'

Ruby was sitting at the kitchen table with Jim and Sergeant Williams, who was taking everything down in his policeman's notebook. The day that she had looked forward to and planned for so long was utterly ruined. It wasn't often that the whole family managed to get together and this was the first time little Alma had been in her home.

Rachel and Percy had taken May and the baby for a walk as soon as the police arrived. Everybody thought it best to shield May from what was going on, as far as it was possible. Rex was still next door and would stay there until the undertaker came to remove the body. The only outward signs that something had happened were the fact that every window in the house was thrown wide open and a lone constable stood guard by the gate.

'Mrs Searle?' Sergeant Williams repeated. His voice brought Ruby back to the here and now. 'When did you last see your neighbour?'

'Monday,' said Ruby dully. 'No, Wednesday. That was the day Mrs McCoody went to see her friend in the nursing home.'

'Wednesday was the day I went to see the doctor,' Jim corrected.

Ruby gave him a quizzical look as she struggled to comprehend.

'You came with me,' Jim insisted.

'Oh yes,' said Ruby. She kept remembering the flies and the awful smell. Why hadn't she gone round when Biscuit kept worrying her? Why hadn't she put two and two together?

'Do you know which nursing home?' asked Sergeant Williams.

'Umm?'

'The nursing home where Mrs McCoody's friend was,' said Sergeant Williams.

Ruby shook her head. She had been told once, but she couldn't remember it now.

'What was her friend's name?' Clearly the sergeant didn't want to give up.

31

Ruby shrugged and then exclaimed, 'Elsie. Her name was Elsie.'

'Elsie who?'

Ruby frowned crossly. 'I don't know.' She looked away. Why didn't the man go away, with his stupid, unanswerable questions? She felt a gentle hand go over hers and looked up at her mother.

'Darling, you'll wear the bottom of the cup out, if you don't stop stirring that spoon.'

Ruby glanced down and took the spoon out of her tea.

'Do you think all this could wait until tomorrow?' Bea asked. 'Only my daughter looks exhausted.'

'No, no,' said Ruby, coming back to life. 'I'll be fine.' She took a deep breath. 'Jim's right. We were at the doctor's on Wednesday, so I must have talked to her last Monday.'

'And you, sir?'

Jim grunted and shrugged his shoulders. 'Weeks ago.'

'We were never close,' said Ruby quickly, 'but we got on all right. We helped each other out, if we had too many guests, but we didn't spend much time in each other's houses.'

She suddenly felt awful again. Perhaps, if she'd been more caring, she might have noticed that Mrs McCoody's washing had stayed on the line for the best part of a week.

'There were so many flies . . .' said Ruby quietly.

'She had the electric fire on,' said Sergeant Williams. 'The room was very hot.'

Ruby shuddered. 'How did she die?'

'It appears to be natural causes,' said Sergeant Williams.

'How old was she?' Ruby asked.

'Fifty-two,' said the sergeant. 'Do you recall if she had any relatives?'

Ruby shook her head. 'Mr McCoody died some time ago. He had TB. As far as I know, Mrs McCoody has always been on her own.'

Sergeant Williams closed his notebook. 'I know this has been a traumatic time for you, Ruby, but you mustn't blame yourself in any way. There was probably nothing any of us could have done.' He rose to his feet. 'If you think of anything else I should know – no matter how small – you know where to contact me.'

Ruby gave him a thin smile. 'Oh, Mum,' she said as he left the room, 'why on earth didn't I twig? Do you think I could have saved her, if I'd been more neighbourly?'

'You heard what the sergeant said,' said Bea. 'You mustn't go blaming yourself, darling. We all lead such busy lives.'

Her mother was right, but it was of small consolation to Ruby. She hated the thought of Mrs McCoody all alone in her sitting room for perhaps as long as four or five days, with only the flies for company.

Ruby laid her head on Jim's shoulder. They were alone and she was sitting on the arm of his chair. Her mother, Rex and May had just gone, and Percy, Rachel and little

Alma were halfway home already. Ruby was feeling utterly drained.

Jim patted her leg tenderly. 'You mustn't blame yourself, love,' he said quietly.

'I can't stop myself thinking about that washing,' she said, returning once again to the same old question. 'Why didn't it register with me that it had been there since last Monday?'

'Monday isn't the only day you do the washing, when you have a guest house,' he said. 'You know that yourself.'

'But she didn't have any guests.'

'You know that now,' said Jim, 'but she didn't always tell us when she'd got boarders in, did she? Ruby, it's not your fault.' He turned his head to look at her. 'It's not your fault.'

Something stirred between them. His hand on her thigh seemed to gain heat. He lifted his head as she lowered hers and, as their lips met, a pulse of electricity was unleashed. That first kiss was clumsy, but she was aware of his hand cupping her cheek and then he pulled her head towards him. His tongue probed her mouth and Ruby responded eagerly. This was the first time in what seemed like a lifetime that he'd kissed her like this. It had been so long – too long. Every cell in her body ached for him. Her heartbeat had gone through the roof and she could already feel herself expanding and moistening her panties. God, she wanted him. She wanted him so badly. His hand found its way into her blouse and she moaned softly as he touched her bare

34

skin. Her hand followed the line of his body, unfamiliar now, travelling from his chest to his waist and on towards his crutch. 'Oh, Jim . . . Jim . . .'

But the moment she touched him, his whole body stiffened. Confused, Ruby covered his face with kisses as she murmured his name. He shifted in the chair and grasped her wrist. 'No, Ruby,' he said gruffly, pushing her away. 'I can't.'

Ruby was devastated. 'Darling, please.'

'I can't face it. My legs – they're not up to it. It'll be too painful.' He pushed himself out of the chair and stood up with his back to her.

'Even if we don't . . . you know,' Ruby began desperately, 'we could still have a cuddle, couldn't we?'

'I'm tired,' he said, avoiding her eye. 'I'm going to bed.'

She reached out for him, but he'd picked up his sticks and moved away. She wanted to burst into tears and scream, *What's the matter with you? Aren't you a man any more?* But instead she sucked in her lips and bit back the tears as she watched him shuffle towards the door.

'Do you want me to make a drink for you?'

'No thanks,' he said, without even turning round, and as he left the room and closed the door, she was left staring at the wood. She cried for a bit; silent tears, but every bit as painful as those with sound. What had happened? For one wonderfully glorious moment she had thought the old Jim was back, but just as before, he would only go so far before the feeling evaporated.

She'd always thought the male sexual drive was the one that needed taming, but she was left with every fibre in her switched on, hungry for satisfaction and with nowhere to go.

Ruby washed her face and combed her hair before she entered the bedroom. Jim was already under the covers and pretending to be asleep. Part of her wanted to make a scene, even shout at him; but then she thought that perhaps if she gave him another chance, maybe, just maybe . . . She undressed, but didn't put her nightie on. Climbing into bed, she switched off the light and moved closer to him. With her arm over his waist, she kissed the back of Jim's neck and his left ear. There was no response, so she pressed herself suggestively into his back.

'Ruby, stop it,' he said.

'Jim, darling . . .'

'I said no.' His voice was harsh. 'Behave yourself.'

'Behave myself?' she said crossly. 'Are you made of lead or something? We're married, for God's sake.' He didn't respond. Hot tears sprang into her eyes again. 'Jim, talk to me.'

But there was only silence.

Ruby moved away and, sitting up, reached for her nightdress under the pillow. 'Is this how it's going to be for the rest of our married life?' she demanded. 'I'm not made of stone, you know. You treat me like a leper. What's wrong with you? There was a time when you couldn't keep your hands off me.'

Her husband remained infuriatingly silent. Ruby banged her pillow and threw herself back down on the bed. 'Answer me, Jim.' By now her voice was bordering on the hysterical. 'Why don't you want me any more?' What's wrong with me? Don't you love me any more?'

'For God's sake, Ruby,' he said in an exasperated tone, 'do you have to be the drama queen every time?'

Ruby felt her face flush with pent-up anger. 'Jim, it's been more than two years.'

He turned over angrily. 'Yes, it's been two years.' The light was off, so she couldn't actually see his face, but as he spoke she could feel a fine spray of spittle coming from his mouth. 'Two years and four months, since you persuaded me to go to that damned rally at the pavilion and I ended up with half a ton of people falling on top of me.'

Ruby opened her mouth to say something, but Jim wasn't finished yet.

'Ever since that day, I've endured such hell,' he spat. 'I've lost my livelihood, I've lost everything I ever dreamed of, I can't work – and I can't even bloody walk properly. I tell you, I'm sick of it.'

'Well, it's hardly been a walk in the park for me, either,' she snapped.

'I can't see why not,' he retaliated. 'You've got everything you want: this house, the guests. You rule the roost, don't you? Mrs Congenial Landlady, woman of means.'

'Are you punishing me then?' she cried in disbelief.

'Me, me, me,' he said. 'It's always about you, Ruby.

All about what *you* want. All about what makes *you* happy. What about me?'

He turned his back again, and Ruby was left gobsmacked and trying to understand his stinging rebuke. Was she really that selfish? She had moved heaven and earth to care for him. Why was Jim so angry with her?

'Do you really hate me that much?' she asked quietly.

'I don't hate you, Ruby,' he said, his voice muffled by the pillow. 'I just want to be left alone. Now go to sleep.'

Go to sleep? How could she go to sleep when he'd just said all those things? She'd always thought that, in some respects, they were lucky. It had never dawned on her that Jim actually blamed her for what had happened, but clearly he did.

The guest house relieved them both of the worry about where the next penny was coming from; and, if they didn't have the guest house, they wouldn't have anything like this standard of living. Jim had got some sickness money from an assurance policy he'd taken out, but that only lasted for two years. He'd paid into a slate club at the pub as well, but that only gave him a few shillings a week and would come to an end shortly.

Trembling, Ruby lay there and, trying to grasp the enormity of Jim's bitterness, struggled to recall the sequence of events on that fateful night. He was right: she had been the one to suggest going to the British Union of Fascists meeting at the Southern Pavilion, but only because she was concerned that, after so many survivors of the regimental firing squad had themselves

38

been murdered, Colonel Blatchington might be in danger as well. Jim had never supported her in her investigations. In fact he'd pooh-poohed the idea and told her she would be labelled a crank. Ruby had suggested that, by warning the colonel, he would be on his guard.

When they had seen the number of bodyguards at the pavilion, their sense of urgency had rapidly diminished. These men were tough-looking athletes – some of them boxers – and they all gave the impression that the BUF could look after its own. She, Percy and Jim were actually on their way home when the colonel stumbled at the top of the steps, bringing other people down with him as he fell – and Jim was underneath them all. The hot tears that now filled her eyes rolled across her face and onto the pillow. It hurt to think that Jim thought it was all her fault. His legs had been damaged, and that's why he didn't want to make love to her. Perhaps his feelings for her had changed as well. She thought back to those wonderful nights in their marital bed in Newlands Road. How sweet and tender he had been back then – a considerate, yet powerfully exciting lover. Was it so wrong to want the old Jim back?

'Jim,' she said softly into the darkness, 'I'm so sorry I hurt you, darling. Please forgive me?'

She held her breath and listened, but the slow rhythmical sound of his breathing told her that her husband was already asleep.

CHAPTER 3

It was hard for Ruby to go back to a normal routine. She struggled to come to terms with what had happened over the past few days. She hadn't been close to Mrs McCoody, but she worried that her neighbour might have been sitting in her chair, feeling ill and calling for help, for a long time before she died.

'Ruby, you don't know that happened,' Bea reassured her. 'Mrs McCoody always gave the impression that she was hale and hearty.'

'But what on earth could have caused such a sudden death?' said Ruby.

Until a post-mortem was done, nobody knew; but that sobering thought made Ruby face up to her own mortality. Mrs McCoody had got up one morning, washed and dressed and eaten her meals. In all probability she made plans for tomorrow and another tomorrow, not knowing that that day would be her last on earth. It was a morbid and scary fact that any day could be your last.

'These things happen,' her mother said. 'Don't dwell on it.'

But Ruby found herself imagining her own demise, or how awful it would be when her mother died, and that upset her even more.

It was also hard to come to terms with Jim's reaction to her clumsy attempt to make love again. Jim was the only man she had known, in the biblical sense. Much of their bedroom activity had been accomplished by instinct and his more practised lead. Bea had never talked to her about marital relations, not even before Ruby's wedding day; and apart from a few titillating suggestions from her friend Edith Parsons, when Ruby got married she was woefully ignorant about such things. She still didn't have any idea how things were done. Should a wife always wait for her husband to make the first move? Was it right to try and seduce him? Jim had apparently been shocked by her advances and had told her to 'behave'. Did that mean she was being lewd or disgusting?

Edith was engaged to Bernard Gressenhall, who worked at Potter & Bailey's grocery store, but as far as Ruby knew, Edith was still a virgin. The only girl who might know what to do was Cousin Lily. Although she wasn't married, Cousin Lily was an experienced woman of the world. However, there was one major snag about talking to her. Lily was hopeless at keeping secrets. She didn't mean to gossip, but she loved to share things, 'in the strictest confidence'. Ruby knew that anything she told Lily would eventually reach Jim's ears, so she was always guarded with what she told her cousin. The problem was: if Jim continued to rebuff her, Ruby knew she was doomed to a miserable and childless marriage, and just the thought of it brought fresh and bitter tears.

The house next door was strangely silent, once the police had gone. Biscuit made no attempt to go back home. He had adopted Ruby and Jim and was settling in quite well. Mrs McCoody was with the undertaker, and because her only relative, a nephew, was nowhere to be found, it was decided that her solicitor, Mr Collins, would arrange the funeral. He was anxious to get it over and done with, because he was about to retire. Ruby wanted to offer to host the wake, but soon discovered that it was to be held in the solicitor's favourite pub – at Mrs McCoody's expense, of course.

The day before the funeral, Ruby noticed a man and woman knocking on Mrs McCoody's front door. Unable to get an answer, they walked down the side of the house and tried the back door. Concerned that they might be friends of her dead neighbour, Ruby came out of her kitchen and called over the low fence. 'Excuse me, can I help you?'

'We're looking for the landlady,' said the woman. She was about fifty, heavy-set and wearing a tweed suit. She wore stout shoes, and Ruby couldn't help noticing her hairy top lip and rather masculine hairstyle. 'Eton crop' they called it. The man with her was completely different. A little older than Ruby, he had an athletic build and dark curly hair. When he smiled, a long crease appeared on each side of his face and, even when he wasn't smiling, he had merry eyes. She noticed that he carried a small leather case.

'Then I'm afraid I have some rather bad news,' said Ruby softly. When she told them what had happened, they were both visibly shocked. 'The funeral is tomorrow.'

'I'm sorry,' said the man. 'Were you very close?'

Ruby shook her head. 'Just neighbours.'

The woman glanced at her companion. 'What on earth do we do now?'

'We'll have to look elsewhere,' he said with a shrug and, looking at Ruby, he added, 'I don't suppose you know of any other guest house nearby?'

'As a matter of fact,' said Ruby, 'I run a guest house myself. Mrs McCoody and I had an arrangement. She often used to send a guest to stay with me, if she was full up, and vice versa.'

The pair looked at each other, then at Ruby.

'In that case,' said the woman, 'could we make an appointment to see you? After the funeral perhaps?'

Bea studied herself in the mirror. She was still the same person as she had been when she was married to Nelson Bateman, but now that she was married to Rex Quinn, her life was totally different. As Nelson's wife, although she had lived in her own house, it was difficult to keep clean and at times she struggled with the housework. She had suffered with her chest for years and dreaded the chilly, damp winters when she seemed to get cold after cold. Now that she was a doctor's wife, her living standards were much higher. Her house was warm and dry, and Rex employed a daily woman, which meant that Bea didn't even have to deal with the drudgery of housework and washing. They had electricity, an indoor bathroom and hot running water.

In keeping with just about every other housewife in the country, Bea had no idea how much her husband earned, but she never lacked for money and was slowly beginning to relax and enjoy life's little luxuries. It meant that she was able to indulge herself by setting a pretty table with matching serviettes, and she had plenty of time to embroider her own tablecloths and chair backs. For someone like Bea, used to managing on a very tight budget, her weekly allowance was more than enough.

Socially it was a little harder to find acceptance, and sometimes she felt as if she was tiptoeing through a minefield. She struggled with the snobbery of some of Rex's acquaintances, as well as with the reticence of some of her old neighbours to still treat her as a friend. Her biggest problem was boredom. When Rex was working, Bea could always go to a matinee at the pictures, but without the company of a female friend, it wasn't really the done thing. Her old friends from Newlands Road would be working or couldn't afford an afternoon at the cinema, and she soon discovered that it embarrassed or offended them if she offered to pay.

Whenever he was free, Rex did his best to remedy the situation. They went for country jaunts in his 1934 Morris Eight, and he invited fellow GPs and their wives to dinner. But Bea was only too aware that the women tended to look down on this fisherman's wife made good.

All that changed when Bea met Mrs Euphemia ('Do call me Effie') Rhodes. Rex had been invited to dinner by Effie and Augustus (known to his friends as Gus), and Effie took to Bea straight away. She was older than Bea by perhaps as many as fifteen years, a kind of jolly-hockey-sticks type of woman, the no-nonsense sort who dressed in tweed skirts and sensible shoes. Tonight, however, she was elegantly dressed in a maroon silk frock, which complemented the three stands of genuine pearls that she wore over her ample bosom. She was well built, but not flabby. She kept active on the tennis court and enjoyed walking. Gus was a congenial fellow with a handlebar moustache, which he twisted to a point on each side of his face. He was a smaller man than his wife, of wiry build and a keen model-railway enthusiast. He spent hours with his model trains and had built in his study a station set in a large landscape. Always smartly dressed in a suit with a waistcoat, Gus had a pipe permanently in his mouth. He made them laugh as he confided that he never smoked it, but in his younger days someone had told him it made him look sophisticated, and now he couldn't bear to give up the habit. Gus had been in the Colonial Office abroad somewhere, but had now retired.

As they enjoyed their aperitifs, Effie asked Bea about her family. 'I saw you and your daughter the other day when we were motoring along Marine Parade,' she said.

'I think you had probably been on the beach. A pretty child. How old is she?'

'Almost eleven,' said Bea.

'She's doing quite well at school,' said Rex, as Gus handed him a drink.

'She'll soon be moving to Worthing High School,' Bea chipped in.

'Well done,' said Effie. 'And what about your other children?'

'Percy, my son, and his wife live in London,' said Bea proudly, 'and my other daughter runs a guest house at the sea end of Heene Road.'

'Ah, yes,' said Effie, 'I think you told me about her. Her husband is an invalid, isn't he?'

Bea nodded.

'She sounds like a plucky girl, if she runs a guest house as well,' said Effie admiringly.

'She certainly is, Effie,' Rex agreed heartily.

'Do you have children?' Bea asked.

She was puzzled by the glance Effie and Gus gave each other. Perhaps that was too personal a question. She hardly knew the woman, after all. Then Effie said rather stiffly, 'Sadly not, but we comforted ourselves that children might have hindered Gus's career.'

Bea was immediately embarrassed. She wished she hadn't asked. She had obviously opened an old wound. 'Yes, yes, of course.'

'Gus and Effie were working in Cameroon for years,' said Rex, coming to the rescue.

'Nearly twenty years,' Gus nodded. 'Back then

Kamerun was in German hands, governed by an old friend of ours – Karl Ebermaier. Do you know him?'

Rex shook his head.

'Capital fellow,' Gus smiled. 'There's still a sizeable German population working out there. Beautiful country.'

The maid called them for dinner and, after an enjoyable meal with compliments flying all around, the four of them settled down with coffee.

'What did you used to do for amusement in Hastings, my dear?' said Effie, leaning back comfortably in her chair.

'I sang in the church choir for a while,' said Bea, 'but it wasn't really for me.'

'You joined the Townswomen's Guild, didn't you, darling?' Rex added.

'Oh yes, I did,' Bea agreed. 'I enjoyed it.'

'I don't think we have a branch in these parts,' Effie remarked.

'Anybody fancy a few hands of whist?' said Gus.

Rex and Bea were not really bothered, but Effie and Gus moved from the loungers to the table and got out the cards. Effie went first, drawing the six of clubs as they cut to deal. Bea drew the two of hearts.

'Looks like I'm the dealer,' said Gus, after he'd drawn the jack of spades and Rex had the ten of clubs. He shuffled the pack and gave everyone thirteen cards, before putting the final card, the three of diamonds, face up and declaring that diamonds were trumps.

Sitting on Gus's left, Bea led with the first trick. Effie

won it with a trump card and led the next trick, and for a while they simply concentrated on the game. At the end of thirteen tricks they paused for more drinks, and Rex blew Bea a kiss when their guests weren't looking.

'How's business, Rex?' asked Gus. 'Got enough patients yet?'

'Not quite,' said Rex. 'I've added most of Dr Carter's old patients to the list, but I don't have very many affluent names.'

'I could name a few, if you like,' said Gus.

'Seriously?' asked Rex.

'Mind you, I haven't seen them for donkey's years,' said Gus, chuckling. 'I hope they're still alive.'

'Oh, Gus,' Effie scolded. 'You can't say that!'

'Why not? He wants live patients, doesn't he?' He grinned mischievously. 'What about Ivy Robinson? She sprained her wrist twenty years ago. Dr Warner told her to keep the bandage on. I saw her last week and, I kid you not, she still had the bloody bandage on!'

Bea gasped. 'You mean she's kept the same bandage on for twenty years?'

'Well, not the same one,' Gus conceded, 'but she's kept it covered all that time.' He glanced at Rex. 'Two visits in twenty years – she'd be no trouble.' He lowered his voice to a mutter, 'Mind you, she won't bring you much income, either.'

'Oh, Gus, behave,' Effie scolded again as everybody joined in the laughter.

'Then there's the major,' said Gus, clearly on a roll

now. 'Ol' Doc Brasher asked him for a sample, and he turned up with it in a whisky bottle. The doc said that, judging by the smell when he unscrewed the lid, the major hadn't bothered to wash it out first. Either that or his pee was pickled.'

The two men guffawed and Effie rolled her eyes. 'You know, my dear,' she said to Bea, 'you should think about starting one around here.'

'Sorry?'

'Something like the Townswomen's Guild.'

Bea was taken by surprise.

'Why not?' said Effie. 'You said you were a member. You must know what's expected.'

'Come on, everybody,' Rex interrupted. 'The night is still young. Let's have another game.'

The evening finally broke up at around eleven. 'Thank you for coming, my dear,' said Effie, giving Bea a peck on the cheek.

'Next time you must both come to us,' said Bea.

Gus and Effie stood at the door and waved. As they left, Effie motioned to Bea, who wound down the window of the passenger door. 'Do have a think about what I said, Bea dear – about starting a club for ladies. I promise to be your first member.'

'What was all that about?' said Rex as he drove home. When Bea explained, he was very enthusiastic. 'I think you should do it.'

'Do you really think I could?' she asked as he pulled up in the driveway.

Rex switched off the engine and, drawing her into

his arms, kissed her lips softly. 'You always did under-estimate yourself, my darling,' he said, nuzzling her neck. 'You are perfectly capable of doing anything you set your mind to.'

In the last hour before they went to bed, Effie and Gus were busy stacking everything on the kitchen draining board. Dirty pans were filled with water to soak off any dried-on food, the cutlery was left in a dish of cold water, and the glasses were lined up by the sink. They didn't wash anything – the daily woman would do that when she came in the morning – but Effie liked to have her dining room free of crumbs and dirty plates, in case they encouraged the mice.

Having shaken the tablecloth outside the back door, Effie found Gus scraping leftovers into the waste bin.

'So what do you think of Bea?' she asked.

'I think she'll do nicely,' he said. 'Compliant, grateful to be noticed, hard-working . . . Yes, I reckon you've chosen well, old thing. She fits the bill perfectly, but don't sound too keen.'

'I didn't,' Effie snapped indignantly.

'Yes, you did, old gel,' Gus insisted. 'The trick is making the lackey think it's his idea in the first place.'

Effie gave him a self-satisfied grin. 'Oh, don't you worry,' she said, 'she will.'

CHAPTER 4

Jim was on his way to the shed – which, like the washing line and compost heap, was behind the hedge at the bottom of the garden – when the two people who had been banging on Mrs McCoody's door earlier in the week came back to the house.

'This is Mr Searle, my husband,' said Ruby as they brushed past each other.

The woman put her hand to her chest. 'Miss Bullock,' she said, repositioning it immediately. 'Pleased to meet you, and this is Mr Balentine.' The three of them shook hands. Jim, supporting himself on the back of the wheelchair, grunted. The monkey was balanced on the seat of the wheelchair in its cage and was half-covered by the blanket.

'My husband caught the little monkey that was running around in Rowlands Road,' Ruby said, by way of explanation. 'He's busy making it a bigger cage.'

Miss Bullock seemed astonished. 'You actually caught it?' she gasped.

Jim pulled the covering right back. 'I set a trap,' he said, with the vaguest hint of a smile.

'How extraordinary,' said Miss Bullock. 'I think most people thought the animal was dead. Nobody has seen it for days.'

'We never did find the owner,' said Ruby.

The monkey chattered away in its too-small cage, as Jim excused himself and set off down the path.

'My husband had an accident,' said Ruby, as Miss Bullock turned to her with a quizzical expression. Mr Balentine gave her a sympathetic smile.

It turned out that Miss Bullock and Mr Balentine were helping to organize a cultural exchange between two schools, one in Worthing and the other in Germany. With Mrs McCoody unable to take the boys she'd promised to have, they first had to report back to their committee, before making any other moves. Having seen the accommodation on offer, Miss Bullock and Mr Balentine seemed delighted. When they all came back downstairs, Ruby showed them into the sitting room and offered them a cup of tea. While she pottered about in the kitchen, she accidentally on purpose left the sitting-room door slightly ajar.

'This place is a fair step from the school,' said Miss Bullock.

'It's only next door to the original guest house,' Mr Balentine remarked languidly.

'I suppose so,' Miss Bullock replied with some reluctance. She lowered her voice. 'But do you think it suitable?'

'What's wrong with it?' asked Mr Balentine. 'She seems a nice enough woman and the place is spotless.'

'But her husband is in a wheelchair,' said Miss Bullock. 'So?'

'So,' said Miss Bullock with a sigh, 'I'm not sure how boys who are growing up with the idea of being Aryan supermen will feel about living with a cripple.'

Overhearing what was being said, Ruby bristled.

'Then perhaps,' Mr Balentine replied tartly, 'they should find out how things are done over here.'

'I suppose beggars can't be choosers,' Miss Bullock conceded with an exaggerated sigh. 'They're young, and the school isn't that far away, I suppose. Besides, I have it on good authority that they are extremely fit. A longish walk will give them a good chance to look around.'

'Look around?' said Mr Balentine faintly.

'Around the town,' Miss Bullock said quickly. She laughed nervously. 'And why not? Worthing is a lovely place.'

As Ruby walked into the room, Miss Bullock's gloved hand rested on the mantelpiece. Instinctively Ruby knew she had been checking for dust. She put the tray of tea on a low table beside it and began to pour.

Miss Bullock explained that the boys who would be staying with her were members of a drama group from a German school. 'They're coming to the Assembly Hall to perform a play called *Der Unsichtbare Elefant*.'

Ruby handed her a cup of tea and, as Miss Bullock sat down, Ruby struggled to recall what the word *unsichtbare* meant. Of course *Elefant* was the German word for elephant. That was easy enough . . . *The Something Elephant*.

Miss Bullock obviously noticed her puzzled expression, because when Ruby glanced up at her, she chuckled. '*The Invisible Elephant.*' Ruby was about to explain that she was in the process of learning German herself when Miss Bullock added, 'Do forgive me, my dear. I quite forgot that someone like you, with little or no education, wouldn't have a clue what I was talking about.'

Ruby felt her face flare with indignation and it took all her willpower not to snap. How dare she? The patronizing cow! But much as she wanted to be just as rude to Miss Bullock, she couldn't afford to be. Instead she handed Mr Balentine his tea, aware that he was shifting uncomfortably in his seat.

'You needn't worry about entertaining them, Mrs Searle,' he said as he took the cup. He was clearly embarrassed by his colleague's attitude. 'They speak good English, and we want them to talk to you and your husband as much as possible. It will be good practice.'

Ruby nodded. 'I understand.'

'Besides, they will be fully occupied whilst they are here,' he went on. 'We shall collect them by coach on Thursday morning for a full programme, and they'll perform their play in the Assembly Hall in the evening.'

Ruby liked him. He had an open and honest face.

'All that is required is an evening meal on Wednesday when they arrive,' Miss Bullock interrupted, 'a hearty breakfast on Thursday, and breakfast and a packed lunch for Friday – the day they leave. They will eat their evening meal with the rest of the school on Thursday.'

'So you would like to book the room?' said Ruby.

'Yes, please,' said Mr Balentine. 'Normally we offer our exchange pupils accommodation with a family, but for some reason these boys preferred to be in a guest house.'

'Then I shall do my best to make sure their stay doesn't disappoint,' said Ruby with a smile.

The three of them sipped their tea. 'I suppose,' Mr Balentine began again, 'that with all this sabre-rattling going on between Germany and this country, it must seem odd to you that these boys should be coming at all.'

Ruby hadn't liked to say so, but her thoughts had travelled along those lines.

'The boys from Worthing High School went to the German school last year,' Miss Bullock said, taking over from her colleague. 'They performed *Twelfth Night*. That's Shakespeare, you know.'

Ruby knew perfectly well, but swallowed hard and said nothing. Although she didn't like the woman, there was little point in antagonizing her; after all, she wasn't the one who was going stay in her house.

'And Mr Martin, the headmaster,' Miss Bullock continued, 'is keen to keep open the lines of communication between our two countries.'

'Very commendable,' said Ruby. 'I guess we all have to do our bit for world peace, however small.'

'Quite right too, Mrs Searle,' said Miss Bullock, holding her gaze. 'However small.'

They left soon afterwards and Ruby wasn't sorry to see them go. As they walked through the gate, Cousin Lily was coming up the road. Ruby waved to her. Mr Balentine turned his head as Lily walked past him. Ruby thought he was admiring her neat figure – plenty of men did – but then, lifting his trilby, he smiled at Ruby, who was waiting by the gate. Miss Bullock stared ahead, her back ramrod-straight.

As Lily drew near, Ruby was concerned to see that she was apparently upset. Oh no, Ruby thought to herself, don't tell me the wedding is off. She and Lily belonged to the same family, but they had little in common. Bea and Lily's mother, Vinny, were sisters, with a rather volatile relationship at times, although they would happily do anything for one another. Ruby and Lily got on well, but they were as different as chalk and cheese. Ruby was a steady girl, unafraid of hard work, eager to make a go of life and always anxious to please those she loved. Lily was more flighty. She was very pretty, and she knew it. Judging by the look Mr Balentine had thrown in her direction, Lily hadn't lost any of her charms. She had already been engaged three times and had broken the engagements off, each time keeping the ring she'd been given. Now she was engaged again, but until now she had seemed genuinely prepared to marry this fiancé. Nick Wilkins had certainly lasted longer than the others, and their wedding was set for April 17th.

'What wrong?' asked Ruby as her cousin walked through the gate.

'I can't marry him,' said Lily tearfully.

'Oh, Lily,' said Ruby sympathetically. 'What's happened now?' They linked arms and the two of them walked up the path together.

'Where's Jim?' Lily asked anxiously as they went inside.

'Down in the shed,' said Ruby. 'He's sawing wood and things, so he won't hear us. Do you want a cuppa?'

Lily shook her head. 'Oh, Ruby,' she sniffed, 'I love him so much, but I can't – I just can't.'

Ruby was well aware that she and Nick were already sleeping with each other. Lily had already given herself to Albert Longman, a previous old flame, and when Nick came along she had fretted that he would know she wasn't a virgin. Sometime after she had confided in Ruby, Lily had told her that she was now sleeping with Nick and he was so besotted with her that he didn't appear to have guessed that she had already had a lover.

'I don't understand,' said Ruby. 'What's happened?' Whenever she'd seen Lily and Nick together, Ruby had been convinced that they'd have a marriage made in heaven.

'Nothing,' said Lily. 'Nick is just perfect. I've got my dress, and when we're married we're going to live in two dear little rooms in a big house in Portland Road. The banns are to be read at the end of this month, but I can't let them do it.'

'Lily,' said Ruby, 'you're talking in riddles. If you love him and he loves you, and all your plans are falling into place, why on earth can't you marry him?'

'Because,' said Lily irritably, 'he told me about the certificate.'

'What certificate?'

'Oh, Ruby,' she said. 'Do pay attention. The wedding certificate.'

'I'm sorry,' said Ruby. 'I still don't understand.'

'He told me I'll have to sign it.'

'Well, of course you will,' said Ruby.

'Then I can't marry him.'

Ruby frowned.

'Well, I can't just put an X on it, can I?' wailed Lily. 'Everyone will know I can't read or write.' She burst into tears.

Ruby put her arm around her cousin's shaking shoulders. 'Oh, Lily, is that all that's worrying you? Then let me help you. We've still got a few weeks till the wedding. Let me teach you how to sign your name.'

'I went to school until I was twelve,' said Lily, reaching up her sleeve for a handkerchief and blowing her nose. 'When I left, I still couldn't do it. I'll never manage to write my name in just a few weeks!'

'I bet you weren't really trying back then, when you were at school,' said Ruby with a smile. Lily turned her tear-stained face towards her. Ruby squeezed her shoulder. 'You've got a real reason to do it now. So let's give it a go, shall we?'

A hundred miles away from Worthing, on the outskirts of a village called West Moors in Dorset, Eric leaned against the bonnet of the van and took a long drag of his cigarette. He craned his neck to see if she was coming. He'd worked up quite a sweat gathering together a pile of large stones, which he'd put in an old sack that he kept in the back of the van. Where the hell was she? Hanging around here made him nervous. In the distance he heard the clock on the church tower chime three. She said she'd be here by half-past two. Perhaps she hadn't been able to get away after all. They'd disagreed about when to make the move. He'd said she should slip away in the dead of night, but she'd had other ideas.

'Supposing Christine wakes up and cries,' Lena had said. 'Mr West's a light sleeper. He's always padding around the house at night. If he catches me halfway down the stairs with the baby and a suitcase, he'll make sure I never see her again.'

Eric threw his dog-end down and ground it with his foot, before reaching into his pocket for another Woodbine. A ciggie was supposed to calm your nerves, but he felt worse than ever. He cupped his hand around the end as he struck a match and drew on the cigarette. When he looked up again, there she was, coming round the bend in the road with the Silver Cross pram gliding in front of her. She was walking briskly. Eric's heart thudded in his chest. Was she being followed? Dear God, he hoped not. He walked round the van and opened the passenger door, just in case she had to make a run for it.

She was wearing a coat, but it was open and flapping in the cool spring sunshine. Her dress clung to the contours of her slim body as she came closer, and he felt himself harden. Content that no one was behind her, he walked along the path to meet her, his feet crunching on the gravel beneath his shoes. She had all her stuff on the tray underneath the pram. It wasn't much. The little girl was sitting upright and looking around. She was a pretty thing, with a mop of light-brown curls and big, innocent eyes, but Eric only glanced at her. It was Lena he was here for. As they met, he pulled her roughly into his arms. 'Lena – oh, Lena.'

''Ang on, lover boy,' she said. 'Let me get me breath back.'

He silenced her protest with a hungry kiss and kneaded her breast with one hand. As he released her, she laughed softly.

'Oh, Eric. Get away with you, you great lummox. There'll be plenty of time for that later.'

'Are you sure you want to do this?' he asked gruffly. 'Once you get into that van, there's no going back.'

'Course I'm sure,' she said. She looked down at the child. 'This is Jean. Say hello to your new daddy, Jean.'

'Jean?' said Eric.

'Yes,' said Lena. She ran her finger lovingly along the child's face. 'Jean is her proper name. The one I gave her. Isn't she sweet?'

Eric grunted congenially. As they turned to go, her foot slipped on the mud at the side of the path and he grabbed her arm to steady her. They smiled at each other, and Lena lifted the child out of the pram. He took the suitcase from the tray underneath and they made their way to the van. Flinging the case into the back, he helped her into the passenger seat and put the little kid on her lap. Then, walking back down the path with the sack of stones, he threw it into the pram. He pushed the pram towards the river bank and so far down, then gave it a hearty shove. It rolled away quickly, but just before it hit the water, the wheels came up against a ridge. The pram upended and the rocks tumbled into the hood. Instead of sliding into the water, the whole thing turned over and went in hood-first. It sank, but not as much as Eric had intended. The wheel rims were visible in the water. He thought about sliding down the bank and giving it another shove, but there was no time to lose. They had to get away as soon as possible, and trust that no one would think of coming down this way until they were long gone. Cursing under his breath, Eric hurried back to the van and climbed into the driver's seat.

'All right?' said Lena.

Eric started the engine. 'Fine.' Jean clapped her hands and he grinned. 'That's right, little one. Hurrah! This is where we begin the rest of our lives.'

CHAPTER 5

Ruby was on her way back from Lonsdale House in Rowlands Road, where Mr and Mrs Bennett had a lending library. For a shilling a month, she could borrow up to two books a week.

'Yoo-hoo, Ruby.'

Ruby turned sharply to see her old friend Edith Parsons running towards her. She and Edith hadn't met up for ages. As the two of them hugged each other in the street, Ruby realized how much she missed her old friend, but somehow the pressures of running the guest house and Edith's wedding preparations had got in the way. The pair of them laughed and danced around each other like two excited schoolgirls.

'It's so good to see you,' cried Edith, when at last they both stopped to catch their breath.

'And you,' said Ruby. 'Have you got time to come home for a cup of tea?'

Edith pulled a face. 'Oh, Roob. I'm so sorry. I'm on my way to Mrs Kinson's for another fitting for my wedding dress, and I'm late already. Can you come with me?'

Mrs Kinson lived in Heene Corner, which was on the way back to Sea View, but Ruby shook her head. 'I'm sorry,' she said, threading her arm through Edith's. 'I'll walk with you for a bit, but I can't come in. I'm expecting a couple of schoolboys. They're staying in the guest house, so I have to get back.'

The two women walked together in companionable friendship. They had worked together as chambermaids in Warnes Hotel before she and Jim got married. Back then, they had rooted for each other, especially when their supervisor, the dreaded Mrs Fosdyke, was around. Mrs Fosdyke could be heartless and cruel. Many a time she emptied the linen cupboard onto the floor, just as they were about to go off-duty. At times like that, it was good to have a friend like Edith.

'Been shopping?'

'I've just been to Timothy Whites to get some liniment for Jim's back,' said Ruby and, holding her books aloft, added, 'and the lending library.'

Edith squeezed her friend's hand. 'How is dear Jim these days?'

'About the same,' said Ruby. 'I don't think anything will change. Not after all this time.'

'Oh, Roob, I'm so sorry,' said Edith.

Ruby shrugged. 'That's life,' she said with a small sigh. And then, realizing the air of melancholy she'd brought between them, she added, 'Not long before your big day.'

Edith's eyes sparkled. 'Just over six months,' and then she added conspiratorially, 'although, just like any Potter

& Bailey customer, I've already sampled what's on offer.' The pair of them sniggered and laughed. Edith's fiancé, Bernard Gressenhall, was a manager in Potter & Bailey's, one of the largest grocery shops in the area. Although Ruby and Edith had never openly discussed sex, a few nights before Ruby's wedding they had talked about what it might be like.

'Bernard showed me his thingy,' Edith had told her. 'It was huge.'

Ruby had shivered. 'So is Jim's,' she'd confided.

'And hard,' said Edith, then she and Ruby had giggled helplessly.

Thinking back to that moment and their wide-eyed innocence, Ruby wished she could turn the clock back. Anything would be better than this nagging desire that she had – a desire that was destined never to be fulfilled. She quickly changed the subject.

'Everything going smoothly for the big day?'

'Yes,' said Edith. 'This is my first fitting for my dress. The bridesmaids' dresses are already being done. I wish you had agreed to be my maid of honour.'

'With Jim the way he is, I was afraid of letting you down at the last minute,' said Ruby.

'I understand,' said Edith. 'Mum tells me you've always got the *No Vacancies* sign up, so you must be very busy.'

'What about you?' Ruby asked. 'How is life at Warnes?'

'Much better now that Mrs Fosdyke has gone,' said Edith. 'I'm in charge of the linen cupboard now.'

Ruby tapped her best friend's arm playfully. 'Ooh, get you, Edith Parsons. What would the old dragon say to that?'

'"Call that tidy, Parsons?"' said Edith, mimicking their former manager perfectly. '"Piles like that won't impress the management."'

Ruby laughed. 'I wonder what happened to her. Is she still around?'

'I heard she works for some rich chap in Goring. Something to do with the government, so I've been told. What's all this about German schoolboys?'

'They were going to stay with Mrs McCoody, but . . .'

'Oh yes, I heard she'd died,' said Edith. 'Someone said you found her.'

Ruby nodded. 'It was horrible. I still think about her the minute I wake up.'

'How awful,' said Edith, giving her arm a squeeze. 'Did they ever find out what happened?'

'Natural causes, as far as I know,' said Ruby. 'Nobody's ever said any different. The place looks just the same. It's not sold or anything.'

'What Bernard and I wouldn't give for a place like that,' Edith sighed. 'We're going to have to start off in Mum-in-law's house. She's letting us use the front parlour.'

Ruby caught her breath. 'What about our old place in Newlands Road?'

Edith stopped walking and stared at her. 'Do you mean that?'

'There's someone living there at the moment,' said

Ruby, 'but I know for a fact that she's only stopping there while she visits her husband in the hospital. She's a patient of my father, and Mum's kind-hearted like that.'

'Ooh, Roob,' said Edith, 'a place of our own would be wonderful. Would you ask her for me?'

'Look,' said Ruby, anxious not to build up her friend's hopes too high, 'I can't promise anything, but I'll certainly try.'

'Thanks, Roob,' said Edith. 'You're a brick.'

On Wednesday March 24th the boys arrived at Sea View. Miss Bullock brought them in her car. Albrecht and Franz clicked their heels and gave Ruby a quick nod of the head as they were introduced. Ruby held out her hand to shake, but it was ignored. The boys were much bigger than she had expected them to be. Albrecht was roughly the same height as herself, but Franz was much taller. In fact he was bigger all round. Thickset and with bulging thighs and hairy legs, he seemed much older than his supposed fourteen years. Both boys were blond and wore their hair shaved close to the side of the head. They were dressed in a long-sleeved brown shirt with a lanyard tied to the shoulder and ending in a pocket on the chest, leather shorts, a belt, long khaki socks and stout walking shoes. Ruby knew from what Rachel had told her that the Scouting movement had been outlawed in Germany, but the boys' uniform looked strikingly like it.

As soon as Miss Bullock left, it became apparent that

Albrecht was the more confident of the two. 'We have travelled from London,' he said in impeccable English and with only the faint trace of an accent. 'The countryside at this time of the year is very good.'

'I love springtime,' Ruby agreed. 'Everything looks so fresh and green. Let me introduce you to my husband.'

Jim was doing the crossword in his paper. He pulled it down to acknowledge the boys, but said nothing. The monkey, now housed in a much larger cage, regarded them with a curious expression as Albrecht and Franz clicked their heels once again.

'I'll show you to your room,' said Ruby as she led them upstairs. Each boy carried a small suitcase. 'I'll leave you to unpack. Your meal will be ready at six.'

Albrecht nodded curtly and she left them to it. She had gone to a lot of trouble to ensure their comfort. Each boy had his own towel, and she had put some children's books beside the bed. Now, having seen what they looked like, she was afraid that they would seem far too babyish. She was mildly surprised when, almost as soon as they had entered the room, they both thundered downstairs and out of the house. The front door swung on its hinges. With a tut of disapproval, she followed them to close it again.

'We go to the sea,' shouted Franz, as he saw her following them to the door.

'Be back by six,' she cautioned.

They ran very fast and in no time at all they were almost at Marine Parade. Ruby had thought that perhaps they were going for a swim, but then she saw their cameras swinging from a strap around their necks.

'What the devil are they up to?' said Jim, coming up behind her.

Ruby closed the door, feeling a tad uneasy, although she couldn't really say why.

The boys arrived back at the house in time for tea and set about their meal with gusto. Ruby served them shepherd's pie with jam roly-poly and custard to follow, but already she worried that she might not have enough. They had enormous appetites.

Because of the language barrier, the conversation at the table was stilted, but they managed. There was no mention of the present difficulties between their two countries. Albrecht explained that they were on a fortnight's tour of the country with their play, and that when they left Worthing they would be heading along the coast.

'Tomorrow,' Franz told them, 'we will go to your town hall. We see the mayor.'

'Then we go to the gymnasium,' said Albrecht. 'We are very good.'

Ruby suppressed a smile behind her hand. And modest with it, she thought to herself.

'Where were you two haring off to just now?' asked Jim.

Albrecht looked puzzled. 'Haring?'

'He means running very fast,' said Ruby. 'You were in a terrible hurry, but you didn't go into the sea.'

'I wish for picture,' said Franz.

'We wanted to photograph the sea front,' said Albrecht, 'but it was already too black.'

'Too dark,' Jim corrected. They sat in silence for a while, then Jim said, 'You are both very fit. I don't think I've ever seen a boy run so fast.'

The chests of both boys swelled with pride. 'We have to run sixty metres in twelve seconds,' said Albrecht.

'And we must run over the country for one day and a half,' said Franz.

Jim pulled a face. 'I'm impressed.'

'We have a performance book,' said Albrecht.

'I see,' said Jim. 'Sounds like a good idea.'

'Oh yes, of course,' Albrecht agreed. 'We German youth are strong and healthy.'

'And when you've done all this keeping fit,' said Jim, 'what is your reward?'

Franz looked puzzled. 'Reward?'

'For this we wear the brown shirt,' said Albrecht, 'our Jungvolk badge and the shoulder strap.'

'I see,' said Jim gravely. Everyone fell silent. 'Would a postcard do?' asked Jim. The boys seemed puzzled. 'Instead of your photograph, would a postcard do?'

'Ah, this is good,' said Franz enthusiastically. '*Ja.*'

There was a knock at the door. When Ruby got up to answer it, Cousin Lily stood on the doorstep. 'I've come for my lesson,' she whispered conspiratorially.

'We're just finishing our tea,' said Ruby. She was about to introduce Albrecht and Franz, but they excused themselves and went up to their room, although not before Ruby noticed Franz giving Lily a rather lustful stare. Fortunately her cousin didn't appear to notice. Lily helped Ruby with the washing up, until Jim decided to go into the sitting room with his paper. As soon as he'd gone, Ruby got out the writing pad and, having written Lily's name in a lovely copperplate hand, left her at the kitchen table to copy it. It took all Lily's concentration, but she managed a fair attempt. Ruby encouraged her to take the test paper home and bring it back when every line on the page had her signature on it.

'All this writing gives me such a headache,' Lily groaned.

'Well, you'll have to put up with it, if you don't want Nick to know you can't read and write,' said Ruby.

Lily shrugged despairingly. 'I suppose so.'

'Night then, love.'

Ruby's voice came softly towards him in the darkness, but Jim didn't answer. He lay on his back, staring at the ceiling and sighed inwardly. His right leg was throbbing again and although he had already taken an aspirin, he knew that until it stopped he would have little sleep. He stretched out his left leg and a sharp pain caught him just below the knee. He jerked it back up until it was slightly bent and tried again, this time moving much more slowly.

He didn't want Ruby to worry, but he was concerned about their schoolboy guests. Why were they singled out from their classmates? The rest of the group were being boarded out with families in the town, and yet Franz and Albrecht had been sent to a seaside guest house far away from the supervision of their teachers. It just didn't add up. Jim couldn't help remembering the look of relief on Miss Bullock's face when Ruby brought her into their home. Was it more than simply relief to have found somewhere so quickly?

The two countries, Germany and Britain, were supposed to be friends. The cultural visits between schools in Germany and the home-grown variety were encouraged, to cement good relations between the nations, but there was no getting away from the fact that everybody was talking about war. It seemed a bit unlikely that the same thing wasn't happening in Germany and, if that was the case, was it possible that Franz and Albrecht were in Worthing with a totally different agenda – or was that a little fanciful?

The year before, and after all his promises not to, Hitler had invaded the Rhineland. This had been classified as a demilitarized zone left over from the last war, and designed to stop German aggression breaking out again. That strip of land bordered the Netherlands, Belgium, France and Switzerland. It wouldn't take much to invade those countries and, if he was tempted, how long would it be before Hitler set his sights further afield, especially now that Germany, Italy and Japan had formed an alliance?

Was he the only person in the country who could see the dangers? And now here he was, with two of that madman's worshippers under his own roof! Having thought things through, Jim decided to keep a close eye on the lads. He noticed that, on their first night here, they spent a lot of time outside. After they'd been to the beach, they sat on the garden wall in what seemed like deep conversation. Tomorrow he would rig up his only camera, the Contax that Mr Kendrick had given him as a gift after his prize-winning stay in Wimborne, in such a way as to take a picture of the gate and the wall. If nothing else, it would be a record of the boys and their habits.

He still hadn't told Ruby about the letter from Percy. It contained an introduction to a friend of his who was a watchmaker in Tarring. At first Jim had been annoyed when he saw it. He resented Percy's interference, and he was irritated that his brother-in-law had obviously been talking about him behind his back. What right had Percy to do that? However, as the day wore on, his feelings mellowed a little. The man was only trying to help. But Jim didn't want to be a repairer of watches. He knew sweet-all about clocks, but he hated being dependent on his wife's earnings. That being the case, he supposed it could be an opportunity to make a living again, but there was another problem. He had been experiencing other symptoms. Both his thumbs were permanently numb and he occasionally had a shooting pain down the back of his left hand and into his ring finger, which made him jerk. How could he work on something as delicate as a watch, with jerking limbs?

He listened to Ruby's slow, soft breathing and was filled with loathing. It wasn't directed towards his wife.

72

It was because of Franz and Albrecht. Why should he put up with those two ruddy Germans at his table? They were so cocksure and clean-cut, and he hated their condescending attitude when they realized he had difficulty in walking. He supposed that, in Hitler's Germany, someone like him would have been put away. That's what Rachel had said: 'There's no place for imperfection in an Aryan society.' Jim thanked God that Ruby was such a dedicated worker. He knew that, but for his wife, he would have been in the workhouse long ago.

And another thing: those boys were supposed to be fourteen, but with biceps like that, they looked more like eighteen or nineteen. He'd seen the way Franz stared at Ruby. What's more, Franz's eyes were virtually popping out of his head when Lily arrived. What was that headmaster thinking of – inviting Nazi sympathizers to a place like Worthing at a time like this? His blood began to boil when he thought of Albrecht and Franz, sleeping only feet away from his own bed.

Ruby murmured in her sleep and turned over. Jim felt his own body tense. He should never have married her. She deserved better.

He did his best not to think about the accident. On the one hand, he still blamed Ruby for what had happened to him; on the other hand, he hated what he was doing to her. He was well aware that he could be very unkind, but he couldn't seem to stop himself. Ruby did her best to make him comfortable and never complained, but funnily enough, that made him resent her even more. In fact he didn't want a wife at all. That night outside the Southern Pavilion when Colonel Blatchington fell on the steps, taking down several other Blackshirts, he had been hit in the back and had somehow swung around the rail at the bottom, with one leg curled underneath his body and the other wrapped around the part of the rail that was anchored to the ground. The weight of the heavyset bodyguards on top of him in this position had done untold damage to his body. Jim had not only lost the proper use of his legs, but – although he'd never managed to bring himself to tell Ruby – also the ability to get his dick up. The desire had died, as well. He never masturbated, and even when he thought back to their wedding night and other nights of passion, it did nothing for him. If he tried to relive the moment, he felt as if he was watching a Hollywood film, or someone from a past life. It did nothing to stir his loins. This wasn't how he'd envisaged his life. What was the point of it all?

This brought him back to the watchmaker in Tarring. Damn it, he was a photographer – and a bloody good one too. He knew nothing else. Even if he went to see this watchmaker, how would he get to Tarring to work? If Ruby was busy getting the guests their breakfast, who would wheel him all that way? Aha, Percy, you hadn't thought of that one, had you?

Jim turned over and banged his pillow. It seemed that just about everyone in the family had a good idea. Rex, his father-in-law, had suggested bookkeeping, but for Jim that sounded like a fate worse than death. He never did get the hang of sums at school, and he didn't like writing, either. He could feel the black cloud coming over him again. If he continued thinking things over, they would envelop him like a heavy wet blanket, sucking the life out of him and pulling him down to the dark abyss. He stared ahead at the brick wall in front of him and, as he drifted into sleep, thought that staring at a brick wall just about summed up his future.

CHAPTER 6

BOURNEMOUTH DAILY ECHO
Fears grow for missing child and nanny

A pram thought to belong to Christine West, aged two, who went missing last week, has been found upside down in the Moors River near Woolslope Farm in West Moors. Police are investigating. Dorset Police say they are 'very concerned' for the child's welfare, after she and her live-in nanny went missing. Christine West is the daughter of Mr and Mrs West, from Avon Road in West Moors. Her nanny, Miss Marlene Amberley, is described as twenty years old, of slight build, with dark hair and brown eyes. She had been working for Mrs West for six months. 'She always seemed a really caring girl and came highly recommended,' a tearful Mrs West told our reporter last night. 'I am positive that she would never harm Christine. It's a mystery what's happened.'

Detective Pressley is urging people to be vigilant and report any possible sightings immediately. The main focus for enquiries is around the villages of West Moors and Ferndown, after the child's pram was found tossed into the Moors River. Detective

Pressley said: 'Dorset Police are grateful for the assistance from members of the public so far, but concern for little Christine's well-being is increasing, the longer she is away from home.'

Christine, who went missing from her home at about 3.30 p.m. on Tuesday, is described as two and a half years old, with long mousy-coloured hair, which may be tied up with a ribbon. She was wearing a pale-blue dress and white cardigan and a brown coat with a matching bonnet. She was carrying her favourite toy, a grey knitted rabbit with long yellow-and-grey striped legs.

*   *   *

Albrecht and Franz were up early. Ruby had already cooked a plate of eggs, bacon and fried bread, which was waiting for them on the table. There was also tea and toast, with either marmalade or gooseberry jam. They both had healthy appetites and tucked in at once, with Ruby keeping an eye on them while they ate.

They spoke mostly in German, unaware that she understood a lot of what they were saying. Their conversation was inconsequential: they talked about the plan for the day, which Ruby gathered was to include a gymnastic display at Worthing High School, and then they would meet the mayor, Alderman William Tree, for lunch. After their meal they would be given a coach tour of the Sussex villages, before stopping at Steyning for tea in the village hall. In the evening Albrecht and Franz would be performing their play in the Assembly Hall. Ruby pricked up her ears when she heard them complaining that there was little time to see the pier or the centre of town. 'And we still have to find the gas-works . . .' said Albrecht in his own tongue.

Gasworks? Why on earth would they want to see the gasworks?

Ruby leaned over them and put a plate of apples and bananas onto the table. 'Do help yourselves,' she said brightly. 'Take one with you, if you like, just in case you feel peckish.'

'Peckish?' Albrecht was frowning. 'What does this mean – peckish?'

Ruby smiled. 'Oh, sorry. It means if you feel slightly hungry.'

Albrecht nodded. 'Ah.'

As she moved away from the table she heard him mutter in German, 'Why does she look at me like that? She's always looking at me.'

Inside, Ruby froze, but to all outward appearances she made herself carry on as if she had no idea what he'd said. Had she been staring? She wasn't aware that she had been, but it was possible. There was something about these boys that made her uneasy.

'I reckon she's not getting enough,' said Franz in his own language. 'That husband of hers looks pretty feeble.'

Ruby bristled. How dare he? The cheek of it! And what right had he to be so personal about Jim?

'She might want me for a lover,' said Albrecht. 'That's understandable, but I'd much sooner have an hour with that blonde tart we saw yesterday.'

They both chortled.

'Everything all right?' Ruby asked sharply.

'Yes, yes, thank you, Frau Searle,' said Franz, politely if a little too quickly. 'You treat us well.'

Ruby turned back to the stove and began to put Jim's fry-up on his plate. He had made it clear that he preferred to eat alone in the sitting room whilst the German boys were staying. Ruby picked up his tray, saying, 'Excuse me for a minute. I need see to my husband.'

'Believe me, he needs seeing to,' said Albrecht in his own tongue as she left the room, and Franz gave his arm a playful slap.

When they had left, Ruby worried about Albrecht and Franz all day. They were supposed to be boys, but they behaved like grown men. Their voices were still a little high, but Franz had a distinct Adam's apple; and she'd happened to see Albrecht coming out of the bathroom that morning: he was well-built – too well-built to be a child. He had seemed embarrassed to bump into her, clad only in his vest and shorts. He had apologized, at the same time running his fingers through his hair, and she couldn't help noticing his hairy armpits. At what age did boys get hair under their arms? There was no sign of shaving paraphernalia in the bathroom, but she couldn't very well rummage through his things, could she? And, come to that, why would two schoolboys prefer to be in a guest house rather than staying in a Worthing home, with young lads of their own age? How come they had been allowed to? It did seem rather odd.

Everyone was aware that the relationship between the British Isles and Germany was hardly convivial.

Despite Hitler's promises to the contrary, the newsreels were full of pictures of goose-stepping jackboots, and of dire warnings of the consequences of further aggression. Ruby couldn't help thinking that, under the circumstances, maybe this visit wasn't a very good idea, but her other observations worried her even more. In the end she talked it over with Jim while he was cleaning out the monkey's cage.

'I was thinking the same thing,' he said. 'If those two are only fourteen and fifteen, I'll eat my hat.'

'So what are they up to?' asked Ruby. At Jim's suggestion, she was giving the animal a little bit of raw egg. It seemed to be enjoying it.

Jim shook his head. 'Search me.'

The boys arrived back home quite late. Apparently the play had gone down very well and they had received a standing ovation. They said they were too tired for cocoa, so they excused themselves and went straight to their room. The strange thing was that they crept back downstairs and went outside to sit on the wall again. Ruby wondered if they might be smoking, although she hadn't smelled smoke on their clothes. After watching them for a while, she went back to her work.

Jim had spotted them too. He couldn't hear what was being said, of course, but he did notice a car drawing up, and the boys appeared to be talking to the passenger. At first Jim thought the occupants were simply asking for directions, but then he wasn't so sure.

* * *

Ruby didn't sleep that night because she was listening out in case Albrecht and Franz were creeping about. Fortunately the house stayed quiet. Breakfast was uneventful and Ruby prepared them both a packed lunch. The coach arrived at ten, and Ruby stepped outside with them to see them off. When she saw the rest of the boys in the coach, they all looked physically larger than English boys of their age. Perhaps her suspicions were the result of an overactive imagination. Maybe all German boys were more powerfully built than English boys, but even the other German schoolboys were not as well developed as Franz and Albrecht.

As Albrecht and Franz climbed aboard the coach, Jim struggled down the path using his walking stick. 'You forgot your packed lunches,' he called after them.

Ruby tapped on the window to tell them. Their knapsacks stood in the road, waiting for the driver to load them into the storage area at the back of the coach. Jim undid one and shoved the lunch inside. The driver was stacking it as Franz came back down the steps.

'It's all right, mate,' shouted Jim. 'I've put it in the bag.'

Franz clicked his heels and nodded sharply, before climbing back on board. A minute or two later the driver was back in his seat and the coach moved off. Although nobody was looking, Ruby and Jim waved them out of sight.

'Did you do it?' she asked.

Jim nodded. 'The cameras were right on top,' he said. 'All I needed to do was open the back. If they were spies, any photographs they've taken of the town will be ruined, when the light gets in.'

'Do you think we should tell someone?'

'What should we tell them?' asked Jim. 'That you heard them talking about the location of the local gasworks?'

'It's not the usual thing that a tourist wants to photograph,' said Ruby.

'We've done what we could,' said Jim.

Ruby looked thoughtful. 'What if they weren't spies?

'Then I imagine their teacher will tell them they should be more careful with their cameras in future.'

Bea had thoroughly enjoyed throwing herself into organizing the first meeting of the proposed Townswomen's Guild, and today was the day. She had begun by making a list of ladies she thought might be interested. They were mainly the wives of people Rex knew well, but she had also picked out ladies from two local churches, the woman from the chemist's shop, who was very chatty and friendly, and some friends of Effie Rhodes. They gathered in the Parish Rooms on Heene Road, because Bea thought a neutral setting would seem less daunting. Also, if any lady felt uncomfortable, she could make good her escape unnoticed.

She had funded the cost of hiring the hall out of her own money. If something was worth doing, she felt she should be willing to take the risk. About a week and a half before the big day, Bea had written to Mrs Dawson, who was a leading light in the Hastings Townswomen's

Guild, asking for advice. She was hoping to receive a letter that she could read out to anybody who turned up, but to her absolute delight, Mrs Dawson decided to come in person.

Bea met her off the train just after noon and, after taking Mrs Dawson to lunch at her place, the two of them walked the short distance to the Parish Rooms. Mrs Dawson looked smart and businesslike. She was wearing a black-and-white checked suit with wide white lapels. The long jacket had a wrapover panel in the front and large pockets. The skirt was a stylish length and she had a black hat with a white flash on the brim. By contrast, Bea was wearing a red ensemble. Her jacket had wide sleeves over the wrist and it covered her hips, and was complemented by a small black belt. The skirt, worn to mid-calf, was slightly flared with an open kick at the front. Her matching red hat had a black band and a saucer brim, which she wore low over her right ear. She carried a small black clutch bag and wore black patent shoes.

When they arrived at the hall, Effie was busy organizing everybody. The room was set and ready to go. To Bea's amazement, most of the women to whom she had given invitations had turned up, and Mrs Dawson gave a spirited account of what was required.

'I have never been one to rest on my laurels,' she told them as she finished her talk. 'If you ladies would like to be a part of this, we should get the ball rolling, don't you think?'

By the end of the meeting everyone who wanted a

branch of the Townswomen's Guild in Worthing had agreed to pay an annual subscription of fifteen shillings, or one and sixpence per meeting. Casual guests would pay slightly more. Mrs Dawson, who had temporarily taken the chair, suggested that they set about selecting a committee. Bea was concerned that not knowing each other would prove to be a problem.

'I realize that some of you ladies have only a fleeting acquaintance with each other, and that the rest of you don't know each other at all,' Mrs Dawson said, as if reading Bea's mind. 'I suggest you propose any of your friends that you deem suitable, and if you yourself would like to volunteer for membership of the committee, you should make that known.'

A few minutes later Bea was one of fifteen ladies standing in front of the assembled crowd. Given a piece of paper with the number six written on it, she was asked to say a few words about herself, and what she thought she could bring to the Townswomen's Guild. After hearing from all the others, each lady then took part in a secret ballot. When the votes were counted, Bea was chosen alongside seven others to be on the committee. Although shaking her head with what seemed to Bea like false modesty, Effie Rhodes was voted in as the new chairman.

'Well, ladies,' said Mrs Dawson with a satisfied smile, 'it looks like the Heene branch of the Townswomen's Guild has come to Worthing.' There was a round of applause, after which Bea stood to thank Mrs Dawson for coming and to announce that they would meet once a month on a Tuesday afternoon. After that, Effie offered to hold the committee meeting in her spacious home on Richmond Road and then they broke up for a cup of tea.

'You were marvellous, my dear,' Effie cooed in Bea's ear, 'and I should like to ask you to consider being the treasurer. Would you do that for me?'

With Mrs Dawson standing close by, what else could Bea say but yes.

'Splendid!' cried Effie, 'I always knew you were the right woman for the job.'

Bea was happy to do it, but she had the feeling that somehow or other she had been slightly sidelined. As the women made their way home at four o'clock, the newly formed committee was asked to convene in a small huddle to finalize the date and time of their first meeting.

'I hear that your daughter has been looking after some German schoolboys,' Effie whispered as they waited for the last two ladies to join them. 'I do so admire her. The country needs all the help it can get, if we are to maintain world peace, don't you think?'

Bea felt a little blush of pleasure reach her cheeks, and at that moment she quite forgave Effie for manoeuvring herself into the position of chairman. The committee seemed a nice bunch of ladies – eight including Bea herself. Only one person made her feel ill at ease. She knew Effie, of course; and she had had a meal with another lady, Cynthia Raymond. Mrs Dawson had suggested that, for the sake of decorum, they should refer to each other in the Guild by their surnames; and so, going around the circle, each woman said her name by way of introduction: Mrs Quinn, Mrs Rhodes, Mrs Wilmot, Mrs Raymond, Miss Horton, Miss Taylor, Mrs Crockerton. The final lady stared steadily at Bea, and she felt herself give an involuntary shiver as the woman said her name: 'Mrs Fosdyke.'

CHAPTER 7

Now that Franz and Albrecht had gone, Jim took down the camera that he'd rigged up by the sitting-room window. He had waited behind the curtain on their last night and had taken several pictures of them. He'd been there when the car pulled up, and he saw Franz hand what looked like a small package to the front passenger. As he'd clicked the shutter, Jim had shivered with excitement. He'd been right all along: they were up to something.

Not wanting to worry Ruby, he had waited until now to retrieve the film. Much as he wanted to, he couldn't develop the film himself. When he had disposed of his darkroom, he had given his chemicals away to friends. One friend had a small photography business in Crescent Road. It was time to call in a favour.

On April 17th the weather on Cousin Lily's wedding day was bright but blustery. She and Nick Wilkins married in Christ Church, a flint building with brick dressing in the very heart of the town, bearing the distinction of being Worthing's first parish church. It was also the only church in the town centre with its own graveyard. Nick's grandfather, a man who had attended the church all his life, was buried there. A popular place of worship, Christ Church had been at the forefront of social care for the people of Worthing ever since it was built in 1843. The congregation, which included Nick's mother, had run a soup kitchen nearby until quite recently; and the south gallery was known as the Fishermen's Gallery, and was kept aside for boatmen who might not smell so good when they came to church in the morning after a night out on the water. The high-backed wooden pews in dark wood had tall ends and large fleurs-de-lys, the roof was of pitch pine and there was geometric tiling on the floor – all of which made it seem rather dark inside. Nevertheless the atmosphere in the church was warm and inviting.

Nick had a large family, so his side of the church was quickly filled. It seemed to Ruby that half of Worthing was a cousin, uncle or aunt. Nick's mother, Edie, was a gregarious woman who made friends easily, and Ruby took to her at once.

Lily's side of the church wasn't quite so full. Percy and Rachel had come down from London with little Alma, who looked delicious in a pale-pink dress. Aunt Vinny was dressed like a duchess. She was wearing a long-sleeved mauve print dress with a large lace collar and a string of imitation pearls. Her cloche hat was the same colour as her dress and she carried a lightweight stole and a small clutch bag. In the years since Ruby's own wedding, Aunt Vinny had got herself an admirer.

Bert Cable worked at the same laundry as she did, in South Farm Road, north of the railway line at the central station. A portly man with a large belly, Bert was one of the drivers. He laughed a lot – a loud cackle that resounded around the room, attracting attention and encouraging others to join in. To add to the hilarity, occasionally his top set of teeth clattered against the bottom set at the same time. When Aunt Vinny introduced him, Bert shook Ruby's hand warmly. She liked him. He was an honest man. What you saw was what you got, and because Cousin Lily's father had died many years before when she was only a child, Bert had volunteered to give the bride away.

Lily had two adult bridesmaids, friends from the cinema where she worked as an usherette. They were in knee-length lilac dresses, and the sash around each waist sported a large floppy rose. Their picture hats set off their ensemble very well. Ruby's sister May, now almost eleven, was also a bridesmaid. This was her first time, and for May it was hugely exciting. She had grown into a rather plain child and was becoming a little chubby, so her smaller version of the same dress wasn't quite as flattering as it should have been. But of course nobody told her that; everybody was very complimentary, and May loved every minute of the occasion. As for the bride herself, she was radiant in an ankle-length satin dress with a sweetheart neckline. On her head she wore a heart-shaped cap and veil. Her bouquet was made up of carnations and lily of the valley.

Lily made all her promises looking directly into Nick's

eyes. And as he returned her gaze, Ruby felt her own eyes smarting with tears. It all looked so perfect from here. Cousin Lily was a beautiful bride, and Nick was as proud as a peacock to have her. Ruby's heart ached as she watched him reach out and tenderly take Lily's hand in his, as he slipped the ring on her finger. Only three years ago she and Jim had been just like that, standing side by side and making those same promises. 'For better, for worse; for richer, for poorer; in sickness and in health . . .' She felt a tear trickle down her cheek and prayed to God that Lily's marriage wouldn't turn out to be as difficult as hers had been. She sighed. If only Jim would talk to her.

After the wedding ceremony, Lily walked confidently into the vestry to sign the register, and the brilliance of her smile as she re-emerged into the church convinced Ruby that all those weeks of frustration, and yet more practice, had been worthwhile.

The reception was held in Christ Church hall, just a few steps away from the church itself in Portland Road, and the wedding party was for around fifty people. It was an opportunity for everyone in the two families to catch up with cousins, uncles and aunts. This wedding was so different from her mother's. When Bea had married Rex, it was as if his relatives and friends had taken over the whole of Worthing. The reception had been a really posh do in Warnes Hotel, and a five-piece band played as they ate. Ruby had wondered if Rex's family might disapprove of her mother. After all, Rex was a doctor and an educated man, and her mother was the widow of

90

a fisherman. But she needn't have worried. Without exception, they were thrilled to meet Bea and to see Rex happy at last.

'No sign of any babies yet?' said Aunt Vinny, as she cornered Ruby by the tea hatch.

Ruby felt her face colour. She shook her head.

'You'll have to tell that husband of yours to get a move on.'

Ruby smiled but said nothing. Aunt Vinny, along with so many others, had no idea how much her probing questions hurt. She would love to have a baby, but with things the way they were, there was little chance. Only the other day her mother had hinted that perhaps Ruby should see her doctor, even suggesting that if she was too shy to do so, she could have a word with Rex on Ruby's behalf.

'Don't you dare!' Ruby hissed. The thought of baring her soul to her own father was too embarrassing to imagine. Besides, what was the point, when Jim had made it clear that he didn't even find her attractive any more?

When her mother had approached her, Ruby knew that should have been the moment to confide in her. They had always had a good relationship and Ruby respected Bea's opinions, but somehow she couldn't do it. This was too personal, too intimate. Not only was she embarrassed, but ashamed as well. What sort of wife was she, when the man she loved wasn't interested any longer?

'Oh dear,' said Aunt Vinny, as if suddenly aware of

Ruby's stricken expression. She put her hand on Ruby's arm and leaned towards her in a confidential manner. 'Is everything all right with you and Jim?'

'Of course!' cried Ruby and then deliberately changed the subject. 'The tables look very nice. Did you make the wedding cake?'

After a few more minutes of small talk, Aunt Vinny excused herself to attend to other guests.

'That photographer is bloody useless,' said Jim, wheeling himself up behind Ruby. 'He's forgotten half of what he's supposed to do. He should have done one with the groom's parents and Aunt Vinny, and he—' He stopped as Ruby turned around. 'You've been crying.'

'Daft as a brush, aren't I?' Ruby joked.

'Many a true word,' said Percy, joining them. He kissed his sister on the cheek. 'How are you both?'

'Fine,' said Ruby. 'How about you and Rachel?'

'Business is good,' said Percy, 'but there's a lot of resentment against the Jews in some parts of London. The Blackshirts are stirring up trouble. Looks like we'll have to move again.'

'Oh no,' said Ruby. 'Where will you go?'

'Rachel wants to live down this way,' said Percy, 'between Worthing and Brighton perhaps. There's a synagogue in Brighton, and Rachel misses her community.'

'Oh, Percy, how lovely,' Ruby cried. And, spotting Rachel and Alma, she hurried to join them, but there was little time to do more than tickle Alma's cheek before the best man called everybody to the table and the wedding breakfast got under way.

The sandwiches, kept moist under damp tea towels, were delicious and the cakes were as good as any you could find in a Lyons tea room. After the speeches, with plenty of bride-and-groom jokes ('What are the five essential words for a good marriage? Answer: "I'm sorry" and "You are right"') and sound advice ('Remember that if you put all your problems on the back burner, they're bound to boil over'), the cake was cut.

A little later everyone got up from their chairs and, whilst the women stacked the dirty plates by the food hatch, for those in the kitchen doing the washing up, the men put the trestle tables away. On the small raised platform that doubled as a stage Eddie Lawrence was warming up on the melodeon. Eddie had at one time worked as a farmer, but after he lost his legs in the Great War and following years of struggle, he had become an auctioneer, although his talents as a musician were also in great demand. A man Ruby had never seen before made his way to the platform with a fiddle under his arm, and someone else was setting up the drums. When the music started, Ruby clapped her hands in delight. Dancing! It had been an age since she'd danced. The caller got everybody ready and then they began with some old Sussex dances, which meant that everybody – young and old – could join in.

'How are you getting on with that chair?' Percy asked Jim. He handed his brother-in-law a glass of beer and sat down next to him.

'Wouldn't be without it,' said Jim.

With Ruby gone, Percy became a man on a mission. 'You didn't go and see my friend, the watchmaker.'

'There was little point,' said Jim truculently. 'I can't pull myself on the wheels all that way in the chair. You have no idea how hard it is.'

'You won't get rich sitting on your fat arse all day,' Percy blurted out.

It was obvious from the expression on Jim's face that he was furious. 'Just leave it, Percy. This is my life now – and that's all there is to it.'

'But you're still young,' Percy insisted. 'Do you really want to spend another thirty or forty years doing nothing?' He sipped some of his beer. 'What about bookkeeping?'

'I'm no good with sums,' said Jim.

They watched the dancers. Ruby was threading her way between the groups, hand over hand, and then twirling as she reached the end of the line. When Bob Knight twirled her again unexpectedly, she threw back her head and laughed. Jim felt a frisson of irritation.

'What if I set you up with a tobacconist's kiosk?' said Percy, interrupting Jim's dark thoughts.

'And how am I going to get there in the morning?'

'For God's sake,' replied Percy, exasperated. 'Hire some little lad who could do with a bob or two, to push you there before he goes to school.'

Jim stared sullenly ahead.

'Do you know what?' said Percy. 'I get the feeling you don't want to work.'

Jim glared at his brother-in-law.

'I mean, look at ol' Eddie Lawrence up there,' Percy went on. 'Did he let the fact that he's got no legs stop him?'

Jim's knees knocked against the table and Percy's beer wobbled. 'Why don't you damned well mind your own business,' said Jim, turning to leave.

Percy grabbed the armrests. 'Look here, Jim,' he said in a more conciliatory tone. 'What happened to you was grossly unfair, and you didn't deserve it, but you've got to pull yourself together, man. Are you really going to sponge off my sister all your life? What happens when she has a baby?'

'Let go of me,' Jim spat through gritted teeth. 'It's all very well for you, with your flash car and all your money.'

'And how do you think I got them?' said Percy, his voice rising. 'Nothing fell into my lap. I got it by hard graft.'

'Let go of the bloody chair!' Jim shouted. People began to turn round.

Ruby stopped dancing and froze to the spot. One of the ushers went over to them. 'Now then, lads,' he said. 'No argufying. This is a 'appy occasion and I'll be thanking you to keep it such.'

'Sorry,' said Percy, straightening up. 'Jim and I were just having a heart-to-heart.' He waved his hand towards the staring guests. 'I apologize, everyone. Please carry on with the dancing.'

But Jim wasn't in the mood to let it go. 'Ruby,' he shouted, as the melodeon struck a chord, 'take me home.'

'But she's enjoying herself,' Percy protested mildly.

'Piss off!' said Jim, jerking his chair away. 'It's none of your business.'

'Look, I've said I'm sorry,' said Percy. 'Let me take you home. I'll run you back in the car.'

'Ruby,' Jim shouted.

'Come on, Jim,' said Percy, 'let the girl have a bit of fun.'

Ruby stopped dancing and looked over at them.

'We're going home,' said Jim.

'That's right,' Percy hissed in Jim's ear. 'Ruin everything. You can't enjoy yourself, so don't let anyone else have any fun, either.'

Jim's face flamed with rage. Not caring whose toes he ran over, he headed towards the door.

Ruby had collected her handbag and was saying her goodbyes.

'Come on, woman,' her husband said tetchily. 'Get me out of here.'

CHAPTER 8

There was only Jim to cook for on Sunday morning, so once he had eaten, Ruby decided to go out.

'I just want to pop down to my mother's,' she said. 'You coming?'

Jim shook his head. 'I'm doing the crossword,' he replied, shaking out the Sunday paper.

She was still annoyed with him for spoiling her fun at Lily's wedding, but they didn't speak of it.

The night before, the atmosphere between them had been tense. Why was he behaving like this? Ruby decided not to speak to him until he apologized and had taken to walking out of the room when he came in, but Jim made no reference to what he had done. He even made a point of pretending to be asleep when she came to bed. Ruby lay in the dark for ages, angry and upset, and trying to shirk off the pangs of hurt and disappointment.

As his gentle snores filled the room, Ruby turned her thoughts to the dance. Oh, what fun it had been to get up on her toes and twirl her skirts. She'd loved dancing with Bob as a partner. He was so light on his feet, a past master on the dance floor, who could skilfully steer her in the right direction whenever she forgot the next move. She had been enjoying herself in a way she hadn't done in a long time, and it had been wonderful.

Robert Knight (known to everyone as Bob) had never married. Some said he was afraid of commitment, while others thought he had simply never met the right girl. She couldn't think why. He was every girl's dream: tall, good-looking, attentive and fun to be with. After a while, every time she touched Bob's hand, Ruby felt a buzz of excitement, which quickly became sensual. She started to anticipate the warmth of his big hand around her waist or on her back, and the pull of his strong arm as he twirled her around. She felt light-headed and giggly. The wheeze of the accordion, the melodious voice of the caller and the closeness of Bob's body all merged into one. For a few wonderful moments on the dance floor she forgot the difficulties of life. She forgot her frustrations. She even forgot Jim and the guest house. The moment was filled with music, the dance and Bob. Then Jim had to go and spoil it all. Ruby had drifted off to sleep thinking of Bob. He was all the things Jim had been – long, long ago.

She left her husband studying the crossword. The monkey, now called Wilfred (after Pip, Squeak and Wilfred, the children's comic cartoon characters), sat beside him, chattering away. Jim had made a small harness for the animal, so that it had the freedom to run around safely on a leash. The two of them were in the garden. For once, Ruby didn't bother to kiss Jim goodbye. He probably wouldn't be bothered anyway, she thought to herself acidly.

The photographs of Franz and Albrecht were not very good. Jim had received them in the post yesterday morning, and so far he had managed to keep them from Ruby.

It was difficult to make out the face of the person in the car, although he had caught the exchange of the packet quite well. Because the print wasn't very clear, he toyed with the idea of throwing it away, but instead found himself looking around for a tin. He stumbled across one in his shed. The photographs and the negatives fitted in it quite nicely. The tin was marked 'Humbugs', and somehow that seemed rather appropriate.

It didn't take long to get to Bea's house. Percy, Rachel and Alma were staying with them for the weekend. When she arrived, Ruby went round the back and opened the kitchen door. The delicious smell of grilled bacon wafted towards her.

'Hello, darling,' her mother cried. 'Come on in.' Ruby kissed her cheek. 'Is Jim with you?'

Ruby shook her head.

'Your father and Percy have already been for a long bike ride and have come back starving,' said Bea. 'Just let me take this to them and I'll be right with you. Have you eaten?'

Ruby nodded, although it wasn't true. She'd felt much too churned up inside to eat.

'Rachel is feeding the baby in the sitting room,' said Bea, cracking an egg over the frying pan. 'Why don't you go and talk to her. We'll chat later.'

Her sister-in-law and her niece looked the picture of contentment, as Ruby knocked softly on the door and went in. 'Darling,' said Rachel, patting the sofa beside her, 'come and join us.'

Alma cast a lazy eye towards her aunt, but was too eager for her milk to stop drinking. She sucked Rachel's breast with greedy little gulps, every now and then making contented sighs. Ruby laid her hand gently on Alma's head. 'Hello, poppet,' she whispered. 'Looks like you're enjoying your breakfast.'

Rachel was looking at Ruby with just a hint of suspicion. 'Is everything all right?'

'Of course,' said Ruby. She smiled brightly, but Rachel wasn't fooled at all.

'I'm sorry about Percy having a go at Jim at the wedding reception,' she said, grasping Ruby's hand and giving it a loving squeeze. 'I'm afraid once he gets a bee in his bonnet he gets a bit carried away.'

'It wasn't Percy's fault,' said Ruby. 'Jim is a bit down at the moment. Photography was his life, and he hates not being able to do it.'

'Why can't he do it from the wheelchair?' asked Rachel. 'I know he can't stand, but . . .'

'It's not so much the standing,' said Ruby. 'He gets

the shakes as well. He finds it difficult to hold the camera still.'

'Oh,' said Rachel. 'Now I understand.'

'It's all so unfair,' Ruby sighed. 'Jim only ever wanted to be a photographer, and now it's all gone.'

Alma had finished feeding and, with a deft move of her hand, Rachel covered herself and put the baby onto her shoulder to rub her back. 'But if he can't do it,' said Rachel, 'he has to think of something else. He can't sit around doing nothing for the rest of his life.'

'I know,' said Ruby. 'It's just that he finds it so hard.'

'We all have to face difficult things,' said Rachel, 'but it's no good moping over things that can't be changed.'

To an outsider, her words would have seemed harsh and uncaring, but Rachel knew more than most what it meant not to be able to turn the clock back. Hadn't she seen her own sister and her baby murdered by the Hitler Youth, back in Germany? And hadn't she been forced to flee for her own life? That was why she was in England.

'What about you?' Rachel went on. 'Has he ever stopped to think how all this is affecting you?'

Embarrassed, Ruby looked away. How could she answer such a question? No, of course Jim didn't think about her feelings, as he was too consumed with his own misery. But to say that out loud seemed totally disloyal.

They heard Bea coming along the hall. Rachel tugged at Ruby's arm. 'I think you and I need to talk,' she said. 'Not now. Later. Just you and I.'

Ruby smiled thinly and nodded her head.

'Now,' said Bea coming into the room, 'who's for a cup of tea?'

Jim had wheeled himself to the window of the sitting room, with Wilfred on his shoulder. Absent-mindedly he fed the animal bits of raw carrot. Biscuit, the cat, rubbed himself against Jim's leg and eventually jumped onto his lap.

Jim was still smarting from what Percy had said to him at Lily's wedding. Jumped-up cocky bastard – what right had Percy to judge him? He wasn't the one stuck in a wheelchair and in constant pain. Jim was well aware that he had to do something with his life, but what could he do? He had gone over his options, few as they were, again and again. The shake in his hand was definitely getting worse. It wasn't there all the time, but it seemed that just as he was trying to do something that required concentration, it would start. He was good at making things – he'd built the trap for the monkey, and its cage and harness – but everything took a long time. And as for trying to make stuff on a scale that could bring him in some money, he knew he could never stand the pressure.

As he'd told Percy, he was no good at sums, and the thought of using pen and ink filled him with horror, so what other options were there? Shop work, working in a bar or, as had been suggested, manning a tobacconist's kiosk all required standing for long periods. It was all very well for Percy to sit in judgement; and it didn't help much to see how efficiently his wife managed without him. He thought back to the previous night, remembering how happy Ruby had looked as she danced with that Bob Knight. Right now Jim hated the man, with his white flashy teeth and his floppy hair falling over his eyes. If he'd had the strength, he would have stood up and socked the blighter on the jaw.

He hated having complete strangers in his house all the time, especially when he caught them eyeing him and feeling sorry for him. Their self-centred conversations bored him. There would have been guests here now, but for the wedding. Sea View was becoming so popular that Ruby often had to turn people away.

He had also been unsettled by an article in the paper, which said that his old orphanage was being pulled down. There were lots of private houses going up on the old Goring Hall Estate, and The Shieling was being demolished to make room for new buildings. The council had never kept it in a good state of repair, and time had caught up with it. He had shown the article to Ruby, but she wasn't really interested. With her out of the house, Jim decided to take a taxi over to Goring to see it one last time.

The big gates were wide open when he got there. The neatly trimmed garden where he had been forced to spend much of his childhood working on the borders, had been left to grow wild. Vandals had left their mark too. He was strangely upset by the peeling paint and broken windows. This was the only childhood home he'd ever known. He asked the taxi driver to wait and, using his sticks, walked around the building. He had so many memories. The coke room where he had been required to load up a scuttle with coke and, having opened the furnace door, tip it into the hungry flames. As a grown man, it didn't seem so difficult, but as a twelve-year-old boy the roar of the fire had been terrifying. He walked past the shed where he'd been made to stand for hours, having committed some minor misdemeanour; and the common room where Father Christmas gave him his one and only present every year. To his surprise, when he got back to the taxi, his cheeks were moist with tears.

'I wondered if that was you,' a voice said behind him. Jim turned to see Mr Brown, one of his former teachers. He was older, of course, but those smiling eyes and the broad shoulders, although a little more rounded, were still the same. He was shorter than Jim remembered, but the warmth of his personality remained. 'Come to say goodbye?'

'Something like that,' said Jim.

Mr Brown looked down at the walking sticks. 'What happened to you, lad?'

Jim explained briefly.

'I'm sorry to hear that,' said Mr Brown. 'I knew about the accident, of course. It was in all the papers, but I thought you had long since recovered.'

They turned to look at The Shieling one last time. 'Odd name,' said Jim. 'Where does it come from?'

'It's a mountain hut used as a shelter by shepherds,' said Mr Brown. 'This will be a pile of rubble by the weekend.' He sighed. 'I spent most of my adult life within those walls.'

'And I the whole of my childhood,' said Jim.

'I always thought what happened to you wasn't right,' said Mr Brown. 'Would you like a drink? There's a pub just up the street.'

They climbed into the taxi and Jim paid the man off when they reached the Bull Inn on Goring Street – a charming, if rather old-fashioned, public house. They sat by the inglenook fireplace and Mr Brown bought them both a beer. They didn't have a lot of time. The licensing laws meant the place would close at three.

'What did you mean, when you said what happened to me wasn't right?' Jim asked.

'Most of those kids didn't have a soul in the world,' said Mr Brown. 'You had a mother and a father.'

Jim stared at him in amazement.

'Don't tell me you didn't know?' said Mr Brown.

'I didn't,' said Jim. He frowned. 'A mother and a father?' So how come he'd ended up in an orphanage? Were they sick or something? Had they abandoned him and, if not, then why didn't they come back for him? He'd never had so much as a Christmas card or a birthday card from anyone outside the home.

'Yes, that's right,' said Mr Brown, clearly unaware of the devastating effect his revelation was having on his former pupil. 'They were quite well-to-do. They went abroad somewhere.'

Well-to-do? It got worse. Jim lifted his beer glass. His

hand was trembling and some of his drink spilled down his shirt. 'So why did they leave me there?'

Mr Brown shrugged. 'No idea, lad. Perhaps they thought you'd be better off.'

'Better off?' Jim gasped.

'I'm sorry,' said Mr Brown, looking up at him. 'I thought you knew.'

'Did you ever hear a name?'

'I can't say I did.'

Jim stared ahead. 'Why on earth didn't the council let me be adopted, or something? I could have had a proper home. It must have cost the ratepayers a fortune to keep me there.'

'Didn't cost the council a penny,' said Mr Brown. 'The fees came every month. Regular as clockwork.'

CHAPTER 9

'Ruby darling, is everything all right between you and Jim?'

Rachel was in the garden putting Alma in her pram, when Bea caught Ruby by the arm. She had just brought their cups out into the kitchen to wash up.

Ruby swallowed hard. She and her mother had a good relationship and they had been through some difficult times together. When Nelson, the man she had thought was her father, died, Ruby realized just how difficult it had been for her mother, trapped for years in a loveless marriage. It was even more humbling to realize that Bea had put up with it for the sake of her brother and herself. Whereas Ruby knew she still loved Jim, or at least she thought she did, her own marriage was being far from easy.

Just one look at her mother's sympathetic expression was enough for it all to come tumbling out: the black moods; the constant battle to help Jim; his fight against the crippling pain; the resentment her husband felt because he blamed her for the accident; and the pressure of having to keep up appearances for the sake of the guests. Bea held Ruby close and smoothed her hair gently, as her daughter leaned on her shoulder. She listened without interrupting, then they cried together. Although they heard someone come to the kitchen door, nobody disturbed them. Eventually Ruby blew her nose and sat up straight.

'I hardly know what to say,' Bea confessed, 'but I promise to support you in whatever decision you make.'

'I can't leave him, Mum,' said Ruby, 'and I can't chuck him out, either.'

'Then let me give you a hand from time to time,' said Bea. 'We'll make a pact that you get a day off every now and then, or at least some time to yourself.'

Ruby nodded. 'Thanks, Mum.'

'I'm so sorry I didn't think of it before,' said Bea. 'You must have been struggling to cope for ages.'

That hadn't occurred to Ruby, either. It was probably the relentless, unchanging routine that had got her down. She hadn't the courage even to mention the lack of sex. It felt too awkward bringing up such a subject in front of her mother, but after she'd talked about everything else, Ruby felt a bit better. She wasn't angry with Jim any more. She told herself that, from now on, she had to look at things from his point of view. Under the circumstances, it must have been very difficult for the poor man to watch her dancing with Bob Knight.

'Ruby,' Rachel said cautiously, 'I know you're having a busy time at the guest house, but is it still all right for you to take some more Jewish people?'

It was late afternoon when Rachel pulled Ruby aside in Bea's garden. Alma was still in her pram sleeping soundly, and Bea had gone indoors to answer the telephone. Ruby made a shrewd guess that at any minute her mother would be breaking up the conversation that her father and her brother were enjoying in the greenhouse. No doubt that call was from a patient who was in trouble, somewhere in the town.

Ruby and Rachel had walked across the lawn and were sitting in the summerhouse. It wasn't yet warm enough to spend a lot of time outside, but with a cardigan around her shoulders to ward off the freshness in the air, it was quite pleasant. If Rachel had heard Ruby crying in the kitchen with Bea, she made no reference to it.

'When are they coming?' Ruby asked.

'They dock at Southampton in five days' time,' said Rachel. 'Several members of the Deborah Committee will travel down to meet them and then we'll disperse them around the country.'

'Is it really getting that bad over there?' asked Ruby. She thought back to the time when Albrecht and Franz had stayed with them. They had spoken only in glowing terms about Hitler's Germany.

'Really bad,' said Rachel. 'Jewish people have been stripped of their citizenship. They're not allowed to go on the buses and trams now, and they can't even sit on a park bench.'

'You're joking!' cried Ruby.

'We should have guessed the way things would turn

out, when Hitler refused to shake Jesse Owens's hand at the Olympic Games last year,' said Rachel.

'That was because he was black,' Ruby remarked.

'Blacks, Jews . . . ' said Rachel. 'Hitler hates them all. God knows where it will all end.'

Ruby gave an involuntary shiver.

'I'm worried about you,' Rachel said suddenly.

Ruby frowned. 'Why?'

'Something's wrong, isn't it?' said Rachel. 'Between you and Jim. You're not as perky as you used to be.'

'Things are bound to be different now,' said Ruby. 'Since Jim's accident . . .' her voice trailed off. 'And it doesn't help when Percy keeps on and on at him.'

'Percy just wants to help,' said Rachel. 'It can't be good for Jim to be stuck indoors all the time. I dread to think how you'll cope when babies come along.'

Ruby laughed sardonically. 'There's little chance of that!' As soon as she'd blurted it out, she regretted it. Consumed with embarrassment, she felt her cheeks flame.

'What on earth do you mean?'

Ruby looked away, tears pricking her eyes.

'Oh, Ruby,' said Rachel. 'You mean that you and Jim . . . ? What – never? But you're so young.'

With that, Ruby burst into tears again. Damn, damn, damn; she hadn't meant to do that. Her sister-in-law moved into the chair beside her and put her arm round her shoulders. 'Don't tell anyone, will you?' Ruby said brokenly. 'I couldn't bear it if the rest of the family knew. Rachel, Jim doesn't want me any more.'

'I can't believe that,' she replied.

Ruby looked stricken. 'I don't want Mum to know. Promise me you won't tell her.'

Rachel glanced towards the house. 'Perhaps,' she began cautiously, 'Jim just needs a little reminder of how it once was.'

Ruby blew her nose noisily.

'Tell you what,' Rachel said decisively. 'When I come for your refugees, we'll take the afternoon off. We'll go shopping in Brighton and have our hair done, and then we'll buy some lingerie and some perfume.'

Ruby managed a weak smile. 'Do you really think that'll make any difference?'

'Trust me,' said Rachel. 'No man can resist a pretty girl dressed in silk.'

They were interrupted by Bea calling her husband. 'Rex darling, that was Mrs Vane on the telephone. Her daughter's waters have broken, and the midwife said to call you.'

At the other end of the garden Rex Quinn stood up wearily. Left on his own, Percy headed towards the summerhouse. Rachel squeezed Ruby's arm conspiratorially. 'Don't worry, darling. We'll soon have that man of yours eating out of your hand.'

Jim was still brooding about his parents. The fact that he had a mother and a father, and that they had paid to keep him in the orphanage, was difficult to deal with. He wondered if he'd been born on the wrong side of the blanket. Perhaps his mother wasn't married to his father. Maybe that was why they'd gone abroad. But that didn't explain why they had never given him the chance to grow up in some other family.

If they didn't want to let him go, why didn't they keep in touch? His parents had missed all the milestones of his life: when he was fifteen and leaving school; when he was twenty-one and came of age; when he married Ruby . . . They could have been there – been a part of it. Had his father put his mother up to it? Or was it as he feared: his mother had been unfaithful? Jim sighed. If Ruby was unfaithful, what would he do with her child? He didn't know, but he was certain he would never put him or her in a home, to languish and wonder. He knew how that felt. It was unfair and painful. He'd been unwanted and unloved. He swallowed hard and, even though he was a grown man, it still hurt. God, it hurt.

The first Jewish refugees, Rivka and Elisheva, arrived at Sea View at the end of the month. Rachel drove them to the guest house from Southampton, where their ship had docked. Both girls were well dressed and well educated. Rivka seemed about seventeen, with shoulder-length black hair and large, sad eyes. She looked very tired and was clearly frightened. Elisheva was older, perhaps twenty-three or twenty-five, and she wore her dark hair tied back in a chignon. Her well-manicured hands told Ruby that she was middle-class and unused to manual work. They each carried one small suitcase.

Ruby showed them to the room they would be sharing

and left them to unpack. Back downstairs, she made her sister-in-law a cup of tea. As she did so, Rachel explained that both girls had an affidavit of support, but they were only allowed to stay in the country if they worked as domestic servants.

'Quite frankly,' said Rachel, 'neither of these girls has done a day's work in their lives. I know it's not part of our agreement, but do you think you could give them a crash course on running a home?'

Ruby gasped. 'You mean ask them to work for me? But I thought they were to be my guests.'

'In one sense they are,' said Rachel, 'but they have to move on. They cannot stay here indefinitely. They both understand that Mrs Whichelow has found a placement for one girl working in Pulborough, and we are actively looking for another position for the other.'

'I feel a bit embarrassed,' Ruby confided.

'Don't be,' Rachel said firmly. 'This is the only way to save their lives.'

Ruby gave her a quizzical smile.

'Honestly, darling,' Rachel insisted, 'I'm not being melodramatic. Even when I was over there, people were disappearing. Hitler has already begun his grand plan, and that doesn't include Jews, Gypsies or the disabled. I get the feeling it's going to get a lot worse before it gets better.'

'Judging by the look of them,' said Ruby, raising her eyes to the ceiling, 'the pair of them need a good long rest first.'

'Perhaps for a day or two,' Rachel conceded, 'but

then we must crack on. We need to get them into place-ments as quickly as possible. We've a shortage of people willing to sponsor the girls, and there are so many who need our help.' She sounded frantic with worry.

Ruby rubbed her arm comfortingly. 'You mustn't take the troubles of the whole world on your shoulders,' she said gently.

'I know,' said Rachel, relaxing a little.

'How long have I got?' asked Ruby. 'To train them to be domestic servants?'

'A week,' said Rachel.

'A week!'

'Ten days at the most,' continued Rachel. 'Their visas are only valid if they are working, remember?'

Ruby was beginning to understand the urgency, and how much this was going to interfere with normal life. Most likely the girls had little English, and yet she'd have to help them get to grips with the English way of life, and cooking English food, which would most likely be totally alien to them. Ruby had always thought it would be helpful to have help in the guest house, but if the girls had to be watched all the time, it was prob-ably going to make more work than it saved! 'Oh, Rachel, it's awful,' she sighed.

Rachel's eyes grew wider. 'You mean you can't do it?' she said.

'No, no,' cried Ruby. 'I mean for those poor girls.'

'Listen,' said Rachel, moving closer and speaking confidentially. 'You and I must put aside all sentimen-tality. We must be businesslike. There's no future for them in Germany. At the moment this is the best option they have. It's either this or go back to Hitler.'

Ruby nodded. 'I'll do my best.'

Rachel patted her arm. 'The fact that you speak German will be useful.'

'It'll be good practice for me too,' said Ruby with a smile.

'But,' Rachel cautioned, 'get them to speak English as much as possible.'

'By the time they leave here,' Ruby quipped, 'you'll be able to get them a job with the BBC.'

CHAPTER 10

The Heene branch of the Townswomen's Guild was taking off. Bea and the rest of the committee had organized a programme for the rest of the year. At each meeting there would be a speaker, followed by cups of tea and home-made cakes. The ladies were so eager to show off their culinary skills that there was no shortage of offers to go on the rota. It amazed her how these women – strangers just a few weeks ago – had slotted in and found their place. Mrs Raymond was good at organizing the kitchen. Miss Taylor was the first at the sink to do the washing up and, as soon as the Parish Room was opened, Mrs Crockerton and Miss Horton were busy getting the chairs out and arranging the room; and Mrs Wilmot was a diamond when it came to organization and getting a speaker. The only woman who did nothing was Effie Rhodes.

Bea had been appointed treasurer. She sat at the table just inside the door and checked everybody in. Each lady paid a subscription of fifteen shillings a year, which could be paid as a lump sum or at the slightly higher cost of one and sixpence per meeting. In the beginning they had decided on one shilling and sixpence a meeting, but that was deemed unnecessary because of the high number of members. One and thruppence a meeting was more than adequate to cover the cost of the hall, all the running costs and the fees commanded by their speakers. The members who were paying annually were allowed to miss meetings, but all the others had to pay, whether they attended or not.

Effie obviously relished being the chairman. She always dressed well, but she excelled herself for the Guild meetings. Today she wore a pale-blue dress with a large bow at the neck and long sleeves and an ankle-length pleated skirt. The brim of her jaunty hat was pulled over her left ear and she wore dark-blue suede court shoes.

She sat in the middle of the top table, complete with gavel, and brought the meeting to order. Today they were having a guest speaker who was giving a talk on foraging food from the hedgerows. Bea wondered vaguely how someone could fill forty-five minutes on such a subject but, according to Mrs Wilmot, the woman's talk to the WI in Goring had brought a standing ovation.

As it turned out, the speaker was very interesting, although Bea wasn't too sure that Rex would appreciate having nettle soup or baked hedgehog on his table. He might, however, be tempted by sloe gin and blackberry-and-apple crumble. As the meeting broke up, Effie came over to the treasurer's table.

'How are our finances, Bea dear?'

'Good,' said Bea, 'but they could be better. I was wondering if we could do a raffle each time.'

'My thoughts exactly,' said Effie. 'By the way, how is that daughter of yours? Still looking after German schoolboys?'

'She's taking in refugees now,' said Bea proudly.

Effie arched her eyebrows. 'Refugees?'

'Some girls who have been brought over by the Deborah Committee,' replied Bea. 'Things are really bad . . .'

Effie was distracted as she caught sight of another woman that she wanted to talk to. 'Oh, I simply must catch Lady Paget,' she said, hurrying away. 'Talk to you later, dear.'

Things had been slightly awkward at the first committee meeting when Bea and Freda Fosdyke had been put together. Bea remembered the harsh way Mrs Fosdyke had treated Ruby while she worked at Warnes Hotel, and how rude she had been when Ruby had returned as a guest with her father. She felt sure that some of it stemmed from vindictiveness. When Bea had got herself pregnant by Nelson Bateman, he and Freda had been stepping out together and planned to marry. It was common knowledge that Freda was hopelessly in love with him, and when Bea and Nelson *had* to get married, it broke her heart.

The irony was that Bea's shotgun wedding was never a happy one. Perhaps if Nelson had been able to marry Freda, things would have been very different. When they broke up for tea, Bea made a valiant attempt to paper over the cracks. 'I haven't seen you in ages, Freda. What is it you're doing now?'

'We're supposed to call each other by our surnames, Mrs Quinn,' said Freda haughtily.

'Yes,' said Bea faintly, 'I'm sorry. I just thought that as we've known each other for so long . . .' Her voice trailed off.

'I'm very well, thank you,' said Freda, not really giving an inch. 'I work for Sir Hubert Temple now. At the moment he's renting a beautiful home in Rustington.'

'Oh?' said Bea. 'Someone told me he lived in Goring.'

Freda shook her head. 'Marama suits him better.'

'You've come a long way,' said Bea. 'Isn't there a branch of the Townswomen's Guild in Rustington?'

Freda's face coloured.

'Or perhaps the WI?' suggested Bea.

'I prefer to come here,' said Freda.

'It sounds like you've got a very responsible job,' replied Bea.

'He only employs the best,' said Freda. 'As you well know, I had a very responsible position at Warnes.'

The barb in her comment didn't go unnoticed.

'Freda.' Bea began again. 'Mrs Fosdyke, all that was a very long time ago, and I am truly sorry for all the pain I caused, but it takes two to tango, you know. Nelson is gone now and we are both older and wiser. Can we not start again?'

Freda Fosdyke gave her a long stare. 'Maybe,' she conceded, 'but only for the sake of the Guild.'

'Just as you please,' said Bea, doing her best to hide her disappointment.

At the top table, Effie Rhodes banged the gavel. 'Ladies,' she said, 'I have just had a wonderful idea. I think we should have a raffle at each meeting. It will raise much-needed funds and we can also do our bit for a charitable cause.'

There was a collective buzz of excited chatter.

'I would ask each of you then,' Effie went on, 'to bring something for the raffle, if you can. And as Mrs Wilmot has graciously agreed to postpone the talk with Mrs Lambourne on American quilt-making, at the next meeting we shall be having Mrs Forbes as our speaker. Mrs Forbes happens to be a dear friend of mine, who collects handkerchiefs. She has been doing so for more than twenty years and has a collection of more than five hundred.'

Oh, my word, thought Bea with an inward sigh. That sounds riveting.

*　　*　　*

Wife and Home magazine
Our Agony Aunt, Audrey Hindley,
answers questions sent in to our problem page,
'Ask Audrey'

Dear Audrey,

I am soon to be a mother and I am worried sick. I am currently looking for a reliable nanny and have interviewed several very respectable young ladies, but in view of the recent missing baby case, how can I be absolutely sure that the person I employ is completely trustworthy?

Yours sincerely, Worried of Hampshire

Dear Worried of Hampshire,

I completely understand your concerns and I would urge you first of all, for the sake of your unborn child, to stay calm. It might be less stressful if you found someone to help you with the interviews. Your mother, perhaps? As for making the right choice, it is better not to rely on first impressions. Ask for references from any previous employer, and contact that person in writing. Ask the prospective candidate where she trained, and make contact with the school. Organizations like Norland or St George's train their girls to a very high standard, and persons of quality recommend them highly. I wish you luck in your newfound state, and I am sure that following my advice you will find a capable, conscientious and trustworthy nanny.

Yours sincerely, Audrey Hindley

*   *   *

'You never said you were going to the orphanage.'

Ruby and Jim were alone in the house. Rivka and Elisheva had gone with Rachel to meet the other members of the Deborah Committee. The Derby family had left in the morning, and the Webb family weren't arriving until tomorrow. Ruby had prepared a nice piece of plaice for their dinner and they sat together in the kitchen.

Jim played with his fish. 'It was a spur-of-the-moment thing,' he said, 'and it was a bit upsetting, if I'm honest.'

'That's understandable,' said Ruby. 'They're pulling it down, and you said you were happy there.'

'It's not that,' said Jim. 'I met up with one of my old masters.'

Ruby listened, her face agog as he told her about his bumping into Mr Brown. 'That's amazing!' she cried. 'You should have invited him over.'

Jim sighed. 'The thing is, he told me I had a mother and father.'

'We've all got one of those,' she quipped and then, seeing the look on his face, she immediately regretted her flippancy. 'Oh, Jim, I'm sorry. Is there something wrong?'

'They paid to keep me there,' he said simply.

Ruby stared at him. 'What?'

'Mr Brown remembered that they were well-to-do,' said Jim. 'Ruby, I stayed in that place all my life because they paid the fee.' His voice broke as he came to the end of the sentence.

Ruby got up and stood beside him. She drew him close to her and wrapped her arms around his head and shoulders. For once he didn't push her away, but sank into her welcoming embrace. 'Oh, Jim, that's awful.'

After a few minutes he said, 'Why would someone do that, Ruby? If they didn't want me, why not let me be adopted?'

'I don't understand it myself,' she said, 'and you're absolutely right, darling. But if you had been adopted, we might never have met and married.'

'Even that might have been better,' he said, his voice muffled by her body.

'You mustn't think like that,' she cried. 'The day I married you, I did it because I love you. Life has given you a raw deal, but if I could go back, I wouldn't do any different. I have no idea why your parents did such an awful thing, but it was their loss, not yours.'

He looked up at her, his eyes red and teary. 'You are a remarkable woman, Ruby Searle.'

She smiled down and then planted a kiss on his forehead. 'Have you only just realized that, Jim Searle?'

It didn't take Ruby long to realize that teaching the German girls how to become good domestics wasn't going to be easy. She had to start with very basic stuff, such as how to clean the carpet with the Vactric or a carpet sweeper, and how to dust shelves without breaking things. She was surprised that she even had to teach them how to wash up, but, when faced with a sink full of dirty dishes, Elisheva had thrown up her hands in horror. Left to her own devices, she failed to use hot water and, having handled the dishcloth with her fingertips, was surprised to discover that it didn't remove all the grease. What's more, she started by washing the pans first, so she had to change the water to wash the plates. Ruby couldn't understand why they were so inept, until Elisheva confided in her that this was the first kitchen she had ever been into in her life. She had no idea that she was supposed to put soda in hot water and plunge her whole hand underneath, with the dirty dish.

Ruby taught the girls how to store food – meat in the meat safe, vegetables on the dry stone floor, if there was no refrigerator in the house. She was aware that some people with posh houses, even if they had several servants, couldn't always afford new gadgets.

'Stand the milk bottles in a pail of cold water in the cool larder during the summer months,' she said. 'If it's really hot, it might be better to boil the milk with a little saltpetre when it arrives. It won't taste quite the same, but it will stop it going off.'

Some of the old home remedies were the best, so she showed them how to scrub larder shelves with sand in warm water, and how to clean and polish windows with vinegar and newspaper.

Even having to deal with Jim, with his tetchy moods, was quite helpful. Ruby didn't bother to apologize for her husband's behaviour. She knew that any prospective employer might be just the same, and the girls would have to learn how to deal with it.

'You won't get much time to yourself,' Ruby warned them, as she introduced them to the tedious job of cleaning the cooker with bicarbonate of soda and vinegar. 'I used to get one day a week off when I worked in Warnes, and I considered myself lucky. Some live-in domestics only have a half-day a fortnight.'

Rivka's jaw dropped. Ruby touched her arm sympathetically. 'It may not be as bad as that. My sister-in-law is doing her best to find you a really good situation.'

Rivka wiped away a tear with the heel of her hand. 'I hate this. I wish I could die,' she murmured.

'Then you must go back home right now,' said Elisheva, rounding on her, 'and your wish will come true.' Her chin quivered and she burst into tears.

It was an emotional moment for them all. Ruby felt helpless and, seeing their distress, she found her own throat tightening. All she could offer was a shoulder to cry on and a clean handkerchief. Then she needed one herself.

'I'll never remember all this,' Rivka blurted out.

'Then we'll spend the afternoon together and you can write it down.'

Elisheva looked up with a tiny ray of hope in her eyes.

'And don't forget,' Ruby said softly, 'I am always here at the end of the telephone, or you can write me a letter. Although Rivka was her junior, Elisheva was older than Ruby, but their helplessness and vulnerability brought out her mothering instinct. Ruby could hardly imagine what they were going through: far from home, in a strange country and having to struggle to master a foreign language. They were constantly being asked to do things that were completely alien to them. On top of all that, they were frantic for news about their family and loved ones who had not yet reached safety. Every moment of the day the girls dreaded that they had already been sent to Hitler's camps. They were all living in perilous times.

For the most part, Jim kept out of everybody's way. Ruby couldn't help feeling slightly irritated that he seemed to spend all his time reading the paper and doing crossword puzzles. The only time he ventured out was when he leaned over the back of the wheelchair to post a letter at the end of the road. Ruby wondered vaguely who he was writing to, but with all the pressures of the daily routine, she kept forgetting to ask him.

Almost two weeks later and by prior arrangement, Rachel came round. She surprised Ruby by saying that she and Percy were about to move to Shoreham, about six miles away, where they had just bought a modest house near the docks. There was a plot of land nearby and Percy was busy creating a lorry park. He planned to run his fledgling haulage business from a small cabin on the site, and was busy looking for someone who could run a tea van for the drivers. Ruby was very excited at the thought of having them so close.

'You must come over as soon as you can,' Rachel said.

The real reason for her visit was to collect the two girls. Their work permits had arrived and they were to leave at once. Rivka was going to work for a businessman and his wife in Pulborough, and Elisheva was heading for a position in Goring.

Tearfully, the girls hugged Ruby and thanked her.

'Don't forget to write, will you?' she said as she swallowed the lump in her throat and went to the gate to wave them off. Jim had shuffled out to the gate with them and shook hands stiffly, while Rachel put their cases into the boot of the car.

With the car loaded up, Elisheva sat primly in the

126

front, while a tearful Rivka sat in the back. Jim headed off to the postbox.

'When I get back,' Rachel said to Ruby, 'we'll go to Brighton for that special shopping trip.'

Ruby glanced at her husband, who was already halfway down the road, leaning over the wheelchair. Silk knickers and perfume – what would he say to that?

'I don't suppose you and Jim . . . ?' Rachel whispered in Ruby's ear as she kissed her cheek.

Ruby lowered her eyes, blushed and shook her head.

Rachel winked. 'You soon will be.'

CHAPTER 11

Ruby and Rachel went to Brighton the following Thursday. Rachel drove like a madwoman. They moved from the relative calm of Worthing along the seafront to Shoreham, where the traffic increased as they approached the port. Heading towards Hove, the houses were larger and people strolled along the waterfront. Brighton itself was teeming with life, a mixture of a modern seaside resort and genteel living. They passed large hotels, Victorian lamp stands and Regency buildings, before coming to the somewhat seedier part of the town. Several times during their car ride to Brighton, Ruby gripped the edge of her seat and prayed, as a sharp corner loomed or an oncoming lorry came perilously close to them. A couple of car drivers gesticulated and one man flashed his headlights, but Rachel seemed impervious to them all. She took Ruby to the heart of the shopping area and parked in a small side-street.

The shop, on the edge of the area called The Lanes, was down in the basement. They went down a steep flight of steps and the proprietress, a personal friend of her sister-in-law, greeted them warmly. As the two friends caught up with each other, Ruby gazed in wonder at the beautiful things hanging from the rails. Such delicate colours: silks and the new material she had read about that was all the rage – rayon. There were petticoats with delicate edging, nightdresses with matching bed jackets, and silk panties in fabulous colours like peach, pale blue and lavender; definitely not the sort of thing you would buy in Woolworths.

'I want you to give my friend a complete wardrobe,' Ruby heard Rachel saying. 'Don't bother about the price tag. I want her to look sensational.'

Ruby looked up, startled. What was Rachel saying? She could never afford all that. Having glanced at the price tags, she might manage a couple of pairs of panties and perhaps a petticoat, but that was all.

'This is your twenty-first birthday present from Percy and me,' Rachel said. 'Now enjoy yourself.'

'Oh, Rachel . . .' Ruby began.

'I mean it, darling,' said Rachel. 'Come on, where shall we start?'

Ruby could have wept. 'I hope you're not expecting me to show Percy first,' she quipped.

The three women enjoyed the joke and set about choosing beautiful things. An hour and a half flashed by, and Ruby emerged from the shop weighed down with bags. She had chosen a nightie, a couple of brassieres, some panties, a petticoat and a silk dressing gown, and she couldn't wait to see Jim's face when she put them on. Surely now she would be irresistible.

'I think I might keep it all in my drawer until my

birthday,' Ruby confided. 'It would feel very special then.'

'Why not,' said Rachel. She winked and nudged her sister-in-law in the ribs. 'You're sure to get a real birthday treat then.' Ruby felt herself blush a deep crimson.

They made the most of their time together by looking around the other shops, and ended up having lunch together in Hanningtons department store. On the way back home, although Rachel's reckless driving meant Ruby found herself praying she would live long enough for Jim to see her in her lovely things, she began to ponder on bringing in some changes. She hadn't thought about her husband or the guest house for a whole morning. It had been such fun – and fun wasn't really part of her vocabulary any more. There were times, if she was honest, when she resented Jim. He couldn't do anything about how things had turned out and she knew that, but the fact that he was such a drain on her life made it doubly difficult. Many was the time she wished for some respite from the drudgery of doing the same thing, day in, day out. She didn't normally allow herself to dwell on it too deeply, because it upset her to think that was the way it was going to be for the rest of her life. This morning had made Ruby realize that she needed some time to herself. She had been behaving as if life had already passed her by, and it wasn't doing her any good. She had to get a bit of balance back into her life.

'We're expecting some more girls in the next couple

of weeks,' said Rachel, interrupting her thoughts. 'Do you think you could help me out again?'

'No problem,' said Ruby, 'and there's no need to worry about asking me again.' She went on to explain that, with the help of Rivka and Elisheva, she had cleaned out the attic and made a cosy space up there. 'If I already have guests,' she continued, 'the girls will have a place to stay whenever they come, even at short notice.'

'You are amazing,' said Rachel. 'We are so grateful, and the fact that you are willing to teach them is an added bonus.'

Ruby dismissed the compliment with a wave of her hand. The fact was: she had loved doing it. Even though Rivka and Elisheva had been traumatized and afraid, she enjoyed the company of women and the opportunity to help those who were down on their luck. The best times were always in the kitchen. She not only taught the girls how to cook, but showed them how to carve a joint, prepare a crab and make a pouring custard. Custard was a completely alien food to the Germans, and although the girls both made up their minds not to like it, as soon as Ruby poured it out of the double saucepan and put it into a jug, everyone agreed that they never knew egg yolk, milk and sugar with a dash of vanilla could taste so delicious.

Elisheva, who had taken the English name of Elizabeth, had written to Ruby to say that her employers treated her well. But Rivka hadn't fared so well. She had refused to change her name and worked long hours for an inconsiderate employer who, when Rivka didn't understand what was required, simply shouted the same incomprehensible instructions over and over again. Ruby advised her to stick it out for a bit, to get a good reference, and then look for another job.

A week or so later, Worthing – along with every town, village and hamlet in the country – was in celebratory mood. The previous year had not only been a trying year for Ruby and Jim, but also a time of heartache for the country. It began in January, when the solemn news came that King George V had died. Once the old king had been laid to rest, the country looked forward to, and began preparations for, the coronation of his eldest son. But in December of that same year a surprise announcement had left everybody stunned. King Edward VIII had abdicated, because he was not allowed to marry a divorcee. 'I have,' the King told his people, 'found it impossible to carry the heavy burden of responsibility and to discharge my duties as King as I would wish to do, without the help and support of the woman I love.'

It was only then that everyone in the country realized that although half the world knew what was coming, the British press had kept quiet until just two weeks before the announcement was made. At the cinema the audience scrutinized the face of the King's lover, with varying opinions. Mrs Simpson was well groomed and attractive, in a rather austere kind of way. Because she liked the King, Ruby wanted to like Mrs Simpson; but once the secret was out, rumours abounded – the most

132

bizarre of which was that Wallis Simpson was, in fact, a man.

Jim muttered darkly that the King should do his duty, whereas Ruby had a softer, more romantic view. 'Everyone has the right to be happy,' she said, but that was before the country was told about Wallis Simpson's failed marriage (not one, but two) and her many other lovers. One mistake, most people agreed, might have been forgiven; but the nation shook its collective head in disbelief. The King was totally besotted by her and was actually giving up his throne to marry a loose woman.

The new king was Edward's brother, the Duke of York. He was to be known as King George VI. He seemed to be a gentle man, nervous, fond of family life, but hardly the sort for public office. For a start, he had a terrible stammer. In this matter people kept their thoughts to themselves, but his speeches – peppered by long pauses and audible gulps – made uncomfortable listening. Fortunately for the King, everyone loved his wife, especially the people of Worthing. The Duchess of York had won the hearts and minds of the people of Worthing after she had opened the Queen Alexandra Hospital Home for disabled ex-service personnel, known as Gifford House, just around the corner from Ruby's guest house in May 1934. These men were the forgotten casualties of war: men who could no longer look after themselves and were doomed to lie forgotten in lonely rooms. Gifford House offered them comradeship, companionship and a chance to enjoy their lives again, as well as giving them the very best care available.

The country also loved the beautiful little daughters of the new King and Queen, the Princesses Elizabeth and Margaret Rose.

When, after a few more months of uncertainty, coronation day – May 12th, 1937 – finally arrived, coachloads of people, including Cousin Lily and her new husband, along with Aunt Vinny, left Worthing in the small hours of the morning from the seafront, to be part of the crowds in London. Ruby knew they wouldn't be back until tomorrow morning, but hopefully they would have a day to remember.

As for the rest of the family, they had decided to have a get-together and enjoy the procession through the town. The coronation service was being broadcast live on the radio waves in the Odeon cinema. It was free to anyone, but Ruby said she preferred to wait for the newsreel film, which was being flown to Shoreham airport later in the day and would be screened that evening in the Odeon, the Rivoli and the Plaza cinemas. Ruby guessed the cinemas would be packed out for the first couple of evenings, so everyone planned to go on Saturday.

The plan for the day itself was to enjoy being together under one roof and catching up with each other's news; to have a meal and then to gather on Heene Road to watch the procession as it went past. They should have a good view. It might not be as exciting as seeing the King and Queen in person, but there would be marching bands and floats and a carnival atmosphere. Ruby was looking forward to it.

She and her mother had shared the preparation of the meal. Rex staggered in with a roast beef joint, which Ruby covered in greaseproof paper and put into an old-fashioned hay box to keep warm, alongside the roast potatoes, parsnips and other vegetables.

As the people gathered in the street, a van drew up outside Mrs McCoody's old place. Bea and May were keen to cross over the road and watch the procession from the other side, because without overhanging trees in the way, they would be able to watch the procession coming down the road for a lot longer. Rex wheeled Jim across, and it only remained for Ruby to join them. Instead she stood still and watched as a man aged about twenty-five climbed out of the car and walked up Mrs McCoody's driveway. He knocked on the door. Getting no answer, he stood by the window and peered in.

Ruby had to do something. He obviously had no idea what had happened. He must be a guest and had booked to stay with Mrs McCoody some time ago. As she followed him up the drive, the man moved back to the front door and crouched down.

'Auntie,' he shouted through the letter box, 'Auntie, are you in there?'

'Excuse me,' said Ruby, by now right behind him.

Startled, the man nearly jumped out of his skin.

'I'm so sorry,' Ruby apologized. 'I didn't mean to make you jump. Are you Mrs McCoody's nephew?'

The man straightened up and backed away slightly. 'So what if I am? What's it to you?'

'Oh dear,' Ruby began. 'I'm afraid I have some very bad news.'

The man stared at her in amazement. They could hear the sound of distant music. The marching bands must be on their way.

'I live next door,' Ruby went on. 'I wonder, would you like to come in for a minute? It might be better to tell you indoors, rather than outside on the street.'

'Tell me what?' the man insisted. 'Just say what you have to say.'

Ruby had no choice. 'I'm sorry to tell you that your aunt has died.'

She could tell at once that it was a body-blow.

'She went very peacefully,' said Ruby, anxious to give the poor man a crumb of comfort. 'Her solicitor has been trying to find you . . .' Her voice trailed away as an angry voice interrupted them.

'Oi, you there!' A policeman was waiting by the gate. 'Yes, you, sunshine.' The man looked even more startled. 'The parade is on its way,' said the policeman. 'Get this van out of the way.'

'Parade?' said the man faintly.

'We're having a coronation carnival,' said Ruby quickly.

'You can pull it up onto the drive,' said the policeman. 'There's nobody living in that house, but get it off the street – and look sharp about it.'

'This man is Mrs McCoody's nephew,' Ruby explained, as the pair of them hurried back down the drive.

'Oh,' the policeman nodded curtly. 'I'm sorry for your

136

loss,' he said crisply, 'but you need to get this van out of the way.'

The music was getting louder all the time. Given another five minutes, the parade would be upon them. The man climbed hurriedly into the driver's seat and swung the van off the road. Ruby could see a woman and a little girl inside. Should she stay and help them? In the end she decided that if they were still in the van when the parade had passed, she would offer to tell them the name of the solicitor. He would most likely have the key, but he probably wouldn't be back at his desk until tomorrow. Coronation Day had been declared a national holiday. Ruby waved at them, then hurried across the road to find the rest of her family.

The procession wasn't long, but everybody enjoyed watching the floats and seeing friends and neighbours taking part. May was on the back of a lorry, with all her friends from the ballet class. When she saw her mother and Ruby she gave them a shy wave as they cheered her on. The floats continued on towards the seafront and the centre of town. By the time the parade reached Homefield Park, Rex would be waiting there to bring May back home in the car.

The day itself was fine, but there was still a bit of a chill in the air. Everyone had their fingers crossed that in London it would be warm and sunny. After the Year of the Three Kings, the whole country was eager to settle back down to normal life, even though they knew in their hearts that across the Channel the whole of

Europe trembled. In Spain the Civil War raged on, with thousands feared dead; in Germany, Hitler was gaining the admiration of other leaders, like Benito Mussolini; and just a few days before, in America, the majestic airship the *Hindenburg* had crashed while attempting to dock, killing thirty-five people.

It took about thirty minutes for the rest of the parade to pass and then everyone in Heene Road drifted back home. Ruby glanced over at Mrs McCoody's driveway. The van was still there, but there was no sign of her nephew or his family. She was suddenly concerned for them. If they had come from a distance, the likelihood of having had anything to eat was remote. There was certainly no food at all in the house. Ruby, at the behest of the solicitor, had removed everything from the kitchen and larder, to discourage rats.

'You go on in, Mum,' said Ruby. 'I just want to check that they're all right. I may invite them to join us to eat.'

Bea nodded and Ruby headed up the path. She knocked for some time before the woman came to the door, and even then opened it only a crack. Ruby could see just half of her face, but she looked pale and tired. Her hair hung loose and was badly in need of a wash.

'Oh, hello,' Ruby said brightly. 'I'm sorry to intrude, but I spoke to your husband before the parade. I live next door. I was just wondering if you would like to come and eat with us after your journey. You'd be most welcome.'

'No thanks,' said the woman dully.

Ruby didn't want to give up. 'My little sister was on one of the floats in the parade,' she said. 'I'm sure she would love to play with your little girl. Have you come very far?'

The woman seemed a bit alarmed. She closed the door firmly.

Ruby was stunned. How rude! The man was coming down the street carrying what looked like fish and chips wrapped in newspaper. They met by the gate and Ruby smiled. 'I'm so glad you had a key to get in. I've just asked your wife if you would all like to pop round to my place for a drink and something to eat. You'd be most welcome.'

'We've been on the road all day,' said the man. 'We're too tired.'

Ruby felt a bit affronted. No 'thank you', no acknowledgement of her kindness? 'I'm so sorry you've come here to find bad news. Were you and your aunt very close?' she asked, determined to be pleasant. 'My name is Mrs Searle. Let me know if there's anything I can do to make your stay a pleasant one.'

But the man walked right past her and up the path. Ruby stared after him. How odd. What strange people.

Once in Mrs McCoody's house, Eric put the fish and chips on the kitchen table. Lena had found plates, knives and forks and had laid the table.

'I'll repair the kitchen door tomorrow,' said Eric. 'It only needs the hinge replacing.'

Lena nodded and sat Jean on a cushion on the chair, then pushed her closer to the table.

'Keep away from that nosy cow next door,' said Eric, unwrapping the food. 'She asks far too many bloody questions.'

CHAPTER 12

Cousin Lily came by the next evening to tell the family about her coach trip to London with Nick and Aunt Vinny. She looked very tired, but it had obviously been the trip of a lifetime. Ruby sat her at the kitchen table, and she and Jim listened with rapt attention.

'When the coach dropped us,' Lily said, 'we managed to find a spot along Northumberland Avenue.'

'Where's that?' asked Ruby. She had never been to London, and although she knew the names of all the greatest landmarks, she'd never heard of Northumberland Avenue.

'It's a road that leads to Trafalgar Square,' Lily explained, and at last Ruby got her bearings.

Even though they had arrived in the capital very early in the morning, the crowds were already four or five deep. 'I was so disappointed. Even if I jumped up, I still couldn't see over the heads of the people,' she said, 'so Nick bought me a periscope.' She produced it from her bag. It was a long white tube with a mirror at one end. Ruby was fascinated when her cousin showed her how to use it. 'It was the only way to see anything,' said Lily. Ruby thought it was a very clever idea.

'We're going to see it on the newsreel on Saturday,' said Ruby. 'They're showing it from tonight, but Mum and I thought we'd wait until all the fuss has died down.'

'Good idea,' said Lily, 'but it won't be nearly the same as the real thing.'

Ruby was forced to agree, especially when Lily talked of the marching bands, the colourful uniforms, the Indian army, the New Zealanders and the Scottish pipe-bands of the British army.

'And when we saw the golden coach,' said Lily, her eyes shining with excitement, 'we all waved our hankies and cheered like mad.'

How Ruby wished she'd been able to be there too. She sighed inwardly. It sounded wonderful.

The last time he'd been in this church, Jim was just a kid. Every Sunday the children in the orphanage walked here in a crocodile to attend the morning service. They'd also take the same route on Good Friday and on Ascension Day – which, for some reason he'd never quite fathomed out, was always on a Thursday.

He looked around, but the person who had wanted to meet him wasn't waiting outside. Jim pushed the wheelchair towards the door of the church. Most of the services here had been fairly nondescript, but there was one that stuck in his memory. That was the Sunday when the children had been invited to the christening of Mr Starling's baby. He smiled to himself. That baby would be in her twenties by now. They'd arrived a bit too early, and while the well-behaved children waited in a neat line along the path, Jim and his friend Danny took the opportunity to skip off and wander around the churchyard. Jim remembered that it had seemed like a fantastic place. In places the grass was almost up to his waist, and the whole area was a haven for dragon-flies and bees.

He smiled as he recalled the moment when he'd found the frog. It was hidden in a damp area and sitting so still that he'd almost trodden on it. He picked it up and fell in love with it straight away. Danny had wanted to hold it, but Jim decided it was his, and his alone. They put the frog on a tombstone and encouraged it to jump. That frog was a brilliant little jumper – it leapt for miles. Hearing the master shouting at the boys to 'keep in line', they made their way back to the others. They'd hardly been missed, certainly not by the staff anyway.

Jim pushed the heavy oak door now and, manoeuv-ring the wheelchair awkwardly, managed to get inside. It hurt his back as he went down the deep step, but he made it. These places hadn't been built for people like him. You had to be hale and hearty to get inside God's house, it seemed.

As usual, the inside of the church smelled musty and damp. Jim remembered spotting a birdbath-thing just inside the door. It was the font, of course, but he didn't know that at the time. Curiosity drew him there and he lifted the lid and dipped his finger in the water.

'Don't let old Brown see,' he'd whispered to Danny, and then he'd put the frog into the water. He and Danny watched it doing breaststroke, until one of the masters came over and clipped Danny on the head and told them to sit down. A few minutes later Mr Starling's family arrived, complete with the bawling baby.

Jim pushed the wheelchair down the aisle and found the very pew where he and Danny had sat. He stared at the high altar, recalling the moment the vicar turned up and the ceremony finally began.

'Hello, Jim.'

Mr Starling's sudden appearance made him jump. Jim wouldn't have recognized him in any other setting, but seeing him standing next to Mr Brown, he realized that this wizened old man was indeed his former teacher. The years hadn't been kind to him.

They exchanged pleasantries and talked a little of their memories of the home and then Mr Brown said, 'Walter, Jim wanted to know about his parents. You were in the office a lot of the time – can you tell him anything?'

Jim hadn't known Mr Starling was called Walter. It felt strange knowing such an intimate detail. It made his former teacher something more than just the voice of authority. It made him somehow more human.

'I can't tell you much,' he said. 'It was all very hush-hush.'

'Were they healthy?' Jim asked. 'I mean, did they have something physically wrong with them, that they couldn't look after me?'

Mr Starling shook his head. 'Not as far as I can remember.'

'Then if they didn't want me, why didn't they let me go for adoption?'

'I don't know,' said Mr Starling. 'I'm sorry. It was all so very long ago.'

'Did you ever see them?'

'No.'

Jim stared at the floor. 'Then you can't help me much.'

'I can give you the name of the solicitor who dealt with the legal side of things.'

Jim's head shot up. 'Is he still alive?'

Mr Starling shook his head. 'I don't know, but the offices are still there, and the same name is on the board outside. It's Naiper-Raikes. His offices are in Liverpool Terrace.' He told them he had to get back. He didn't often leave the house and, if he was gone too long, his daughter would be missing him.

'When I came in, I was remembering her christening,' said Jim, as the three men walked back up the aisle. 'Us boys held our breath when the vicar lifted the lid on that font.'

'I always wondered,' said Mr Starling, 'did you plan it?'

Jim shook his head. 'Your baby was yelling her head off and, as the vicar cupped cold water all over her head, the frog took his chance for freedom.'

'Oh yes,' said Mr Brown. 'I remember now. It landed on the edge of the font and sat there, croaking gently and looking around.'

Jim smiled and Mr Starling actually laughed. 'It landed on the vicar's sleeve. Half of my relatives legged it to the back of the church, and my mother was so shocked that she all but fainted.'

'What happened to the frog?' Mr Brown asked.

'It went under one of the pews,' said Jim. 'Us boys cornered him halfway down the aisle and, while everyone else tried to calm everybody down, I took him back outside. I was sad to let him go.'

The two old men chuckled. 'You were a bit of a tyke, Jim Searle,' said Mr Brown.

'I meant no harm,' said Jim. 'I was just curious.'

They helped him out through the awkward doorway and set him back on the path. 'It's been nice seeing you again, lad,' said Mr Brown. 'Good luck with the solicitor.'

'If you take my advice,' said Mr Starling, 'you'll let sleeping dogs lie. It might not do you any good, knowing the truth.'

'I know,' said Jim as they all shook hands, 'but I feel driven to do it.'

Ruby could hardly wait for Saturday evening to come, when she would see the pictures of the coronation. She'd kept a lookout for the family next door, but they hadn't even drawn their curtains back. The van was still on the driveway, so they must be inside, but they kept themselves to themselves. Pity – if she'd managed to catch them, she would have asked them to join them at the cinema.

She cleaned the rooms, once her overnighters left after

breakfast. She had some more people coming on Sunday afternoon and they were staying until the following Friday, so she was facing a busy week. The trip to the Odeon this evening would make a welcome break. Jim had refused to come – as usual. Ruby was a little annoyed, because he never seemed to want to do anything together these days. He spent money they could ill afford on more and more magazines and, apart from sitting in the garden for a while, or playing with the monkey, he was doing crosswords. It frustrated her and she grumbled every now and then, but he would make her feel bad by reminding her that the way he was wasn't his fault. She dropped hints to find out where he'd gone that afternoon, but he wouldn't tell her anything. It was as if he couldn't talk about it.

She had planned to wait until her actual birthday before wearing her lingerie, but late that afternoon she changed her mind. She might save the nightie, but she would put on the underwear. She was only going to the pictures with her mum, Aunt Vinny and Lily, but she didn't care. Tonight she wanted to feel a bit special. The material felt lovely against her skin. She smiled as she pulled her dress over it. Her hair was looking good as well, and her hands were beginning to feel a lot more attractive too. Following Rachel's advice, Ruby had been creaming them thoroughly at night. She'd even worn cotton gloves in bed, so that her skin would reap the benefit of the moisturizing hand cream she'd put on. She heard voices downstairs and knew that her mother, aunt and cousin had arrived with her father and May as well. They were going to walk down to the town together, and after the pictures they planned to drop into the licensed bar underneath. As she walked downstairs and said goodbye to Jim, Ruby felt more alive than she had done in ages.

As soon as they'd gone, Jim sat at the kitchen table with a pencil, a ruler, paper and a dictionary. It was time to put his plan into action. The family might think him idle, but he had spent the past three months doing detailed research. He loved doing crosswords. Since the accident, it was his passion. Some were easier than others, but it hadn't occurred to him for ages that each crossword puzzle was tailored to the readership of the magazine he was reading. A crossword in a magazine was easier to tackle than the one in *The Times* or the *News Chronicle*. Another thing that hadn't occurred to him, until he'd made it his business to find out, was that the templates were similar. Eventually, by buying the magazines on a regular basis, he had worked out that each one probably had only ten or twelve templates, which were used in rotation.

Jim spent hours poring over them all and, when Ruby wasn't around, copied the templates very carefully. The hard bit was putting the answers down. It could be tricky trying to find a word with an 'e' or an 'f' in the right place, so that it fitted in and matched up with another word going up or down. He messed up several templates before he worked out how to do it. Once the answers were in place, all he had to do was write down the questions. Cryptic crosswords were the biggest challenge.

He enjoyed doing it most with the monkey sitting on his shoulder, or on the back of the chair; and once he got going, he worked steadily. He'd have to do a lot of crosswords if he was going to make decent money at it, but he was convinced that once he got into a routine he could bring in anything from two to five pounds for each crossword that was accepted. For the first time in an age he felt he was getting somewhere. Concentrating on the words helped him forget the pain and discomfort. He'd never make a watch repairer or even a sign-writer, or any of the other jobs that the family had bandied about at one time or another. And he'd kept his plans from Ruby because he didn't want her to build up her hopes and have her end up disappointed again. He knew he was a rotten husband, but he really, really cared about her, even though he could no longer show her. There were still times when he wished he'd never married her, but only because she deserved better than this.

His money from the slate club had already run out and the small policy he'd taken out while he was still a photographer, to help him if he ever got sick, was almost exhausted. He'd sold his photographic equipment, apart from the Contax camera that Thomas Kendrick had given him after he'd won a prize to spend a week under his tutorage in 1934. Soon he would be totally reliant on Ruby's earnings and the thought turned Jim's stomach. He had been emasculated, in more ways than one. This was why it was so important to him to find a way of making a living for himself. Perhaps the crosswords would be a start. He glanced up at the clock. Ruby would only be gone for two or maybe three hours. He'd better get cracking, but first he would drop a line to Mr Naiper-Raikes, the solicitor Mr Starling had told him about.

The Odeon cinema, which had been opened in March 1934, was supposed to resemble the sleek lines of an ocean liner. Just off the main shopping street in the centre of Worthing, its tall tower was illuminated at night. There was a large cafe in a curved extension in front of the cinema, with the foyer right behind. Inside, the auditorium was stunningly modern, with a huge multi-layered chandelier and an organ that came up out of the orchestra pit as it was being played during the interval.

As they waited in the queue to go in, Ruby pulled her mother aside and broached the subject of Edith Parsons' need of a home. She had already mentioned it once, almost as soon as Edith asked her, but Bea was understandably cagey. Her lodger, a patient's wife, was using the house while her husband battled for his life in hospital. Under the circumstances, Bea didn't want to talk to her about leaving the property.

'It seems rather insensitive,' she'd told Ruby. 'I don't want to add to the poor woman's problems.'

'Of course not,' Ruby had agreed at the time, but now that Edith's wedding was fast approaching she felt she had to ask again.

'It seems terrible to say this,' Bea began, 'but it shouldn't be long now. He's in the final stages, but please don't say anything yet, darling.'

Ruby nodded. It was ironic that one person's sorrow was another person's joy. Of course she wouldn't say anything to Edith, but she was excited for her. It looked as if her friend could start her marriage in her own home, after all.

Ruby, Bea, May and Rex were lucky to find a seat. As it was, they were unable to sit in the same row. Rex was in the row in front of them. The cinema was buzzing with excitement. When the Pathé News started, Ruby was glued to the screen as the soft voice of the King making his promises filled Westminster Abbey; and when the Archbishop of Canterbury lowered the crown onto King George VI's head, the whole place erupted in spontaneous applause. The two little princesses, Elizabeth and Margaret Rose, looked so sweet in their long dresses with little bows all down the front. They each wore a crown themselves and were flanked by their grandmother, the majestic Queen Mary, and by the Princess Royal. When the main Pathé News presentation was over, the cinema-goers were in for a treat. There was another film of the coronation – a bit shorter than the first, but this one was in colour. Now Ruby could appreciate what Cousin Lily was talking about. The whole of London came to life as she saw the flags in The Mall and the colourful uniforms. She loved all the red and gold and was so lost in the film that it almost felt as if she'd been there herself.

When the show was over, Ruby spotted Bob Knight coming out of the cinema at the same time. He was with a group of friends, but when he saw Ruby he came over to say hello. Everyone made polite conversation, mostly about Lily's wedding and how nice it was; but all the while Ruby was very aware of Bob's closeness, and of her silky underwear. Her heart was racing and she felt dizzy with excitement. His dazzling smile as he left them seemed to be specially for her, and she knew her cheeks had gone pink. As she turned away, her mother said in a low breath, 'Behave yourself. You're a married woman, remember.'

Hugely embarrassed, Ruby blushed and looked away.

When she got back to the guest house, Jim was already upstairs. Ruby kept the light on as she undressed, to make sure he was looking at her.

'Where the hell did you get that?' he asked as she took off her dress. She was standing in front of him in her peach-coloured brassiere and matching panties. She fingered the lace on the leg. She loved the fact that it went all the way round, and that the long slit on her thigh went almost up to the elastic on the waist.

'Do you like them?' she said, parading before him. 'This is what Rachel and Percy are giving me for my twenty-first birthday present. I bought them the day Rachel and I went to Brighton.'

Jim's brow furrowed. 'Your brother bought you that?'

'Well, he didn't actually see it,' Ruby chuckled, 'but

it was a present from them both. It's real silk, and it feels lovely. Go on, feel it.'

Jim's expression was frozen and Ruby suddenly felt uncomfortable. 'What's the matter? Don't you like it? It was very expensive.'

'You look like a French tart,' he spat.

Ruby was devastated. 'I'd only wear things like this for you, Jim. I thought you'd like it.'

'But you've been wearing it tonight,' he said. 'I can't say I like the idea of my wife parading around the town looking like that. Supposing you had an accident and had to go to hospital – what would people think? Take it off, and put on some proper underwear.'

Tears sprang to Ruby's eyes. She walked to the bed to get her nightdress from under her pillow, but then thought better of it. Jim had his head turned away from her, so she opened her drawer and took out the silk nightie. She had planned to save it until her twenty-first birthday, but when she slipped it over her shoulders, it fitted her like a dream, flattering her slim figure and perfectly complementing her complexion and her dark hair. Her breasts were slightly pushed up and the lace trim set it off beautifully.

'Look, Jim,' she said softly. 'I'll never wear this, other than in our bedroom. This is just for your eyes.'

Her husband turned his head and his jaw dropped. Ruby smiled. This was exactly the reaction she'd wanted. He had been sitting on his side of the bed while he took his socks off. He was ready to swing his legs up and pull the covers over himself. Instead he walked slowly

153

around the bed. She smiled up at him as he approached, her eyes bright with happiness. He snatched at the top half angrily and she felt the stitching go. Then he drew back his hand and slapped her across the face – hard.

'I don't know what you think you're doing,' he said in a cold, measured tone she'd never heard before, 'but I told you before, Ruby: the answer is no. Now get it into your head – it is not going to happen.'

She was crying now. Her face hurt so much it felt as if he'd split her cheek, but as she could see herself in the mirror, she knew her skin was still intact, even though it was already very red. Her head was spinning too. She supposed it was because the force of the blow had made it jerk sideways. With her hand on her flaming cheek, she watched in disbelief as Jim went back to his side of the bed and sat down. Although deeply shocked and surprised, her heart was pounding. She wanted to hit him back, scratch his eyes out, call him every foul name she could think of. But instead she could only stand and weep as a big black cloud of despair enveloped her. Dear God, *for better, for worse* – was this it? Did she have to put up with this for the rest of her life?

There was a terrible silence in the room and, when she finally found the strength to speak, her voice was quiet.

'I hate you, Jim Searle, and I wish to God I'd never married you.'

He leaned forward and put his head in his hands. 'So do I, Ruby. Believe me, so do I.'

CHAPTER 13

Jean wasn't very well. She had been fretful and off her food for a couple of days and Lena was worried. They had woken up to find her hot and sweaty, her hair plastered to her head.

'She's got a temperature,' said Lena as she picked her up. Jean whimpered. 'We have to get a doctor.'

'No doctors,' said Eric. 'If I get a doctor, there'll be questions.'

'We don't have to tell him everything,' said Lena. 'She's our baby and we came here to see your auntie – what's wrong with that?'

'No doctors,' said Eric. He was beginning to get a bit browned off with the way things were going. He was crazy about Lena and would have done anything for her, but spending every waking hour in a locked-up house was not his idea of fun. They had to keep their heads down until everything calmed down, but he wanted to get out, get a job and have a normal life. They'd been in Worthing almost two weeks now and, apart from the occasional stare from the nosy cow next door and a word with the bloke behind the counter where he bought groceries, he hadn't spoken to a living soul.

As the day wore on, the toddler was very limp. Her face remained flushed, even though Lena constantly sponged her down with a cold flannel. By lunchtime things hadn't changed.

'We have to do something, Eric,' she wailed. 'I don't want my baby to die.'

'Nobody's going to die,' said Eric. 'Just let her sleep it off. She'll be fine.'

'If she dies, I shall tell the police it was all your fault.'

'You're the kid's mother,' he retaliated angrily.

'And I shall say you kidnapped me and held me here against my will.'

Eric stared at her in disbelief.

'Well?' she challenged. 'You never let us go outside the front door, do you?'

'I don't want nobody asking questions,' Eric insisted.

'Mummy . . .' Jean whimpered. 'I want my mummy.'

'I'm here, darling,' said Lena. 'Mummy's here.'

Jim was consumed with guilt. He couldn't understand why he had reacted the way he did. For some reason the sight of that nightdress had sparked something truly ugly, deep down inside him – something that he had no idea was even there. Of course he knew that was no excuse, but he wasn't a man given to violence or bad temper. He had always prided himself that he had control over his emotions. It wasn't so terrible, what Ruby had done, but when he'd seen her dressed like

156

that, it was as if all the frustration and anger he'd been trying to subdue these past months had boiled over. May God forgive him – he'd hit a woman. He had always despised wife-beaters, and now he was one of them. He couldn't get the thought out of his mind. He churned it round and round for hours on end, until he felt emotionally crippled and exhausted.

He couldn't concentrate on his crosswords. He was too angry: angry with himself, and angry with Ruby for starting all this up again. The trouble was, she honestly believed that a kiss and a cuddle would make everything all right. She was a romantic, but when it came to the harsh realities of life, she was still so naive. Why couldn't she simply accept that he just couldn't have sex. He didn't want it. He couldn't do it. He couldn't get it up any more. It was unfair and it was lousy, but there it was.

Right now, he couldn't bear to look at her. It was a mixture of hurt and shame, but he was hard pushed even to understand his own feelings, he felt so mixed up. Sometimes, when he was sure that he was on his own, when she'd gone to the shops or something, Jim wept. He wept for his parents; he wept for what might have been; and he wept because he couldn't redeem himself.

Ruby wept too. She wept because the moment Jim slapped her face, something in their relationship died. The trust was gone. And if she couldn't trust him, how could they ever be happy again? She didn't want to, but she always ended up going over and over everything that had happened in those awful months after the accident. She was no paragon of virtue herself, but she had made a bit more of an effort to save their marriage than he had. She'd tried to get him back on his feet. Look at the hours and hours she'd spent massaging his legs when he first came out of hospital. In the end he'd told her to stop, and when the family nagged him for not doing the exercises any more or refusing to go to the swimming baths, she'd stuck up for him.

She'd given Jim everything for his comfort, but whatever she'd done, it wasn't enough. She'd encouraged him the best way she knew how, but he'd simply given up. It was as if he didn't want things to get any better. And now he'd turned violent. Was it so wrong to do what she'd done? All she'd wanted was her husband back again. Rachel had told her there were other ways of doing it. She'd blushed when her sister-in-law had been so frank, but she was grateful at the same time. Apparently Jim didn't have to work with his legs.

'When he's ready for you, why don't you sit astride him,' Rachel had said. 'Lower yourself onto him. That way you can both enjoy each other, and it won't put Jim under any strain.'

The more Ruby thought about it, the more it made sense. She would have told him her idea that night, but Jim wouldn't even discuss making love. That slap had done a lot more than hurt her cheek. She felt broken inside; broken, unloved and doomed to live out this childless sham of a marriage. She couldn't bring herself to look at him. Their conversation was monosyllabic, and she spent her days either avoiding him or going out of the room when he came in.

When the Sunday-to-Friday guests arrived, Ruby knew she would have to give them a plausible explanation for the bruise on her cheek. It had gone from red to blue and, worst of all, she was left with a very distinct finger mark.

'You'll have to excuse the way I look,' she said with an apologetic smile, 'but as you can see, my husband has difficulty in getting around. I saw him stumble and went to grab him, but unfortunately I ended up as the casualty. I look a bit of a sight, but everything is perfectly fine.'

She wasn't sure how much of her story they believed but, having arrived on Sunday, they told her on Monday evening they would be leaving in the morning after breakfast, because 'Something has come up'. Ruby guessed they had spent the day searching for another guest house. That made her even more annoyed with Jim. Now he was losing her business, as well.

Whenever she walked into the room, Wilfred the monkey eyed her nervously. It was as if he sensed the tension between her and Jim. Biscuit behaved as normal, but then as long as he had food, Biscuit was anybody's. She and Jim never spoke about what happened that Saturday night. When she had washed it, Ruby folded her lovely underwear and put in towards the back of the drawer. Through her tears, she did her best to mend the nightdress, but the lace around the neckline was irreparably damaged. It was such a shame. Perhaps she would never have anything so beautiful again.

With the *Vacancies* sign up in the window and no guests, Ruby was free to do as she pleased for at least a couple of days. Rachel was bringing two more refugees on Friday, but in the meantime Ruby decided to catch the bus to Chichester. As she walked towards the gate, she heard her mysterious neighbour calling from Mrs McCoody's. She hadn't seen much of the family since they'd arrived. They'd kept themselves to themselves more than most, but now Mrs McCoody's nephew looked worried.

'Excuse me, love. Do you know where's the nearest doctor? Only our Jean has been took bad.'

'Oh yes,' said Ruby. 'Dr Quinn is at the other end of the road. There's a sign outside the door. You can't miss it.'

The man went to get in the van.

'I've got a telephone,' said Ruby. 'It'll be quicker. What name shall I say?'

'Er . . . Bill Tucker.' He hesitated. 'You're all right, love. I'll use the van.'

As she turned to go back into the house, he tried to start the engine, but a couple of weeks sitting idle in the driveway had made it difficult to start. When Ruby came back out to tell him that the doctor was on his way, Mr Tucker was sitting in the driver's seat with the bonnet up.

'Would you like me to come and see if I can help with the little one?' Ruby asked. She was aware that

160

Jim had followed her to the door and was just behind her, watching.

'No!' said the man, getting out of the van quickly. Ruby was startled, so he added in a softer tone, 'You never know, it might be catching.'

A few minutes later Rex drew up outside the door and hurried up the path, carrying his doctor's bag. Both men went inside the house.

Bea had been on a voyage of discovery. Now an avid reader, she had stumbled across an article about a philanthropist called Andrew Carnegie. First she had to look up the word 'philanthropist' and found out that it was to do with being generous to people. She then went on to discover that Andrew Carnegie had strong connections with Worthing.

Born a Scot, Carnegie moved to the United States as a boy and rose to become one of the richest people in the world. After he sold his Carnegie Steel Company in 1901 for a reputed $250 million, he devoted the rest of his life to building libraries (one of which was Worthing's) and making donations to worthy causes. To show their gratitude, Worthing Council not only named a road after him, but also made him a Freeman of the Borough.

Andrew Carnegie had died some eighteen years before, but the residue of his enormous fortune was still being shared out, and the Townswomen's Guild had been allocated £800 to develop an interest in craftwork among its members. Armed with this information, Bea first approached Effie about holding a craft fair to raise funds for Gifford House.

Although she listened, Effie wasn't very encouraging. 'My dear, it will be an awful lot of hard work. Have we got time to do it this year?'

'I'm sure our ladies will be up for it,' said Bea, bursting with enthusiasm. 'There's so much terrible news these days – it will help to lift our spirits.'

'But think of the extra cost.' Effie frowned.

'From what I can gather,' said Bea, handing over the paperwork, 'we could get a small grant to help us set it up.'

Effie scanned the piece of paper she'd been handed and grunted in a non-committal fashion.

Bea wasn't about to give up so soon. 'If I may make a suggestion,' she began, 'think of it as a modern-day parable of the loaves and fishes. We've got extra funds from the sale of teas and coffees to get us going, and the money we make from the raffle is excellent. If we could get our share of a grant, I'm sure each lady will pull her weight.'

The rest of the committee was just as enthusiastic, when the idea was mooted to them. That was just as well because by then Bea had already secured the church hall across the road for the day Effie deemed suitable, Saturday, October 3rd. The Parish Rooms was barely big enough for the monthly meetings, let alone for holding a sale for members of the public.

'This will lift our spirits in these dark days,' Effie told the members at the next meeting. 'Each lady can use her skill to make something and enter one of the competitions.'

There was a murmur of approval as she spoke.

'We shall offer a small prize for first, second and third places, and hopefully encourage others to join us or, at the very least, to take up a hobby of their own.'

By now the murmur had become a hum of excitement.

'Mrs Fosdyke has a clipboard with a list,' Effie went on. 'We are looking for helpers for the day, and for volunteers to put up posters.'

By gleaning information from friends and patients who had run church bazaars or WI fundraisers, Bea had formed a comprehensive plan. Not only was the bigger hall secured, but she had also costed out the publicity posters, ordered certificates and badges and, with the help of Mrs Crockerton, the branch secretary, had constructed an entry form for the exhibitors. Miss Horton and her team organized who was doing what concerning the catering on the day, and decided there would be teas and coffees served through the hatch. She also made sure there were enough tablecloths to cover each table, and enough white sheets to cover the trestle tables for the exhibits. A red ribbon pinned to the table would mark off each bay, and the classes would include making an apron, embroidery, needlepoint, making a child's toy, best-dressed doll, creating a wild-flower arrangement, a pincushion, a sun hat (although by the time of the sale, summer would be over), a knitted article, and a novelty class – in case someone made something that didn't really fit in any of the other classes.

'Hopefully,' Effie told her starry-eyed members as she presented Bea's plan to the meeting, 'these categories will ensure that everybody has something they'll enjoy.'

Mrs Wilmot had some good ideas about publicizing the event; Mrs Raymond suggested having a bumper raffle; and Miss Taylor was put in charge of collecting prizes. The hum of excitement rose to a buzz.

'The thing we need above all else,' Effie told them, 'is someone of note to open the fair.'

The women looked at each other with a sense of hopelessness.

'We could try Councillor Bentick Budd,' someone called out. But as a member of the BUF and a controversial figure, some feared that he might attract the wrong sort of person.

'There's Matron from the hospital,' suggested Mrs Wilmot, but that idea was quickly dismissed, as she might be far too busy. Several other suggestions were put forth – and even Rex's name was bandied about – but for one reason or another, none was deemed suitable. When the conversation had died down, Effie stood up again.

'I have been talking to Elsie and Doris Walters,' she said rather smugly. 'I don't know if any of you are aware, but they both live in Steyning. I believe they are free to come on Saturday October the seventeenth. Is that a good day for our fair? Would you like me to ask them?'

'Oh,' said Bea. 'I thought you wanted October the third.'

'Did you, dear?' said Effie. 'Whatever gave you that idea? Anyway, Elsie and Doris can only come on the seventeenth. I do hope you can change it, dear; if not, we'll have to put it off until sometime next year.'

The other members of the committee looked at Bea, disappointment written all over their faces. Bea struggled to control her tongue. The cow! Effie had done it on purpose, hadn't she? 'I'll do my best,' she said, tight-lipped.

Effie smiled. 'So does everybody agree that if Mrs Quinn can correct her mistake, I should ask Elsie and Doris?'

The suggestion was greeted with great enthusiasm. Elsie and Doris Walters – better known as 'Gert and Daisy' – had been musical artists for many years and were very well known. As for the date, everyone agreed that to do a summer fair would be far too much of a rush, but October 17th meant they would be in good time for Christmas, and yet there was every possibility that the weather would still be good.

Mrs Crockerton, who was sitting next to Bea, whispered, 'I've got a gramophone record of Gert and Daisy with Stanley Holloway. They are very funny.'

'Now that I know everyone is in agreement,' said Effie, 'I shall get on the telephone as soon as Mrs Quinn has rectified her mistake.'

Rub it in, why don't you? thought Bea acidly. Everyone applauded and, as she joined in, despite being angry, Bea couldn't help having a sneaky admiration for Effie.

She certainly knew how to play to the crowd and manipulate everything to her own advantage.

'I want you to think of this,' Effie shouted over the noise, until everyone quietened down, 'as the story of the loaves and fishes. If we give what we can wholeheartedly, it will multiply and help many needy people.'

As the meeting broke up for refreshments, Mrs Wilmot leaned over towards Bea. 'Isn't she a ruddy marvel,' she said in a loud whisper. 'Where does she get all those wonderful ideas from?'

'I really can't imagine,' Bea sniffed.

CHAPTER 14

It was amazing what a shepherd's pie could do. The day Jean was taken ill, Ruby cancelled her bus trip to Chichester and made one for Bill Tucker and his wife. When it came out of the oven, she tried knocking on the kitchen door; but getting, as she had suspected, no answer, she pushed a note through the letter box and left the shepherd's pie on the step. By the time she'd reached her own back door, although her neighbour's door remained firmly closed, Mrs Tucker had taken the dish in. She called over with the empty dish a couple of days later.

'Come in, come in,' cried Ruby when she saw who it was. 'I'll put the kettle on.'

Mrs Tucker hesitated for a second or two but, to Ruby's delight, she came in. She was very young, maybe eighteen, but no more. Her short blonde hair was fluffed up at the sides, parted on the left and with a deep wave on the right. She had big brown eyes and an innocent face.

'I can only stay a minute,' she said. 'I have to get back to Jean.'

'How is she?' asked Ruby. Rex made a point of never discussing his patients, so Ruby knew better than to ask him what was wrong with the baby.

'She had tonsillitis,' said Mrs Tucker. 'It was quite nasty, but nothing too serious.'

'Oh, I *am* sorry.'

'She's on the mend now,' said Mrs Tucker. 'Lots of jelly to eat. Right now she's helping her daddy with a jigsaw puzzle.'

They smiled at each other. Ruby pushed a cup of steaming tea in front of her neighbour. 'I didn't know your husband's aunt very well,' she began, 'but she seemed a nice woman. We sometimes shared guests. If she was too full, I would take hers; and if I was all booked up, I'd send them next door.'

Mrs Tucker lowered her eyes. 'Sadly, I never met her. Eric used to come and stay with her when he was a boy. There was an old man living in this house then.'

'Eric?' said Ruby.

'My husband,' said Mrs Tucker. 'He's Eric and I'm Lena.'

'Oh,' said Ruby, surprised. 'I thought your husband's name was Bill Tucker.' She laughed. 'I can't think where I got that idea from.'

Lena seemed surprised too. 'Our name is Farmer,' she said, her face colouring slightly.

Ruby was puzzled. How odd. She needed to change the subject. 'The old man your husband remembered living here was Linton Carver,' she said. 'He always seemed old to me while I was growing up in the town, but in actual fact he wasn't that old. He had war injuries.'

'Shame,' said Lena, finishing her tea quickly. 'Well, thanks again for the pie. It was lovely.'

'You're welcome,' said Ruby, sensing Lena was about to go. 'Look, when Jean is better, why don't you both come round for a cup of tea? My husband has a little monkey. I'm sure Jean would enjoy feeding it.'

'A monkey!' cried Lena. 'But aren't they dangerous?'

'It was wild when he caught it,' said Ruby, 'but it's quite tame now. It sits on his shoulders most of the time.'

'Well, well,' said Lena, standing to her feet.

Ruby watched her walking back down the path and gave her a little wave at the gate. She seemed a nice enough woman. Who knows, given time they might become friends.

Ruby woke with a flutter of excitement in the pit of her stomach. Today was her twenty-first birthday. She had come of age. There were no plans for the morning, but she had been told to go to her mother's house for 3.30 p.m. Nothing had been said, but she guessed there would be a little family party, with presents and cake. Ruby felt as excited as a silly schoolgirl.

She had kept the calendar free that day, although she would be having another set of refugees the following Saturday, and on that score things were going well. By now she had worked out what jobs were the most difficult ones for the girls to comprehend, when it came to going into service, and had put together the know-ledge she had gained into a small booklet. The only trouble was, it was laboriously slow writing it all out by hand over and over again. Rachel suggested getting a typewriter, but it still meant making numerous dupli-cate copies. For that reason she thought about getting it properly printed, but worried about the cost. She had a stream of visitors and she was getting faithful returners, so she knew her reputation for a clean house and a comfortable stay was growing all the time. Perhaps in a few more weeks she could contemplate getting a booklet priced up by the printers.

As for the problem with Jim, mostly they kept out of each other's way. He had gone back to doing his crosswords, although he was often distracted by the comments on the letters pages. Sometimes he agreed with what the letter-writer had to say, but more often they had him reaching for his own pen to make a reply. There was one name that stood out from the rest. Those letters were always signed 'B. Simmons Jr'. The writer came from Upper High Street, Worthing (the *Herald* printed his address in their columns), but his letters were also in the pages of several other newspapers and magazines. Jim studied the way B. Simmons Jr wrote his letters.

The subject matter varied. It seemed that the man had an opinion on just about everything, and Jim began to understand that his letters were the answer to an editor's prayer. Terse and almost abrupt, they contained no waffle, no fanciful turns of phrase and no awkward sentences. Brief and to the point, the letters penned by B. Simmons Jr were easy enough to slip into any small space on the page. 'The football-pools winnings should be taxed,' he thundered in the *News Chronicle*. Although he didn't do the pools himself, Jim was irritated by that letter and, when he found himself reaching for his pen to write a reply of disapproval, he suddenly realized why B. Simmons Jr was so successful. A strong opinion evoked a response; that response meant selling more papers, and increased sales would keep the shareholders happy.

Not only did the same letter-writer crop up in the national dailies, but he also had an opinion on local issues. After he pressed for more seats in Homefield Park, and got them, he won the admiration of the people of the town. Jim made a conscious decision to channel his own efforts into something worthwhile. He might not be able to achieve much in the physical sense, but he could wield a pen and take up a cause.

He and Ruby still shared a bed, but after all that had been said on that fateful night, they had started off by sleeping at the very edge of their own side. As the weeks went by, although they no longer kissed each other goodnight, they were more relaxed under the sheets. They still didn't touch, but now they both slept soundly. Neither of them discussed what had happened, which meant that the bitterness of heart they both felt – albeit for different reasons – remained.

For her birthday, Jim had bought Ruby a birthday card and a necklace. She guessed he must have asked her mother or Rachel to do the actual shopping, because Ruby was sure Jim hadn't been into town for months. It didn't really matter. It was the thought that counted, and they were both very pretty. She thanked him, but didn't give him a kiss.

The postman brought a flurry of cards: one from Edith and Bernard, a couple from the girls she used to work with at Warnes, one from Mrs Whichelow on behalf of the Deborah Committee, and even a card from Isaac Kaufman, the German-Jewish refugee who had lodged with them at Newlands Road. She couldn't think how he had remembered her birthday, unless her mother had told him.

Ruby treated the day as any other and stuck to her usual routine until two-thirty, and then she washed and changed her frock. She wore a royal-blue waltz frock that she'd bought in Smith & Strange with money that Bea and Rex had given her. It had a sweetheart neckline and puff sleeves. Gathered under the bust, its panelled skirt swung out attractively as she moved. As it happened, the necklace Jim had given her complemented it perfectly. By three, she and Jim were on their way to her mother's house, with Ruby pushing him in the wheelchair. As they approached Heene Parish Rooms, Rex, looking smart in a dark-blue blazer and white open-necked shirt, stepped out in front of them, giving Ruby a surprise.

'Happy birthday, darling,' he said, taking her into his arms.

Immediately Ruby felt the tears welling up. All those

years when she'd wished her father would hug her and say, 'Happy birthday' and had been disappointed . . . But now here he was. She still couldn't quite believe it.

Percy stepped out onto the street behind him.

'What are you both doing here?' Ruby squeaked.

'We'll sort Jim out,' said Rex. 'You go on inside.'

Her brother bent his head and gave her a peck on the cheek. 'Happy birthday, Sis.'

'Are we in the Parish Rooms?' said Ruby incredulously.

Playfully the two men pushed her through the door, where she was met by a sea of faces – friends, relations and neighbours all calling out 'Happy birthday!'

Ruby could hardly believe her eyes. All the people who mattered to her were here. Her mother and her sister May; Cousin Lily and Nick; Aunt Vinny and her man friend, Bert Cable; and Rachel and Alma. The room was filled with women in colourful afternoon dresses, men in casual suits and children in pretty party frocks. Everywhere she looked, people were smiling at her and wishing her many happy returns. Ruby was hugged and kissed to death. Huddled together in a corner, she spotted Edith Parsons and Bernard, Florrie Dart, Phyllis Dawson and Doris Fox, the girls she had worked with at Warnes all that long time ago.

'How wonderful to see you!' she cried. The sister from the ward where she'd worked in the hospital was there too, and then she spotted Isaac Kaufman.

'But you sent me a card this morning,' cried Ruby as she hugged him.

'I didn't want you to guess that I was coming,' said Isaac. 'It was a little surprise.'

'A lovely surprise,' Ruby smiled happily. He was sitting with Rivka and Elisheva, the first two girls she had schooled to become domestics. Elisheva, who now called herself Elizabeth, looked well; but Rivka had dark circles under her eyes, and although Ruby could tell she was putting a brave face on it, she didn't look happy. Ruby longed to talk to her, but there wasn't time. Already her mother was tugging at her arm to come and see the birthday cake. It was truly amazing. Florrie Dart, her old neighbour, stood beside the table, grinning from ear to ear.

'Did you do this, Mrs Dart?' said Ruby, guessing full well that she must have done.

Florrie nodded.

'It's . . . it's absolutely incredible,' said Ruby. The cake was actually three square cakes on top of each other, each at a different angle. Florrie had decorated the sides with a wallpaper look and with fashionable ladies dressed in summer dresses, fur stoles and evening gowns. The top bore the inscription 'Happy Birthday, Ruby, 21' and the whole thing was covered with edible roses. It must have taken hours. Mrs Dart wasn't the sort of person she hugged, but Ruby couldn't resist it. Florrie let out a little squeal of delight and hung onto her hat. When Ruby let her go, she blushed a bright crimson.

Her other former neighbours were there too: Susan Marley, who had surprised everybody in the town by

174

marrying the policeman, Sergeant Len Williams, in the early spring; and Cecil Turner, the coach driver, now the proprietor of a coach company with four vehicles; as well as some of Nelson's old fishing friends.

Her younger sister, May, presented Ruby with a beautifully painted card that she had made all by herself. Ruby loved it.

'Oh, Mum,' she said, her bright eyes dancing with happiness, 'this is the best birthday ever.'

'You deserve it, darling,' said Rachel, standing next to them. 'Doesn't she, Bea?'

Bea smiled. 'She certainly does.' The three of them stood, smiling sheepishly at each other, until Bea tugged at her daughter's arm. 'Now go and enjoy yourself.'

So enjoy herself Ruby did.

After a period of time during which everyone caught up with old friends, they played silly games like Guess the Legs, when all the girls had to take off their shoes and stand behind a large blanket being held up at each end by two people. The husbands, who had been sent outside while they got ready, were then brought in and asked to find their wives, just by looking at their legs. It was great fun, made even more hilarious when Percy chose one of Rachel's legs and the leg of the woman standing next to her.

They also played Wink-Murder, Musical Chairs and they danced the 'Hokey-Cokey'. Bea and Rachel had organized a buffet tea and, when the covers came off, the table was groaning with food. There was a rule in the Parish Rooms hiring conditions that no alcohol was allowed on the premises, but that didn't stop the women from lacing their tea; and the men kept disappearing outside, where they had put a beer barrel in the outside shed. No one got drunk, Rex saw to that, but everyone was very merry.

At 5.30 p.m., or thereabouts, Ruby cut the birthday cake, but that wasn't the end of the party. The night was still young. Everyone cleared away the tables for dancing and, this time, Jim didn't make a fuss. It was 10.45 p.m. by the time Percy pushed Jim back home, with all Ruby's presents loaded onto his lap. Ruby, tired but happy, trailed behind.

Once they were in bed, it didn't take Ruby long to drop off, but sleep came slowly for Jim. He lay staring at the ceiling for a long time. He should have told Ruby about the letter he'd had from the solicitor, who had also turned out to be one of the trustees from the orphanage. Considering the length of time that had passed, Mr Naiper-Raikes had replied quite quickly. Ruby would be surprised, but perhaps he wouldn't tell her today. His wife had enjoyed her birthday and he was glad. His frustration with life was still there, but it was more under control at the moment. That said, he would have given anything to have danced with Ruby again.

He thought back to the time when they'd danced together at their own wedding and he'd whispered sweet nothings in her ear. It felt like a hundred years ago. He rolled over. Ruby hadn't quite closed the curtains and the moonlight was bright on her face. Jim watched her sleeping. He had married the girl, and now he was in the same bed with the beautiful woman. How lucky was that? She was funny and clever and faithful. Stop this, he told himself. What good would it do? Even now his phallus was limp. He sighed. It wouldn't be long before he could show her that, although he could never be the husband she wanted, he wasn't a total waste of space. He'd surprise her and make her smile again.

CHAPTER 15

When Jean was tucked up in bed, Eric and Lena talked. Their money was almost gone and Eric knew he had to get a job, but he worried about leaving the pair of them on their own. Jean had recovered from her tonsillitis, but she was still very pale. She had no playmates but, apart from that, since she had been in Worthing she had settled down nicely. The doctor had told them that all she needed now was lots of fresh air and sunshine. It was wise advice, but as soon as they were out of the house, Eric began to fret.

'We'll be fine,' Lena reassured him. 'We need to get out and about now. We'll only make ourselves more conspicuous if we stay in all the time.'

'But supposing someone recognizes you?'

'The story is dead,' said Lena. 'We've been all over the country, and now we're a hundred miles away. Now that we're married and I've changed my name, who would guess?'

'I can't go back there, Lena,' Eric said, shaking his head. 'I'd rather kill myself than go back to prison.'

'You won't have to,' she soothed. '*If* – and I mean

if – anyone out there is still looking, then they're looking for me, not you. No one ever knew you existed. Relax.'

So he'd found a job at the railway-station coal yard. It was hard work, but the pay was reasonable. They were better off than some. They had no rent to pay. The solicitor, Mr Collins, had told Eric that under the terms of his late aunt's will, as her only living relative, the house was his. As luck would have it, the paperwork had only just been signed when Mr Collins himself went to meet his Maker. Over-worked, they said.

It was Saturday afternoon when Eric and Lena discussed reopening the house as a guest house, but Eric didn't want strangers living with them.

'It's a big house,' said Lena. 'We could even live on the ground floor and rent the top floor to lodgers.'

But Eric said 'No', and there was an end to it.

He'd been in his job at the coal yard for almost a week when Lena told him that Ruby had offered her work next door. His face paled.

'It'll be perfectly safe. I shall either clean the rooms after the guests have gone,' she told him, 'or I shall be in the kitchen.'

'All right, but don't get too chummy,' Eric cautioned. 'Be careful what you tell them.'

'You worry too much,' she said. She kissed him until he was fully aroused and then, with Jean asleep in her cot, they found satisfaction and comfort in each other's bodies.

* * *

Bea looked down at the embossed invitation to check the address once more. Yes, this was the house. It was very impressive, with a large front garden and a pretty red-and-black tiled path leading to the front door. It was late-Victorian and probably had five or six bedrooms. There was a gabled porch and some stained glass in the door. She was surprised that Mrs Hayward, a member of the Townswomen's Guild, would be the mistress of such an impressive house, but there it was in black and white on the invitation:

> Dear Mrs Quinn,
>   I would be delighted if you could have tea with me at 3 p.m. on Saturday afternoon. There will be a few other hand-picked friends with me, and I have a small proposition to make to you all. I do hope you can come.
>   Yours sincerely, Mrs Hayward

Bea had been curious. Mrs Hayward was a delightful woman. Bea had no idea how old she was, but she was closer to Ruby's age than her own. She was sensible, well organized and full of life and enthusiasm. Effie had assigned her to kitchen duties on TWG evenings, but anyone could see that Mrs Hayward was capable of doing far more than the washing up.

Bea lifted the brass door knocker and gave it three sharp raps. A few minutes later the door was opened by a maid in uniform and Bea stated her name.

She was invited into a wood-panelled hallway that smelled of lavender polish. There was a long oak table on one side and a crowded hat stand on the other. A laconic spaniel ambled towards her, wagging his tail. The maid showed her into a chintz sitting room, where Mrs Hayward was surrounded by several other women. Bea recognized Miss Horton from the TWG and Mrs Crockerton, but the rest were strangers.

'Ah, Mrs Quinn,' cried her host, 'I'm so glad you came. You know Miss Horton and Mrs Crockerton, don't you?' The ladies nodded to each other and then Mrs Hayward introduced Bea to everyone else.

As soon as everyone was perched on a chair, the tea was served. They started with small sandwiches, then moved on to scones and jam and several delicious-looking cakes. The conversation was cautious, but enjoyable. As the second round of tea was being served, Mrs Hayward tapped her china cup with her teaspoon to get everyone's attention.

'As some of you know,' she began, 'Mrs Crockerton's husband works for the fire service, Miss Horton is chief librarian in Worthing library, Mrs Quinn's husband is a doctor . . .'

As she went on to list either their capacity as the wife of a professional (dentist, hotelier or banker) or as a woman with her own skills, such as a nurse, matron of an old people's home, corsetiere or teacher, Bea was beginning to feel a little alarmed. Why on earth had she been summoned here? With all the talk of war and mayhem in the world, was this some sort of fifth column?

'I've asked you here,' Mrs Hayward went on, 'because,

181

as you know, our country is in a precarious position. An aunt of mine, Stella Charmoud, Lady Reading, has been asked to spearhead a women's organization, to help in time of need.'

There was a distinct hum of approval in the room.

'She's planning an organization that will take a leading role in pulling together other volunteers to help people, should the unthinkable happen,' Mrs Hayward continued. 'Early next year the Air Raid Precaution Department will be extended to include women.'

'What exactly will this organization do?' someone asked.

'My aunt thinks that women could act as a link between governmental departments and the general public,' said Mrs Hayward.

The women looked around at each other in mild confusion.

'I'm afraid I can't be specific at the moment,' she apologized. 'Things are very much in the planning stage, but I've asked you here because I think every one of you has something to offer and I want you to think about what you might be able to contribute.'

'My skills are very limited,' said Mrs Crockerton.

'But your husband is in the fire service,' said Mrs Hayward. 'Should there be a war, the fire service will come to our aid of course, but some women wouldn't have a clue what to do in the case of a fire. They may never even have used a telephone and, as a consequence, they may not know how to use the new nine-nine-nine service.'

Following a disastrous fire in 1935 when five women were killed in London, a neighbour who had rung for the fire brigade was frustrated to be left in a queue by the telephone exchange. The incident outraged the whole country. No doubt, if she had got through to the fire brigade more quickly, lives could have been saved. Although not yet countrywide, there were plans to make the new 999 service available to everybody.

Bea was beginning to get the point. 'My husband is a doctor,' she said. 'Should I ask him to organize first-aid classes?'

Suddenly the room lit up with helpful suggestions. Bea wished Ruby was here. She was good at thinking up ideas.

'Has anyone else got a suggestion?' asked Mrs Hayward.

'In 1933,' Bea went on, 'my daughter started a second-hand clothing swap to help poor neighbours. It was very successful.'

'That's just the sort of practical thing I mean,' cried their host.

'I suppose, if people lose their homes and all their possessions,' said Mrs Crockerton, 'they are going to need all the help they can get.' The hum of conversation rose again.

The young woman sitting next to Bea said confidentially, 'Do you really think war is inevitable?'

'Who knows?' said Bea quietly. 'But if it is, we'll be ready.'

The woman wrung her hands in her lap and nodded.

'My father died in the Great War. The Battle of the Boar's Head. I never even met him.'

'"The Day Sussex Died",' whispered Bea.

There wasn't a person in the county of her generation who didn't know of that battle, which began on June 30th, 1916. It was fought by three Sussex battalions, the 11th, 12th and 13th Southdowns Battalions of the Royal Sussex Regiment, and by part of the 116th Southdowns Brigade of the 39th Division. The Germans had known they were coming and when the bitter fighting was over, in just five short hours, 60 per cent of all those who had gone over the top had been killed. Bea couldn't remember the actual numbers, but she would never forget the newspaper headlines, which told her that twelve sets of brothers had perished, three from one family. And this poor young woman had lost her father among them.

She squeezed the girl's hands. 'I'm so sorry.'

The young woman's eyes were rimmed with tears, but she smiled grimly. 'The sad thing is, we really believed they had died in the war to end all wars.'

It seemed to Ruby that the summer of 1937 sped by in a blink of an eye. She was working flat out at the guest house, with barely a moment to breathe. She didn't mind, though. She'd enjoyed making sure that her guests were happy.

That summer season in Worthing was shorter than most. Along with the deterioration of the weather, large amounts of seaweed that had washed up onto the shingle beach lay rotting in the sun. The pungent smell, rather like that of rotten eggs, was accompanied by a plague of little black flies, which hatched from eggs laid in the weed. Some days the coastline looked as if it was suffering from some sort of biblical plague. The smell was so strong, it permeated the shops and local homes, including Sea View. Until local farmers carted the seaweed away as free fertilizer for their land, fewer people than usual ventured into the water, because to get there they were forced to walk over the stinking mounds, which could easily be several feet deep in places. Visitors left the town in droves and everybody knew that the late-season day-trippers wouldn't be returning next year.

With the help of Lena and the German girls, Ruby managed to keep her visitors a little longer than most. In fact, during the summer months, another four girls had passed through her doors. She had become adept at calming their fears and imbibing them with enough confidence to be able to make, if not an excellent job, a reasonable stab of success as live-in help. When the time came, they were always sad to leave her. She equipped them as best she could and, although she had found time to laboriously copy out four more of her booklets, she really couldn't face doing it again.

Jim was still doing his crossword puzzles. One morning when he opened the post, he let out a cry of joy. 'I've done it, Ruby. I've done it!'

He waved two pieces of paper in the air and, when he showed her what was in them, Ruby's jaw dropped.

185

He had actually managed to sell a couple of crosswords to two magazines. After months and months of trying, it was his first success. The money wasn't huge, a two-pound postal order for one and a four-pound postal order for the other, but he was as excited as a footballer winning the FA Cup. Now at last Ruby understood what he'd been aiming for. She was pleased for him, not only because of the cash incentive, but also because at last he had found a sense of purpose.

She and Jim lived together in a sort of amicable friendship. She knew that if she made another approach towards her husband, she would be rebuffed, and while she was busy Ruby could live with that. But by the end of August the numbers in the guest house were beginning to slacken and, with less to do, the frustration came back. Some days the desire for sex drove her mad. She didn't exactly lust after the baker's boy when he brought the daily loaf, and neither did she lie in wait for the postman, but she did fantasize. Lena seemed so content and happy with Eric that Ruby, whilst not desiring her friend's husband, envied that. And her mother and father, although in their late forties and early fifties, looked so happy together. She loved the way Rex would stand at the garden gate and watch Bea walking up the street, and she wished with all her heart that Jim would do the same for her.

She and Lena got on well. Lena was older than she looked – in her early twenties, Ruby guessed – and told Ruby she had known Eric for five years. Apart from that, Ruby didn't know much about her. She seldom spoke about her past and Ruby didn't like to pry. Once, over the washing up, Lena had mentioned that her mother and father hadn't wanted them to marry. Her father had refused to give her his permission.

'Oh, how awful,' said Ruby.

'I didn't care,' she said defiantly. 'I was determined to marry him, so we waited until I didn't need his permission.'

'It must have seemed like a long time,' said Ruby.

'When you really love someone,' Lena told her, 'you're willing to wait forever.'

Ruby didn't disagree. Look how long Edith had waited for her Bernard from the bacon counter. Edith had loved him since before Ruby and Jim got together and, although their wedding was now only a week or so away, and Bea had agreed to let them have the long-term tenancy of the house in Newlands Road, they were still waiting.

Lena used to bring little Jean with her when she worked. She was a delightful child and played happily in a corner with her dollies while her mother worked. She refused to be separated from her favourite toy, a knitted animal of some sort with long stripy legs, that she called Chewy. When she was tired, Jean rubbed the end of her nose with one of the legs until she fell asleep. Occasionally Ruby would offer to read her a story and the little girl would curl up on her lap. As she read, Ruby would breathe in the smell of her hair as it tickled her nose. It was always a bittersweet moment, because it reminded Ruby of what she could never have.

'And the prince and princess lived happily ever after . . .'

The days didn't seem nearly as long, with Lena working in the house. Ruby enjoyed her company more and more. They often had a good laugh together, but Lena never took advantage. She maintained the careful demarcation line between employer and employee, although their relationship was relaxed and friendly. It wasn't long before Ruby found herself sharing things she hadn't told anyone for years. When Lena asked her about her father, Ruby talked about her difficult years with Nelson and his subsequent death. She also told Lena about the day she'd discovered that her father wasn't Nelson, but Rex Quinn.

Lena was a good listener, but said little about her own background or her past. It was never glaringly obvious, but when Ruby sat down to think about it, she knew nothing about Lena's private life.

'Where did you grow up?' They were stripping the beds after a guest had left.

'Oh, I'm a country girl,' said Lena. 'I'm used to early mornings and hearing the cows right under my bedroom window on their way to be milked.'

They each tucked a piece of clean sheet under the mattress. Ruby picked up the top sheet and shook it out, ready to pull it over. 'Sounds intriguing,' she said.

'My relations were all country folk,' said Lena. 'Uncomplicated. Ordinary.'

The top sheet was tucked in and they tackled the blanket.

188

'I remember once that our neighbour, Mrs Salt, told my mother that her daughter was getting ideas above her station,' Lena went on. 'It turned out that she was horrified that her daughter wanted a clean plate for her pudding instead of – and this is what she said – "turning her dinner plate upside down, like decent folks do".'

They both laughed and, by the time the counterpane was straightened, the bed was made. It wasn't until later that Ruby realized she *still* didn't know where Lena came from.

Now that Eric had gained more confidence, he decided to get a second job. He would use his evenings and his day off to garden. His own vegetable plot had given him an appetite to be out in the open, and there were always people desperate for others to work their unruly gardens. Soon after he made the decision, he spotted a card in the newsagent's window:

Gardener required.
Four hours a week. Richmond Road.
Good rates of pay.
Contact Worthing 392.

Richmond Road was ideal. It was only a stone's throw from their house and would probably only take a ten-minute walk to get there. Eric lost no time in applying for the job.

*   *   *

If her heartache over Jim wasn't enough to worry about, Ruby – along with everyone else in the country – lived in fear of another war. People talked about peace, politicians travelled abroad in search of peace, but it seemed that the country was moving inexorably towards another conflict. In May, Neville Chamberlain had become Prime Minister, and in June the Duke of Windsor, as Edward VIII was now known, had married his Wallis Simpson at the Château de Candé. There had been a terrible coal-mining disaster in Staffordshire, and an Act of Parliament had added insanity and desertion as legitimate causes for divorce. Ruby had sighed. What about withholding conjugal rights? If she were a man, she had no doubt she could get a divorce for that, but what would the world think if a woman complained of the same thing? Could she go that far? Probably not, because the thought of such a thing getting into the papers as salacious gossip was too much to bear.

The TWG fair that her mother had organized was on Saturday. Ruby knew how tirelessly Bea had worked, first to get the thing off the ground and then to make sure everyone knew exactly what they were doing. Ruby was looking forward to it and had saved a little money to splash out on the day.

At the last meeting before the TWG craft sale, Ruby had helped her mother iron out the few remaining problems.

'Of course,' Bea told her daughter, 'Effie will be looking after our celebrity guests. She has a wonderful way with people. It's a gift.'

Ruby made no comment. From what Bea said, Effie was meticulous with her instructions, anxious that everything reflected well on her. Anyway, Ruby was proud of her mother's achievements.

'I'm thinking of getting my booklets printed,' Ruby said as they packed up. 'Where do you get the stuff printed for the TWG?'

'Caxton Printers,' said Bea. 'It's in Portland Road. They are very reasonable.'

CHAPTER 16

The print shop was halfway down Portland Road, opposite the Christ Church hall where Cousin Lily and Nick had held their wedding reception. It was small, with a deep step going down into the shop. The bell jangled as Ruby opened the door. The whole place had a rather cluttered feel. A Quaker Oats tin overflowing with pens stood on the small counter next to the cash drawer. A dirty cup and saucer gathered mould beside it. The only sound, a mellow tick, came from a large wooden clock on the wall in front of her, and the whole place smelled of machinery and ink. Ruby was tempted to sit in the customer chair beside the counter and look at the posters lining the walls, but as usual she was in a hurry. Somewhere in the back she heard the distant sound of machinery starting up.

Absent-mindedly putting her handbag on the counter, Ruby picked up a small booklet and leafed through the pages. This was just the sort of thing she wanted, although considerably smaller. She scanned the back for a price, but there didn't appear to be one. She looked around. No one was coming. There was a brass bell on the counter. Should she use it?

The posters on the walls were obviously samples of past work. One advertised Cobham's Flying Circus, an exciting air show that was popular along the south coast in summer; another was for Billy Butlin's 'Centre of Happiness' in Bognor; and there was one extolling the virtues of 'Sunny Worthing'. There was also a more up-to-date poster, advertising Oswald Mosley's forthcoming visit. After the Battle of Cable Street in October 1936, when 5,000 Fascists were prevented from marching through the Jewish quarter of the East End of London, Ruby had hoped that enthusiasm for Mosley and his crew might have been quelled. It might have been dampened down in the rest of the country, but Worthing was still a hotbed for Mosley's followers and clearly the man was nowhere near finished yet. As she stared at those small, piercing eyes and the proud, jutting jaw, Ruby gave an involuntary shudder.

'Hello, Ruby.'

She spun round and came face-to-face with Bob Knight. As normal, his dazzling smile totally disarmed her. He was in his shirt sleeves. His biceps bulged under the rolled-up material and his chest was slightly exposed. She couldn't help staring at the dark, curly hair and glistening skin.

'What can I do for you?'

She blinked like a flustered schoolgirl. 'Um . . . I . . .'

Wiping his hands on a piece of rag, he came a little closer. She could smell his warm body and the printer's ink. 'It's lovely to see you again,' he said, clearly enjoying the discomfort he was causing her. 'It's not often you come into my shop.'

'I've never been in your shop before,' she said.

Her voice was breathy and she hoped he couldn't hear her heart pounding. This was embarrassing. She hadn't expected him to be here. She had no idea he was a printer. She should have asked him what he did for a living when they'd danced at Cousin Lily's wedding. If she had done so, she could have spared herself this meeting. There were plenty of other printing shops in Worthing.

'I was wanting to enquire about getting a booklet printed,' she went on. 'I don't have a clue how much it will cost and I may not be able to afford it, but my sister-in-law suggested I find out. It takes forever to copy it all out by hand. I've already done six copies and I can't bear the thought of doing it all over again.' She was gabbling and she knew it. Her heart was still racing and she was acutely aware of how close together they were standing. She glanced up at Bob's face and her heart lurched.

'Would you like to show me the booklet?' His voice was soft and sensual.

Ruby felt her face flush. Her fingers were trembling as she reached into her bag and drew it out.

He took it from her and began to flip through the pages. 'I don't see that this will be a problem,' he said. 'I can probably get it all on one sheet of paper. How many copies would you require?'

Ruby stared at him with a blank expression. 'Oh, I don't know. I hadn't thought that far ahead. A few.'

He laughed. 'It'll work out cheaper if you take fifty or more.'

'Fifty it is then,' she said, regaining her composure.

They discussed paper and size, and the cost, which Ruby was surprised to learn was less than she'd expected.

'They'll be ready in a week.' Bob smiled that disarming smile and she looked away quickly. As she reached the door he said, 'Don't forget your bag.'

Ruby paused. Taking a deep breath, she turned back to fetch her bag but, as she did so, she turned awkwardly on the steep step. The next thing she knew, she was falling. He rushed to save her, but it was too late.

'Don't get up too quickly,' he cautioned as Ruby landed on the floor. 'Get your breath back. Take your time. Does anything hurt?'

'My ankle,' she said weakly. 'It hurts like mad.'

He covered her ankle with his warm hand. 'May I?' Ruby watched as he examined it expertly. 'I don't think anything is broken, but it looks as if you're going to get one hell of a bruise.' He helped her to her feet. 'Can you put weight on it?'

'I'll be fine,' said Ruby, anxious more than ever to get going. She got up, but when she tried to walk, she cried out in pain.

'Sit on the chair,' he said, 'and slip off your stocking. I'll go and get some cold water.'

Obediently she did as he said, and moments later he

was back with a small enamel bowl of water and a towel. The water was soothing as he gently splashed her throbbing ankle.

'I think I'd better strap it up for you,' Bob said. 'If it swells up, you may not be able to get your shoe on.'

He left her again and reappeared with a bandage. Ruby could hardly breathe as he laid her wet foot on the towel on his lap and gently patted it dry. He bandaged her foot expertly, cutting the end of the bandage in half and carefully tying it around the top of her ankle. She could immediately feel the support.

When he had finished, he looked up at her. 'How's that?'

The electricity between them was palpable.

'I think you know how I feel about you, Ruby,' he said quietly.

She became acutely aware of her foot still resting in his lap, and his warm hand was on her calf.

'Bob, don't.' He moved his hand until it was touching her knee. She shivered with excitement. Don't kiss me, she thought. Please don't kiss me or I am undone.

He stood to his feet and took her hand. 'Can you stand on it now?'

She rose to her feet. They were standing so close together. Too close. She kept her head down as she tried to put weight on her foot. It still hurt, but the bandage definitely helped.

I can probably manage to hobble home, Ruby thought. 'Thanks,' she whispered. 'I'm sure I'll be fine now.'

She looked up at him and suddenly his lips were on hers, warm and sensual. Her pulse began to race again. Her knees felt like jelly. A small voice in her head reminded her: You're a married woman . . . But an even louder voice drowned it out: Don't stop. It's just a kiss. Only a kiss . . .

'Come into the office,' he said. 'You can rest your foot for a bit.'

They both knew that if she went into the office, it wouldn't be to rest her foot, but Ruby allowed him to help her all the same. Bob stopped only to shoot the bolt over the shop door and then, with his strong arm around her waist for support, they moved slowly into the little office at the back. Once they were inside, he kicked the door shut behind them.

Ruby's first impression was one of chaos. There was a desk awash with papers, and pamphlets in piles on every surface, including the windowsills; and the drawers to the filing cabinet were open and bulging with stuffed paper files. There was an old-fashioned couch under the window covered in bits and pieces – paper, a coat, some used rags. Bob let go of Ruby and, with one deft move, swept everything aside. The papers fell in a haphazard way, littering the floor, then he lowered her down. As Ruby looked up at him, he cupped her face gently in his hands and began to kiss her. She knew she should stop him, but it was delicious and she hadn't been kissed for so long. Bob was so passionate that she could hardly draw breath and the longer she let him do it, the harder it became to stop him. It was exciting. He was so powerful and eager. All reason and restraint went out of the window. She was becoming aroused. So was he.

When he lay her down, it seemed like the most natural thing in the world. She felt her skirt going up, but she hardly knew how her panties came off. She made a small protest – 'Don't . . .' – but they both knew she didn't mean it. He paused for a minute, as if giving her time to push him away, but instead she relaxed and parted her legs. Then his fingers were probing her and the only thought in her head was 'Don't stop.' They looked each other in the eye as he mounted and entered her, gliding in on a sea of expectation and excitement.

'Oh, darlin',' he breathed. 'You are so lovely . . .'

He was an expert lover, moving slowly and with such control, careful to give her as much pleasure as he was getting himself. She was aware of every move he made, licking her raised nipple, then kissing her mouth; breathing her name in her ear, then raising and cupping her buttocks so that he slipped even further in. Closing her eyes, Ruby let him create a rhythm between their bodies that carried her to some exotic pleasure paradise, where every touch only served to bring her to a more acutely sensual place. Her body felt more alive than it had ever done. The sensation became more and more fantastic as he thrust deeper and harder. At last she cried out and came, a split second before he did, so that the pulsating of his member kept them both at the point of ecstasy for some wonderfully delicious seconds.

Spent and satisfied, he became a dead weight on top of her. Ruby tried to push him off, but she was pinned down until Bob could gather enough strength to lift himself from her. Staring at the stained paper on the ceiling made what they had just done seem dirty and sordid. Oh Lord . . . what had she done? She should have stopped him. He'd given her the chance to push him away, but she'd egged him on. And now she'd been unfaithful. She was an adulteress.

He leaned up on one elbow and smiled. 'Well, Ruby Searle. You're quite some gal, ain't you?' He kissed her cheek; not the tender kiss of a lover, the smacker he planted there made her feel cheap and used. Bob pulled himself to his feet and stood up, tucking his member inside his trousers and doing up his flies. Ruby reached for her own underwear and sat up. As she pulled her panties on, he tucked his shirt into his waistband and grinned at her in an over-familiar way.

'Never expected someone like you to 'ave such tasty panties,' he smirked.

Ruby burned with shame. 'I don't usually behave like this,' she said haughtily.

'Of course not, darlin',' he said. 'Bloody good, though, wasn't it?'

Ruby's eyes smarted.

'Now don't look at me like that, sugar,' he said, cupping her chin in his hand. 'You were gagging for it as much as I was.'

She batted his hand away angrily. 'Shut up. Shut up.'

Bob pulled the braces over his shoulders. 'Have it your own way, but I bet that cold fish of a husband never gave you a good time like that.'

'I happen to love my husband,' she retorted.

'Suits me, gal,' he said with a shrug, 'but everybody could do with a little bit of fun now and then. Don't take life so seriously.'

Somebody tried the shop door and then knocked on the glass.

Bob ran his fingers through his untidy hair. 'Better go. Customer. Take your time, darlin', no hurry.'

As he left the room, Ruby leaned forward on the couch and put her head in her hands. She wanted desperately to cry, but at the same time she didn't want to give him the satisfaction – he might think what just happened mattered. He had used her, hadn't he? Taken advantage of her predicament. If he hadn't been so damned nice, she wouldn't have . . . She closed her eyes despairingly. Oh God, what had she done?

She heard Bob slide the bolt back on the shop door and then he said, 'Hello, darlin'. What can I do for you?'

Ruby put on her stocking on her good leg. All she wanted was to get out of this sordid place as quickly as possible.

'I should like to order a couple more wedding invitations,' said a very familiar voice.

Ruby's head jerked up. It was Edith Parsons. She felt sick. Oh Lord, she mustn't let Edith find her here. Whatever would she think? With a trembling hand, she tidied her hair.

'We seem to have forgotten some relatives who simply can't be missed out,' Edith was saying.

200

'Oh dear,' said Bob, in his usual easy way, 'we can't have that, can we? You don't want to start a second world war, do you?'

Edith chuckled. Ruby could hear Bob rustling papers.

Suddenly Edith said, 'Isn't that Ruby Searle's handbag?'

Ruby held her breath.

'I'm afraid it is,' said Bob in a contrite tone. 'Mrs Searle was just leaving the shop when she fell down the step. I had to take her into the back room and bandage her ankle. That's why the door was locked.'

'Oh, my goodness,' cried Edith. 'How bad is it?'

'She says it's very painful,' said Bob. 'I'm thinking I may have to take her home.'

'In here?' said Edith, and the next minute she was in the back room. Ruby was fully dressed and lying back on the couch with her bandaged foot over the armrest. She had her hand across her eyes. 'Oh, Roob,' Edith exclaimed, 'you poor thing. Can you walk?'

Ruby pulled herself up. 'I hope so,' she said weakly, 'but now that it's bandaged I can't get my shoe on. Such a silly accident.'

Bob stood behind Edith with a knowing smirk on his face. Ruby avoided his eye.

'Here,' said Edith, 'let me help you.'

Ruby struggled to her feet. Her ankle was still painful, but all she wanted to do was get out of the shop and away from Bob. With Edith's help, she hobbled outside and onto the street. They had only gone a few steps when she heard the bell on the shop door go again.

'Oh, Mrs Searle,' Bob called. Ruby froze. 'Don't forget your other stocking.'

She turned back. He was holding it up, for all the world to see.

Snatching it, she said tartly, 'Thank you, Mr Knight. You've been most helpful.'

'Always glad to be of service, Mrs Searle,' he added lecherously. 'Any time you need me, I'll be here.' Ruby felt her face colour.

'Come on, Roob,' said Edith, 'let's get you home.' And, leaning on her friend's arm, Ruby hobbled away.

CHAPTER 17

The Townswomen's Guild fair was held in the church hall that belonged to St Columba's Church in Heene Road. The church itself was in St Michael's Road, just around the corner. A few minutes before Elsie and Doris Walters arrived, Bea and Effie stepped out of the front door to meet them.

Effie took in her breath noisily and tugged at Bea's arm. 'Look, dear. That bunting has fallen down.'

Bea frowned. How strange – it had been perfectly in place when she'd walked through the door on her arrival, but somehow or other the string had been pulled away from the drawing pin at one end, and about three feet of bunting hung on the ground. Bea examined the pin. It had been trodden flat.

'I'll have to get another one, and a chair to stand on,' she said.

'Hurry up, dear,' Effie hissed. 'They're here.'

It was all a bit of a rush, but Bea soon had the bunting back in place, then she climbed off the chair and hurried back inside with it.

Carol Crockerton and May waited by the entrance

with two bouquets for the guests. Effie shivered. Taking her bouquet from May, she said to her, 'Pop into the hall and fetch my jacket, will you, dear? It's on the chair by the stage.'

Although she was an obedient child, May went inside reluctantly.

There was no doubt about it, the entrance to the church hall looked wonderful. Thanks to the committee's unstinting behind-the-scenes work, the whole place had been transformed. Effie smiled with smug satisfaction. This would definitely put her in the public eye.

A small crowd waited outside and inside the lychgate and cheered as Elsie and Doris Walters climbed out of the car. The women weren't glamorous. In fact they looked rather homely and middle-aged, and a bit like somebody's mother and favourite aunt. Since 1930 they had carved out a very successful career in variety, as two cockney pals called Gert and Daisy. Their humour wasn't the rib-tickling sort, but was drawn from real life, and the characters they'd created were easily identifiable.

As they stood and waved to the crowd, Doris was wearing a pink floral blouse with a brooch at the neck, while Elsie wore a plain pale-blue blouse with a loose tie and a string of pearls. They were in identical dark suits.

With Bea somewhere in the building replacing the chair, Effie went out alone to meet them, an expression of smug self-satisfaction written all over her face. The rest of the Townswomen's Guild committee waited just inside the door and, as Bea returned, the young Mrs

Raymond winked at her. Everything was going exactly as they had expected. The only blot on the landscape was in the street outside, where men from the water board were digging up the pavement. When she'd seen them, Effie had been furious.

'Why on earth dig up the road today, of all days?' she'd fumed. 'It's Saturday. We've got a very important craft fair and sale in here . . . for Gifford House.'

'Can't 'elp that, Missus,' said the foreman. 'When there's a leak in the pipe, it's gotta be fixed.'

After some more hand-waving, smiles and posing for the photographer from the local paper, when their guests came into the building, little Carol Crockerton and Sylvia, the granddaughter of Effie's latest prodigy, stepped forward to present Elsie and Doris with a bouquet each. Bea and the other members of the committee had expected to be introduced, but Effie sailed past with her nose in the air. 'Do come this way, Miss Walters and Miss Walters . . .'

Bea thought it was rather unfortunate that Effie's flame-coloured suit clashed wildly with Doris's pink floral blouse as the three of them strode inside. She scoured the crowds for Ruby, but she didn't seem to be there.

May appeared from the direction of the main hall and was distraught to find that the bouquets had already been presented and that Sylvia had taken her place. Bea couldn't believe what had happened. Rex, who had followed Elsie and Doris Walters through the door, was livid. 'Mrs Rhodes did what? Where is she?'

As she drew May into her arms, Bea laid a restraining hand on his arm and shook her head. Together they comforted the child, speaking softly to her and drying her eyes. When May was calm again, she went off with her friends and Bea took her husband to one side.

'I hope you're not thinking of letting that woman get away with this, are you, Bea?' Rex demanded loudly. 'Because I won't hear of it.'

'No, I'm not,' said Bea in a much quieter tone, 'but there is a time and place. I don't want to create a scene.'

'That bloody woman needs taking down a peg or two,' Rex spat. 'Look at the way she's treated you? Taking all the credit for your hard work – and now this!'

'I promise I won't let her get away with it,' said Bea.

'I'm coming with you when you do it.'

'No,' said Bea. Rex gave her a startled look. 'I know you mean well, darling, but I need to do this myself.'

'You're far too soft,' he said, his eyes still blazing with rage.

'Calm down,' she soothed. 'Yes, you're perfectly right. I don't have to put up with the bullying any more. And I have turned a blind eye – but not when it comes to my child.' She squeezed his arm. 'Rex, I need to do this myself.'

For a second he was thrown. 'Well, just see to it that you do,' he said grumpily.

'Oh, I will,' she replied.

The Misses Walters were very appreciative of the warm welcome they'd been given and spent several minutes walking around and admiring the exhibits, which were in some cases quite spectacular. There were first, second and third places in each category, and one star prize, which was called 'Best in Show'.

During their deliberations before the event, Effie had suggested putting herself forward as judge, but Bea had arranged for Mrs Dawson from the Hastings guild to send some judges who were completely impartial. These women were also very skilled needlewomen and crafts-women in their own right, so Bea was confident they would know what to look for. She also hoped they might find something good enough to be passed on to the countrywide exhibition later in the year. The TWG had very exacting standards, because they believed in being the best.

Bea had managed to get second prize in the best-dressed doll category and, considering the exceptionally high standard of the winner, she was more than pleased with her own efforts. She had wanted to show her eldest daughter, but Ruby still hadn't put in an appearance. Elsie and Doris Walters were generous with their praise. After a short speech, once they had finished looking around, Doris Walters cut the blue ribbon across the doorway and declared the craft fair open. The public poured in. May and Rex were thrilled with Bea's effort and congratulated her warmly.

'I should have brought the Box Brownie,' Rex lamented. 'It's wonderful, darling.'

Effie invited Doris and Elsie onto the stage, where the members had put a table and some chairs. Bea was still struggling to control the anger she felt over what had happened to May. How could Effie be such a bitch? At one time how nice she had been! One thing was for sure: Bea was very impressed with the way May had handled the situation. She had cried, which was perfectly natural, but from that moment on she had behaved with dignity, even when other members of the committee had commiserated with her misfortune. However, Bea wouldn't forget it. She had lived with a bully for long enough when Nelson was alive. Being with Rex had given her confidence and she wasn't about to get into that position again.

'I have arranged for you to have some tea and cakes,' Effie gushed as their honoured guests reached the steps by the stage.

Elsie said that she wished to use the facilities, and Effie turned, about to show her the way.

'No – no need for you to come,' said Elsie, clearly annoyed by Effie's smothering attitude. 'Just point me in the right direction. I'll find it.'

So Effie let her go. She was confident everything would be all right; after all, she had insisted that the toilet be thoroughly scrubbed, with such illustrious guests on their way. Once she was satisfied that Miss Horton had made the Ladies clean enough, Effie had produced a carefully written notice: 'No one – absolutely no one – is to use this toilet.'

'Put this on the toilet seat,' Effie had told her. 'And put all the cleaning stuff in the other toilet and shut the door.'

'What about everyone else?' Miss Horton had cried.

'They can use the outside toilets,' said Effie, with a sweep of her hand. 'I don't want anybody else to sit on that seat.'

Elsie Walters seemed to take ages in the toilet and, when Bea was dispatched to see if she was all right, she could hear the sound of a bucket being moved about behind the door. When she emerged from the Ladies, Elsie looked a little flustered.

'Is everything all right, Miss Walters?' Bea asked.

'Quite, thank you,' said Elsie, in a tone a little less cordial than before.

As she walked in front of Bea on the way up to the top table, Bea couldn't help noticing an ugly ladder in the back of her stockings.

'Excuse me.'

Bea turned round to find Lena smiling at her. 'I just came to tell you that Ruby is sorry, but she can't be here. She's had a little accident and hurt her ankle, so she's resting at home.'

Rex had joined them. 'Hurt her ankle? How?'

Lena explained what had happened. 'She's resting with her foot up,' she went on. 'It's very swollen, because she had to walk all the way home from the printer's.'

'I'll pop round and see her,' said Rex.

'She said to tell you not to worry,' replied Lena. 'She wants you to enjoy the show.'

'Thank you,' said Rex, 'for giving us the message.'

'I know she's very disappointed not to be here,' Lena went on. 'The German girls and I have offered to look after the guest house, but fortunately there are no more guests until the end of next week.'

Rex squeezed Lena's elbow and nodded. 'Tell her we'll come round as soon as the fair is over.'

Effie was holding a plate of bread and butter in her hand as Elsie arrived back onstage. 'Would you like a cup of tea, Miss Walters?' she gushed.

'Ooh, lovely,' said Elsie.

Handing her the cup, Effie smiled broadly. 'I thought you might like to have your tea now.'

Mrs Wilmot showed them to their seats.

As Bea arrived a few minutes later, Effie hissed, 'Where on earth have you been?'

'I think you may owe Miss Walters an apology,' Bea whispered urgently. 'She didn't use the toilet that was supposed to be for our guests.' She handed Effie the notice, which she had found on the closed lid of the pan.

'Why on earth didn't you take it down?' Effie snapped. 'Oh, really. Do I have to do everything around here?'

'I was busy with the bunting, if you remember,' said Bea.

Effie tutted irritably.

'It seems,' Bea went on, 'that our guest had to clamber over the mop and bucket in the other toilet, and she's laddered her stockings.'

Despite the hiccup over the Ladies' loo, the visit was a resounding success. Before they enjoyed their tea, and with an audience gathered below the stage, the two sisters had become their characters, Gert and Daisy, and given the people in the hall an impromptu performance.

'Did you see that lovely needlework they've got over there? I had a go at making a tray cloth once. It wasn't very good. The window cleaner thought it was his duster.'

'Well, you get ten out of ten for trying, Gert.'

'Oh yes, my Wally says I'm very trying.'

Everyone laughed heartily.

'Did I tell you: the other day, Bert and I had this terrible quarrel.'

'Oh dear, what happened?'

'He said to me, "You know, I was a fool when I married you." So I said, "Yes, I know, but I was so in love with you, I didn't notice."'

The audience loved it.

After their performance, Doris sat down in Effie's seat, but they all enjoyed the high tea that the committee members had laid on. It went well, although Effie was a bit perturbed, because she couldn't find the plate of bread and butter. She'd had it in her hand a moment ago. Perhaps, she reflected, as Elsie and Doris tucked into the scones and cream, they didn't really need it.

Bea took the opportunity to seek out Rex and May again. 'I can't wait to get over to Ruby's.'

'Darling, you heard what Lena said,' said Rex. 'She's resting. She's a sensible girl. It's the right thing to do.'

'I'm going to be ages here,' Bea lamented. 'We've got to clear up the place before we leave.'

211

'May and I will go home in a few minutes,' said Rex. 'You come when you're finished. Don't worry.'

With the tea over, Elsie and Doris stood to leave. Effie led the way through the crowds. Bea was behind them.

'Um, Effie . . .' Bea said anxiously. She had come up beside Effie and put her hand to the side of her mouth, to speak confidentially.

Effie batted her away. 'Not now, dear.' This was her finest hour, and no one was going to spoil it for her. She smiled with satisfaction as she heard some in the crowd making little gasps as she led the way. At the door, Effie thanked Elsie and Doris, who waved to the cheering crowds.

'We are so grateful to you for coming,' Effie said.

'Oh no,' said Elsie, 'we should thank you. You have done a magnificent job today. I wish you and all your members every success.'

Effie nodded in a gracious way, but as the two women walked towards their car, her mouth gaped and she stared in horror. She was forced to put her hand to her mouth to suppress a cry of despair.

'I tried to tell you,' said Bea, coming up beside her. 'You must have put the plate on your own chair, and then Doris changed seats after the performance.'

The back of Doris's lovely suit was covered in small triangles of bread and butter, which peeled away from her bottom as she walked.

Effie prayed that she wouldn't notice, but as Doris Walters got into the car, she smoothed down the back of her skirt – and Effie knew she was undone. To give her her due, Doris Walters said nothing, but as the car moved off, she turned to look at Effie, her face red with fury.

When Effie turned to remonstrate with Bea and the other members of the committee, she found herself alone on the doorstep.

CHAPTER 18

It was nearly six before Bea had an opportunity to speak out – Rex and May having decided to wait outside until Bea had 'had a word'. Only the members of the committee remained in the hall. Everyone was working with brooms, dustpans and brushes as they put the finishing touches to the big tidy-up. The only person not doing anything was Effie, but, as their chairman, she was bursting with pride.

'This has been the most wonderful occasion, even if I do say so myself,' she said, sweeping her hand around the empty room. 'Mrs Quinn, how much did we make on the day?'

'One hundred and twenty pounds,' said Bea.

'One hundred and twenty pounds,' Effie echoed, saying the words slowly and with emphasis. She raised her head and closed her eyes, as if waiting for a round of applause. When none was forthcoming, she opened her eyes and glared. 'I think that merits a little clap of appreciation, don't you?'

No one moved.

'I should like to talk about the mix-up with the

bouquet,' said Bea. She had made up her mind to remain perfectly calm as she challenged Effie. She had seen others try to stand up to her, but they'd ended up in tears; and somehow, even if the point had been proven, it always seemed as if Effie had won.

'A regrettable incident,' said Effie dismissively. 'It was a good job my friend's granddaughter was on hand, to step into the breach.'

'Personally,' said Miss Taylor, 'I think you planned it that way.'

'Rubbish!' said Effie.

'I do, too,' said Bea, beginning to feel the heat rising inside her. 'In fact I think it was a downright despicable thing to do to a child.'

'Here, here,' said Mrs Raymond.

'Now look here,' Effie began indignantly.

'No, Mrs Rhodes,' said Bea, 'you look here.' Her heartbeat quickened and she heard the other ladies around her take in a collective breath. 'This organization is worthy of better behaviour than we've witnessed today,' Bea went on. 'It's not for people like you to lord it over all of us, like some sort of Lady Muck.'

'How dare you!' Effie spluttered.

But Bea hadn't finished yet. 'We are women of the twentieth century and, as such, we are worthy of respect and equal opportunity,' she continued. She was willing her voice to stay strong and not waver. 'You not only disappointed my daughter, but you let the side down and embarrassed all of us, in front of two highly respected women of the theatre.'

There was a deafening silence. Effie looked around and glared, but luckily for Bea, the other women held her gaze.

'Women of the theatre,' Effie scoffed. Her face was scarlet with rage. 'I hardly think so, dear. They are only variety actresses . . .'

'There you go again,' said Bea. 'What gives you the right to look down your nose at anybody?'

Effie pursed her lips. 'Well, if you don't like it, *Mrs Quinn*, you can always resign,' she said acidly.

'I fully intend to,' said Bea defiantly, 'but not before I've had my say.'

Effie began to collect her things. 'And do you really think I'd be interested in hearing the views of a jumped-up madam like you? I think not. You may be a doctor's wife now, but I know all about you. There was a time when you were nothing more than a common fishwife.'

For a second Bea was thrown by her nastiness.

'Speaking for myself,' Miss Taylor interrupted, 'I have enjoyed working with most members of the committee, but I shall not be continuing with my membership.'

'Nor I,' said Mrs Crockerton.

'I'm afraid I am tending my resignation as well,' said Mrs Raymond.

'Please,' cried Bea, regaining her composure, 'don't do anything hasty on my behalf. I really don't give a fig for Effie's opinions.'

'So . . . you've all ganged up on me,' said Effie. She

turned to Bea and said savagely, 'I'm assuming this was your idea.'

'No, it wasn't. That's not my style, so don't you dare tar me with your own brush, Effie,' Bea replied, over the murmur of protestation from the others. 'I don't manipulate people for my own ends. The only plan I had was to confront you with what you did to May.'

'I did nothing to May,' Effie gasped. 'The child wasn't there to present the bouquet and someone else stepped in, that's all.'

'She wasn't there because you had asked her to fetch your jacket,' said Bea. 'You knew full well that she wouldn't have time to get to the stage and back again before the presentation. You wanted to impress that woman. I call that manipulation.'

The other women agreed.

'Call it what you like,' said Effie indignantly. 'And if that's the way the land lies, you can keep your stupid club.' She turned on her heel, ready to sweep out of the room. 'You'll have my resignation before the next meeting.'

She slowed as she reached the door, as if she expected someone to rise to her defence, but nobody moved. 'After all I've done for you – you ungrateful bitches.' Then, thrusting her head high, she stalked out of the room and slammed the door.

Everyone was slightly stunned, but seconds later they heard footsteps coming from the stage area. Freda Fosdyke, her nose high in the air, sailed between them all and headed out of the door. 'Effie. Effie, wait for me.'

'Well, I never,' said Miss Taylor. 'I didn't expect that.'

'I can't say I'm surprised,' said Bea. 'Mrs Fosdyke has always been very close to Mrs Rhodes.'

'I meant Mrs Rhodes resigning,' said Miss Taylor.

'You don't have to resign because of me,' said Bea, looking around helplessly. 'In fact, now that she's gone, none of you needs to go.'

'If we stay,' said Mrs Raymond, 'would you be our chairman?'

Bea shook her head. 'As a matter of fact, I've been asked to be involved with another organization. I'd still like to be a member of the TWG, but not quite so involved.'

'That's that then,' said Miss Taylor.

'I can tell none of you really wants to leave,' said Mrs Wilmot. 'Why don't we give it another try?'

'We still need another chairman,' said Miss Taylor.

'Then let's put it to the membership,' said Mrs Wilmot. 'We've all done a really good job here today, despite Effie. I think we have bags of potential.'

The women looked at one another, with an obvious sense of relief, and nodded.

Jim was worried about Ruby. Edith had brought her home with a twisted ankle. He'd asked Ruby if she wanted the doctor, but she'd shaken her head and, when Edith left, she'd stayed in the kitchen, staring into space. He felt helpless. She seemed awfully upset about something, but when he tried to show his concern, it only made matters worse.

'Talk to me, love,' he said gently.

Edith had told him that Ruby had fallen down a step in the print shop, but the way she was behaving made him sure it was more than that. Had she had a row with someone? Had someone pushed her? How could he help, if she wouldn't say anything? Eventually he shuffled back to the sitting room and his writing.

He'd had a measure of success with the crosswords, and – taking a leaf out of B. Simmons Jr's book – was becoming something of a local celebrity with his letters to the *Herald* and *Gazette*. He complained about the lack of progress on the road-widening schemes in the Tarring area, where Princess Avenue was supposed to link up with the Littlehampton road. Progress was very slow, and Jim wondered what the council were doing about it. Once his letter had been published, several other people wrote in with the same complaint, prompting a comment from the Borough Council. He was anxious to keep fanning the flames with his next letter, but his mind kept drifting back to his wife. He was sure he could hear her crying softly.

Ruby's mother and father turned up at the guest house as soon as the craft fair was over. Jim shuffled back to the kitchen to join them. Bea's pink paisley dress was smudged with cake stains and she had a piece of fluff near the waistline. As she was normally immaculately turned out, Jim realized she must have been working hard. She looked a little flushed and tired, but had

219

obviously enjoyed the experience. Rex, dressed in a casual blue blazer and cream trousers, was as dapper as ever; and little May's dress was covered in sticky sweet marks and ice-cream splatters. Apparently the whole day had been a success; and, when her mother told them, everybody enjoyed the tale about the bucket in the toilet and the incident with the plate of bread and butter.

'How embarrassing,' Ruby exclaimed. She was smiling again, Jim was pleased to see.

'I'm sure that will find its way into their routine,' laughed Rex.

Everyone was very impressed with the way May had coped with losing her chance of presenting the bouquet.

'I was a bit upset,' she admitted, 'but everybody else was so nice. Miss Taylor and Mrs Crockerton gave me a sweetie, and Mrs Hayward gave me some talcum powder.' She produced a tired-looking tin that was probably only half-full, but everyone admired it and said they loved the smell.

'Let me look at your ankle,' Rex said to Ruby.

May crossed the room to show Uncle Jim her trophy, while Rex examined Ruby's ankle carefully and admired the bruise.

'As soon as I got home,' said Ruby, 'I put some witch hazel on it.'

'That's good,' said Rex. 'It'll help reduce the swelling.' He studied her face. 'Are you all right otherwise? No other injuries.'

Ruby avoided his eye as she shook her head. There

was no cure for what she had done and her heart hurt more than her ankle. 'Would you like to stay for something to eat?'

'I think we've eaten too much already,' said Rex, patting his stomach. 'All that cake . . .'

Ruby laughed.

'How are you going to manage with the guest house and that ankle?' her father asked as he re-bandaged it a little more firmly.

'Fortunately we don't have anyone here for a few days, and Lena has said she will come round tomorrow to give me a hand.'

'You'd be lost without that girl, wouldn't you?'

Ruby nodded. 'I certainly would. She's a marvel.'

* * *

Tit-Bits Magazine
Tit-bits from all the Interesting Books, Periodicals, and Newspapers of the World

Where is baby Christine?

The mystery deepens surrounding the disappearance of two-year-old Christine West, who has not been seen since she and her nanny, Miss Marlene Amberley, set out for a walk last March. Christine's pram was found dumped in the West Moors river a few days later, but there was no sign of the child or her favourite toy, a grey rabbit with long stripy legs. Her mother, Mrs Agatha West, is pictured by the front gate of their home in West Moors.

'Christine is adopted,' the broken-hearted

mother said. 'As soon as we saw her, we knew we wanted her for our child. I love her as much as I would have done if I had given birth to her myself.'

There has been a great deal of speculation as to what happened to Christine. Some have suggested that she was kidnapped for ransom; and one clairvoyant in America believes she has been abducted by aliens.

* * *

Ruby's ankle took a couple of days to stop hurting, and a week before she could walk any distance on it. She was careful not to do too much, because by the end of the day it would be puffy and sore. After two weeks, with two new German girls arriving, she was faced with the problem of collecting the booklets from Caxton's. She asked several people if they were passing that way, but it seemed nobody was. She would have to go herself.

She planned the move carefully. She decided to go on Friday, giving herself only a very short space of time before she had to be back at the guest house for weekend visitors arriving. She would go on her bike, rather than on the bus like last time. It would be the perfect excuse not to stay – not that she would, of course. By the time she reached Portland Road, Ruby felt as nervous as a kitten. What if Bob invited her out to the back again? What if he touched her or . . . kissed her? What if he suggested they meet some other time? Her feelings were all jumbled up. One minute she was anticipating the thrill of seeing him again, and the next she was reliving the shame and guilt that had settled on her shoulders like a heavy cloak. It made her feel terrible. She knew it was wrong, but she wasn't sure if she could resist him.

Jim had been so kind when she'd hobbled in on Edith's arm. That made her feel even worse. She told herself she didn't want to think of Bob Knight and what they had done together; but then the memory of the way he'd touched her inner thigh, that engaging smile of his, the memory of . . . No, no, she mustn't keep remembering.

Her hand was trembling as she pushed open the shop door and the bell jangled. There was an older man behind the counter. For a second she was thrown, but she stated her business and waited whilst he found her order. The booklets were perfect. Small enough to slip into a pocket for easy and instant reference, and yet clear in their contents. Bob had bound each volume in a pretty green cardboard cover, and her name was on the front: 'Hints and Tips for the Domestic by Ruby Searle'. The moment she saw it, she loved it.

'Is Mr Knight here?' she asked.

'I'm afraid not, madam,' said the assistant. 'He's taken an order to Fittleworth. Why, is there a problem?'

'No, no,' cried Ruby. Her heart sank. Fittleworth? That was miles away. 'It looks wonderful. I just wanted to thank him, that's all.'

She paid her bill and the man handed her the books in a brown paper bag. 'I'll be sure to tell him.'

Ruby looked up sharply. 'Tell him what?'

'That you were pleased with the order,' said the man.

*   *   *

223

Eric pushed open the pub door. A warm wall of smoky beer-soaked air welcomed him in. A couple of men at the bar turned round and acknowledged his presence.

'Hey up, Eric. What'll it be?'

But already the barman was reaching for his favourite mug and, before Eric reached the bar itself, was filling it with a pint of best draught bitter. Eric grinned. Life was good. This was what he had dreamed about, all those long months he'd spent in jail: he and Lena, with a place of their own, a good job and a bit of money in his pocket. He didn't come to the pub every night, but as soon as he'd saved up enough money to buy himself a bike, a whole new world had opened up for him. He didn't ask for much: a couple of pints, a game of darts and a bit of a laugh with his mates, that was all.

He'd just been paid a bonus for his gardening job. His employer had been pleased with Eric's hard work and his garden was now looking tip-top, even if he did say so himself. He'd started a bit late in the year, but the runner beans were almost ready for picking, and he'd managed to keep the cabbage and lettuces relatively bug-free. He'd covered the raspberry canes with netting, to keep the birds away, and he'd kept the grass mowed. The Missus had flowers for the house, and the hollyhocks around the front looked a picture.

Eric had worked hard, but he'd enjoyed every minute and it gave him great pleasure to realize that he had brought not one, but two, gardens up to scratch – the one he was getting paid for and his own. He would use the bonus to give Lena and Jean a day out somewhere.

Perhaps they could take one of those coach trips that were becoming so popular these days. The Devil's Dyke sounded thrilling; or the New Forest, or maybe Beachy Head. He had no idea what any of them were like, but with a bit extra in his pocket, he could soon find out.

The men waiting at the bar had become his mates. Eric enjoyed their company. He wouldn't tell them about his bonus, but he would enjoy sharing a little.

'Landlord,' he said importantly, 'the next round is on me.'

CHAPTER 19

Ever since the editor of the *Gazette* came in person to ask him to write a weekly piece under the banner 'The way I see it', Jim couldn't wait to get started.

'I'll have free rein to bring up any subject I want,' he told Ruby, 'and so long as I am respectful of other people's views, the editor doesn't care if I stir up a hornets' nest.'

His first effort had been to make a comment on the Church of England's new ruling to accept the theory of evolution. The response in the letters page caused hardly a ripple, but when he began a lively discussion on the state of the country and the solution to the problems in Europe, the editor's postbag filled to bursting point. Some wrote of impending doom, especially as the daily papers were reporting an aurora borealis that stretched right across Europe as far south as Gibraltar, which had caused a great deal of alarm. Some people called it a 'curtain of fire', while others gave it a more religious significance, calling it a sign of God's disapproval.

Jim saw his opportunity to fan the flames. 'Is this a heavenly sign?' he asked readers. 'Has Hitler got a hidden agenda?' To back his theory, he recalled the school visits of the previous year when a coachload of German youths had stayed in the town, and he made a vague suggestion that all might not have been as it seemed. 'Some of those Germans bicycled along the beach here in Worthing,' he wrote. 'Could they be "spy-clists"?'

The suggestion had divided the town, and the letters poured in.

Writing of a visit to Germany the year before the schoolboys came to Worthing, Mr R.G. Martin, the headmaster of the school, was quoted as saying, 'We have a deep debt of gratitude to Germany. Those of us who went from Worthing to north Germany were received with the greatest friendship and open-handed generosity.' And the mayor reminded everyone, 'I told them I hoped that when they went back to their coun-trymen, they would tell them that the English extended the hand of friendship. We don't,' his letter continued, 'want to go back to the old days.' And a 'Patriot of Goring' wrote, 'That visit was culturally inspired.'

On the other hand, several readers were alarmed to discover that Germans were even being allowed into the country. Doris Avon of Durrington wrote, 'My husband died of wounds he received at the Somme, after nearly twenty years of suffering. How can we offer a hand of friendship to such people? Hitler and his cronies are not our friends, and nor should they ever be.'

With the drawers of his small desk already bulging,

Jim kept everything important in an old storage box for 78 rpm records that Ruby had picked up for a song at a jumble sale. However, as he acted as both referee and agent provocateur, the post brought yet another envelope and a postal order even bigger than the last payment.

Ruby couldn't be absolutely sure when it started, but by the middle of November she could hardly face getting up in the mornings. There were a few guests – a couple of travelling salesmen, and of course the girls sent by the Deborah Committee – but having to cook a fry-up every morning was becoming a nightmare. The nausea came in waves and she felt dizzy and light-headed. Somehow or other she managed to cope, and was highly relieved to see Lena when she came to help. Most of all, Ruby looked forward to the days when she had nobody staying with them. On those days Jim had toast for breakfast.

Ruby was pregnant.

On a bad day she understood how Miss Russell must have felt all those years ago. Imogen Russell had been staying in Warnes Hotel when Ruby worked there as a chambermaid. She had found Miss Russell in a terrible state one morning: she had had a miscarriage, and Ruby helped her get to hospital without her father knowing. Now it occurred to Ruby, for the first time, that it was possible Miss Russell had procured an abortion. Ruby didn't want to, but perhaps she should do the same. There was Jim to think about. He still needed looking after. How would she cope with a baby as well as her sick husband and running the guest house? And another thing: how could she tell Jim she was expecting a baby? It would destroy him. They'd only been a married couple for a short time before the accident, but she knew that, back then, he wanted a family. Could she ask him to help her bring up another man's child? What if he divorced her? And what of Bob Knight? Everybody said he wasn't the marrying kind, but just supposing she was free: would he be prepared to make an honest woman of her? The whole thing went round and round in her head until Ruby thought she would go barmy.

A few days later she remembered Mrs Pickering, who had lived in the same road as Ruby when she was young and had looked after women who were in trouble. That was never talked about, but somehow or other, it was common knowledge. And so one Wednesday afternoon Ruby told Jim she was going out for a bike ride, and rode over to Newlands Road.

When she got there, she leaned her bicycle against the wall and knocked on the paint-blistered front door. A few minutes later Trixie Pickering, a girl Ruby had gone to school with, opened the door. Immediately Ruby's face burned with shame.

'I'll put your bicycle around the back, if you don't mind,' said Trixie cheerfully. 'You don't want anybody recognizing you, now do you? You go on inside. Mother's in the kitchen.'

Mrs Pickering had her back to Ruby as she walked in. The room smelled stale, with a hint of fish. It was gloomy, despite the fire burning in the old-fashioned blackleaded range. Some stockings and woollen socks were draped on a wire over the mantelpiece, and a large cat had its leg in the air, doing its toilet on the only chair in the room. Mrs Pickering appeared to have something boiling on the kitchen range. She stood at the kitchen sink, where she was peeling potatoes. Her hands were clean, but Ruby couldn't help noticing that her finger-nails bore the marks of garden work. She wondered if she should mention this. She didn't want the woman giving her an infection. It all seemed a bit odd: cooking a meal and performing an abortion at the same time.

'Come on in, dear,' said Mrs Pickering, taking a handful of potatoes to the saucepan and dropping them in. 'You're late. There's not much time. My husband will be back home soon, and I don't want you here when he comes.'

Ruby was puzzled. She hadn't made arrangements to be here, and yet the woman was behaving as if she was expected. She must think she was someone else. Ruby cleared her throat and Mrs Pickering turned round.

'Oh!' she cried. 'It's Ruby Searle. You gave me quite a start. I thought you were—'

There was a sharp rap on the door and Mrs Pickering drew in her breath. 'That's her. Where's Trixie?'

'She's taken my bike around the back,' said Ruby.

'The silly mare must have thought you were my customer,' said Mrs Pickering, pushing Ruby towards the sitting-room door. She was a small woman with a very weathered face, obviously used to being outdoors. 'Ruby love, you'll have to go in here and wait for me.

I shan't be a tick.' She went to close the door and then, leaning back in, said confidentially, 'I hope I can rely on you to be discreet.'

The knocking on the kitchen door was becoming more urgent.

'Coming, love,' Mrs Pickering called.

She hadn't quite closed the sitting-room door, so Ruby shrank behind the floor-length curtain that kept out the draughts and listened.

Mrs Pickering's voice was muffled, but Ruby heard her say, 'Got the money, dear? Put it on the mantelpiece. Right, now take off your knickers and lie on the table, there's a good girl.'

Ruby heard the saucepan being moved and then she heard the sound of running water.

'I always boil everything first, to make sure it's clean,' Mrs Pickering said. 'Just have to cool it a bit under the tap.'

There was a long silence, then another voice said nervously, 'Will it hurt?'

'It might be a little bit uncomfortable, dear,' Mrs Pickering said, 'but after this, all your troubles will be over.'

Ruby couldn't resist slipping into the little corridor between the two rooms to see what was happening. Peeping through the crack in the half-open door, she couldn't see who the woman was, although she lay on Mrs Pickering's kitchen table with her legs akimbo. When Mrs Pickering came into view, she was holding something that looked a lot like a knitting needle. She

231

blocked Ruby's view as she stood facing the woman's private parts. Bending low, she manoeuvred the needle into place. Ruby closed her eyes and shuddered as she heard the woman cry out in anguish, and then Mrs Pickering said, 'All done. You can get dressed now, dear.'

Then Ruby heard crying.

'That's enough of that, dear,' said Mrs Pickering sharply. 'You don't want to go outside with your eyes all red, now do you?'

The woman blew her nose. 'How long before . . . ?' she asked.

'I expect it'll all come away tonight,' said Mrs Pickering. 'Bit of a tummy ache, that's all. Now off you go, dear.'

Ruby heard the door close and dashed back into the sitting room before Mrs Pickering returned.

'Sorry about that, dear,' she said. 'I'll give Trixie a shout. She always waits in the garden until it's all over. It's nice of you to pop by.'

Ruby headed back into the kitchen.

'Got time for a cup of tea?' Mrs Pickering asked, after she'd opened the back door and called her daughter.

Ruby tried not to look at the splatter of blood on Mrs Pickering's hand and on the front of her apron. This was a bad idea. She knew now that she would never tell Mrs Pickering the real reason she'd come. Who knows what infections she would get, if she put herself in the hands of this woman. Having a baby was bad enough, but submitting to a knitting needle being stuck into her private parts to get rid of it was quite another.

232

Back in the kitchen, Mrs Pickering rinsed her hands under the tap and began to lay the table for their meal. Ruby declined the tea and didn't even wait for Trixie to come in from the garden. 'I only popped in to say hello,' she said. 'I'd better go. I've got to get back in time to give Jim his tea.'

When she opened the front door, Trixie was putting Ruby's bike against the wall. She smiled at Ruby, then looked concerned. 'Will she be all right riding back home, Ma?'

'Ruby only came in for a chat,' Mrs Pickering chuckled. 'Trust you to get the wrong end of the stick.'

Ruby turned the bike round and sat astride it.

'Bye, Ruby love,' said Mrs Pickering. 'Come back again, won't you?'

With a quick wave, Ruby sped off. Not if I can help it, she thought.

'I have never been so humiliated in my life.' Effie Rhodes leaned back in her chair, hugging a brandy and soda to her chest.

It was late evening and, having enjoyed a delicious dinner, she and Gus were relaxing in their sumptuous sitting room. Gus, who had spent the day trying out a new model train, was enjoying a malt whisky, and in the background Beethoven's Piano Concerto No.4, performed by Myra Hess, was playing on the gramophone. He sighed. He'd heard the story a dozen times before, but it still rankled his wife.

'It was a little unfortunate . . .' Gus began.

'Unfortunate!' she retorted. 'If I had known Bea Quinn harboured such feelings, I would never have recruited her in the first place.'

'Don't worry about her,' said Gus casually, but Effie had only just got going.

'I was never one to blow my own trumpet,' she said, getting up to refresh her glass, 'and it embarrasses me to say this, but that sale would never have happened without yours truly. Who organized the troops? Who got Elsie and Doris Walters to come along – not my choice, I assure you, but they were chosen by popular consensus. Who kept everybody on their toes all day?' She threw herself back on the sofa and lowered her eyes.

Gus leaned over and gripped her shoulder. 'Steady on, old gel.'

Effie snatched herself away. 'And yet after all I did,' she said, with a break in her voice, 'that damned woman encouraged everyone to gang up on me.'

'Strange, isn't it?' her husband said languidly. 'Bea came over as a rather mousy woman the night we all had dinner together.'

'And that's just where we were both wrong,' said Effie tetchily. 'The things that woman said! I tell you, the whole damned thing was nothing less than a bloodbath.'

They sipped their drinks in silence.

Eventually Effie said, 'It's not fair, Gus. It's not bloody fair.'

'I know, old thing, but there it is.'

Her head snapped up and she glared at him. 'Is that all you can say? "There it is"?'

'Look, my dear,' he began again, 'I know it's disappointing, but quite honestly I can't think why you even bother with such people.'

'Because I want to be somebody in this town,' she wailed. 'Can't you see that? All my life I've had to do what someone else wanted me to do. If it wasn't the Colonial Office, it was you. When we came here, you promised me this was *my* time. Well, it's about time people sat up and took notice of me!'

'I understand that,' he said, 'but why bother with people like Bea Quinn and Freda Fosdyke? They are such small fry, Effie.'

'We've been away for nearly twenty years, Gus,' she said, jumping up and pouring another brandy. 'I don't know anyone any more. I need to be in the best circles. I need—'

'Then create it yourself,' he interrupted.

'What?'

'If you want to be at the front, old gel, you'd better take the lead. Give the best parties. Invite famous people. Stop worrying about silly little autumn fairs, and turn yourself into the person whose parties everybody wants to go to.'

Effie sank back on the cushions as if she'd been winded. Lavish parties? Fabulous guests? She could see it all now. Gus was right. If she was going to become a force to be reckoned with in the town, she had to make herself the person to be seen with. Her eyes glistened with excitement. Gus moved a little closer.

'We'll have to spend quite a bit of money,' she began cautiously.

'We've been more than adequately rewarded for our services,' he said, putting his hand on her thigh.

'We'll get some really good caterers,' she said, her mind racing ahead. 'Bentalls, or perhaps a firm from Brighton.'

Gus had lifted her skirt and had his hand on her suspender and stocking top. If she had looked down, she would have seen that he was already fully aroused. He leaned into her neck and nuzzled her ear. 'Anything you want, old thing.'

In her head, Effie was already writing out the guest list. She would choose some really important people.

Gus kissed her hand, palm up, and then gently brought it down towards his crutch. She was suddenly aware of him and he puckered his lips for a kiss.

'No time for all that nonsense now,' she said, sitting bolt upright. 'We've got a guest list to write.'

CHAPTER 20

Ruby was in turmoil. She couldn't hide her pregnancy for much longer, yet she didn't know what to do about it. She had toyed with the idea of just telling Jim straight out, but she was scared of his reaction. He'd be angry, of course, but what then? Would he throw her out of the house, or make her go away and give the baby up for adoption? Or perhaps denounce her to the whole world? None of these prospects was very appetizing. At the same time she burned with shame at the thought of her mother knowing what she had done.

True, Bea had not been married to Rex when she'd conceived Ruby, but they had the excuse of wartime, an uncertain future and a cruel and heartless husband. What excuse could Ruby give for a five-minute fling with a man she hardly knew? She was frustrated that Jim rejected her in the bedroom, but he couldn't help it. It wasn't done out of any sense of malice. She had a good home and a well-run business, which brought them a comfortable living. She was a respectable land-lady, but now she'd thrown it all away for a brief moment of unguarded lust. She knew she was being hard on herself, but even that suited her. The guilt weighed heavily on her shoulders because, even though she tried hard not to, in her mind she went over and over the experience. The dreadful thing was: she had enjoyed every moment.

If she couldn't tell Jim, maybe Bob was a better bet. He was unmarried, and an exciting lover. She knew divorce was expensive and they'd have to find someone to act as co-respondent, but if eventually she and Bob were married, she could have night after night of the same passion. He didn't own the printer's where he worked, but he was good at his job. Perhaps they could both talk things over with Jim and come to some sort of arrangement. If she lived with Bob, they'd have to leave Worthing, of course, but perhaps in another place they could make a happy life for themselves. Ruby rationalized that Lena would look after Jim. She might even run the guest house, if Ruby made an attractive enough offer. Lena didn't appear to have any other ties – no family or commitments elsewhere. Ruby had tried to find out about her past life, but Lena remained tight-lipped. It had even crossed Ruby's mind that perhaps Lena already had a husband somewhere and that she and Eric had run away together.

Christmas was only three and a half weeks away. Ruby planned to spend that afternoon doing the first of her Christmas shopping. The shops in Montague Street were already looking festive. Wrapping her scarf around her neck and pulling on her woollen gloves, she set off just after two.

In Woolworths she bought a box of handkerchiefs for Lena and a pretty nightdress for Jean. Ruby had been knitting a cardigan for May, so she stopped by at Mason's Wool and Toy Shop for some buttons to match. Thus she found herself only a stone's throw away from Caxton Printers.

Screwing up every ounce of courage, she decided it was now or never. Bob had to know that he was soon to become a father. She wondered how he would react. Would he be angry with her, or upset that she hadn't told him sooner? By the time she was standing outside the shop, she was convinced that he would be delighted. She was carrying his child. What man wouldn't be pleased? Although the sign on the door was turned to *Closed*, it hadn't been properly shut. The bell stayed silent as Ruby stepped into the shop. She could hear muffled voices in the back room. She was about to call out, but something stopped her. One voice was female. The pair stopped talking and then Bob laughed. When Ruby had been in his arms, it was a pleasant sound. She closed her eyes, remembering.

'Lovely,' she heard Bob say. 'Oh, sweetheart, that's lovely.'

Reluctantly Ruby moved towards the door. She could see two shadowy figures through the glass and they were awfully close together. Her heartbeat began to quicken and her stomach fell away. The pair of them were on the horsehair sofa. She couldn't see who was underneath him, but Bob's bottom was bare and pumping up and down.

'Lovely,' Bob was saying. 'I'm so glad you came into my shop, darlin'.'

Tears sprang into her eyes as Ruby dropped her shopping bag and clamped her hand across her mouth, to stifle the cry of shock as she stumbled backwards. Some papers fell onto the floor as she brushed past them.

She heard the woman say anxiously, 'What was that?'

'Nothing, sugar,' said Bob. 'I put the sign on the door, remember?'

Her chin quivering with disappointment and rage, Ruby sprinted into the street and slammed the door so hard that the sound of the jangling bell followed her halfway down the road.

She felt sick. What a fool she had been. What a stupid idiot! So much for Bob 'doing the right thing'. She was nothing more than another trophy on the horsehair sofa.

She found herself heading towards the sea. The chilly December air cut through her open coat and wrapped itself around her body, but she was so numb that she hardly felt it. It took some time before she realized how cold she was. Eventually she buttoned up her coat and, hugging herself tightly, walked onto the pier. The kiosk was closed for winter, so she was spared having to find tuppence to promenade. She was frozen to the marrow by the time she reached the Southern Pavilion. The bright lights of the tea rooms drew her inside.

'We're closing in half an hour, madam,' the waitress said pointedly as Ruby sat by the bow window. There

240

were still a few customers in the room, but they appeared to be finishing their meals.

'Is there still time to have a pot of tea?' Ruby asked.

The waitress didn't look too happy. Obviously she was hoping to do the clearing up and finish early, but she hurried away to get Ruby's order. Ruby stared out of the windows. On the shore, the lights on Marine Parade twinkled in the gathering gloom. Out to sea it was already getting quite dark. Low cloud threatened the town with rain, or maybe the first snowfall of the winter. The heaviness of the weather matched Ruby's mood. Unbidden, a tear trickled down her cheek. She quickly swept it aside with her hand. What a mess she was in. Clearly she had been as stupidly naive as a sixteen-year-old, when it came to Bob. Hadn't she been warned about his reputation? Hadn't her mother, having spotted her dreamy expression, reprimanded her for staring at him? She had no other course open to her now but to tell Jim what she had done and face the consequences. In her head she began to rehearse what to say. The more she thought about it, the more she dreaded his reaction.

All at once Ruby realized she had been sitting staring out of the window for nearly twenty minutes. Her tea was cold by the time she drained the last dregs in the cup. The waitress came over to the table as soon as Ruby stood to her feet and began to pull on her coat. As she did so, the waitress gathered Ruby's cup and saucer, the milk jug and teapot onto a tray. They both hesitated and their eyes met.

'Sorry to hold you up,' said Ruby brokenly.

The waitress shook her head and added softly, 'It might not be as bad as you think, love.'

Ruby managed a weak smile, before picking up her purse. When she reached the door, the waitress added, 'Happy Christmas, love, and . . . good luck.'

Bea opened the book and stared at the flyleaf:

First aid to the injured. The authorized textbook of the St John Ambulance Association, being the ambulance department of the Grand Priory in the British Realm of the Venerable Order of the Hospital of St John of Jerusalem.

She blinked. Bit of a mouthful, she thought.

'Two hours a week, for six weeks, should do it,' said Mrs Hayward. 'Of course, only members of the medical profession can be instructors.'

'Of course,' Bea agreed.

They had been having tea in Hubbard's. It had been a most enjoyable experience, with tea served in a silver teapot, bone-china cups and a three-tiered plate of the most wonderful fancy cakes. Bea knew she shouldn't but she'd succumbed to two.

Her new-found friend was brimming with enthusiasm. It seemed that the Air Raid Precautions organization in Worthing was going to be bowled over by her suggestions and, given the awkwardness of the male contingent, she proposed to run an all-female arm of the organization.

But first, she had explained to Bea, she had to have dedicated and committed women in the ranks.

'I'm sick of men telling me the women will be more worried about their hats and getting home to their husband's tea than fire-watching or evacuation,' she told Bea. 'Women can make a valuable contribution to the country, should we go to war.'

'I couldn't agree more,' said Bea, 'but where do we start? The task seems enormous.'

'Getting our ladies to do first aid would be a start,' said Mrs Hayward pointedly.

Bea glanced down at her hands. The blue hardback book was set out as a series of lectures. She supposed the idea was to do one a week. She let it fall open and came to the fourth lecture:

Insensibility – when breathing is absent (asphyxia) . . . practical instruction – artificial respiration.

She could see the sense of it all. Right now, if she found someone who wasn't breathing, she wouldn't know what to do. Under those circumstances, the best she could offer was a scream for help. She still didn't know how to administer artificial respiration, but the lessons would make her better equipped. There were illustrations throughout the book: a picture of a dislocated elbow, the St John tourniquet (a piece of webbing with a buckle and a twister) – although why on earth you would need such a thing, she hadn't a clue – and a diagram of the circulation of the blood. It all looked rather daunting and she felt slightly queasy.

Mrs Hayward was watching her. 'Do you think you can help us out?'

'I can but try,' Bea said.

'That's not all I want,' Mrs Hayward said, leaning forward and resting her palm on Bea's hand. 'Did you know that, if war comes, the government is planning to disperse hundreds – maybe thousands – of people out of the cities all over the country?'

'I've heard rumours,' said Bea faintly, 'but I wasn't sure if there was any truth in it.'

'Oh, believe me, Mrs Quinn, there is,' said Mrs Hayward stoutly. 'If push comes to shove, we have got to be involved. I'm trying to find out about it.'

Bea put her hand up. 'I admire your enthusiasm, my dear,' she said gently, 'but one thing at a time.'

Mrs Hayward wiped the corner of her mouth with her napkin. 'You are so right, Mrs Quinn,' she chuckled. 'I do get carried away, don't I? First aid first.'

The manageress was hovering nearby. Mrs Hayward looked at her watch. 'Oh dear,' she said, 'it's almost five-thirty. I think we've outstayed our welcome. My car is parked outside. Can I give you a lift, Mrs Quinn?'

'That would be most kind,' said Bea.

They gathered their things and walked from the restaurant. 'You know,' said Mrs Hayward over her shoulder, 'we need as many people as we can get.'

'I'm positive I can muster at least ten women,' said Bea, 'but where shall we hold the meetings?'

'Farncombe Road,' said Mrs Hayward. 'St John's have a headquarters there.' They stepped out into the dark evening and she smiled broadly. 'I'm so glad you've caught the vision, Mrs Quinn. I believe with all my heart that, between us, we could make a formidable team.'

As Mrs Hayward led the way to her parked car, Bea smiled to herself. A formidable team – she rather liked the sound of that.

Jim had decided to go and look at the sea. The guest house wasn't far from the front, but the high shingle bank hid the water from view. It was a pleasant evening and Ruby was at her mother's, so he pushed the wheelchair himself, leaning over the back and placing his hands on the armrests. When he got tired he could sit on the seat until he'd mustered enough strength to make his way back. He knew he had to exercise his legs, but he had also learned that if he did too much they would throb at night, robbing him of sleep, and his knees would 'give way' the next day. There was nothing more scary than putting your weight on a leg that suddenly wasn't there any more. He didn't often hurt himself badly, because the experience had taught him to go with the fall rather than resist it.

He crossed Marine Parade and found his way up a slope onto the walkway. The wind was keen but the sea sparkled. A few fluffy clouds wandered high above his head, but the sky was relatively clear. Couples strolled by arm-in-arm on the beach. A few diehard day-trippers were putting their empty flasks into their bags and making their way up the beach. Sandy-faced children, tired and complaining, followed in their wake. To his left as he faced the sea, Worthing pier with its magnificent Southern Pavilion and its newly added sun-screen reminded him of happier times, and of the summer. He recalled the day of Ruby's birthday a couple of years back and the first tentative steps he'd made towards her on his walking sticks. Oh, he had had such high hopes of a complete recovery back then. Now it seemed like a lifetime ago.

Jim took a deep breath. Overhead, gulls swooped and dived, their raucous call reminding him of fishing boats and seaside photographs. He aimed for a bench facing the sea a little further along. A lone woman sat there, but the seat was plenty big enough for two people, and she might have moved on before he got there. If it felt intrusive to join her, he could always go another fifty yards and sit down on the wheelchair.

As he got closer, she looked familiar. Closer still, he realized it was Edith Gressenhall. Her head was bent low and she seemed deep in thought.

'Hello, Edith.'

She looked up and he was startled to see that she'd been crying. She wiped her eyes quickly and blew her nose. 'Hello, Jim. How nice to see you.'

He sat on the other end of the bench, slightly embarrassed, and wondered what to say next. 'Are you all right, love?'

To Jim's consternation, Edith burst into tears.

Jim froze. 'I'm sorry. I didn't mean to upset you.' She stood up. 'No, no, don't go, Edith. Is there any way I can help?' He saw her hesitate. 'Please sit down again. Tell me.'

She lowered herself onto the seat and wiped the end of her nose with her already sodden handkerchief. Jim fished around in his pocket and handed her his freshly laundered one.

Edith took it gratefully and, shaking it out, dried her eyes and blew her nose again. 'I don't know what to do,' she said brokenly.

Oh God, he thought. She's going to tell me there's something up with her marriage. 'I'm not as clever as Ruby,' he began.

'I can't pay the rent,' she blurted out.

He stared at the top of her bent head. Oh dear. She must need some lessons on looking after money. Funny, he'd never had her down as a girl who was frivolous with her money.

She opened her bag. 'I went to the fishmonger to buy a mackerel for Bernard's tea and tried to pay him with this.' She handed Jim a five-pound note. 'I wanted the change, do you see? I've got the rest of the rent money in the book, and I planned to come to your place to settle up. Save Ruby a journey. Only Mr White, the fishmonger, says this is a forgery. And now I can't pay the rent.'

Jim examined the note. He'd never seen a forgery before and he'd only ever seen a couple of five-pound notes, but somehow this one didn't feel right. He held it up to the light, but it seemed normal. He studied it more carefully. Was he missing something? Britannia was on the left-hand side at the top. The numbers were repeated on the note twice: A 223 and 03016. He'd have to check the numbers with a bank to be absolutely sure, but if the fishmonger had spotted something, then – without being offensive – it had to be something a little more obvious. The signature of the Bank of England's Chief Cashier looked fine: K.O. Peppiatt; and the note promised to 'pay the Bearer' and all that. But then he saw the glaring mistake: the date written on the cheque was February 29th, 1933. He pointed it out to Edith.

'It's the date,' he said. 'This must have been what Tobias White noticed. 1933 wasn't a leap year. That was 1932, and then again last year. Where did you get it?'

'Bernard gave it to me.'

'And where did he get it?'

'I think it was from the man who bought one of his model engines,' said Edith. 'He paid him with three of them. Bernard will be heartbroken.' Her husband had been making model engines for some time as a hobby. Everyone agreed that he was very skilled, and each engine took the best part of a year to make.

Jim raised his eyebrows and sighed. 'You should take

them back,' he said. 'You'll have to tell the buyer they were dud notes.'

'What if he doesn't believe us?' said Edith. 'We've got no proof they came from him.'

'If the chap can afford to pay fifteen pounds for a model engine,' said Jim, 'he can afford to put it right.'

'And if he won't?'

'Then you and Bernard need to go to the police.'

Edith nodded dully. 'In the meantime, what am I going to do about the rent? I know you and Ruby are our friends, but I don't want to take advantage.'

'You say you've got some of it?' said Jim.

'We pay monthly,' Edith explained. 'I'm one pound ten shillings short.'

'Give me the book and what you've got there,' said Jim. 'I'll put the one pound ten shillings in when I get back home. You can pay me back as and when.'

Her jaw dropped. 'Oh, Jim,' she said, her fingers trembling over her mouth, 'you would really do that?'

He put his hand out for the rent book and she handed it to him.

'Ruby always signs it for us,' said Edith.

'Ruby is out at the moment,' said Jim. 'I'll tell her you came and that you'll stop by for it tomorrow.'

Edith regarded him gratefully. 'Thank you.'

He stood to go.

'Would you like me to push you back home in the chair?' she asked.

'I'll be all right,' said Jim. He took a few steps, then

looked back. 'By the way, this is just between you and me, right?'

'Right,' she smiled.

Ruby was late getting the tea ready. She had decided to have sausage and mash, Jim's favourite. As she'd come up the road she had seen Jim leaning over the back of the wheelchair on his way to the postbox with another batch of letters and crosswords. He was getting a steady stream of acceptances now. Last week he had made almost five pounds. That was more than Eric next door made at the railway depot.

Ruby had visitors staying, but they would be out until late – a family wedding. That meant it was just her and Jim for dinner. By the time Jim got back, the sausages were in the pan waiting to be cooked and Ruby was chopping up some onions. Jim loved fried onion. All she had to do now was put a light under the potatoes and greens and she was well on her way. Jim walked in the door just as Ruby blinked back another tear. Not only was she upset about the baby and Bob, but it had just dawned on her that she'd left her Christmas shopping at the printer's. Would Bob recognize it? Had she left anything inside the bag that would bring him to her door? Oh God, she didn't want him turning up with it. She had no reason even to be in the shop.

'Won't be long,' she said cheerfully. She stopped to blow her nose. Biscuit rubbed himself around her legs and she pushed him away crossly with her foot. 'Stop it, Biscuit, you silly old cat.'

Jim took off his coat and hung it up. He kicked off his shoes. 'What's wrong?'

Ruby looked up. 'Wrong?' she said innocently. 'Nothing. I'm peeling onions, that's all.'

'You're pregnant,' he said quietly. The atmosphere in the room became suddenly charged with electricity.

Ruby's jaw dropped. 'How . . . how did you . . . ?' The words died on her lips.

'I'm not a fool, Ruby,' he said. 'I hear you being sick every morning; you're tired; you don't like doing cooked breakfast; and you're always in the toilet. You're having a baby, aren't you?'

She pressed her hand over her mouth. Her throat felt as if she'd swallowed a whole orange. 'Oh, Jim,' she squeaked.

He lowered himself onto the chair opposite her. He couldn't meet her eye. His hand trembled slightly as he put it to his forehead and rubbed it, as if trying to remove the worry lines. 'Are you going to leave me?'

She shook her head vigorously. 'No, no.'

He seemed relieved, which made her feel guilty again. 'I only did it the once, I promise,' she said, quickly hanging her head. The silence between them grew.

'Whose is it?' he said eventually.

'Please don't ask me that, Jim,' she said. 'He means nothing to me.'

Silence again.

'Have you told him?'

She shook her head. 'He doesn't know.'

The ticking of the clock seemed to grow louder by the minute.

'So,' said Jim, looking up at her for the first time, 'what happens next?'

'I guess that's down to you,' she choked. Her eyes filled with tears again. 'I've reached the end of my options, and I have nowhere to go.'

For a split second she thought he was going to reach out to her, but he simply stared. 'Do you want him?' Jim's face was expressionless.

Ruby shook her head again. 'No – a thousand times no.'

He said nothing for several minutes, so she said, 'It was a God-awful stupid mistake. I'm so, so sorry. I went to see Mrs Pickering,' she blundered on, 'but I can't bring myself to get rid of it, either. I'm too scared. I'll go away if you like, Jim. We'll make something up. I'll have the baby and I'll give it up for adoption.' She was crying now, hot miserable tears that ran off the end of her chin.

'But you want children,' he said.

'I wanted your child,' she said desperately.

'And I can't give you one,' he said.

They sat in silence again, then Jim said, 'Have the baby here, Ruby. We'll tell everyone it's mine.'

She gulped audibly and, wiping her eyes, stared at him in disbelief. Her head began to spin. She felt dizzy with joy. 'Oh, Jim . . . I don't deserve you.'

'Don't be daft,' he said, standing to his feet. 'But we tell no one, right?'

'Right,' she said breathlessly.

He shuffled towards the door but, on reaching it, turned round again. 'The bloke,' he said, 'does he look anything like me? Will people think it's my baby?'

She hesitated for a second, then she said, 'I suppose he does look a bit like you, Jim.'

'Then we'll say no more about it,' he said, leaving the room.

CHAPTER 21

Rivka managed to find a few moments' peace and quiet between serving the courses. Her employer was a hard woman and, since she'd had the German girl in her employ, she'd had Rivka in tears more than once. Although Mrs Hobden had a reputation for wonderful Christmas parties and lavish gifts, that day – and, for that matter, the week leading up to it – hadn't been very enjoyable for Rivka.

'Of course, you being Jewish, you don't celebrate the season, do you?' Mrs Hobden had said. 'There's little point in buying you a present.'

Rivka didn't much care about presents, but she did care that Mrs Hobden had her on the go from six in the morning until gone midnight.

'For heaven's sake, girl, put your back into it. At this rate you'll never get all the silver polished by four.' 'Rivka, where are my red slippers?' 'No, not the brown coat, stupid girl. Can't you see I'm wearing my best hat!'

Mama and Papa never treated our servants so shabbily, Rivka thought ruefully. Furthermore, she was doing the work of three people. And there was so much to remember: small white apron when people came in the afternoon; washing on Monday; ironing on Tuesday. It was a good job she wasn't expected to do the cooking as well. A cook-housekeeper came in most days, but she was a sullen woman who said as little as possible.

Rivka had been working for Mrs Hobden for nearly nine months and she was desperately lonely. The only joy in her life came when Ruby wrote to her. At first Ruby had written two or maybe three letters a week. They had tailed off now, probably because Rivka could only manage to reply once or twice a month. It took her so long to compose a letter, and there was very little spare time. Ruby's letters didn't tell her much, but they were most welcome. It was comforting to know that at least one other person in the world was thinking of her. Ruby had even sent her a Christmas card. Inside she had written, 'I hope you have a wonderful first Christmas in England.' She meant well, but the hopelessness of the sentiment made Rivka cry.

It was when Mrs Hobden had dinner guests that she hated it the most. Cook prepared everything beforehand, so all she had to do was put the meal in the oven at the right time, but her workload almost doubled. Not only did every room have to be spotless, but she had to lay the table with the best china, and wash everything up and put it away before she was allowed to go to bed. It wasn't easy. She was at her employer's beck and call the whole time: 'Rivka, more coffee.' 'Put more coal on the fire, Rivka.' 'Where are the clean stem-glasses, girl? We can't drink out of tumblers.'

If the guests stayed until midnight, Rivka had to be available and, when they had gone, there was still all the clearing up to do. The next day Mrs Hobden would have a lie-in, but there was no lie-in for Rivka. Even if she'd gone to bed at two in the morning, she still had to be up at six to see to the fires and get breakfast.

Today was Christmas Day, and her employer had been more exacting than ever. Rivka was homesick and exhausted. She was in the middle of washing up the dinner plates when she heard a footfall behind her. A middle-aged man holding a large cigar in one hand and a half-full whisky glass in the other swayed in the doorway.

'Is there something I can get you, sir?'

'Toilet,' he slurred.

The toilet? What on earth was he doing looking for the toilet downstairs in the kitchen? Rivka dried her hands on the tea towel and went to the doorway. 'This way, sir.'

The man didn't move. For some reason, Rivka felt a little uneasy. She recalled Ruby's cautionary tales and realized that she couldn't get past him without touching his portly belly. 'Never allow yourself to be compromised,' Ruby had warned her. 'Be polite, but always keep your distance. Remember: some men take advantage, and if you are seen in an awkward situation, a man is likely to blame you, to save his own skin.'

She took a step back. 'It's down the passageway and to the left,' she said, indicating with her arm.

The man touched his forelock and grinned. As he turned to go, she heard a quiet burp. He walked unsteadily down the corridor and Rivka went back to her dishes. The saucepans were kept on the high shelf and, as she reached up to place one above her head, she felt a hand on her breast. The pan landed on the shelf with a clatter, and Rivka cried out in shocked surprise. The man pushed himself against her, pinning her to the edge of the draining board. She tried to hit him away, but his hands were all over the place, and from that moment it seemed like he had the strength of ten men. One minute he was tugging at her dress, and the next she felt his hand on the inside of her bare thigh and moving towards her crotch.

'No,' she protested. 'No, no . . .' but her anxious cries only seemed to inflame him all the more. When he started fumbling with his own clothes, she could feel that he was fully aroused. She tried to reach the saucepan again, planning to bring it down on his head, but the pan spun away and the handle slipped from her grasp. Then he pushed her head down onto the draining board and splayed her feet with his own leg. Her face was pressed hard against the plate shelf. The thick ring on his finger cut into the side of her ear, and she wept helplessly as she felt his clumsy hands pulling her knickers down.

When it was all over, he finally stepped back and adjusted his clothes. Rivka was sobbing with the pain.

257

She felt as if she had been ripped in two, and moaned slightly as she straightened herself up. Her lip felt as big as a balloon and her right eye was half-closed. Her cheek throbbed where he had pushed her face against the plate rack. There was blood coming from her ear, but that was nothing compared to the raging agony she felt between her legs. She turned to look at her assailant. He had his head down as he brushed the front of his white shirt; there was a splatter of her blood on the end. Snatching up the drying cloth that she was still holding in her hand, he dipped the end into the washing up water and sponged the blood away. 'Bloody German tart!' he muttered.

Tasting blood, Rivka licked the inside of her mouth and became aware that one of her teeth was loose.

Properly dressed again, the man picked up his drink and examined his cigar. It was almost bent in two. 'Oh, bugger, look at that,' he complained.

Their eyes met for a split second. Rivka held his gaze long enough to gather all the spittle she could and then she spat in his face. In a flash he raised his arm as if to hit her, but behind them both a woman's voice called out, 'Are you still in the bathroom, darling? Are you all right? You haven't been taken ill, have you?'

Rivka bent painfully to pull up her knickers while the man, using the same tea towel that he'd used to wipe his shirt tail, soaked up the globule of saliva on his chin and tie. 'Just washing my hands,' he called casually. 'I'll be half a tick.'

Rivka had her back to Mrs Hobden when her

employer came into the room. 'I was getting worried,' she said. 'You were gone such a long time. There's still time for another rubber, if you want one.'

'Why not,' he chuckled. Mrs Hobden ignored Rivka and they left together.

As soon as she was sure she was alone, Rivka made her way painfully up the back stairs to her room. About half an hour later Mrs Hobden rang through for hot chocolate. Ten minutes after that she went to the kitchen to see what was keeping her employee. The kitchen was still in a state of chaos, but there was no sign of her serving girl. On the way out of the room Mrs Hobden noticed a few spots of blood on the floor. Her hand automatically went to her throat. Don't tell me the stupid girl has cut herself, she thought acidly; if she's got blood all over my sheets, I'll damn well take it out of her wage. It didn't occur to her that in all the months she had worked for her, Rivka had never once received a wage.

When Mrs Hobden burst into Rivka's attic room, she wasn't there, either. As she stood in the middle of the room, completely nonplussed, the wardrobe door swung open. The coat hangers swung together. The wardrobe was empty.

For Ruby, Christmas turned out to be a family affair, but with two foreign guests. Ruby's latest girls from the Deborah Committee had arrived five days before the holiday began. As it was impossible to move them on during the season, they were still at Sea View. Sisters

Heidi and Frida were only in their teens. They had escaped from Germany, but they knew their parents – both professional people – had been taken to a concentration camp. Terrified and traumatized, they were relieved to find that Ruby was kind to them. As Jews, they didn't celebrate Christmas, but these were exceptional days and they were glad to be included with the family and, above all, safe.

Of course May was far too old to believe in Father Christmas, but he had finally heard her request for a yellow bicycle. First thing in the morning, having opened a rather flat-looking envelope, she was over the moon to find a note telling her to look outside, where she found a yellow bicycle at the side of the house. She biked down to Ruby's place to show her sister, and throughout the day spent every moment she could riding around the empty roads.

The whole family met at Bea and Rex's home to spend the day together. Percy and Rachel had motored from Shoreham during the morning, bringing little Alma and her presents with them.

As usual, the family opened their presents before dinner. Alma, now just over a year old – one year and three weeks old, to be exact – was alert, although slightly puzzled by the celebrations. She managed to tear the wrapping from a couple of her presents, but in the end she liked the box that her bricks had come in better than anything else. When she hit the side of it with her fist, it made a satisfyingly hollow sound, and yet she was strong enough to pick it up and wave it around.

May had given everyone a carefully drawn picture, and Rex had given Bea a string of pearls, which were greatly admired by everybody. Rachel had a fox-fur stole from Percy, and Ruby got a hand-knitted cardigan from Jim. 'Lena made it for me,' he whispered as she unwrapped the tissue paper. 'Good, isn't she?'

Ruby nodded and pecked his cheek.

'Shall we do it now?' he asked.

Ruby shook her head. 'Teatime,' she said.

Their Christmas meal was amazing. Bea had enlisted the help of Ruby's German girls and they had the luxury of a chicken, which they ate with roast parsnips, carrots, cabbage and roast potatoes. Bea had made the Christmas pudding herself and carried it to the table on a silver platter in a blue haze of flaming brandy, to a round of applause and some cheers.

By twenty past two, everyone was feeling full and the men were a little sleepy. While Bea, Ruby and Rachel did the clearing up in the kitchen, the German girls were sent outside with the children – May on her bicycle and Alma in her pram – for a walk by the sea.

'You should have asked them to do the clearing up,' said Rachel. 'It would be good practice for them.'

But Bea had wanted it this way. It was a good opportunity to be alone with her girls and to catch up with all their news. She was delighted to hear that Rachel and Percy were doing very well with the transport business. Rachel was still doing her best to rescue those who had fallen foul of the authorities in Germany, but it was becoming more and more difficult.

'I'm not sure how many more the Deborah Committee can get out,' she said, scraping the leftover food into the pigs' bin by the sink. 'There are fewer and fewer travel permits being issued. These two may well be the last.'

'What then?' asked Bea. She was drying up and putting things back into the kitchen cupboards.

Rachel stared somewhere into the middle distance. 'You know, I've got a horrible feeling Hitler wants to kill every single Jew in Europe.'

'Surely not,' said Bea stoutly. 'This country would never allow it.'

'You really think war is inevitable then?' asked Ruby.

Rachel and Bea glanced at each other. 'I'm afraid so, darling,' said Bea.

'We may not be seeing too much here, in sleepy old Worthing,' said Rachel, 'but children in council residential schools around London already have to have compulsory gas-mask practices.'

'I've given up being treasurer of the Townswomen's Guild and I'm joining the ARP instead,' said Bea. 'As soon as the new year starts, we'll be actively preparing for war, and Mrs Hayward says she wants us Worthing women to be at the forefront of preparations here in the south.'

'Mrs Hayward?' said Ruby. 'I've never heard you mention her before.'

'Haven't I?' said Bea. 'She's a lovely girl. About your age. You'd like her.'

'Some of the women I know in Shoreham who joined

the ARP have already packed it up,' said Rachel. 'The men seem to be reluctant to give them anything to do, except make the tea.'

'Typical!' said Bea, pulling a face. 'Don't they realize that when war comes to this country, we're going to need every single person we've got, if we want to stop Hitler coming across the Channel?'

Ruby, who was setting the tea tray, gave an involuntary shiver.

'If you can spare the time,' said Bea to Ruby, 'why don't you join us, darling?'

Her reply was lost when Rex called from the sitting room, 'The King's speech is coming up.'

They carried the tea tray in. Everyone made themselves comfortable and, just in the nick of time, the German girls came back with May and Alma. The baby was fast asleep in her pram, so Rachel left her in the kitchen. May came and sat at her mother's feet with a bar of Cadbury's chocolate and her new drawing pad. Rex turned the radio up and everyone fell silent, but it was a little uncomfortable listening to the King's message. Although he didn't stammer or stutter once this time, it was clear from his slow and awkward delivery that he was struggling to get the words out.

'Many of you will remember the Christmas broadcasts of former years when my father spoke to his people as the revered head of a great family. His words brought happiness into the homes and hearts of listeners all over the world. I cannot,' the forty-two-year-old king went on, 'take his place.' Then, referring to the promise that he and the Queen had made at their coronation, he said, 'We have promised to try and be worthy of your trust and this is a pledge we will always keep.'

Ruby shifted in her seat as the King went on to speak about the world being in the grip of shadows of enmity and fear. At the end of the speech he wished everybody 'God's blessing, health and prosperity in the year that lies ahead'. And, as the radio fell silent, everyone breathed a sigh of relief.

Rex stood up and switched it off while Bea served more tea. The mood in the room was sober.

'Ruby and I have something to tell you,' Jim suddenly blurted out.

Ruby tried to stop him, but it was too late. She blushed deeply as everyone turned to look at her. 'I'm going to have a baby,' she said, lowering her eyes.

The room erupted in happy squeals and kisses. Jim was slapped heartily across his back by the men, and Rex got out his best malt whisky and some decent sherry. May seemed slightly bemused by all the excitement, but she looked pleased. It took a couple of minutes for Heidi and Frida to cotton on, but they were just as delighted as the rest of the family. The men raised their glasses and the women their sherry, as they toasted Ruby and Jim. Jim seemed to be enjoying every minute, but Ruby could only manage a rather self-conscious smile.

When all the fuss had died down a bit, Rachel leaned into her and, giving Ruby a hearty nudge, whispered in her sister-in-law's ear, 'What did I tell you? No man can resist a pretty pair of silk knickers.'

On Boxing Day the weather had deteriorated, but they did it all over again, only this time at Percy and Rachel's place. It was the first time Ruby and Jim had been to the house in Shoreham. Percy and Rachel lived in an impressive Edwardian house, spread over three floors. It was just off the seafront and, with central heating, was lovely and warm. Rachel had decorated it beautifully. The sitting room was cream and rose-pink with a light-green carpet in the middle of the parquet floor. There were three deeply squashy sofas. Percy's office had oak panelling and the furnishings were russet-red. Upstairs Alma's room was a delight in pale yellow, with a huge mural of a fairy castle. The kitchen was twice, maybe three times, the size of Sea View's and very modern. The flooring was of a geometric design while the cupboards were green, and the tins, bread bin and canisters had a jazzy red pattern. There was a modern electric oven and two sinks.

They ate in the dining room, which had a huge oak table that seated everyone comfortably. Rachel introduced the family to gefilte fish, which was stuffed carp poached with onions, eggs, seasoning and vegetable oil; it was delicious and much lighter than the meal they had all enjoyed the day before.

In the afternoon they left Alma with her nanny and took May to the pantomime. This year it was *Cinderella* and it was held in the newly opened Odeon theatre. A beautiful and modern building, its facade was clad in faience tiles and had a series of six projecting ribs in the centre over the entrance. May loved the show and she wasn't the only one. Bea nudged Ruby, who nudged Rachel as they caught sight of Rex, totally absorbed and shouting, 'He's behind you' during one of the routines. They sang the silly songs and ate ice cream in the interval. Ruby thought she had never been happier, and even Jim joined in with the actions during the final sketch.

When they came out of the Odeon, it was snowing. On their way back, Rachel squeezed Ruby's hand in the back of the car.

'Promise me,' she whispered, 'if anything happens to Percy and me, you'll take care of Alma.'

Ruby was puzzled. 'Why – what's likely to happen?'

'Promise me,' Rachel urged.

Ruby was alarmed to see a tear glistening in her eye. 'Of course I will,' she said.

Rachel sighed and, patting her sister-in-law's arm, said, 'Thank you, darling.'

By the time they set out for Worthing, Ruby and Jim were ready for their beds. Once they got home, Ruby filled a hot-water bottle for Jim while he fed Wilfred and put down a dish of food for Biscuit. They were just about to go up to bed when Ruby looked at Jim with a quizzical expression.

'What was that?'

'What was what?'

'That scratching sound,' said Ruby.

'Obviously the cat trying to get in,' said Jim, but just then Biscuit wandered across his feet and headed for his saucer. Jim pulled a face. 'It's just the wind,' he said.

'There it is again,' said Ruby and, picking up the poker, she went to the back door. 'Who is it?' she called through the wood. 'Who's there?'

She thought she heard something. It was barely audible and almost like a small sob. Cautiously, and with Jim right behind her in the wheelchair, Ruby opened the door. The freezing night air rushed in, but there was nobody on the doorstep. Ruby was just about to close the door when they both heard a small moan and then she looked down. A bundle of rags lay on the path. A hand came up and Ruby was filled with compassion. It must be some poor old tramp who had nowhere to go. It was Christmas, for heaven's sake. Jim would never allow him in, but she could at the very least give him something hot to drink, and maybe some warm clothing, before sending him on his way.

It was only as she drew closer that she saw they didn't have a tramp on their doorstep. It was Rivka.

CHAPTER 22

Rex slipped his arm around his daughter's shoulders. 'Are you all right?'

Ruby nodded dully. They were sitting in the waiting area outside the ward. It had been a very long night. As soon as Ruby had realized it was Rivka lying on their back doorstep, every other thought had been shelved. It had taken every ounce of her strength to get the girl inside. Totally exhausted, Rivka was a dead weight and frozen to the marrow. Somehow or other Ruby hauled her into the chair by the range, and she and Jim swathed her in a blanket. By now Rivka was drifting in and out of consciousness.

'How did she get here?' Jim asked.

'Walk,' said Rivka in one of her lucid moments.

Jim and Ruby glanced up at each other. Walked – all the way from Pulborough? But that was twelve miles or more. When had she set out? She must have walked all night to have arrived by lunchtime. Had she been on the back doorstep all afternoon and evening?

'When did you set out?' Jim asked, but Rivka had closed her eyes and her head lolled on his chest.

To make her more comfortable, Ruby eased off her shoes. 'What could have happened, to make her walk all that way?' The girl's feet were swollen and bleeding, and blue with cold. Her footwear was totally unsuitable for outdoor walking, especially at this time of year. 'I think we'd better call my father.'

Jim nodded.

Thank God for the telephone. In a little under twenty minutes, Rex was on the doorstep with his doctor's bag. He had no hesitation in making the decision that Rivka should be in hospital and phoned for a St John ambulance.

Rivka didn't regain consciousness until much later in hospital and by that time the doctors had decided that she needed to go to theatre. As they wheeled her in, Rex came to Ruby with the bad news.

'She's been brutally raped,' he said simply.

Tears sprang to Ruby's eyes. 'How could someone do that to a vulnerable young woman who has been brought here to keep her safe?' She shook her head in disbelief. 'I thought everyone had been vetted by the Deborah Committee.'

'You can't know what's in someone's mind,' said Rex. 'It's appalling, but it happens.'

'How is she?' Ruby asked.

'In a bad way,' Rex sighed. 'There's some internal damage and she's lost a lot of blood. Walking all that way didn't help.'

'But she will survive, won't she?'

'I hope so,' said Rex. 'She's in good hands, and right

269

now I'm more concerned about you. Come on, I'm taking you home.'

'I'd like to be here for her,' said Ruby.

'And so you shall,' said Rex, 'but not now. In your condition you need to get some sleep, and Jim will be worried sick about you. You can come back later today at visiting time.'

It was two days later and Rivka was still in hospital when Ruby finally contacted her sister-in-law. Rachel and Percy had been up to London to visit friends, and Ruby caught the bus to Shoreham to tell her face-to-face. Rachel's jaw dropped when she heard what had happened.

'But that's terrible! Are you absolutely sure she was raped?'

'How can you ask such a thing?' said Ruby crossly. 'She wouldn't be lying in a hospital bed with half her insides in shreds if it weren't true, now would she?'

'She could have egged him on,' Rachel muttered.

'Rachel!'

Her sister-in-law had the grace to look ashamed. 'Yes, yes, you're right. I'm sorry. It's just that I met Mrs Hobden myself. She seemed a bit snooty, but she's highly respectable. I'm just surprised it happened in her house, that's all.'

'Well, obviously she didn't do it personally,' Ruby snapped. 'What was her husband like?'

'Respectable,' Rachel repeated. 'He's in politics. Quite ambitious, by all accounts. They're a bit stingy, but I suppose that's how these people stay rich. God this is awful – rape . . .'

'One thing is for sure,' said Ruby, 'you can't send her back there.'

Oh, absolutely,' replied Rachel, 'but under the terms of her visa, Rivka has to be employed.'

A few weeks later Ruby and Jim were in Lena and Eric's home for another celebration. This time it was Jean's birthday. Along with May, they were the only guests. Rivka was convalescing at the guest house and Bea was looking after her.

When it was time for the cake, Lena struck a match and lit the three candles. Calling out 'Ready?', she heard Eric drawing Jean's attention to the kitchen door.

Lena had spent all the previous evening decorating the cake, which she had made all by herself, and she was justly proud of her achievement. It was only a Victoria sponge, but she had pressed into the middle half a doll that she'd picked up from a jumble sale, and had made the cake look as if it were her ballgown. Each of the pink-and-white icing-sugar stars had a silver ball in the middle, and Lena hoped the magnificence of the dress would detract attention from the doll's slightly sunken right eye.

As she stepped over the threshold and everyone sang 'Happy birthday to you', Lena placed the plate carefully in front of a starry-eyed Jean.

'Blow the candles out and make a wish,' cried May.

271

'I don't think she understands about making wishes,' said Ruby.

'Yes, she does,' May insisted. 'Jean, tell us what would you like most in the whole wide world?'

The little girl seemed puzzled. She pulled her toy rabbit to her face and rubbed his stripy leg against her cheek. Lena held her breath, thinking: Please don't let her say anything. She never talks about Mr and Mrs West; surely she must have forgotten about them by now.

'You told me just now,' May prompted.

'It doesn't matter,' Lena interrupted crisply. 'Blow out the candles.'

Jean's face suddenly lit up with a broad smile. 'Ice cream! I wish I had ice cream.'

Everyone laughed – Lena with a sense of relief.

Although they didn't know a lot of children, she couldn't let Jean's third birthday go by without some sort of celebration, and since they had become good friends with Ruby and Jim, it seemed safe enough to invite them. Ruby's younger sister loved mothering Jean when she came round. Sometimes May brought a school friend with her, but today she was alone.

Jean blew out the candles and everybody clapped. Lena couldn't have been happier. This was everything she'd ever dreamed of: her own home, with Eric and Jean. She felt more relaxed than she had ever done before. Coming to Worthing had been the right thing to do. Next year she would be confident enough to make sure Jean had some friends of her own age at her party, but for now it was good just to have Ruby and Jim and May.

They cut the cake and after everyone had complimented Lena on the lightness of her sponge, she went back into the kitchen to get Jean's special surprise. On his way back home from work, Eric had bought a Lyons Maid brick ice cream. It was wrapped in several layers of newspaper and she'd put it on the stone floor to keep it cool. Being the end of January, that wasn't too much of a problem, until they brought it into the warm house. When she unwrapped it, it was very soft, but had kept its shape. Jean was thrilled when Lena walked in with the ice cream and declared to all assembled that her wish (possibly planted in her head by May) had come true.

As they cleared up the party things, Ruby broached Lena about the thing that was uppermost in her mind. 'Lena, now that you know I am having a baby,' she began, 'I wanted to ask you something.'

'I guessed,' said Lena, her face all lit up. 'I was thrilled when Jim told me. Oh, Ruby, I am so pleased for you both.'

'The thing is,' Ruby went on, 'I shall need more help in the guest house.'

Lean put up her hand. 'Whatever it is, consider it done,' she said stoutly. 'Eric is quite happy for me to work for you. I'll give you all the hours you want.'

'I'm all right for a bit,' Ruby cautioned. 'My mother has promised to help when she can, but how do you feel about being the manager when the baby comes?'

273

'No!' cried Lena a little too quickly, then added in a more measured tone, 'I haven't a clue where to start with something like that.' She couldn't possibly be up front in the guest house. What if someone from her village came to stay? What if someone recognized her?

'I'll train you,' Ruby began.

'No,' said Lena firmly. 'I'm sorry, but I can't. Whatever you need done in the kitchen or in the rooms, I'm quite happy to do that, but I don't want anything to do with the guests.'

Ruby was a bit startled. She was about to say something, when Jim came through to the kitchen saying that he was going back home to feed the monkey. 'I brought the rest of the ice cream in,' he said. 'Where shall I put it?'

'It's almost melted,' Ruby observed. 'Won't the children eat it?'

'I think they're a bit too full of cake,' said Jim.

'Would the monkey like to finish it off?' asked Lena.

'I reckon so,' said Jim.

Jim headed for his wheelchair, to lean over the back, and Lena rewrapped the ice cream and put it on the seat.

'Thank you,' said Jim matter-of-factly. 'See you presently, Ruby.'

Back in their own kitchen, Biscuit competed with the monkey for a lick of ice cream. When they'd had their fill, Jim began to screw up the newspaper, but dropped one sheet. When he picked it up, something caught his eye. Lowering himself onto the chair, he let his breath out slowly as he read the article from *Tit-Bits* magazine.

Park Crescent was built in the eighteenth century. It was a series of houses arranged in a serpentine shape, after the fashion of the Georgian crescents in Bath, although not nearly as splendid. When it was built, the houses in Park Crescent would have overlooked farm-land, with an unimpeded view stretching as far as the parish churches of Tarring and Goring. There were fourteen houses altogether, accessed through a triumphal arch on the corner of Richmond Road and Crescent Road. Designed to be used by carriages, the arch was supported by the carved heads of four bearded men. On either side of the main arch was a smaller one for pedestrians, and at either end of the crescent were two Swiss cottages. Effie and Gus Rhodes lived in the south cottage.

The British League of Women was designed to rival the Townswomen's Guild and the Women's Institute. It was intended to embrace the ideals of similar organiza-tions that she'd taken part in, in Cameroon, promoting and celebrating all that was good about *British* women. Effie told her hand-picked guests that it would be a sisterhood of wives, mothers and decent women who would put back the 'great' into Great Britain. Of course she hadn't dreamed that up on her own. Using various manifestos, she had cobbled together a form of words that she believed would be most attractive. Gus had made himself scarce and was upstairs with his model train set. He was trying out the new engine and it was brilliant. It had cost him an arm and a leg, but the chap who'd made it was a master craftsman.

As the meeting began, there were ten women squeezed into Effie's drawing room. With the exception of Freda Fosdyke, who was taking the minutes of the meeting, they all sat with cup and saucer in hand, waiting to hear what their hostess had to say.

'As you know,' Effie began, 'there are a great many new organizations springing up, but only the British League of Women will give the women of this country a sense of belonging and patriotism. We shall lead the way and be a beacon in these dark times.'

'Yes, but what will we actually *do*?' Miss Taylor asked. 'I mean to say, what makes this different from church groups or the WI?'

Effie's eyes narrowed. She was unsure of Lydia Taylor. She had been part of the committee of the Townswomen's Guild, but Effie had never really got to know her. She'd been loyal to the organization and done everything she was required to do, but she asked awkward questions. Effie flicked an imaginary crumb from her dress. How was she to answer that?

'My neighbour says you're part of the British Union of Fascists,' said a voice at the back of the room.

'Absolutely not,' Effie declared. 'I am my own woman and answerable to no one, but that's not to say we won't listen to their point of view.' She took a deep breath. 'We need to educate women. Win over their hearts and minds. But how can we possibly do that if we don't have the full facts?'

She looked around. Every eye was riveted on her. True, she hadn't really thought it through, but this was the answer to that question. Let the WI and the TWG have their silly sewing lessons and their cookery books; she would make her mark in society by being an educator of women. She would show them that there was more to life than having babies.

'As you know, we are spoon-fed by what the government wants us to hear,' she told her starry-eyed followers. 'Hitler is no threat to this country. He wants peace, and yet the whole country is getting geared up for war.'

'Some say he's deluded,' said another voice.

'This is neither the time nor the place to worry about that,' said Effie. 'What we are about is making our country the best in the world.'

No one spoke.

'The truth of the matter is,' Effie went on, 'we women tend to do what our husbands do, or say what other people say. We never get the chance to form our own opinions.'

There was a hum of approval.

'I may be wrong about what I've just said,' Effie went on, confident that her assembled guests would disagree, 'but unless we have all the facts at our disposal, how are we to know what to think?'

'Yes, but what are we going to *do* about it,' Lydia wanted to know.

'We shall do everything to promote peace,' said Effie.

'We shall study and educate other women. We shall convince our men that war is futile, and promote exchanges between the nations.'

She sat back down in a warm glow. The ladies talked among themselves, and by the end of the meeting they had co-opted various people to form a committee and the names of several speakers had already been suggested.

After the main meeting broke up, Effie was left with the chosen few. Although she had protested modestly that she was ill equipped for leadership, she had been voted in as chairman, with Freda Fosdyke as the secretary and Cynthia Raymond as the treasurer.

'It feels a bit like old times,' Effie quipped as she offered them each a sherry.

'I felt quite sure the TWG would fold when you went,' said Cynthia. 'Rose Wilmot runs it now. They meet in the Oddfellows' Hall.'

'Bea Quinn left the committee,' said Freda, 'but she still attends the meetings.'

'That doesn't surprise me,' said Effie dismissively. 'I know I shouldn't say this, but she's a sly, conniving bitch. I can't believe I befriended her! Did you know, I even invited her to dinner in my house. I thought she was all right until . . . Well, look at the way she treated me.'

'If you ask me,' said Cynthia, 'the whole family are nothing but troublemakers.'

'Dr Quinn seems all right,' said Freda with a puzzled expression.

'I don't mean him,' said Cynthia. 'Have you read the

letters in the paper just lately? The ones from that "Worthing Worthy"?'

'I can't say I have a lot of time to pay that much attention to the paper, dear,' said Effie languidly.

'Well,' said Cynthia, 'there's a whole article about do-gooders who are trying to make a name for themselves, and he's got half the town at loggerheads with the other half, over what's happening in Germany.'

Effie turned to Freda. 'Have you seen it?' she asked innocently.

'Oh yes,' said Freda, sipping her sherry. 'There's quite a lively debate going on about the pros and cons of Hitler's intentions, and whether we've laid ourselves open to invasion by being too trusting.'

'So who is this mysterious letter-writer?' Effie wanted to know. 'In my day,' she went on, 'if you believed passionately in something, you didn't hide behind anonymity. You had the courage to stand up and say so in the open.'

'I have a shrewd idea who he is,' said Cynthia smugly.

'You do?' said Freda.

'A little slip of the pen,' said Cynthia, clearly enjoying the air of mystery.

'Well, come on then,' Effie demanded. 'Don't keep us all in suspense.'

'It's Jim Searle,' said Cynthia.

Effie looked at Freda, but was none the wiser.

'He's that chap who got injured at the BUF rally a few years ago,' said Cynthia.

'Yes, I know who you mean,' Freda replied, 'but I thought he called himself by another name.'

'"Concerned of Worthing",' Cynthia prompted. She held up her fingers and checked off the various aliases as she recalled them: '"Concerned of Worthing", "The way I see it", "Worthing Worthy" – it's all the same person.'

'How do you know?' asked Freda.

'He mentioned that his wife gave some German refugees a book about living in this country,' said Cynthia. 'I've seen it. Lottie Langland's maid has one.'

'So?' Effie challenged.

'She was brought here by the Deborah Committee,' said Cynthia, 'and, when she arrived, she stayed in Jim Searle's guest house in Heene Road.'

'I still don't . . .' Effie began.

'Jim Searle is Bea Quinn's son-in-law,' said Freda.

Effie's nostrils flared slightly. 'I think you're right, dear. The whole ruddy family are nothing but trouble-makers.'

*C*HAPTER 23

Rachel had found Rivka another position, this time in Sompting, which was only about three miles away. She was to be the maid for two elderly spinsters. For more than thirty years Estelle Martin had taught students to be teachers in Uganda, with the African Inland Mission, and Constance had worked as a Bible translator. They lived simply and had a reputation for being gentle and caring members of their church community. Now not so robust, they needed someone to help with their day-to-day life, but were still alert and enthusiastic.

When Ruby and Rivka arrived, they found a pretty cottage overlooking farmland in the middle of the village. It wasn't a large place, so straight away they could see that the work wouldn't be too hard. Having been shown around the cottage, Ruby and Rivka sat in the neat little sitting room and had tea.

It had taken Rivka a whole month to recover. Her outward wounds healed quite quickly, but Ruby could see that the mental scars would take a lot longer. She was jumpy around men, even Jim.

'You should try and talk about it,' Ruby had said

one evening, as she and Rivka sat alone in the kitchen. Jim hadn't been feeling too well and had gone to bed early.

Rivka shook her head vehemently. 'I don't even want to think about that dog, but,' she touched her head, 'he is in here all the time.'

'That's why you should talk,' Ruby insisted.

'One day I shall have revenge,' Rivka spat.

'That's the one thing you must never do,' Ruby cautioned.

Rivka tapped her nose. 'They talk. I look straight-face. They think I *nicht* understand, but I do. I know.'

'If you tell the police,' Ruby tried again, 'we may be able to stop him doing it again.'

Rivka shuddered visibly. 'Who believes a German Jew?'

Ruby had said nothing, but she had to admit to herself that Rivka was probably right. Rachel had said that when Mrs Hobden had been confronted with what had happened, she had called Rivka a cheap little tramp and a liar.

'How dare you come here with your filthy lies!' she'd screamed at Mrs Whichelow from the Deborah Committee. 'We are respectable people.'

Mrs Hobden had even gone on to complain that, by walking out, Rivka had left her in the lurch. 'There was no reason why the girl needed to go,' she'd insisted, 'and in view of the fact that I have been badly let down, I'm withholding her wages, in lieu of the inconvenience she's caused.' When she got back to Worthing, Rachel

282

had told Ruby that the whole thing had left Mrs Whichelow with a bad taste in her mouth.

After they'd all had tea and a little chat, the sisters agreed a fair wage and promised to give Rivka a day off every week, with one weekend off every six weeks. Ruby immediately invited her to come back to the guest house whenever she wanted. It seemed a much better arrangement and, by the time she left, Rivka had tears in her eyes, but Ruby knew she would be well looked after.

'You mean they changed the notes with no trouble?' Edith was surprised that the man who had bought Bernard's model engine hadn't made a fuss when Bernard took the forgeries back. 'Did he know who gave them to him?'

'If he did, he didn't say,' said Bernard.

'I wish I hadn't given Jim the other one now,' said Edith. 'I didn't mean to. It was stuffed in with the rent book. I just didn't think. If you'd had it with you, he might have replaced that one too.'

'He replaced it anyway,' said Bernard.

'What?' Edith exclaimed. 'You mean he believed you when you said you had three, even though you hadn't brought the third one back?'

Bernard nodded. 'He seemed genuinely upset that it had happened,' said Bernard. 'Really, he couldn't have been nicer.'

'Did he say anything else?'

'He asked me where it was,' said Bernard, 'so I

explained about Jim and everything, but he didn't ask me to get it back or anything. I told him Jim was an honest man and wouldn't try to get rid of it. He was most apologetic – and that was that.'

'Let's hope he doesn't turn up on Jim's doorstep,' said Edith.

'Why should he?' asked Bernard. 'Besides, he was perfectly reasonable with me, so there's no reason to believe he'll go to see Jim.'

'You don't understand,' said Edith. 'Jim said it was just between us. He didn't want Ruby to know.'

It was a couple of months later and Ruby was in the kitchen finishing off some jobs. Bea had invited her to join the ranks of her new women's group and was waiting for her daughter to get ready to go out. In her condition, Bea knew her daughter might not be able to do a terrific amount at the moment, but, 'If you're with us right from the start,' she had reasoned, 'you'll be more likely to be included, once we get the thing going.'

Ruby left a pile of ironing on the stairs, ready to take it up and put it in the airing cupboard when she got back home. She was looking forward to meeting Mrs Hayward and the other women. Over the past few weeks her mother had told her so much about them.

'She's invited us to her home for the afternoon, for tea,' Bea went on. 'I've told her about you, and what you and Rachel have already been doing for those poor girls. She was most impressed.'

Having taken the ironing basket into the scullery,

Ruby put the iron down in the grate to cool, before putting it away. 'Oh, Mum,' she scolded, 'I hope you didn't lay it on thick.'

'I only told her the truth,' said Bea defensively. 'I'm very proud of you.'

Ruby had no idea how long everything would take, but just to be on the safe side she had told Jim she would be out most of the afternoon. She had been up early this morning. There was a shepherd's pie in the oven, waiting for her to switch it on when she got home. She had the feeling she would be tired and wouldn't feel like preparing the meal from scratch, so the carrots were in a saucepan of water on the stove and all she would have to do was lay the table.

'Is there anything I can get you before I go?' Ruby asked her husband. Her mother had gone outside to wait in the car and Ruby was pulling her coat on, although it was becoming difficult to do up the buttons now. She still felt a little bit concerned about Jim. Although he seemed fine now, he'd had a bad cold which had seemed to hang around for ages. It had left him listless and, up until a few days ago, he'd struggled to do his crosswords.

'I'll be fine,' Jim said. 'I've got plenty to do, and I'm going to ask Eric round for a chat. There's something I need to talk to him about.'

Jim had made a start on his weekly column for the *Gazette*. The monkey was sitting on his shoulder, and Biscuit lay on the chair beside him. She smiled. They looked the picture of contentment. Her marriage wasn't ideal but, with the baby on the way, she and Jim seemed to have found a middle path.

'Well, I'm off now, Jim,' she said rather obviously, although she was sure he hadn't even noticed. 'There's some cold ham on a plate in the meat safe for your lunch.' He half-turned to look at her. 'And you'll find some cheese and a couple of bread rolls in the tin.'

'Fine,' he said.

He was planning his reply to the shoal of letters that he'd received the previous week: 'How dare you!', 'Extremely Annoyed' of Wiston Avenue had thundered; 'What's wrong with trying to promote peace?' the Reverend of the Manse wanted to know. What indeed, Jim remarked, but did everyone share the same dream? As for those visits from German schoolchildren, had that been wise? Could the well-meaning headmaster of the school have been duped?

He glanced up with a wispy smile. 'Enjoy yourself.' He turned back to his typewriter and she made her way to the door. 'Oh, and Ruby.' She stopped. 'There's something . . .' he faltered, then changed his mind.

'Is there something else?' she asked.

'Nothing important,' he said. 'I'll tell you when you get back home.' She looked at him, and he smiled. 'Don't go tiring yourself, will you?'

A flood of affection washed over her and tears smarted in her eyes. She couldn't resist going back and kissing the top of his bent head.

He looked up. 'What was that for?'

Ruby shrugged. 'You're an amazing man, Jim Searle. I just wanted you to know that.'

'Of course I am,' he said teasingly. 'Have you only just realized?'

As she passed through the hall the telephone rang. Ruby picked up the receiver. 'Worthing 206, Sea View guest house.'

'Go ahead, caller,' said the operator.

'Is that Mrs Searle?' It was a man's voice, educated, authoritative.

'Yes, this is Mrs Searle,' said Ruby, reaching for the appointments book and a pencil. 'Can I help you?'

'Is your husband there?'

'Yes, he is, but it will take him a while to get to the telephone. Can I take a message?'

'My name is Sir Hubert Temple,' said the voice. 'I should very much like to speak to your husband. I think it might be to our mutual advantage.'

'Then if you don't mind hanging on for a bit, I'll call him.'

Rex drove Bea and Ruby to the more salubrious part of town. Normally Bea would have driven the car herself, but today Rex needed to be in Littlehampton for a meeting, so it was arranged that he would drop them at the house and pick them up on the way back.

Big houses were going up all over what used to be called the Goring Hall Estate. After about fifteen minutes they came to Amberley Drive and the house where Mrs Hayward lived. Several cars were already in the driveway as Rex pulled up. After they'd said their goodbyes, Bea and Ruby rang the bell. A maid opened the door to them and they were shown into a spacious room where the other women waited.

While Bea caught up with old friends, Ruby stood by the window watching a small spaniel chasing the birds in the garden. He looked so sweet she almost forgot why she was here. It wasn't until she heard her mother say, 'Ruby, I should like you to meet Mrs Hayward', that she turned round. As soon as Ruby saw her hostess, she felt her cheeks flame and her heart skipped a beat. Judging by the look on her face, Mrs Hayward was having exactly the same experience. However, neither woman reacted openly. They greeted each other formally and the meeting got under way.

Mrs Hayward introduced Lady Beryl. 'Lady Beryl Smithers's husband has been Viceroy in Ceylon,' she told them. 'He's now retired and they live in this country.'

There was a round of muted gloved applause.

'I just need to tell you ladies how the women's organization is to function,' she began. 'An announcement will be formally made next month in June, but the mere fact that you and I are here is proof that the scheme is already under way.'

'Do you mean we shall be separate from the ARP?' someone asked.

'The short answer to that is "yes",' said Lady Beryl. 'We shall be known as the Women's Voluntary Service – the WVS. Both the ARP and the WVS will be trained to know what to do, in the event of an air raid, but each organization will have separate duties.'

'Such as?' the same woman asked.

'Should the country go to war, the government is considering the mass evacuation of children, pregnant women and nursing mothers from our major cities, especially London,' said Lady Beryl. 'They are looking for an organization that can coordinate everything, from finding suitable billets, to meeting the children from the train and getting them settled in.'

A hum went around the room until another woman said, 'Surely that would be better organized by the police or the military.'

'My husband is in the police,' said one woman, 'and when it comes to looking after children, he's pretty hopeless. Last Christmas, when he took our Billy to see Father Christmas, he left him sitting in the toilet.'

'Father Christmas?'

'No – our Billy.'

'The evacuation may not be the only thing we're called upon to do,' Lady Beryl continued. 'We must be prepared for anything and everything. How many of you ladies have a driving licence?'

Bea and two other women put up their hands.

'I suggest that every woman in this room should be able to drive,' said Lady Beryl. The hum in the room became a buzz. 'If war comes,' she went on with a shake of her head, 'our menfolk will be called up to fight. Someone will have to drive the ambulances, and the tractors. There may be important communications between the authorities that need something faster than the post.'

Bea leaned towards Ruby, who was getting distracted by the spaniel outside again. 'I'll teach you to drive.'

Ruby pointed to her neatly rounded bump.

'That won't last forever,' said Bea firmly. 'Supposing the Germans invade our coastline, how are you and the baby going to get away? Walk?'

All at once, the full horror of what they were now facing finally hit home. Up until now, Ruby had been rather detached from it all. These past months of sabre-rattling and failed diplomacy had begun to bore her. Now she understood that this was something that might actually affect her and her family. The thought of an invading army rushing up the beach, when she was living just yards away, brought the reality of war into sharp focus. She looked around the room. One young woman was crying, and a couple of others were accusing Lady Beryl of scaremongering. The noise level was getting louder by the minute.

'Ladies, ladies,' cried Lady Beryl, standing to her feet and bringing the meeting to order. 'I don't want anyone to feel alarmed, but think, ladies – ladies, think. If you came across a fire, would you know what to do?'

'Ring for the fire brigade, of course,' someone snapped.

'Worthing has but one fire engine,' said Lady Beryl. 'Just supposing it's already on call, I asked you: what would *you* do?'

The room became a little quieter.

'Just supposing again,' Lady Beryl went on, 'that one of the victims of that fire is your relative. He's badly burned. You know you need to get him to hospital, and you will, but how will you treat him in the meantime?'

This time no one spoke, and it was obvious that everyone in the room was beginning to feel uncomfortable.

'Don't you see? By pulling together and working with a common aim, we can overcome the darkest night,' said Lady Beryl. 'But people will need to learn how to put out fires. They will need to learn first aid. And if we are to lead others, we need to be able to do it ourselves. What I am proposing is this: that we first prepare ourselves, and then we shall be ready to help other members of the community.'

'Supposing we don't go to war,' someone piped up. 'What then? We'll all have wasted our time.'

'Perhaps,' Lady Beryl agreed, 'but at the very least we shall have enjoyed learning a new skill and be better equipped for life, won't we?'

The atmosphere in the room was changing. After confusion and hostility, they had become more enthusiastic.

'I need volunteers,' said Lady Beryl. 'You don't have to do everything, but the more you know, the better it will be. Now, who would like to do a first-aid course?'

As the women put up their hands, she began to write down their names.

Mrs Hayward leaned over to Ruby. 'Mrs Searle, I

wonder if you would come and give me a hand with the teas?'

Ruby stood up as Mrs Hayward threaded her way between the women, and the two of them headed to the kitchen. With the door closed, they turned to face each other, then grasped each other's hands.

'Oh, Miss,' cried Ruby. As soon as she'd seen Mrs Hayward, Ruby had recognized her immediately, as the former Imogen Russell whom she had met at Warnes Hotel. 'I can hardly believe it's really you! I often wondered what happened to you after you got married.'

'And I you,' said Imogen. 'My husband is a solicitor.'

'Children?' Ruby asked.

A shadow crossed Imogen's face. 'No children. You?'

Ruby touched her belly. 'I'm expecting my first.'

Imogen smiled. 'Congratulations!'

'How wonderful to see you again,' cried Ruby. 'It only seems like yesterday that we were standing in that hotel corridor, trying not to let anyone see us.'

'It was a long time ago, Ruby,' said Imogen. 'Almost five years. I've never forgotten what you did for me that day.'

'I only did what anyone else would have done,' said Ruby.

'It was more than that,' said Imogen. 'You saved my life. My father never found out. I told my husband, of course, but the three of us are the only people in the world who—'

They were interrupted by the maid, who had come

into the kitchen. Imogen let go of Ruby's hands and pulled herself up straight.

'We're ready for the tea now, Betty.'

'Yes, ma'am,' said Betty, eyeing Ruby cautiously.

'As soon as the kettle's boiled, you can bring it in.'

Back in the comfortable sitting room, names had been registered for driving lessons and first-aid courses, and the addresses of people who might be interested parties were added to those already on the clipboard. There was a general hum of business being done and new friendships being formed. Lady Beryl was delighted.

CHAPTER 24

Jim was sitting in his wheelchair by the back door as Eric rode his bike up the driveway and home. At the time, it didn't seem odd. It was only later that it crossed Eric's mind that Jim had actually been waiting for him.

'You got a minute, mate?' Jim asked. 'There's something I'd like to show you.'

It was Eric's half-day and he planned to work in the garden but, ever obliging, he said, 'Just let me tell Lena where I am, and I'll be right over.'

To his surprise, Eric found he enjoyed domesticity. He had created an area at the bottom of the garden where he'd planted carrots, cabbages and potatoes. The cabbage was suffering from slug infestation, but someone at the railway yard had told him to half-bury an old soup bowl and put some beer in it. 'They're attracted by the smell and fall in,' the chap said with a grin. 'What a lovely way to go – drowned in a puddle of best bitter.'

Eric had laughed, but he planned to put the man's theory to the test.

*   *   *

Inside Sea View the telephone rang again. Jim hardly ever answered the damned thing because it was usually someone wanting to make a booking. He didn't have much patience and, if the caller dithered, he couldn't hide his irritation, so it was best to avoid answering it. On the other hand, Ruby wasn't in, so he had little choice.

'Mr Searle?' said a man's voice. 'Are you the Mr Searle who writes in the newspaper?'

Jim hesitated. He'd always been keen to keep his anonymity, but after the phone call earlier this afternoon, it hardly mattered now.

'I believe,' the caller went on, 'that you write under the name of "Worthing Worthy" and that you have the column called "The way I see it"?'

'I did . . .' Jim began.

'I'm Grenville Anderson. I'm the editor of the *Surrey and Sussex Recorder*. Can we send the photographer round this afternoon?'

By the time Eric had walked back to Jim's house, Jim was in the kitchen with the back door wide open. As luck would have it, Lena was out, probably down at the beach with Jean. Two bottles of local beer stood on the table. Eric glanced at Jim cautiously, but his neighbour avoided eye contact. Something was up. He sat down at Jim's invitation, but felt uneasy. They chit-chatted about nothing in particular and Jim took the tops off the bottles. Eric's drink was half-gone when Jim pushed a magazine in front of him.

'I don't know if you've read this,' Jim said. 'When I saw it . . . Well, look for yourself and then we'll talk.'

Never one to do much reading, Eric struggled with some of the words. He read slowly, but it didn't take long for the full implication of what he was being shown to hit him. His stomach fell away. Something told him to stay calm. Act like it's nothing. Don't react. He mustn't give any indication that the game was up. He finished the article and looked up with what he hoped was a deadpan expression.

'It was when I got to the bit about the toy rabbit that I thought of your Jean,' said Jim.

Eric said nothing. His brain was working overtime. How many people had Jim shown this article to? Did Ruby know? Where the devil did the magazine come from, in the first place? He looked down at it again and recognized the stains. Of course, it was the paper that was wrapped around the birthday ice cream. Hell's teeth, why hadn't he noticed? 'Why are you showing me this after all this time?' he thundered.

'Hasn't your Jean got a toy rabbit with stripy legs?' said Jim.

Eric's head shot up. 'What the hell are you implying?'

Jim put both hands up in a defensive manner.

'There must be thousands and thousands of rabbits like that, out there,' said Eric. His voice had an edge. 'Just because our Jean's got one, that doesn't make her somebody else's kid.'

Jim leaned back in his chair. 'For someone who is completely innocent, you're getting pretty worked up.'

296

Eric gave a hollow laugh. 'If you were that worried about it, why didn't you show it to me sooner?' He was angry and embarrassed. The only thought in his head was that he must say something – anything – to persuade Jim that Jean wasn't Christine West.

'I would have done,' said Jim, 'but the truth of the matter is, I wanted to check up on a few things first.'

'There must be something wrong with your head, as well as your legs,' Eric snapped.

Jim gave him a wounded look, and Eric immediately regretted what he'd said. He didn't want to hurt Jim, but he couldn't let this happen. 'I've never been to . . .' he picked up the paper to check the name of the place again, 'West Moors in my life. Me and Lena are married, fair and square, and we never took no one.'

Jim lowered his eyes and fingered the pages. 'Then you won't mind if I go to the police?' he began cautiously.

At this, Eric rose sharply to his feet. Knocking the table at the same time, his bottle of beer tumbled and rolled towards the floor. Jim looked up with a startled expression and pushed himself back, as it finally fell to the floor with an almighty smash.

Rex was late and Bea was beginning to feel embarrassed. She was anxious not to outstay her welcome, but surprisingly neither Mrs Hayward nor Ruby seemed unduly worried. After everyone else had gone, Bea suggested getting a taxi back to Worthing, but Mrs Hayward wouldn't hear of it. 'We'll go into the summerhouse,' she said. 'There's a little wood-burner in there and we'll have tea and crumpets until he comes.'

They were in the middle of making small talk when the maid came to say that Rex was on the telephone, wanting to speak with his wife. Bea followed her into the house.

'You know, I can't believe Mrs Quinn is your mother,' cried Imogen. 'I do so like her and she kept telling me about her lovely daughter. I never dreamed it was you!'

'Oh, Miss,' said Ruby. 'I'm so glad everything worked out for you.'

'My father gave me a wonderful summer that year,' said Imogen. 'Paris, Cannes, Venice, Rome . . . I wish you could have come.'

'Me too,' said Ruby, 'but my father had just died.'

'I was so sorry to hear that,' said Imogen. 'I wish I could have helped.'

'You did,' said Ruby, 'and even if I never got to see all those lovely places in the flesh, all your postcards kept me going through the dark times.'

Imogen leaned over and squeezed Ruby's hands.

'I'm glad you had a good time, Miss.'

'Best of all, that was the year I met Ambrose.'

'Ambrose?'

'My husband, Ambrose Lucian Hayward,' said Imogen proudly. 'He's a solicitor. A wonderful man.' She studied Ruby's face. 'So what have you been doing with your life,' she continued, 'apart from getting married and having a baby on the way?'

Ruby gave her a brief outline of her life since they'd last met, ending with Jim's injury.

'How awful,' cried Imogen, 'I had no idea.'

'It's not so bad now,' said Ruby. 'We are happy, in our separate ways. It hasn't turned out the way we thought, but Jim is carving a name for himself and I enjoy running the guest house.'

Bea returned to the summerhouse. 'He's delayed,' she said. 'Some sort of emergency. We'll get a taxi.'

'Sit down and enjoy your tea first, Mrs Quinn,' said Imogen. 'I'll run you both home in my car when we're ready. Ruby has been telling me about the guest house.'

'We don't want to be any trouble,' Bea protested.

'It's no trouble at all.'

Bea sat back down. 'Has Ruby told you she's been helping Jewish refugees?'

'Mum!' Ruby scolded.

'No, she hasn't.' Imogen laughed. 'Come on, Ruby, tell me.'

Ruby explained about the Deborah Committee work that she was involved with.

'Tell her about your little book,' Bea prompted.

Imogen was fascinated. 'You know,' she said, 'that's a book that might even be useful for us. Can I see a copy?'

'Of course,' said Ruby. 'I'll give you one when you drop us home.'

It was already getting dark by the time they arrived back at the guest house. None of them had intended

299

for Bea and Ruby to stay so long, but they had enjoyed each other's company.

'Don't forget to give me one of those books,' said Imogen as she drew up outside Sea View.

Ruby stepped out of the car. 'Shan't be a minute, Mum.'

'I'll come with you,' said Imogen. 'It'll save time.'

They waved to Eric, who had just turned into his gateway on his bike.

'How's it going?' he asked.

Ruby smiled happily. 'Fine, just fine.'

As she reached the front door she turned to Imogen. 'What's that awful smell?' As she spoke, recognition dawned. 'My God . . . gas!'

Ruby fumbled in her handbag for the keys. Oh, where were they? Her bag wasn't that big, but there were times when things slipped down to the bottom and it became cavernous. Infuriatingly, this was one of those times.

Imogen watched her fumbling and waited anxiously. Neither of them noticed, but as Ruby had said 'gas', Eric had thrown his bike onto the path and vaulted the low wall between the two houses. Seeing him jump over, Bea had got out of the car.

At last Ruby found the key and, after another fumble, pushed it into the lock. A heavy, pungent and evil smell wafted out to greet them. The whole house was filled with gas. How long had the gas tap been on? And where was Jim? Automatically Ruby reached for the light switch. At the same time, she felt a sharp blow on her wrist and Eric's voice right next to her ear said, 'No!'

Ruby turned her head, startled.

'One spark from that switch and we'll all be blown to kingdom come,' he said firmly.

She went to step inside, but once again Eric stopped her. Bea tugged at her daughter's arm. 'You'd better not go in there,' she said, 'not in your condition.'

Not in your condition . . . Ruby's hand went to her belly. Eric had grabbed a couple of scarves from the hall stand and was wrapping them around his nose and mouth.

'Back door,' he said. 'Do you have a key?' Ruby stared at him with a blank expression. 'A key, Ruby?' His voice was urgent. 'Is the key in your bag?'

Ruby shook her head. 'It's in the door.'

'Go round the back and break the kitchen window,' Eric told Bea and Imogen. 'I'll go in this way, but I'll have to be quick. There's so much gas, it's a bit of a risk.'

As he headed down the hallway, Imogen, Bea and a couple of passers-by who had followed them up the path ran down the side of the house. There was a galvanized bucket by the back door. Ruby used it when she washed the kitchen floor and the back step. Bea picked up the scrubbing brush inside and banged the glass a couple of times. With the window still intact, Imogen grabbed the bucket and hurled it at the window. At the same time they heard the key in the back door turn, and a second later Eric crashed outside, coughing and retching. He only just had time to yank the scarves from his face before he was violently sick and then he collapsed, gasping for breath, on the ground.

Bea pulled her handkerchief from her pocket and ran it under the outside tap. She washed his face with it and they turned him on his side. He was deathly pale. 'Get a St John ambulance, quick,' Imogen barked at one of the strangers in the path.

Ruby was stunned. She watched helplessly. Her brain was refusing to function. With everyone's attention on Eric, she looked in the back door. Biscuit lay on the mat, his tongue protruding between his lips. His eyes were open and sightless. She bent to touch him, but she didn't go inside. The animal was stiff.

Eric sat up.

'Where's Jim?' said Ruby. Nobody moved. It was obvious to everyone, except perhaps Ruby, that no one could possibly have survived in that toxic atmosphere. 'Where's my husband?'

Putting her handkerchief over her mouth, she stepped into the kitchen. Even with the taps off, the door open and the window smashed, the pungent smell of gas was still overwhelming. Ruby looked around the room. A man she'd never seen before came up behind her. 'Out of the way, love. We'll get him.'

He pushed her roughly to one side and three men, their feet crunching on broken glass on the floor, went into the kitchen. As they bent over the cooker, she saw him. Jim was lying on his stomach, with his whole head and chest inside the oven. The dead monkey, loyal to

the end, was lying on his back. One man threw it carelessly to one side and grabbed Jim's feet. The three of
them lifted him from the oven and took him outside
and into the fresh air. They laid him on the path, face
up. He was a terrible colour. Yellow pus framed his eyes
and his mouth was filled with mucus.

Imogen and Bea began artificial respiration. Imogen
knelt Jim with his head between her knees and began
pulling his arms from his side above his head and back
again, while Bea pushed his chest. Jim made no sound,
but a trickle of yellow mucus came out of his mouth.

'No wonder he can't breathe,' cried Ruby. 'There's
something in his mouth!' She pushed her finger between
his lips and hooked out a wad of paper. A knot of
mucus followed.

Ruby was staring at the paper. 'Why's he got newspaper in his mouth?' she gasped.

No one had an answer. Imogen and Bea continued
to work away.

Not long afterwards they heard the ambulance bell
and then the sound of running feet. The women got up
and moved away to make room, and Ruby watched the
ambulance attendants trying to revive her husband. A
second or two later she became aware that her mother
was crying and put her arm around Bea's shoulder. 'It'll
be all right, Mum,' said Ruby. 'As soon as they get him
to hospital, he'll be fine.'

Bea, her handkerchief pressed over her mouth to
contain her sobs, glanced up at her daughter in disbelief.

Ruby smiled encouragingly. 'It'll be fine. You'll see.'

The ambulance man stood to his feet. 'Can't do anything for this one, Jack,' he said to his colleague. 'The poor blighter's a goner.'

'No!' cried Ruby. Her eyes grew wide. She staggered towards Jim, but then her legs gave way and she fainted.

CHAPTER 25

Eric waited until Jean was in bed before he spoke to Lena. The events of the past couple of days had left them both deeply shocked. The ambulance not only took Jim's body, but also took Eric to hospital. He was immediately put on oxygen and was ordered to have bed rest. He felt light-headed and slightly confused, but apart from a dull headache that lasted about twenty-four hours, he had recovered well. Dr Quinn looked in on him several times and, because of what he had done, Eric was given star treatment by the nurses. When Lena visited him in the afternoon, she told him that Ruby was with her mother and the guest house was shut for a couple of weeks.

Dr Quinn sent a taxi to bring Eric home and, when he arrived, Jean was overjoyed to see him again. He left Lena saying goodnight to their daughter, then braced himself for what would inevitably be a difficult time.

Eventually Lena came downstairs with some washing and put it in the laundry box. Sensing that he was staring at her, she spun round. 'Is something the matter?'

He nodded. 'I need you to sit down.'

Immediately her heartbeat quickened. 'What – what is it?' Without taking her eyes from his face, Lena lowered herself onto a kitchen chair. 'You're frightening me.'

'Jim knew.'

'What do you mean, "Jim knew"? Knew what?' Eric waited for her to work it out for herself. Her face paled and she began to tremble. 'How?'

'He found a story in a magazine.'

'What magazine?'

Eric pushed the copy of *Tit-Bits* in front of her. 'It was wrapped around the ice cream we had at Jean's party. You gave it to him for the monkey, remember?'

Lena started to cry. 'No . . . no. It's my fault, isn't it? It's all my fault.'

Eric leaned forward to grasp hold of her hands. 'This isn't about blame.'

She searched his face, her eyes spilling tears. 'Do you think he told anyone?'

Eric shrugged.

'What can we do?' she cried. 'If he told somebody, they'll take her away.'

'Not necessarily,' Eric replied, his tone measured. He could see Lena was trying hard not to panic, but even he was struggling to remain calm.

'I can't give her up,' she said, blowing her nose. 'I won't. I'd rather die than give her up.'

'And I can't go back to prison,' he said.

She fingered the magazine again. 'When did he give you this?'

306

'I was in there that afternoon,' said Eric.

Her eyes grew wide. 'Oh, Eric, you didn't . . .'

'He was fine when I left,' he said calmly. 'We had a row, but that was all.' He moved into a position to put his arms around her, but she batted him away.

'We'll have to leave,' she said, standing up. 'We'll go tonight. I'll go and pack.'

'Lena, we can't keep on running away,' said Eric. 'I think we should sit tight. It might not be anything to worry about and, besides, the man is dead. How's it going to look if we leg it during the night?'

She stared at him, trying to make sense of it all.

'It's going to be all right,' he said again. His words sounded a bit lame, but she nodded and sat back down. He shifted his feet, before beginning again. 'The thing is,' he went on uncertainly, 'he had some papers.'

'Papers? What papers?'

'He'd got hold of other old newspapers. He had a lot of stuff about – you know – Christine.'

'Don't call her that!'

'He'd got a box full of clippings and letters,' Eric went on.

She gasped. The panicky feeling in her chest was making breathing difficult. She knew the box Eric meant. Jim kept it with him wherever he was working. It was an old storage box for gramophone records. 'What was he going to do with them?'

'I'm not sure,' said Eric. 'He said he wanted to hear our side of the story first.'

'And you told him?'

'What else could I do, Lena? The chap had me over a barrel. The thing is, I don't think he'd told Ruby anything, and I want you to get those papers back before she reads them.'

'Me?' She rose to her feet. 'I can't go rummaging through his stuff.'

'Listen to me, Lena. You've got to. They're bound to ask you to help out in the guest house over the next few weeks, especially with the baby so close. Just pretend to be tidying up his things and have a look at the same time.'

'Oh, Eric, I can't – I can't.'

He grasped her forearms and looked straight into her eyes. 'You have to, Lena,' he said firmly. 'For our Jean's sake.'

For the next few days, when Ruby woke up in the morning, her first thought was one of confusion. Where was she? The powder-blue walls and flowered curtains were unfamiliar. The single bed with its pale-lemon blanket and striped counterpane didn't feel like her own bed, and of course it wasn't. She was at her mother's house. On two of the days the sun streamed in through the window and she could hear birdsong. Another day, soft rain made running noises down the window glass; and the next day the light levels were much lower because the sky was grey and overcast. As soon as she opened her eyes, she had no feeling at all, but then the awful grief would rush in, sucking all the warmth from her body and leaving her with an unbearable crushing pain in her chest. Her mind was flooded with horrible images. They were vivid, but muddled: Jim's bloated and blue face, with mucus coming from his eyes and nose; her mother and Imogen desperately trying to get him to breathe; opening the front door to that terrible pungent smell; Eric being sick on the path . . . The scenes played over and over in her mind, until her throat closed up and her tears fell unchecked.

He had been a good husband to her. If only things had been different. He'd had a hard time and she hadn't helped matters. How she wished she had told Jim how much he'd meant to her. If only she'd been kinder to him. She was devastated to think that the last thing he would have remembered was that she'd been unfaithful.

When she was up, people came and went. They tried to persuade her to eat or drink, suggested going for a 'nice walk' or taking a nap on the bed, and she did what was required of her, but she felt like an automaton. Jim was dead. They were saying that he killed himself. If he did, it was all her fault. He'd been amazing about the baby, but that must have been a front. What other reason did he have to kill himself? Perhaps the enormity of what she had done had finally hit home and he couldn't live with it any more. If that was so, then she had killed him as surely as if she'd turned on the gas taps herself. Oh, Jim . . .

She went over every detail of the day, looking for some clue – some small detail of something he might have said that she'd missed – but there was nothing. On the other hand, hadn't his parting words been full of concern for her well-being? Was that another way of saying goodbye? If killing himself wasn't about the baby, what other reason could he have had to take his own life? He was doing well with his newspaper articles. Why kill yourself when everything was going so well? He was always saying that he had a job to keep up with the demand for his crosswords. Just last week he'd told her he'd got enough commissions to keep him going for another six months at least. True, he still couldn't walk and sometimes he was in pain, but in every other aspect his life was on the up. No, there was no other reason except the baby why he should do away with himself. It had to be the baby. Among his very last words to her had been, 'Don't go tiring yourself.' Was that his way of telling her what he planned to do? It seemed a bit obscure, but what else was she to think?

Someone on the telephone wanted to speak to Jim.

Rachel took a deep breath. 'Who is calling?'

'Grenville Anderson of the *Surrey and Sussex Recorder*.'

Rachel chewed her bottom lip. Probably an editor wanting more crossword puzzles. 'May I ask what this is about?'

'I would prefer to speak to Mr Searle in person,' said Grenville. 'This is his telephone number, isn't it?'

'Mr Anderson,' Rachel began, 'I'm afraid I have some rather distressing news. Mr Searle has passed away.'

There was a slight pause, then Grenville exclaimed, 'What! How – when?'

'I'm not at liberty to say anything more at the moment,' said Rachel. 'It has become a matter for the police.'

'Good Lord!'

'May I ask you what this call is about?'

'Are you his wife?'

'No,' said Rachel. 'I'm his sister-in-law. Mr Searle's passing was only a week ago and, right now, Mrs Searle is indisposed.'

'Yes, yes, of course,' Grenville flustered. 'Please forgive me. I had no idea. Please give Mrs Searle my sincere condolences.'

'I will,' said Rachel, still waiting.

'I was ringing to talk to Mr Searle about the prize he has won.'

'Prize?' said Rachel faintly.

'First prize, in fact,' Grenville went on. 'We have been running it for years. It's hugely popular, and Mr Searle has won the sum of twenty-five pounds. We shall of course send it to his widow, but I need to warn you that, when the paper comes out, there will be a picture of Mr Searle on the front page. I telephoned him about the issue a few days ago. He knew about the prize, but wanted to keep it a secret and surprise his wife.'

Rachel was having problems trying not to break down.

'I think, under the circumstances,' Grenville went on, 'you should break the news to Mrs Searle yourself.'

'Yes, of course,' said Rachel huskily.

'Please accept my sincere condolences,' Grenville repeated.

'What was the prize for?'

'An article,' said Grenville. 'On making the most of life.'

Rachel hung up. Poor Jim . . . poor Ruby.

The inquest into Jim's death was a lot more open-and-shut than either Nelson's or Linton Carver's had been. Rex told the court that Jim was thrilled to become a father, but – faced with his medical record, which showed the hopelessness of his mobility, and the fact that when he lost his photographic business he had lost everything – it seemed inevitable that there could be only one conclusion.

'You say he had problems with his mobility?' the coroner asked Rex.

'He found it hard to walk, and his balance was very wobbly.'

'Did he have falls?'

'He hadn't had one for a while, but I think that was because he would lean over the back of his wheelchair when he wanted to walk. It gave him stability and support.'

'So the bruise on his forehead could have been accidental?'

Ruby looked up. She didn't know Jim had had a bruise. She tried to remember it, but couldn't.

'Could the injury have been accidental?' the coroner repeated.

'Possibly.'

'Possibly or probably?'

'Probably.'

'Why didn't he simply stay in the wheelchair?'

'Jim was a determined man,' said Rex. 'He didn't give up easily.'

'But he did get depressed?'

Rex looked uncomfortable.

'Dr Quinn?'

'Yes,' Rex said reluctantly, 'he did sometimes feel let down by life.'

Ruby tried to redress the balance, by giving evidence that Jim was doing well with his new interest, but when the editor of the *Gazette* read out some of the readers' responses, the vitriolic nature of their opinions only added to the coroner's convictions. The coroner returned a verdict of suicide while the balance of his mind was disturbed, and released the body for burial. Thus it was that, five days later, Jim was interred in the cemetery at Offington Corner.

At his wake, Imogen invited Ruby to come away with her for a few days.

'I can't,' she said, 'I have the baby to consider. I have to get back to the guest house.'

'Is she asleep?' asked Bea.

'I think so.'

Ruby heard her sister-in-law's quiet reply, but didn't open her eyes. She was lying on the couch in the summer-house in her mother's garden. The weather was warm

313

but hazy – the perfect day for relaxing. It was a month or so since the funeral and everyone was still struggling to come to terms with what Jim had done. After she had fainted, when Jim was declared dead, Bea had insisted that her daughter stay at home with her and Rex. Ruby was slowly emerging from the terrible fog of grief that had left her unable to think clearly, but there were times when she didn't want to talk, and this was one of them.

Rachel had filled a zinc bath with warm water. Seventeen-month-old Alma was sitting in it playing with some eggcups, a colander and some spoons, while the rest of the family sat around a small table on the lawn. Rex leaned back in the deckchair with the newspaper over his head. A little way away, Percy was playing croquet with May.

'Poor girl,' said Bea sympathetically. 'How could he do that to her, at a time like this? There was absolutely no reason for him to take his own life.'

'That's what I can't understand,' said Rachel. 'He was about to become a father, his crosswords were selling well and, only the week before, Ruby was telling me he'd been given his own column in another newspaper. It just doesn't make sense.'

Although she didn't join in the conversation, Ruby felt exactly the same.

'He had some odd opinions,' said Percy.

'I'm not sure he believed everything he wrote,' said Rex, his voice muffled by the paper. 'He was a good journalist, that's all. He had a sound understanding of

314

action and reaction, and what he wrote sold news-papers.'

Ruby had heard enough. She stirred herself and immediately everyone was concerned about her.

'Don't fuss,' she scolded as she sat up.

'We're all bound to be worried about you,' said her mother.

'There's no need,' said Ruby. 'And I need to get back to the guest house. I can't afford to lose any more customers.'

The family all looked from one to the other and Ruby guessed something was afoot. 'What is it?'

'Ruby, we all want to help you,' said Rachel. 'In your condition, you clearly can't run the place single-handed, so your mother and I have worked out a rota.'

Ruby blinked in surprise.

'It includes your mother and me,' Rachel went on, 'but it also includes several of your friends who are desperate to be of service.' She handed Ruby a list of names. 'Each person has pledged either a whole day or one morning or an afternoon a week. You don't have to pay anyone. They are simply glad to help.'

'I can't believe it,' Ruby whispered.

'Why not?' said Bea. 'They are all people who have a reason to be grateful for your help at one time or another and, I must say, they were practically falling over each other to be included.'

There was a lump in her throat as Ruby went over the names. Her mother, bless her, Imogen and Lena. She'd half-expected that; but the people listed underneath were a revelation to her: Susan Marley, who had spent a couple of Christmases with Ruby before she remarried; Edith Gressenhall, who was now happily married and renting Bea's old house in Newlands Road; Rivka, who was giving up her one day off a week to help out; and Rachel herself, who had added in brackets next to her name: '(I have a nanny for Alma)'. Then there was Florrie Dart, Olive James, Betty Dawkins and Eileen Hall – all old neighbours from Newlands Road – and finally Cousin Lily and Aunt Vinny. With the volunteers doing either a whole day or doubling up with someone else to do a morning or an afternoon, it seemed that the guest house was completely covered for a fortnight at a time.

'There'll be no need for you to worry about anything until after you've had your baby,' said Rachel.

Ruby's eyes were smarting. Such kindness, such consideration. She almost had to pinch herself to believe what they were doing.

'So you see, my dear,' said Rex, 'you have no reason to run the guest house for a while. Imogen has invited you to go and stay in her home, to have a proper break, and I have to say I think it a splendid idea.'

Ruby had to admit she was tempted. 'There's only a couple of months before the baby is born,' she said, rubbing her hand over her bump.

'Imogen has promised to get you back in good time for that,' said Bea.

Ruby knew she was exhausted, and that made the

offer too good to refuse. She couldn't say the words, but she nodded her head gratefully.

'Shall I help you to go back home and pack a suitcase?' asked Bea.

They all left Bea's house at around six. Rachel and Percy were anxious to get Alma back home and in bed. Ruby hadn't been back to her own home since that awful day. It seemed strange walking up the path, and she felt her heart lurch a little as they opened the front door. She hadn't given much thought as to what she wanted to take, except for one thing. With her case packed, she went into the kitchen, where her mother was wrapping something up to put in the bin.

'There were loads of flies hanging around the meat safe,' she said. 'I had no idea there was a shepherd's pie in there.'

'I made that for Jim's tea,' said Ruby dully.

'Well, it's as high as a kite now, of course,' said Bea. 'I should have checked.'

Ruby picked up the electric iron from the seat of Jim's wheelchair and, winding the flex around it, put it away in the cupboard. She took one last look around the kitchen. It was neat and tidy, but everywhere was dusty and she spotted the odd sliver of broken glass. The floor needed sweeping. Still, she needn't worry about that. The first member of the team, Lena, would be on the doorstep first thing in the morning and, as soon as she was ready to turn the sign back to *Vacancies*, Sea View would be open for business.

CHAPTER 26

A couple of days later, Imogen took Ruby on an excursion. It wasn't far, but it was further than Ruby had ever been before. They went to Bosham, a picturesque village two miles from Chichester.

'In the eleventh century this was the place where King Canute commanded the waves to "go back",' said Imogen.

'Why?'

Imogen shrugged, 'To demonstrate his kingly powers, I suppose.'

'I hope he did it when the tide was on the turn,' Ruby quipped and they both laughed.

'Have you heard of King Harold?' Imogen asked as they pulled up. She was wearing a delightful yellow floral dress in handkerchief linen with a bias flared skirt, short sleeves and an empire-line bust. Ruby felt huge in a wraparound dress in blue, with a matching striped jacket long enough to cover her pregnancy. She nodded. At school she had learned all about King Harold and the battle of 1066.

'Apparently he sailed from Bosham,' said Imogen. 'It's even mentioned in the Bayeux Tapestry.'

Ruby had to admit she was slightly surprised. The place was very small and almost insignificant, even if it was beautiful. They found an area of grass called Quay Meadow where they put down their picnic things. With the church in the background, it was a delightful spot. Imogen put up a folding chair for Ruby to sit on. It wasn't terribly comfortable, but it served its purpose. For the first time since Jim died, Ruby had regained her appetite. They ate boiled eggs, pork pie, cheese and bread, with fresh greenhouse tomatoes.

As yet, Ruby hadn't met Imogen's husband. At the moment he was forced to spend a lot of time in London working on an important case, so he was living with his parents in Highgate. He telephoned regularly, and it was obvious that Imogen adored him.

'When we first married,' she told Ruby, as she lay back on the picnic rug, 'we talked about moving to London, but the air in Sussex is so much nicer.'

'You must miss him,' said Ruby.

'I don't think I could live without him,' said Imogen. She laughed and almost immediately was seized with embarrassment. 'Oh, Ruby, I'm sorry.'

'You really mustn't worry,' replied Ruby. 'I hate it when people feel they're treading on eggshells when I'm around. I've got to get used to it, haven't I?'

'But it must be awful for you.'

Ruby looked away. 'It is,' she said, 'especially when I know it was my fault.'

'You mustn't say that,' cried Imogen, leaning up on

her elbow. 'Of course it wasn't your fault. Why on earth would you think that?'

Ruby hesitated. If she said the words, the terrible secret would no longer belong just to her. In the days since Jim had been gone, it had eaten away at her, tormenting her and making her hate the baby inside her. She had felt frustrated and miserable. Jim had obviously had a change of heart, and it must have been to do with her infidelity. Nobody knew except them, but perhaps he had decided he couldn't deal with it after all.

Their life together had been wonderful when they'd first wed. The sex was . . . well, she didn't want to remember that. Being denied something so exquisitely beautiful was torture. Perhaps if her body had never been awakened, it might not have mattered so much, but it had and it did. With Jim she had discovered love, passion and that wonderful feeling when he'd encouraged her to a climax; and, once sampled, she'd found she couldn't do without it. Of course, being with Bob had been exciting, but nothing like the times she remembered with Jim.

Ruby glanced at Imogen, who was still awaiting her answer. Should she tell her? Should she keep silent? She desperately needed to share it with someone, but who? She had decided against talking to her mother. It was too intimate, too embarrassing. Rachel? She'd be shocked and possibly angry too, especially when she'd gone to such great lengths to help save their marriage. So why not Imogen? She knew Imogen's secret and had never breathed a word to a living soul. Imogen knew she could trust Ruby, but could Ruby trust Imogen?

'Ruby?' said Imogen, sitting up. 'Are you all right? You've suddenly gone very pale.'

The tears came unbidden. Ruby stared at her friend and gulped. 'It *was* my fault.'

'Oh, Ruby,' said Imogen, getting to her feet.

'The baby isn't his.'

There – she'd said it. Her words hung in the air like shards of glass. Ruby hardly dared draw breath as she searched Imogen's face for her reaction.

'Did Jim know?' she asked.

Ruby nodded.

'When did you tell him?'

'Last November,' said Ruby. 'He guessed when I was being sick in the morning.'

Imogen put her arms around Ruby's shoulders. It was almost too much to bear. Ruby burst into tears again. 'But if he knew all that time ago,' said Imogen gently, 'I can't see why he would do away with himself now.'

Ruby blew her nose on her handkerchief and stared at her own hands in her lap. What Imogen said made sense. If Jim was that upset about it, surely he would have committed suicide way back then. That thought made her remember something he'd said at the time. 'We'll tell everyone it's mine, then we'll say no more about it.' Why would he say that, if he didn't mean it?

'Your mother and Rachel told me Jim was thrilled about the baby,' Imogen went on. 'No, there has to be another reason why he did that. What you're saying doesn't add up.'

'You won't tell anyone, will you?' said Ruby anxiously.

'Of course not!' cried Imogen. 'After what you did for me, I always wanted you for my friend. Now we have even more in common than before.'

Ruby's heart leapt. *My friend* – she had always felt there was something special about Imogen, and now she could class her as her friend.

Effie Rhodes's face flushed with pleasure. She read and reread the letter over and over again. Imagine him writing to her in person – and a handwritten letter too. 'My dear Effie,' he'd begun. She ran her finger over the ink. She was in the hallway. Normally she left the post for the maid to bring in, but she'd been on her way downstairs as the letters dropped onto the mat. As soon as she saw the envelope with the BUF flash in the corner, she knew she couldn't wait.

Years ago Effie had invited a woman who studied handwriting to one of her dinners. After the meal, they'd played a game. The woman – Effie struggled to remember her name – had asked each person to write a sentence, and then she'd told them something about their personality just by studying their writing. Effie couldn't remember everything she'd been told, but didn't angular letters (the way she wrote herself) depict a person who liked quick results? And a sixty-degree slant, didn't that mean an intense nature? Even the pressure of the pen on the paper said something about the writer. A heavy

322

hand, like this one, meant that the writer was the sort of person who would act first and ask questions later:

> My dear Effie,
>   Diana and I would be delighted to attend your soirée on Thursday week. We plan to combine it with a visit to Littlehampton in the afternoon, where I have a business meeting with the faithful, and others.
>   I commend you and Gus for all your hard work and devotion to the Colonial Office. I trust you will both enjoy your well-earned retirement.
>   O. Mosley

'Retirement' – she hated that word. It made her feel so . . . old. She took a deep breath. The Leader was coming here: to her home. She had less than a week and a half to prepare but, by God, she would give them an evening to remember. Already her mind was whirling. She knew she was brilliant at organizing, but with this, nothing must go wrong. She would enlist Freda Fosdyke's help. She had experience of getting lazy staff to work harder. She could do all the stuff at grass-roots level – cleaning the house, getting the silver polished, washing the plates, and so on – leaving Effie to do the really important things.

Mosley was a man who liked the finer things of life. She would seek out a quartet or, better still, a quintet of quality. How would she find out what sort of music he liked? And flowers – she would call the florist immediately after she had breakfasted. She stood for a minute, clutching his letter to her chest and dreaming of how good it would be, when she spotted the gardener dead-heading the roses. Opening the door, Effie called out, 'Watson, we must have plenty of colour in the garden.' And she told the startled man, 'Lots of pot plants. Hydrangeas by the front door, and geraniums by the summerhouse.'

Watson blinked and touched his forelock.

Gus was reading his morning paper as she walked into the dining room. 'Hello, old thing. Sleep well?'

'We've had a letter.' She beamed. Was it all right to call him by his Christian name? Why not – they were friends now, weren't they?

Gus put down the corner of his paper. 'Oh?'

'He's coming,' she said breathily. 'Oswald Mosley and Diana are coming to my soirée.'

'It wasn't there!' Lena's eyes were wide with fright.

She had run down the garden, where Eric was busy picking runner beans. He spent every moment he could in the garden and, since the beginning of summer, they had enjoyed the fruits of his labour. Broad beans in May; carrots and peas in June; and now runner beans. Eric had never grown anything before, but by now he was convinced that he had green fingers. His lettuce crop had been spoiled by slugs, and the cabbages had suffered from cabbage-white caterpillars until he'd covered them with old net curtains. One of the men from the yard had told him to put some cider vinegar, sugar and water in a bottle, along with some bits of banana skin. It sounded a bit far-fetched, but when he put one bottle on the ground and hung another from a low branch, sure enough, he bagged plenty of unwanted garden pests.

'Eric, did you hear me?' Lena cried. 'It wasn't there. Jim always kept all his papers in a gramophone-record box and now it's gone.'

Eric scrambled onto the path. 'So who took it?'

'I don't know,' cried Lena.

'Damn and blast it!' said Eric.

'What are we going to do?'

Eric ran his fingers through his hair. 'When I told Jim, he was quite reasonable about it,' he said. 'Maybe she'll be the same.'

'But supposing someone else has taken it?' Lena wailed.

It was obvious from the look on his face that Eric hadn't thought of that. 'Then we really can't leave,' he said. 'If someone like the police took it and we do a moonlight flit, they'll come after us. They might even think I had something to do with Jim's death.'

'They didn't find us last time,' Lena said.

'And I've thought about that long and hard,' said Eric. 'Mrs West could hardly tell them the whole story, could she?'

Lena looked slightly sceptical. 'Oh, I wish this was all over,' she said brokenly.

'I know,' said Eric, slipping his arm around her. 'But, right now, all we can do is sit tight.'

Lena dropped her head onto his shoulder and cried softly.

* * *

Later that night, in her bed at Imogen's house, Ruby reflected on their conversation. Her friend was right. Her own fears about Jim changing his mind about the baby didn't add up. There were a few other things that didn't add up, either. The shepherd's pie worried her, for a start. What she needed was someone to bounce her ideas off – someone who wouldn't pooh-pooh everything away. She had to do some serious thinking; sensible thinking. There was a logical explanation somewhere. Imogen had promised to keep quiet about the baby's father, and Ruby believed she would. Yes, and she could confide in Imogen about other things too. After all, she told herself as drowsiness crept closer, two heads are better than one.

CHAPTER 27

Just lately, Ruby slept a lot. The weather was hot and dry, she was exhausted by her grief and her body was struggling to cope with the last stages of her pregnancy. It was difficult to motivate herself to get on with anything.

She sat in the summerhouse with a jug of fresh lemonade. Imogen's little springer spaniel, Dusty, lay panting at her feet. The only sound came from the breeze as it rustled the leaves of the wisteria and the lilac bushes. Both had long since shed their flowers, but they used the summer months to gain strength and grow taller and thicker. Across the lawn she could see a three-seater bench with wrought-iron legs and a pattern on the back. Behind the seat was a forsythia tree, and a robin, half-concealed by one of the branches, was singing his heart out. Jim once told her that the robin is the only British bird that sings all year round. Fiercely territorial, in the spring its song is not so much for the joy of living as a warning for other birds to stay away. Now, in summer, its song was slightly more subdued. Ruby stretched to ease the discomfort in her back and sighed. Later in the evening a scream of swifts would fill the air as they

327

swooped and dived for small flying insects and flies. Dusty would chase after them, barking like mad, even though he hadn't a hope of catching one.

The thought of actually going through Jim's stuff was daunting, but Ruby had his gramophone box with her. She had to make a start somewhere. She began by separating everything into distinct piles, using the lemonade jug and her glass to stop the papers blowing away. A third pile sat on a chair, with a cushion on the top. The largest pile was correspondence relating to the crosswords. She was surprised to see how appreciated they were – Jim had letters of thanks from readers, as well as magazine editors. There was no need to do anything about them. She had already received letters of condolence from the editors of most of the magazines, so they were well aware of what had happened.

The letters from the newspapers were slightly different. They were quite old. Nothing very up-to-date, and she supposed that was because the police must still have the most recent ones. They had taken papers away from the house as part of their investigations. The subject had been covered by the inquest. Ruby was surprised by how nasty some of the writers were. Several people called Jim a traitor to his country, which – although grossly unfair – was, she supposed, their honest opinion. But she drew the line when people wished him dead, or that someone in his family would get cancer. She read all the letters, just in case there was something she might have missed and, by the time she'd finished, she wanted nothing more than to burn the lot.

'What are you doing?' Imogen's sudden arrival in the doorway made her jump. 'Sorry,' she apologized immediately. 'I didn't mean to startle you. You looked so preoccupied.'

Ruby explained what she was doing.

'Can I help?'

'I've been through that pile,' said Ruby. 'Some of it's pretty awful stuff, but I don't think I need to do anything about it.'

'You should at least take down names and addresses,' said Imogen.

'Do you think so?' asked Ruby. 'Surely they will have made them up.'

'All the same . . .' said Imogen. She hurried indoors to find pen and paper.

Ruby made a start on the miscellaneous pile, and before long came across a small wodge of newspaper cuttings about a missing baby. At first she couldn't make out why it would be of any interest to Jim, but as she read on, she began to feel uneasy, especially when she came across an envelope and a letter from the *Bournemouth Daily Echo*:

> *Dear Sir,*
>
> *I enclose the cuttings you requested on the Christine West case for your perusal. If, at the end, you have any information that could lead to the whereabouts of Christine, this paper is keen to be the first to know. We never pay for information appertaining to a criminal offence, but it*

> *is not beyond our bounds to see that such infor-*
> *mation is rewarded.*
>   *Yours sincerely*
>   *Thomas Bailey-Smith, Editor*

Ruby frowned. Jim seeking a reward? That didn't sound like a characteristic of his. He had very little interest in money. There had to be another reason why he was collecting information on this case.

Imogen was back and was copying names and addresses into a small exercise book, but the weather was about to change and the light levels were becoming much lower. They had just decided to go back into the house when Ruby suddenly said, 'What do you make of this?' She had been putting everything back into the gramophone box when she'd dropped an envelope, and several bits she'd not seen before fell to the floor.

It was hard for Ruby, given her bulk, to reach them easily, so Imogen picked them up. As she thumbed carelessly through the pieces of paper, she shrugged. It was only as a cutting of a knitting pattern fluttered from her grasp that Ruby made the connection. There was a brilliant flash, followed almost immediately by a heavy clap of thunder. The knitting pattern was held by a paper clip to a newspaper cutting about a little girl who was missing.

Ruby drew in her breath noisily. 'Oh no!'

'We'll be fine,' said Imogen, thinking that the storm was frightening her. 'I'm sure we can get back indoors before the rain comes.'

'It's not that,' said Ruby, handing Imogen the knitting pattern. 'My next-door neighbour's little girl, Jean, has got a rabbit just like that; and what's more, she fits the description of the missing child.'

Effie looked around her sitting room and smiled with an inner glow of self-satisfaction. She was surrounded by the great and the good, including Oswald Mosley and his wife Diana, Norah Elam, the BUF County Women's Officer for Sussex, and the Reverend James Crosland, the vicar of Rustington. They were the cream of society, but it didn't end there. She had persuaded Alfred Keene, a former Olympic fencer, to come; and Jessie Matthews, a popular singer. She had tried to get Michael Redgrave, but he was busy on an Alfred Hitchcock film called *The Lady Vanishes*.

She and Gus had spent a small fortune on this evening. She'd virtually bought up the local nurseries. There were potted plants all over the garden, in the driveway leading to the house and dotted around the summerhouse. Watson had shaved the lawn to within an inch of its life specially for the occasion, so it was a great shame that they'd had a violent thunderstorm just before her guests arrived and the grass was far too wet to be outdoors.

As well as everything else she'd been required to do, Freda Fosdyke had made sure there were flowers in every room; but in the event, they had to be confined to the laundry room, because it turned out they made Diana sneeze.

The trio was moderately good, but in Effie's view it was a little unfortunate that the cellist looked like a you-know-what. She hoped Oswald wouldn't notice. She gazed at him admiringly. He was charismatic and charming, and those piercing black eyes of his seemed to look right through you. He noticed her stare and smiled.

'So, Effie,' he said, tearing himself away from the conversation he was having with the local police chief, 'I understand that you and Gus are fairly new on the scene.'

'Actually we were married in Worthing thirty years ago,' said Effie, patting the back of her hair, 'but then Gus was posted to British Cameroon.'

'Ah yes, I remember,' he said. 'You were with the Colonial Office. Twenty years?'

'Yes, well almost.'

'My dear Effie,' he said, 'I can hardly believe it. You must have been a child bride.'

Effie smiled coyly. 'You're teasing me, Sir Oswald. I am no spring chicken.'

As he moved on, she felt a hand caressing her bottom in a most intimate way. Effie hadn't been touched like that for years and she shivered with excitement.

'In my experience, a good rooster will give any chicken – spring or not – a more contented cluck,' he whispered into her hair. 'Well done, my dear. An excellent party.'

Effie blushed modestly, but although she revelled in all the attention and the accolades, she hadn't a clue what he meant.

CHAPTER 28

No matter what position she took up, the ache in Ruby's back persisted most of the night. She tossed and turned, but it wasn't until the first hazy light of a new day seeped through the curtains that she realized she might actually be in labour. The contractions, if they were contractions, were not painful, but she had the distinct feeling of something tightening and then relaxing inside. She lay quietly, glancing every now and then at the clock as the sensation continued. Before long she was uncomfortable again and the pains were returning every five to six minutes. The baby was definitely coming.

She decided against waking Imogen. She would only panic and most likely insist that they went to her mother's place immediately, even though the baby wouldn't be here for hours. No, let her sleep on. Ruby would tell her at breakfast time.

To occupy her mind, Ruby went over the conversation they'd had last night during the storm. She had already guessed that Jim thought Jean was, in fact, Christine West. It wasn't a pleasant thought. She liked Lena and had every reason to be grateful to her, but if she really was Marlene Amberley and had kidnapped her employer's daughter, then there was no getting away from the fact that she was a criminal. She couldn't ignore something as big as living next door to a child abductor, but what was she going to do about it?

Discussing Lena the evening before had given Ruby the courage to open up to her friend. 'Can I bounce a few other things off you?'

'Go on,' Imogen encouraged.

'You won't laugh?' said Ruby.

'I promise,' said Imogen with her hand over her heart.

Ruby could see the smile tugging at Imogen's lips and looked away.

'I'm sorry,' said Imogen. 'Don't be cross. I will listen, I promise. Go on.'

Ruby took a deep breath. 'Let's begin with the shepherd's pie.'

Imogen was startled. 'The shepherd's pie?'

'On the day Jim died, I'd left it in the oven ready to cook for tea,' said Ruby in all seriousness. 'I forgot all about it. When I went back home to pack, before coming here, my mother found loads of flies around the meat safe, and the shepherd's pie was still inside. Two weeks after he'd died! I found Mum wrapping it up to chuck in the bin.'

'So? I don't understand why that should bother you,' said Imogen. 'If it was in the way, when he went to . . . do what he did, he must have put it in the most logical place.'

Ruby shook her head. 'My Jim was a typical male,'

she said. 'It wouldn't occur to him to place it anywhere else but on the kitchen table.'

Imogen looked thoughtful. 'Perhaps, for once in his life, he was just being considerate.'

'He was supposedly about to take his own life,' said Ruby. 'Would putting the pie in the meat safe be uppermost in his mind?'

'Point taken,' said Imogen.

'Come to think of it,' said Ruby, 'I left his lunch in the meat safe, which means he must have died sometime during the afternoon. Which brings me to the iron.'

Imogen leaned back in her chair. 'A shepherd's pie, and now an iron?'

'It was on the seat of his wheelchair,' said Ruby.

'Well, he must have . . . he probably – maybe he . . .' Whatever scenario she conjured up, Imogen could see that it wouldn't work.

'Don't you see? The iron must have been put there after he vacated the wheelchair.'

'Could the police have put it there, after they'd examined the kitchen?'

'I suppose so,' said Ruby, 'but why would you put an iron on the seat of a wheelchair?'

Imogen nodded. It was a conundrum. 'The way I see it, you've got two problems that can possibly be explained away,' she said. 'I hardly think they would merit the police looking into this further.'

'Then there's the monkey,' said Ruby. 'I've been wondering why Jim would take Wilfred and Biscuit with him. He loved those animals, especially Wilfred.'

'What about the note? Did he leave a note?'

Ruby shook her head.

'Didn't you have any inkling that he was depressed?' asked Imogen, shaking her head in disbelief.

'Jim wasn't depressed.'

'They say that people who commit suicide hide their true feelings from those they love,' she observed.

'He wasn't suicidal,' Ruby insisted. 'Why should he be? As I went out of the door, he had a telephone call from someone called Sir Hubert Temple. I bet that was another commission.'

'Can you be sure of that?'

'Well, no.'

'Ring him and find out what he wanted,' Imogen said. 'Have you got his number?'

Ruby shook her head. Imogen picked up the telephone receiver.

'Operator, would you get the number for Sir Hubert Temple, please?' There was a long pause and then she said, 'Are you sure? Thank you.' She replaced the receiver. 'There's no subscriber with that name in the area.'

'Jim had everything going for him, Imogen,' Ruby insisted. 'Why should he want to die?'

'Listen, Ruby,' said Imogen, 'if he didn't die by his own hand, then there's really only one other explanation.'

'Exactly.'

'You're beginning to frighten me.'

'I'm frightening myself,' said Ruby.

They stared at each other in horrified silence. 'But surely,' Imogen began again, 'the police would have realized?'

'They didn't know Jim,' said Ruby, moving the cushion from behind her back as she tried to get more comfortable. 'Ever since that day I've been trying to work out how he got into that oven.'

'He got down and shoved his head right in,' said Imogen. 'How else could he do it? Oh, and he put the shepherd's pie in the meat safe first.'

'Does that sound logical to you?'

Imogen blew out her cheeks.

'He couldn't kneel,' said Ruby. 'Explain to me how someone who can't kneel could turn on the gas tap and then push themselves right up against the jets.' Imogen opened her mouth to say something, but Ruby raised her hand. 'Did I mention that he was under both oven shelves as well? Wouldn't it have been easier to take the shelves out first?'

'I've no wish to be unkind,' Imogen began again, 'but if a man is determined to kill himself, he'll find a way to do it.'

'If my husband had really wanted to do such a thing,' said Ruby, 'there were plenty of strong painkillers in the cabinet. I heard my father warn him once not to exceed the dose. Jim knew they could be dangerous.'

Imogen's eyes grew wide. 'Oh, Ruby . . . I don't know what to say.' She got up and went to the drinks cabinet and poured herself a sherry. 'Want one?'

Ruby shook her head. Imogen came back and sat on

the sofa with her feet curled underneath her. 'So if someone bumped him off, who could it be?'

'I don't know.'

They'd left it there. They had to. Ruby was tired and needed to put her swollen feet up. Now, lying in her bed with the baby coming, she was finding it harder and harder to concentrate on anything else except the pain. Jim had told her Eric was coming to the house later that afternoon. In view of the newspaper cuttings, and the fact that Jim had actually written to the editor of the *Bournemouth Daily Echo*, perhaps Eric . . . No, she refused to believe that. She didn't know why Jim was planning to see Eric that day, but . . . She shuddered. The thought that Eric might be responsible made her feel sick. After a while she told herself it couldn't possibly be him. It would have taken two people to force someone into the oven. Eric couldn't have done it alone – unless, of course, he'd had help. A wave of horror swept over her as another thought came rushing through her mind: Eric and Lena together?

Her tummy muscles tightened and Ruby felt something come away from her. She looked under the sheet and discovered she had passed a sticky, jelly-like plug of mucus. Was this the 'show' that her mother had told her about? This discovery was followed by some more muscular spasms and an increased level of pain. She laid her hand on her tummy and felt it get harder and then relax. Each pain lasted about half a minute.

How she wished Jim was in the bed beside her. But perhaps, she told herself sadly, that wouldn't have been such a good idea after all. Although he'd spared her blushes, the baby wasn't his. Oh, Jim . . . I miss you. In no time at all, her emotions were all over the place. Her labour had started and she didn't want to think any more. Tears trickled down her cheeks and onto the pillow and she cried. She cried for poor Jim, she cried for the baby and she cried for herself. For as long as she could remember she had longed to be a mother, but now she didn't even want this baby. How could she spend a lifetime looking after someone who reminded her of her own infidelity and betrayal? How could she cope with running the guest house and looking after a baby? She would tell everyone that she wanted it adopted. They'd understand. They'd say, 'Poor girl, she doesn't want a constant reminder of her dead husband.'

She heard a movement on the other side of the door in the corridor. Imogen was on her way to the bathroom. She would give her a chance to have a wash and get dressed and then she'd call her.

Ruby's next pain was subsiding when the memory of Jim's bloated face stole across her mind. She shuddered at the thought of that horrible stuff coming out of his eyes, and the egg-shaped swelling on his temple. Her eyes suddenly grew wide again. Yes, the coroner was right: Jim did have a bump on his head. How could she have forgotten? And, more to the point, how did it get there? They had said at the inquest that he must have bumped himself against the side of the oven as he climbed in. She had already established in her own mind that there was no way Jim could have got into the oven on his own.

But suppose he had that injury before the gas taps were switched on? He could have been hit with something, to knock him out first.

She took in her breath noisily. That bruise – Jim must have been hit with the electric iron! She distinctly remembered putting it in the grate as she left the house with her mother. And yet when Bea was getting rid of the shepherd's pie, there the iron was, in the middle of Jim's wheelchair. She shivered. Someone must have picked it up out of the grate and hit Jim on the head, before putting him in the gas oven.

Now she was absolutely positive that Jim had been murdered . . . but why?

May stared crossly at the ceiling. It had been a chaotic morning, and now her favourite time of day was being spoiled.

Her sister had arrived at the house just after ten. She appeared to be ill. Her stepfather helped Ruby upstairs and she was moaning with pain.

'What's wrong?' May had asked, but her mother waved her away.

'Nothing for you to worry about. Run along and play, there's a dear.'

May hated it when she was fobbed off like that, but if she made too much of a fuss the grown-ups sent her to her room and she had to keep the door shut. If she didn't make a fuss, she could gather her things in the dining room and keep the door open. That way she would be able to see anything exciting.

There was a lot of activity in the house, but it wasn't very interesting. A nurse in a blue uniform and a starched white apron arrived, and Mummy took her upstairs. Mrs Dixon, their daily, arrived shortly afterwards, even though she didn't usually come on a Sunday.

A bit later on, Mummy and Daddy came downstairs and sat in the garden room. Mrs Dixon made them some coffee.

'She's a fine healthy young woman,' May heard Mrs Dixon say. 'I'm sure there's no cause for concern, madam.'

May followed her back out to the kitchen, ostensibly to get a drink for herself.

Mrs Dixon handed her a glass of home-made lemonade. 'Now be a good girl, won't you, May? Don't get in people's way. Your mother and father have got quite enough to worry about.'

May was about to ask her how the nurse would get Ruby's baby out of her tummy when she was shooed out of the kitchen.

Back in the dining room, she decided that a chair facing the door would give her the best option to find out what was going on. She could keep an eye on the stairs while she sat at the table with her colouring pencils. The nurse didn't come back down, but her stepfather went up and down twice more, and each time Mummy waited anxiously at the bottom of the stairs until he came back.

'Mummy . . .' May tried once.

But Bea said, 'Not now, dear', before May even had

341

the chance to say anything. Adults could be very annoying sometimes. May knew she couldn't make too much fuss about it, because she had only just signed the League of Ovaltineys' seven promises.

Number one was to do the things parents tell you. When she'd committed herself to that promise, she had no idea it would be so infuriating. The other promises weren't so bad. Number two was to have plenty of exercise; number three was to work hard at school; number four was . . . what was number four? Oh yes, to make sure she had a good sound sleep; number five was to eat everything her mother said; number six was to drink Ovaltine every day; finally, number seven was to be a loyal member of the League of Ovaltineys. It had taken her ages to persuade her parents to let her join the league, so it was important not to disobey the rules. Being a real Ovaltiney gave her the right to wear the badge, have a certificate of merit, the rulebook and, best of all, a copy of the secret code.

Mrs Dixon called her into the kitchen for dinner and May was surprised to find two slices of cheese on toast waiting for her. Normally on Sunday they had a lovely roast dinner, with lamb or beef and crispy roast potatoes and lashings of gravy.

As she tucked in, she tried to coerce Mrs Dixon into telling her what was going on, but her probing questions went unanswered. 'Ask your mummy,' she replied. Or 'Your daddy will explain it all, I'm sure.'

What was the big secret? Had something gone wrong and they couldn't get the baby out? Why wouldn't anyone tell her? May finished her cheese on toast and went outside with her apple. There was no one around to take her to Sunday school, so she decided she would miss it this week. She didn't care that much and besides, she didn't want to miss the strange goings-on in her house.

She mooched around moodily and wished she was more grown-up. For heaven's sake, she was nearly eleven. Surely that was old enough to be told the truth? Halfway through the afternoon, May heard her sister scream. She rushed back indoors, her heart going like the clappers. Was Ruby going to die? What were they doing upstairs? When she burst into the sitting room, her mother was sitting there as calm as you like – knitting! What sort of a mother leaves her child by herself, screaming?

Ruby cried out again. May waited for some sort of reaction. 'Aren't you going to help her, Mummy?'

Her mother looked up and smiled. 'Everything's fine, darling. Don't worry.'

May was flabbergasted. A couple of seconds later her stepfather came back downstairs, rolling down his sleeves. Mummy looked up at him and moved to the edge of her chair. Now, at last! thought May.

'A while to go yet,' said Daddy, and Mummy settled back down again.

'May, ask Mrs Dixon for some tea, will you, dear,' said Mummy, hardly looking up from her knitting.

Having delivered the message, May sat at the kitchen table. Another wail of anguish made its way into the room. 'Is my sister going to die?' she whispered.

'Heavens, no!' cried Mrs Dixon. 'She's having her baby, that's all.'

She bustled out of the kitchen with the tea tray, leaving May blinking with rage. Well, of course she was going to have a baby! Did Mrs Dixon think she was stupid or something? Ruby cried out again, and May shivered. If having a baby meant all that pain and all this fuss, one thing was absolutely certain: she would never ever have one.

CHAPTER 29

The crunch came at around five o'clock. May needed the radio on for 5.30 p.m., when the Ovaltineys would be on Radio Luxembourg, but she wasn't supposed to touch the knobs by herself. By now everyone else in the house was running about like headless chickens, or was on the telephone or something. Nobody was listening to her. Mrs Dixon had prepared a meal, laid the dining-room table and then gone home. Both Mummy and Daddy were upstairs now, and Ruby was still yelling the place down. When, to May's immense relief, Auntie Rachel turned up, May begged her to switch on the radio. As soon as she'd done so, May curled up on the sofa and asked her aunt to join her, but Auntie Rachel bounded upstairs too.

Oh well – now at last she could enjoy something sensible. There were songs: 'We are the Ovaltineys', of course, 'Happy days are here again' and 'Such funny little ways', a nonsense song that made her laugh. And there were jokes: 'Question: Why do you have fouls in football? Answer: Because they have ducks in cricket.'

She didn't quite understand that one, but the children on the radio laughed, so she did too.

At times it was difficult to hear, with Ruby making such an awful racket, but she did manage to copy down the numbers for the secret-code message, just before her mother burst into the room. As soon as the door opened, May was aware of a baby's cry. Her mother was beaming from ear to ear, as she put her arms round her youngest daughter and hugged her tight.

'Oh, May, Ruby has had her baby. She has a darling little boy. You're an auntie now.'

Rested and clean, Ruby relaxed against the pillows. The nurse was tending to the baby and her mother had come into the room with a cup of tea. The baby had a lusty cry and already Ruby was feeling a tug at her heart-strings. While she was in labour she had made up her mind not to look at him, but when the nurse held him upside down and slapped his bottom to encourage him to cry, the urge was too strong.

Ruby and her mother exchanged a loving smile as she sipped the scalding tea. The nurse appeared at her side with a small bundle that looked like an elongated sausage. Bea took the cup from her and, when the nurse leaned over the bed, Ruby automatically crooked her arm to receive him. She looked down at a cherubic face, not wrinkled at all. Bea stroked his dark hair, and he screwed up his eyes and pulled the corners of his mouth down ready to cry.

'Hello, sweetheart,' Ruby whispered near his ear, and he stopped, as if hearing her voice for the first time.

He wasn't exactly handsome, but Ruby's heart was immediately lost. Everything in her body wanted to love and protect this little boy. The rush of feeling was almost overwhelming.

'Oh, darling,' Bea was saying, 'I can hardly believe it. He's beautiful.'

Yes, yes, he was. And he was her son, her precious little boy.

'We'll put Baby back in his cot now,' said the nurse, cutting in. She was a solidly built woman, the brusque and no-nonsense type, but Ruby had felt perfectly safe in her capable hands. 'He needs a rest after his ordeal.' She took him back and Ruby watched her place him in the bottom drawer of the chest of drawers, which they had emptied out and put across two chairs. His makeshift bed would have to do until she got him home to Sea View and his own cot in her bedroom.

The pain and anguish of the past few hours were forgotten as Ruby relaxed against the pillows again. Her father had been with her, and the nurse never left her side throughout the birth. At the very end, Rex had actually delivered his first grandchild himself. Having made sure his daughter was doing well, he was now downstairs drinking a much-needed whisky and trying to remove the ear-to-ear grin that wouldn't go away. Most unprofessional, he told himself.

'What are you going to call him?' May had crept into the room and was staring down at the baby.

'Michael,' said Ruby. 'Michael James Searle.'

In the days that followed, Ruby had a steady stream of visitors and every time she showed them her son, her heart was filled to overflowing with love. She and Michael bonded well and he fed from her breast greedily. Somehow Michael's arrival had helped to soothe her feelings of loss. It would have been much better, of course, if Jim had been here with her, but one look at the baby lifted the terrible ache in her heart and made the days more bearable. Ruby really enjoyed all the attention they both received, but it made her feel uncomfortable when people said things like, 'He looks so like his father' or 'Jim would have been thrilled'. If only she could erase Bob Knight from the picture altogether. If only Michael really was Jim's son.

Imogen turned up, bearing gifts. Ruby was in the sitting room with the window open, getting a bit of fresh air. She tore at the paper and unwrapped a beautiful hand-knitted pure-white shawl and a blue romper suit. 'I had the shawl made,' Imogen said, 'but I bought the romper suit in Hubbard's. If you don't like it, they'll take it back.'

'Oh no,' cried Ruby. 'It's lovely. Would you like to hold him?'

While Imogen cuddled the baby awkwardly, Ruby said, 'I want to ask you something. Would you be his godmother?'

Imogen's eyes grew wide. 'Oh, Ruby, it would be an honour.'

'I've asked Percy and Rachel,' said Ruby, fingering the pattern on the shawl. 'I was going to ask Lena as well, but under the circumstances . . .' Her voice trailed away.

'Yes,' said Imogen, giving an anxious glance over her shoulder, 'what are you going to do about that?'

'I don't know,' said Ruby. 'I need to go through Jim's papers more thoroughly first. I hardly had time to digest them previously.'

'If that little girl has been taken from her rightful mother,' said Imogen stoutly, 'you mustn't wait, Ruby. It's wrong.'

'I know,' said Ruby, 'but I'm sure she's safe and she's happy. Lena is a good mother.'

'But she may not be Jean's mother,' Imogen reminded her.

'I know, I know,' Ruby protested. She was beginning to wish she hadn't confided in Imogen now. She wasn't ready to face the enormity of sorting this out just yet, and she didn't want to feel pressured. Lena, Eric and Jean weren't the only people she had on her mind. She hadn't told anybody her suspicions about the knock on Jim's head being caused by the iron.

'You have no idea what a woman like that is capable of,' Imogen said crossly.

'I'm popping out now,' said Bea, coming into the room. 'It's the Townswomen's Guild this afternoon. Will you be all right on your own?'

349

'I'll be fine,' said Ruby, offering Bea her cheek to kiss. 'Imogen isn't going just yet, and Edith is coming later on.'

Bea stroked her grandson's cheek and smiled. 'What woman were you talking about?' she asked casually and, seeing their puzzled expressions, added, 'When I came into the room, you said you didn't know what she was capable of.'

The two women froze and exchanged anxious glances.

'The person who knitted this fantastic shawl, of course,' said Ruby, holding it up for her mother to admire.

Bea enjoyed the newly formed Townswomen's Guild and, with Rose Wilmot at the helm, it was already expanding. They met in the Oddfellows' Hall in Clifton Road, so it really did feel like a fresh start. The group organized some wonderful talks on a wide variety of subjects, including district nursing, how to build a rock garden from scratch, and the land of Palestine. Occasionally Mrs Wilmot encouraged the elected officers to step down and let others take over the meeting for an afternoon. This gave ordinary members an insight, as she put it, 'into the intricacies of administration'. Women who had never been asked to do any more than make the tea suddenly had their first taste of responsibility and leadership.

Not all TWG meetings were self-indulgent. A great many of the activities that both the TWG and the WI took on were for the greater good of others. They campaigned for women police officers, better conditions for domestic servants and better information, should there be a war.

With the precarious situation in Europe in mind, the TWG decided to initiate classes at which experts could show members of the public how to prepare a room in case of a gas attack. To Bea's mind, Ruby's place seemed an ideal venue, so she put forward her daughter's name.

Thus it was that three weeks after Michael came along, about twenty women squeezed into the downstairs reception room at Sea View. The ladies paid for their refreshments and Ruby laid on tea and cake. The police force, who were giving the talk, paid for the use of the room, which not only augmented her income, but also gave Ruby food for thought. By now she had realized that having a small baby in the house required round-the-clock care. How could she look after Michael twenty-four hours a day and run the guest house? Not only that, but he might well disturb her guests at night. It was time to think ahead, and what better way to generate an income than by hiring rooms out for teaching purposes?

With everybody worrying about what was going on across the Channel, it seemed that a plethora of new women's groups was springing up all over town. She could offer a more intimate setting than a church hall, and she could do the refreshments as well. Not only that, but she could perhaps offer classes herself. They said, if war came, every able-bodied male would be asked to fight. If she rewrote the little booklet she had produced for the German girls, then should war come, it might prove to be useful for ordinary middle-class housewives, who had never so much as lifted a duster. With their domestic servants going to war, they would have to learn how to run their own households.

Michael slept all afternoon, so Ruby was able to sit in on the 'How to gas-proof a room' talk. The title was a little ironic, given what had happened to Jim a few feet away, but she not only took in the talk, but also watched the man who was giving it. If she herself was going to teach, then she needed to study the technique.

They had all introduced themselves while Ruby was preparing the tea trolley, so she missed his name. It wasn't until he was about halfway through his talk that Ruby realized why he seemed so familiar. It was Mr Balentine, the man who – along with Miss Bullock – had brought Franz and Albrecht to the house the previous year. It brought her up with a jolt. What a lot had happened since then. When Albrecht and Franz had arrived, she'd been a frustrated wife with an invalid husband. Now she was a mother and a widow.

She'd remembered that Mr Balentine wasn't exactly handsome, but he had an open, honest face and smiled a lot. He was clearly passionate about what he was doing. Using drawings and diagrams that he had obviously made himself, he told the assembled audience that they should keep a pile of newspapers handy.

'They can be soaked and stuffed on the floor,' he said, although he didn't actually explain why that was a good idea. 'A blanket across a support frame will prevent anything coming down into the fireplace,' he went on, 'and you should use strips of sticky paper to seal along the skirting boards and the windows.'

It all sounded very scary and Ruby wondered how you would know when to do all this. If the gas attack had already taken place, surely you would have succumbed long before you had a chance to seal everything up; and if he was suggesting that they live permanently shut up in an airless room, well, that didn't sound very healthy, either.

'To minimize cuts from flying glass,' Mr Balentine went on, 'stick brown-paper strips across your window panes, and remember to keep a pack of cards handy, to while away the time until the all-clear.'

At the end of his discourse Mr Balentine asked for any questions, but Ruby chickened out. He might not do the talk again if she pointed out the all-too-obvious flaws in the plan.

'Would you be willing to let us use this room one more time, Mrs Searle?'

The meeting had ended and Mr Balentine was packing up his things.

'We shall be using the cottage next door to the police station from the week after next. I'm being allowed in to create a mock-up of what's required, and then we can actually have everything in place for the demonstration.'

Just once more, Ruby thought to herself. 'Of course,' she said.

'I didn't see your husband this time,' he remarked, as he paid the invoice and she showed him to the door. 'I hope he is well.'

Ruby lowered her eyes. 'I'm afraid I'm a widow now, Mr Balentine.'

He looked genuinely embarrassed. 'Oh, Mrs Searle,' he said, 'how clumsy of me. I am so sorry.'

'That's quite all right,' she said pleasantly. 'You weren't to know.'

He gave her a sympathetic smile and tipped his hat. Ruby closed the door behind him and watched him go down the path, through the small window at the side of the door. As he turned to close the gate, she ducked out of sight. He was a nice man. Considerate.

Imogen was shopping in Worthing. She had bought herself a new frock at Smith & Strange and treated herself to some new shoes from Watts'. She had parked the car at the end of Warwick Street and was hurrying back. Her husband was coming home tonight. The big court case in London was finally over and he could return to normal life in Worthing.

When she spotted the woman coming towards her, her heart missed a beat. She had never been formally introduced, but she recognized Ruby's neighbour straight away. Something rose up inside her. Ruby still hadn't challenged this kidnapper – and Michael was nearly a month old, for goodness' sake. She'd had plenty of time to go through Jim's papers again, and yet this woman was still keeping some other woman's child as a hostage. It wasn't right.

Imogen didn't know exactly when she decided to take matters into her own hands. It was a spur-of-the-moment thing, but totally irresistible. As Lena went by, Imogen called her name.

'Marlene . . .'

Lena stopped walking and turned round.

Imogen held her breath and, stepping into the porch of Whibley's, pretended to study the contents of the jeweller's shop window. In actual fact she was using the reflection in the window to see what Lena was doing on the other side of the road.

After a couple of minutes spent scouring the crowd for a familiar face, Lena began to walk hesitantly on.

'Yoo-hoo,' Imogen called again. 'Marlene Amberley.'

Lena spun round with a look of sheer terror on her face, but could see no one she recognized. Imogen glowed with smug pleasure. With one small call, she had proved that Lena was indeed the infamous child-napper, Marlene Amberley. Just wait until Ruby heard this. Or should she go to the police herself?

By now, Lena was running – running down the road and looking behind her in panic. Imogen walked briskly to her car. She had only gone a few steps when she heard the squeal of brakes and a loud bang. When she looked back, a car had stopped in the middle of the street and people were running towards it.

Back in her own car, Imogen pulled out and headed

towards the commotion. As she crawled by, she could see that a young woman had been knocked over by a car. She appeared to be badly injured; at least she wasn't moving, and someone had covered her with his coat. Imogen's blood ran cold as she recognized her. It was Lena.

CHAPTER 30

Whoever was ringing the doorbell was most persistent. Ruby had been settling Michael down after his feed and hurried downstairs as quickly as she could. The doorbell was still going. If whoever it was didn't stop, she'd have Michael crying for hours. She pulled the door open and a man she'd never seen before stood on the step. He was in his thirties, with light-coloured hair and a moustache. He wore a dark coat, which was open, and she could see a smart suit underneath. It was raining hard and his bare head was already wet, although where he now stood in the porchway he was protected from the weather.

'Mrs Searle?'

'Yes.'

'I'm Ambrose Hayward, Imogen's husband.'

For a second she was thrown. Until he said his name, she had it in mind that he was someone looking for lodgings for the night. Despite the awful weather, she would have had to refuse him. She couldn't invite a lone man into her house, now that she was on her own.

Not only would it put her reputation at risk, but it wasn't safe.

'Oh,' she said, and then as a second thought rushed through her head, she put her hand to her throat. 'Imogen, is she all right?'

'Yes,' he said, 'and no. Look, I know it's late, but may we come in?'

It was only then that she saw that her friend was sitting in the car on the driveway.

'Yes, yes, of course.'

Ruby stepped back and left the door open while he went to open the passenger door of the car. When she saw Imogen's face, Ruby was alarmed. Something was clearly very wrong. Imogen's eyes were red and puffy and it was obvious that she was very upset.

'Oh, Ruby,' she said as she walked through the door, 'I've done a truly awful thing.'

Ruby made them both a warm drink while they took off their coats. Ensconced in the sitting room, they cupped their hands around mugs of cocoa.

'It's Lena,' Imogen blurted out. 'I saw her in the street.' Now that she had Ruby's full attention, she glanced anxiously at Ambrose.

'Immie has told me everything about your conversation concerning Lena's little girl,' he said simply.

'I know you told me to leave it,' said Imogen tearfully, 'but I just couldn't.'

'What did you do?' Ruby asked.

'I kept thinking about that poor little girl, without

358

her proper mother, and I knew I had to do something.' She covered her mouth with her handkerchief and looked helplessly at Ruby.

'So what did you do?' Ruby repeated.

'I didn't jump out on her or anything,' said Imogen. 'She walked right by me. I was in Whibley's doorway and she was on the other side of the road.' She put her handkerchief into her lap and began to wind it into a rope.

Ambrose put his hand over hers and gave her a smile of encouragement. 'Go on.'

'I didn't mean to frighten her,' she choked. 'I just wanted to know for sure that it was her.'

'And?' said Ruby.

'I shouted her name,' said Imogen. 'Well, not "Lena", but "Marlene Amberley". You know, as if I was a friend calling.'

Ruby felt slightly relieved. She had been dreading that Imogen was going to say something far worse. 'And what did she do?'

'She must have panicked,' she said. 'She ran away, but kept looking back. I suppose she was scared someone from her past was coming after her. She wasn't looking where she was going, and then . . . and then . . .' Imogen burst into tears.

'She got knocked down,' said Ruby, finishing the sentence for her.

Imogen and Ambrose looked at her in surprise. 'How did you know?'

'Eric told me, before the police took him to the

hospital,' said Ruby. 'The police – and Eric, for that matter – were under the impression that Lena may have tried to kill herself. Do you think she ran in front of the car deliberately?'

'I don't know,' said Imogen. 'I don't think so, but I didn't actually see it happen. I heard the squeal of brakes and the bang, that's all.' She unravelled the handkerchief and blew her nose noisily. 'She was only trying to get away. Is she . . . is she dead?'

Ruby shook her head. 'No, as far as I know, she's not dead.'

Imogen shook with relief and Ambrose pulled her into his arms. Ruby watched them, but her thoughts were elsewhere. She was annoyed with Imogen for interfering, but even crosser with herself that she had allowed having Michael, and getting him into a routine, stop her from dealing properly with this problem. She also felt a sense of relief for Eric. When he had turned up on the doorstep, his face was white with fear, and she could tell that next to the thought that he might have lost her, he dreaded being told that Lena had attempted to take her own life.

'I know I shouldn't have done it,' said Imogen, blowing into Ambrose's clean handkerchief, 'but I just wanted to make sure that little girl was safe.'

'Well, you can put your mind at rest now,' said Ruby. 'She's perfectly safe. As a matter of fact, she's upstairs fast asleep in my bed.'

Ruby could see relief written all over Imogen's face.

'Immie tells me that you have some newspaper cuttings appertaining to the case,' said Ambrose.

Ruby nodded. 'My late husband kept them in a box,' she said. 'I know he saw Eric on the day he died, but I have no idea why.'

'Is it possible that I could take a look?'

She remembered that Imogen had said he was a solicitor. 'Of course.' She stood up to find the cuttings, which she had transferred from the gramophone-record box to a small cardboard folder.

Ambrose worked his way through the cut-out slips of paper with a practised eye. Ruby had got as far as putting them in order and, when he reached the final clipping – a 'Stop Press' notice from the *Bournemouth Daily Echo*, she said, 'When I saw that, although I still don't know the full story, I stopped worrying about Jean.'

'What is it?' Imogen asked.

Ambrose handed it to his wife.

Stop Press

Police have called off their search for missing toddler Christine West. A spokesman said last night, 'Investigations have shown that there is no case to answer.'

*   *   *

Eric walked a little unsteadily into the pub. It had been an appalling shock to see Lena lying there in a hospital bed. They said she'd have to have an operation on her arm and would have to stay in for a week. He had almost keeled over when they said that. The nurse mistook his concern as worry about the cost, but it wasn't that at all. They belonged to the Worthing Hospital Contributors' Scheme at the chemist's and paid thruppence a week for emergencies such as this. The shock was that he could have lost Lena forever.

The landlord pulled his usual and, having dropped a few coins on the bar, Eric went to sit by the window. He wasn't in the mood for talking.

Left alone to his own thoughts, he didn't hear the men come in. He only became aware of them when he heard raised voices.

'You can search the whole bloody pub,' the landlord was shouting. 'I'm an honest man. If that thing was in my takings, it's because some blighter passed it to me.'

Eric looked up. The landlord was holding a five-pound note in the air. He shifted in his seat uncomfortably.

'I can see it's a forgery now,' said the landlord, giving it back to one of the men, 'but you don't expect me to do this every time I get a note, do you? I'll be here all ruddy night!'

'Have you any idea who gave it to you?' asked one of the men at the bar. He was dressed in a smart suit and carried a briefcase.

'No, I haven't,' snapped the landlord, 'and I tell you now, if I ever catch him I'll wring his bloody neck.'

As silent as a mouse, Eric slipped out of the door.

Ruby went to see Lena the next day, having left Jean and Michael in the care of her mother. Jean was making bubble pictures at the kitchen table and Michael was asleep in the porchway, in his pram. The weather was nippy but not cold, and he was well wrapped up. With the pram hood up and the pram itself facing the house, he was warm and snug. The district nurse was pleased with his progress. He had gained weight and, at almost a month old, he was alert and trying to focus his eyes. Jean seemed unperturbed that her mother wasn't around. She enjoyed being at Ruby's place and, so long as she had something to do, she was no trouble.

The hospital had acquired a new front entrance, which had only just been officially opened. Ruby waited outside the ward doors until a nurse opened them, bang on the dot of three, and then all the visitors went in.

Lena was at the far end of the ward. She was sitting up, with her pillows arranged on the backrest of the bed. Her face was bruised and the skin was broken in several places. It was a range of colours: blue bruises going green, and red wounds splattered with yellow iodine to ward off infection. Her arm was encased in plaster of Paris and was held in a sling. She had her eyes closed, but they sprang open as soon as Ruby said her name.

There was a chair beside the bed. Ruby pulled it out and sat down. She had brought oranges and a banana. Apologizing, she explained that she would have brought grapes, but there were none in the shops.

'How are you?'

Lena smiled wanly. 'Not too bad.'

'You gave us all a bit of a scare,' said Ruby. 'I heard what happened.'

'I should have been looking where I was going,' said Lena.

'You were looking for the person who called your name, weren't you?' said Ruby. She was anxious to get this all out in the open. The time for pretence was over.

Lena looked away.

Ruby placed her hand over Lena's. 'Now don't get upset,' she went on, 'but I know all about you and Eric.'

Lena turned and gave her a startled and fearful look.

'It's all right, Lena,' said Ruby. 'You have nothing to worry about.'

'Eric didn't mean to get angry with Jim,' said Lena. 'He was perfectly all right when Eric left.'

Ruby frowned. 'What? I don't understand.' She wasn't expecting any of this. She had meant to say that she knew about Jean.

'The newspaper cuttings,' said Lena. 'Eric told me not to worry. He said he thought Jim was a reasonable man, and he'd go back and see him. Only then Jim did what he did, so he couldn't. My Eric does have a bit of a temper, but he'd never hurt a fly.'

Ruby thought it strange that Lena was talking as if the cuttings were still an issue. Surely, if Eric had seen the last one, he would realize that whatever secret they were hiding, he wasn't in any trouble. Not with the police anyway. She opened her bag and took out the final cutting. When she handed it to Lena, Ruby was surprised by her reaction. As she read the words, the

364

paper flapped as if it were in a force-nine gale and Lena wept silently.

'Didn't Eric tell you about this?' Ruby asked.

Lena shook her head. 'He didn't know. If he had, he would have told me.'

'I'm sure Jim would have shown him.'

'He might have wanted to, but Eric didn't stay long,' said Lena. 'He lost his temper and left.'

'Look,' said Ruby. They were talking in whispers now. 'I know it's none of my business, but can't you tell me what this is all about?'

'They stole my baby from me,' said Lena.

'Who?'

'Mr and Mrs West. I didn't take her. The boot was on the other foot. They took my baby from me.'

'Five minutes,' said the nurse, walking down the centre of the ward. 'Visiting time ends in five minutes.'

Ruby was speechless. 'So Jean really is your child?'

Lena nodded. 'Look, there's not enough time to tell you all about it now, but I will tell you. I promise.' She held the cutting up. 'Can you do me one more favour. Can you give this to Eric for me? He needs to know.'

'Where is Eric?' asked Ruby.

Lena's face paled. 'Isn't he with Jean?'

'I've got Jean,' said Ruby. 'Eric brought her round on his way to come and see you. He was with the police.'

Lena looked shocked. 'They arrested him?'

'No,' said Ruby. 'Not as far as I know. They brought him here to see you. He said he was going to come right back for Jean, but I haven't seen him since.'

The nurse walked down the centre of the ward with a large hand bell and rang it loudly.

Ruby stood up. 'Have you any idea where Eric might be?'

Lena shook her head.

'Why would he run away?'

'He's scared he'll end up back in prison.'

'Prison?' gasped Ruby. 'Why?'

The nurse touched her arm. 'Visiting time is over now,' she said brusquely. 'Come back tomorrow.'

Ruby gathered her things and gave Lena a kiss on her cheek. 'Try not to worry,' she said, but as she walked down the ward, she knew they were both worried sick.

There was a real draught in this room. Even though the window was closed, the curtain moved. Ruby was sitting in the room that Jim called his office. This was the first time she'd spent any length of time in it.

Curious about the draught, Ruby pulled the curtain back. To her great surprise, she found Jim's Contax camera mounted on a bracket on the wall. It wasn't a very good job, so Ruby guessed Jim must have done it himself. The camera had a wire fixed to the shutter button, which hung down level with the chair. Jim had placed it on the wall so that the lens of the camera was facing the street. He must have been taking pictures of people coming or going from the house. But why?

When she took it down, a blast of cold air came into the room, so for now she stuffed the holes up with screwed-up newspaper, but she would have to get a builder in to do the job properly.

She examined the camera. It normally took twelve pictures. There were five frames left on the film. She would get them developed in the morning. Who could be on it?

CHAPTER 31

Bea and Rex were glued to the radio. Their maid hovered in the doorway and the rest of the family sat around, listening hard. On September 30th, 1938, at Heston Aerodrome on the borders of Heston and Cranford in Middlesex, a Lockheed 14 aircraft, number G-AFGN, had just touched down after a flight from Munich airport. According to Richard Dimbleby, an up-and-coming BBC reporter, the pilot was Victor Flowerday, who had now gained entry into the hall of fame because one of his passengers was none other than the British Prime Minister, Neville Chamberlain. The whole country had been on tenterhooks as Chamberlain, worried by the massive build-up of German fortifications in the Rhineland and by Hitler's declared intention for expansion in Europe, had made no fewer than three trips to Germany in two weeks, in the interests of peace.

The family knew what was coming. It had been on the radio all day, but hearing it said by the man himself made this a momentous occasion, and one not to be missed. Percy and Rachel had motored over from Shoreham, picking up Ruby and the two children on the way. Jean was still staying with Ruby, because Lena had picked up a serious infection after her accident and, although she was gradually improving, she was still in hospital. The two older children were playing in May's bedroom, while Michael lay on the mat in front of the fire having a good kick with his legs. Having enjoyed a lovely meal, the adults gathered around the radio. This was a moment of history and they all knew it.

Richard Dimbleby described the occasion so well that they felt as if they were witnessing it with their own eyes. As the plane touched down, they could almost see the crowds pushing good-naturedly through the police cordon, and the flags hanging from every house surrounding the airport. The weather wasn't good. It had been raining, but as Neville Chamberlain appeared at the door of the aircraft, men took off their hats and waved them as everybody cheered.

As soon as he stepped down, the Prime Minister was given a letter from the King. There was no time to read it. The crowd, and indeed everyone in the country, held their collective breaths to hear his voice.

'The settlement of the Czechoslovakian problem . . . has now been achieved,' Chamberlain said. 'This morning I had another talk with the German Chancellor, Herr Hitler, and here is the paper which bears his name upon it as well as mine.' Richard Dimbleby told his listeners that Chamberlain was waving the white sheet of paper above his head, as everyone cheered. 'We regard the agreement signed last night,' the Prime Minister went on, 'as symbolic of the desire of our two peoples never to go to war with one another again . . . My good friends, for the second time in our history, a British Prime Minister has returned from Germany bringing peace with honour. I believe it is peace for our time.'

Somewhere in the distance someone called, 'Three cheers for Neville', and the crowd roared its response.

The family listened for a while longer, but the excitement had already worn off. Everyone was so relieved. The preparations for, and the prospect of, war had rested heavily on everyone's shoulders, although for the sake of one another they had each kept that particular burden to themselves. The only person unconvinced by events was Rachel. There might be peace between the British and German peoples, but the rest of Europe was still in turmoil.

'Is this an end to the APR women's section?' Ruby asked. 'I was looking forward to my driving lessons.'

'You can still have them, darling,' said Bea, 'and no, I don't think the Women's Voluntary Service will end. The evacuation has only been postponed, for now. As for everything else, we're being told to carry on regardless.'

'So it's not lasting peace,' said Percy.

Rex took a cigarette from the box on the table in front of him. 'It's peace for now,' he said sagely.

Jean came into the room asking if she could have a sweetie. Ruby shook her head. 'Not now, sweetheart. Sweeties are on Saturday. Remember?'

The child pouted a little and went back upstairs to play again. The adults gave each other a knowing smile.

'What's happened to her father?' Rex asked. 'Did he ever turn up?'

Ruby shook her head. 'Afraid not.'

'What is the man up to?' said Rex. 'Do you think he had anything to do with the girl falling in front of the car?'

'I should hardly think so,' said Ruby. 'He adores her.'

'Then how come he's deserted both his wife and his daughter?' Rex said drily.

Ruby couldn't answer that one.

A couple of days later Imogen came over to see Ruby. After the accident, Ambrose had taken her to Paris for a relaxing holiday and now she was back. The two women were pleased to see each other again and Ruby enjoyed hearing about her trip. Imogen told her about the second-hand booksellers on the banks of the River Seine.

'They are called *les bouquinistes*,' said Imogen. 'Apparently there have been booksellers there since the sixteenth century.'

Ruby rolled her tongue around the French word for booksellers. '*Les bouquinistes*.'

Imogen went on to describe Javel la Croix, a bar in Montmartre, the artists' quarter, where she and Ambrose would dine before heading off to a jazz nightclub, and it stirred Ruby's long-held desire to travel. Funny how life gets in the way, she thought.

'Is there anything you'd like me to help you with?' Imogen asked.

Ruby had never got round to going through the last of Jim's papers. In fact, since he'd died, she didn't like spending time in the room he called his office. Other members of the family offered to go through everything for her, but she wanted to do it herself – when she was ready. The trouble was, she could never bring herself to start.

'Why don't we do it together?' Imogen asked, when Ruby explained. 'We'll take it at your own pace and, if it gets too much, we'll leave it for another day.'

Ruby nodded gratefully. It was an ideal moment. Michael was having an afternoon nap and, knowing that Imogen was coming, Bea had offered to take Jean to see her mother in hospital.

Jim had been a tidy man. His desk wasn't clear, but each pile of papers was neat and in order. It was only as they started sorting through them that Ruby realized they were in a muddle. It was as if someone had gone through them and put them back in the wrong order. They found a few crossword-puzzle templates, and a little black book containing some half-finished ideas and clues. Distracted for a moment or two, Ruby could see at once how he did the crosswords. A template for *Good Health* magazine already had the answers written in pencil; just before he died, Jim had been working out the clues. There was a well-thumbed dictionary on the desk beside it. The answer for six down was 'prune' – a dried plum, Ruby thought, but then discovered that Jim had chosen 'a regular breakfast food' as his clue. She thought for a minute and realized that he was keeping in step with the ethos of the magazine, which promoted good exercise and a healthy diet. Prunes were an essential food to the reader of *Good Health* magazine. She smiled to herself. No wonder he had been so successful.

Imogen had found an old tin marked 'Humbugs'. 'What's this?'

She shook it, but it didn't rattle. Instead she heard a shuffling sound. Inside they found some grainy photographs. Ruby could see at once that they weren't up to Jim's standard, but she was sure they had been taken by him on the Contax camera. Was he trying his hand at photography again? And why on earth had he kept these pictures? He hated keeping anything that wasn't of good quality.

'Do we keep these?' Imogen asked, her hand hovering over the wastepaper basket.

Ruby examined them more closely. There was a man and a woman walking away from the house. They had their backs to the camera. 'I know them,' she said quietly, but for some reason she couldn't place the names. She instantly recognized Franz and Albrecht sitting on the garden wall, and there was a second one of them in which they seemed to be talking to someone in a car.

'What's that, in Franz's hand?' she asked.

Imogen leaned over her shoulder. 'A package or something.'

'Is he giving it to the passenger, or is the passenger giving it to him?' said Ruby.

Imogen stared harder. 'Taking,' said Imogen, and at

373

the same time Ruby said, 'Giving.' They both laughed. 'Better keep them,' said Ruby.

As she went through Jim's stuff, other memories began to flood in. The shepherd's pie wouldn't go away, no matter how many times she told herself Imogen was right. Imogen was convinced that Jim, for once in his life, was being considerate by putting it in the meat safe before he put his head in the oven, but Ruby still found that hard to believe. She kept a tidy kitchen, and anything not in its rightful place stuck out like a sore thumb. So who put the iron on the wheelchair?

Imogen began looking at the bookcase. It was almost empty, although there were piles of books stacked against the wall. 'Do you want to keep all of Jim's books?'

Ruby nodded. Imogen began filling the spaces on the shelves.

Ruby's mind wandered to Eric and Lena. She was puzzled that Eric hadn't come back. If Jim had shown him the newspaper cuttings, Eric would have known there was no case to answer. Ruby still didn't know the full story, but Lena had promised to tell her when she got home. Eric had no reason to run away unless . . . Her blood ran cold. Could he really have had something to do with Jim's death? She took a deep breath. Don't be silly, she told herself crossly. Why would Eric harm Jim? Hadn't he risked his life to rescue him from a gas-filled kitchen?

'Are you all right?' Imogen asked gently. She'd seen

374

Ruby shiver and was concerned. 'We can stop now, if you like?'

'I'm fine,' said Ruby. She had already gone through Jim's record box of papers some time ago, but now she looked in his desk. It wasn't really a desk, just a table with drawers underneath. There was nothing of any significance in either, but something that had been trapped at the back of the table and against the wall had fallen to the floor. Ruby gasped as she opened it.

'What is it?' Imogen asked.

Jim had saved nearly £130 in a Post Office Savings book. Not only that, but there was a five-pound note and three postal orders waiting to be cashed, at the back of the book.

'Oh, Ruby!' cried Imogen. 'That will make such a difference for you.'

Tears sprang into Ruby's eyes. Yes, indeed it would. Perhaps her most pressing problem since Jim had died had been her lack of income. As a widow with a small child, she would have been eligible for a pension from the government, but that was forfeited because Jim had taken his own life. She was, however, eligible for five shillings a week to raise her son. It would be a joke, if it wasn't so serious. But she was lucky. She had a small savings account, and she knew she could rely on help from her parents and Percy. Other people had a much harder struggle. She had often wondered how an old person managed on a pound a week, especially if they had to find seven to nine shillings' rent out of that sum of money. She lowered herself onto the chair.

'I think it's time for a break,' said Imogen. 'I'll make us some coffee.'

Alone again, Ruby considered her options. She'd already decided she couldn't carry on with the guest house. With a newborn baby to care for, there wasn't the time to give her guests the level of care she wanted to, and she felt far too vulnerable when a lone man knocked on her door and asked for lodgings. Even if she put locks on her private rooms, there was an element of risk that she wasn't prepared to ignore.

Hiring the downstairs rooms for meetings brought in a small amount, but by the time she had supplied tea and cake, there wasn't a lot of profit in that. She could take in a lady lodger, but she wasn't very keen on the idea. She valued the little bit of freedom she had between guests, but if she took a permanent lodger, she would forfeit that freedom for good. She'd be tied to the house twenty-four hours a day. Besides, supposing she and the lady lodger didn't get on? It might lead to some unpleasantness.

She turned the Post Office book over in her hands. She had no idea what her husband was saving for, but he had inadvertently handed her a lifeline. If she used it wisely, the money might last almost a year, and that would give her sufficient time to work out what she was going to do in the future.

Imogen appeared with two cups of Camp coffee and put them on the table. 'Had enough?' she asked.

Ruby shook her head. 'No, we'll carry on for a bit. I'd like to get it cleared up if I can.' She sipped the welcome coffee. 'Thanks for helping me with this. It's so much easier with someone else around.'

'Don't mention it.' Imogen smiled. She gazed into her cup. 'How is Lena, by the way?'

'She's coming home tomorrow,' said Ruby.

'So she's all right?' There was no mistaking the relief in Imogen's voice.

'Her arm is mended,' said Ruby, 'but it will be a little while longer before she's up to scratch. It takes time to build up your strength, after something like that.'

Imogen nodded miserably. 'I still feel dreadful about it.'

Ruby reached over and squeezed her arm. 'Well, don't,' she murmured. 'These things happen.'

'Has her husband come back yet?'

Ruby shook her head.

'Then how will she manage with the little girl?'

'I shall have Jean with me,' said Ruby. 'We'll keep popping next door so that Lena can spend time with her.'

'I could get her a nurse,' said Imogen.

'There's no need for that,' said Ruby, 'but . . .' Another thought came to mind. 'Could you perhaps pay for a daily woman? I haven't been able to do much in the house, what with the baby and looking after Jean, as well as my own house. It needs a thorough going-over in there.'

'Consider it done,' Imogen smiled.

Ruby was just about to put the Post Office book into

her handbag when she noticed there was a name and telephone number on the back.

'I know this name,' she said, pointing it out to Imogen. It was Sir Hubert Temple, the man who had rung up on the day Jim died.

'He's a government minister, isn't he?' said Imogen. 'Something to do with the Foreign Office.'

Ruby explained about the telephone call. 'I only remember him because he sounded so posh,' said Ruby, 'but why did he want to speak to Jim?'

Imogen shrugged.

'Well,' said Ruby, reaching for the telephone, 'there's only one way to find out.'

Eric looked out over the field and shivered with the cold. He hadn't thought for one minute that it would all end up like this. He had legged it all the way out of Worthing, keeping close to the hedges and occasionally jumping down into a ditch if a car went by. He dared not thumb a lift in case the driver asked too many questions. He didn't know the lie of the land, but he reckoned he was about eight miles out of Worthing. Today he'd passed a sign for a village called Patching and had headed towards another called Findon, but he had no real idea where he was. All he knew was that he had to keep out of the way, for Lena's and Jean's sake. What was he going to do? He'd already spent two nights in this barn in the middle of nowhere. He should have got right away, but he couldn't do it. Nobody must see him, but he couldn't bear being too far from his family.

He stank to high heaven. He could smell his own body odour. He needed a proper wash and some clean clothes, but he had no money. He'd spent the last of it on a pie yesterday. His stomach rumbled. He hadn't eaten since then and there was little prospect of food today – not unless he pinched something, but he'd never nicked anything in his life. No matter what they said, he wasn't a thief.

When he had seen the landlord holding up the five-pound note, he knew it was his. It was the note his employer had given him as a bonus. Trust his bloomin' luck. The one time he thought he'd got a leg up, and that happened. He held his head in his hands and tried to think. A thought drifted through his mind. Did his employer know it was a forgery? Eric raised his head, then lowered it again. Na, the bloke was obviously very well off. Why would he want to pass off forged bank notes? Still, he told himself, it was no good brooding over it. What was done was done. He had to decide what to do now. He longed to see Lena. She was his world. She was the only reason he wanted to draw breath. Without her, he just couldn't live; but if he went back to Worthing, the next thing would be the coppers feeling his collar, and he couldn't go back to prison, he just couldn't. He was crying now. What sort of a man cries . . . ? But he couldn't help himself.

CHAPTER 32

Jean was very excited. She had spent a large part of the morning making pictures for her mother. Ruby had done her hair up with ribbons and she was wearing a new dress. She looked lovely. The colour, an attractive crushed raspberry, suited her perfectly. When Bea's car drew up outside the house, Jean could hardly contain herself. Having made sure that Lena was comfortable, Ruby gave them some time alone.

Bea sat in Lena's kitchen, cuddling her grandson, while Ruby put the finishing touches to a meat-and-potato pie and an apple crumble.

'This should do Lena and Jean for a couple of days,' she said as she put them in the oven. As she cleared away the dirty things, Ruby told her mother about Jim's Post Office book.

'A hundred and thirty pounds!' Bea exclaimed. 'Where on earth would he get a sum of money like that?'

'I'm guessing it was from his magazines,' said Ruby.

'Good heavens,' said Bea. 'I had no idea you could earn as much as that.'

'They don't pay a huge amount,' said Ruby, 'but Jim

worked very hard. I'm only just beginning to realize just how hard. He had built up quite a reputation.'

'Why didn't he tell you?'

Ruby shrugged.

'Married couples shouldn't have secrets,' said Bea.

'No, Mother,' said Ruby, giving her a knowing look. Bea had kept the biggest secret of all from Nelson, for most of her married life. Her mother had the grace to look embarrassed when she saw Ruby looking at her, and turned her head away. 'I wanted to ask you a favour,' Ruby went on. 'Can you look after Michael for me next Tuesday? I have an appointment over in Rustington.'

'Who do you know in Rustington?' Bea wanted to know.

'Actually, I've never met him,' said Ruby. 'It's somebody Jim knew.'

'Did you tell him you have a small baby?' said Bea. 'Can't he come to you?'

'If you can't do it, Mother, just say so,' said Ruby irritably.

'I can do it,' said Bea, 'and I'd enjoy it. I'm just a bit concerned about you going over to Rustington to meet a complete stranger.'

'I shan't be on my own,' said Ruby. 'Imogen is coming with me.'

Michael was becoming fractious. Ruby finished wiping down the draining board and dried her hands, before holding her arms out for her son. As Bea gave him to her, he was frantically chewing his fists. He always seemed to be hungry these days. Was he getting enough from the breast? Should she think about giving him a bottle? He wagged his head eagerly until he found her nipple and latched on, and straight away she was listening to his loud swallows and contented gurgles as he gulped her milk. She fondled his arms and legs. They were well filled out and he'd put on quite a lot of weight. Perhaps she was giving him enough, after all. Nevertheless, she would talk it over with the district nurse the next time she came.

'What's happening with the WVS?' Ruby asked Bea. 'Now that we have peace, are they going to disband it?'

Bea shook her head. 'It's only been a month since Chamberlain came back with his piece of paper, but the smiles are already fading. Rex says the flow of refugees has become a flood.'

'Before the Prime Minister came back home, Dad told me if Czechoslovakia went, Poland would be next,' Ruby remarked. At the time it had sounded rather fanciful, but she wasn't so sure now.

'In all honesty,' said Bea, 'I don't think Hitler will take a blind bit of notice of any agreements.'

'Rachel feels the same way,' said Ruby.

'Rachel has good reason to,' said Bea.

Ruby lifted Michael from her breast and sat him up to rub his back. A few seconds later he obliged her with a loud burp. 'Good boy.'

'Do you need any help with Lena and Jean?' Bea asked.

'I'll take Jean back to mine after tea,' said Ruby. 'She

can have her wash and sleep with us for a few nights – just until Lena feels she can cope.'

Bea nodded. 'Where's that husband of hers?'

Ruby shrugged. 'Your guess is as good as mine.'

Later that evening Lena made her way slowly to Ruby's house. She wanted to kiss Jean goodnight before she went to bed. Jean, smelling sweetly of Knight's Castile soap and some of Michael's Cuticura talc, was delighted to see her mother. She wrapped her arms around her mother's neck. 'Goodnight, Mummy.'

'Goodnight, darling,' said Lena. 'See you in the morning.'

Jean hesitated by the stair. 'Will you be here when I wake up?'

'Yes, of course I will,' said Lena.

'Where's Daddy?'

Lena glanced at Ruby, who looked away. 'Daddy had to go away for a bit,' said Lena. 'I'm sure he'll be back soon.'

When Ruby came back downstairs, Lena was still sitting in the kitchen. 'Oh, Ruby, what am I going to do about Eric?'

'I don't know,' admitted Ruby. 'Now, are you going to tell me what all this is about? Why was he afraid of going to prison?'

'It's a long story,' said Lena.

'And I've nothing better to do,' said Ruby.

They curled up in Ruby's sitting room, each with a mug of cocoa.

383

'Eric and I were at school together,' said Lena. 'I think I loved him from the moment I set eyes on him.' Her face took on a dreamy expression. 'He's two years older than me. We just wanted to be together.'

'But your parents had a problem with that,' said Ruby.

'Not my parents,' said Lena. 'They died young. I was brought up by my aunt. She never had children of her own and, quite honestly, I think she only took me in out of a sense of duty.' Lena sipped her drink, her eyes fixed on Ruby over the rim of the mug. 'Looking back,' she went on, 'the only love I ever got was from Eric.'

'I could always tell you loved each other very much,' said Ruby.

'I was fifteen when I got pregnant,' said Lena. 'My aunt was livid, of course, but Eric and I planned to marry when I was sixteen.'

'But she wouldn't give you permission,' Ruby prompted.

'Worse than that,' said Lena. 'She sent me away to have Jean, then she and Mrs West came to an arrangement. A private adoption.' Her hand was trembling slightly. 'Of course I refused to sign,' said Lena, 'but they took Jean away from me anyway.'

'Could they do that?'

Lena shrugged. 'All I know is that they did.'

'Couldn't Eric help?'

'My aunt accused him of stealing something,' said Lena. 'My Eric never stole a thing in his life, but who was going to believe the word of a boy who'd got a

384

nice girl into trouble, over the word of a well-respected and wealthy woman? No one, so he ended up in prison.'

Ruby leaned forward. 'Oh, Lena, I'm so sorry.'

'I managed to find out where Jean had been taken, but I had to bide my time,' said Lena. 'I had no way of looking after her – not with Eric gone. Then, as luck would have it, Mrs West was advertising for a nanny and I applied for the job.'

'Didn't she recognize you?'

'When Jean was taken from me, I never actually saw her,' said Lena. 'I don't think my aunt did, either. It was all very secretive.'

'But how could you be absolutely sure the baby was your Jean?'

'One of the girls from the baby-home was asked to carry Jean to the car,' said Lena. 'She knew the woman. She told me Mrs West used to come to the tennis club, where she did the teas. It wasn't hard to check.'

'So you got a job looking after your own baby,' said Ruby. 'Neat.'

'Except Mrs West thought I was getting too fond of her, so she was going to give me the sack,' said Lena. 'Then, joy of joys, my Eric came back.'

'And you snatched her,' said Ruby.

'What could I do?' Lena cried helplessly. 'She was *my* child.'

'Well, it seems that everyone agrees with you now,' said Ruby. 'A solicitor followed up the newspaper reports, and it seems the private adoption never actually went to court.'

'That's because I never signed any papers,' Lena said again.

'Ambrose explained to us that all legal adoptions must go through the courts,' said Ruby. 'They have to, ever since a special Act of Parliament came in in 1926. And apparently,' she went on, as she rubbed the tips of her thumb and fingers together, 'when they confronted your aunt, it turned out that Mrs West had paid her a large sum of money.'

'Paid her!' gasped Lena.

'I'm guessing this is why the whole thing is not being taken any further,' said Ruby. 'Mrs West has a clever lawyer. They would do anything to avoid a court case.'

'So we can keep Jean?' asked Lena breathlessly.

'Why not?' said Ruby. 'She is your daughter.'

Tears sprang into Lena's eyes. 'Oh, thank you, thank you.'

'It wasn't me,' said Ruby. 'It was Imogen. And you need to know that it was Imogen who spooked you in Warwick Street. She feels terrible about your accident. She didn't mean for it to happen, and it was her husband Ambrose who sorted everything out.'

'I don't know what to say,' said Lena.

'Perhaps you could find it in your heart to forgive her?' suggested Ruby. 'I know it's no excuse for what she did, but if she hadn't done it, none of this would have come to light.'

Lena nodded sagely. She left a little while later. Ruby stood at her door to make sure she got home safely. They waved each other goodnight, but as Ruby turned to go back into her own place, there was a movement out there in the darkness.

She hesitated. 'Eric? Is that you?' There was no answer, but Ruby had the distinct feeling that she was being watched. 'It's perfectly safe now, Eric,' she called. 'You can come back home now. Nothing is going to happen.' She waited a few more minutes before calling into the darkness, 'You're not in trouble.'

But the feeling that someone was there had gone.

On the day she went to meet Sir Hubert Temple, the chauffeur-driven car came for Ruby just after lunch. She and Imogen sat in the back, like a couple of VIPs, and spoke in whispers as they sped through the countryside towards Rustington. Ruby was nervous.

They pulled into the driveway of a very elegant house just across the road from the beach. It had been built in the new Art Deco style, with gently rounded corners and a single turret to the left. The long Crittall windows had elegant arches and, when they stepped inside, it gave the whole place a light and airy feel. The outside of the house was white, and the interiors carried on the same theme. A grand piano stood in the middle of the massive lounge and the furnishings were obviously expensive. On the way down, the chauffeur had told them that Marama belonged to an industrialist-turned-film-producer called Joseph Arthur Rank, but that Sir Hubert had hired it for the winter months. That would explain why the telephone operator had been unable to find his name as a subscriber.

Invited to sit down, Ruby and Imogen perched on each end of a long sofa. Presently a man in his fifties, thin rather than slim, with a bald head and small, round glasses, swept into the room. He held out his hand towards Imogen. 'Mrs Searle,' he gushed. 'Hubert Temple. I am so pleased to meet you at last.'

'I'm Mrs Hayward,' said Imogen, taking his hand. 'This is Mrs Searle.'

'Madam, my apologies,' said Sir Hubert, turning to Ruby and shaking her hand. 'Please, do sit down. It's really good of both of you to come. Mr Searle said you would be along, Mrs Searle, but I expected you some time ago. Still, it's of no consequence. You're here now. And how is Mr Searle? He said he wasn't too well when he telephoned. I trust he is feeling a little better?'

Ruby glanced at Imogen. 'My husband . . .' she began.

'Mr Searle died,' said Imogen bluntly.

Sir Hubert gave her a horrified stare. 'My dear Mrs Searle, I am so sorry. What must you think of me, but really I had no idea.'

Ruby shook her head and raised her hand slightly. The door opened again, and Ruby was surprised by a familiar face. 'Mr Balentine!' she exclaimed.

'You two have already met?' said Sir Hubert, looking at Mr Balentine.

'I first met Mr Balentine when he brought two German boys to my guest house,' said Ruby, smiling at him.

They shook hands. 'It's nice to see you again, Mrs Searle,' he said.

'Balentine, sadly, this lady's husband has passed away.'

'Mrs Searle told me the last time we met,' said Mr Balentine, searching Ruby's face. 'I am sorry, but it's good to see you looking so well under the circumstances.'

He guided her back to her seat and Ruby introduced Imogen as she sat back down again.

'Listen, Balentine,' said Sir Hubert, 'I have to make a few calls. Would you look after Mrs Searle and her friend while I'm gone?' He turned to leave. 'Fill her in.'

As he left, Mr Balentine sat in the easy chair opposite. Ruby was impressed by his appearance. He was dressed in a well-cut suit, complete with matching waistcoat. She thought back to the rather untidy man in a raincoat who had come to the guest house with Miss Bullock. They were two entirely different people.

'I'm sorry Sir Hubert was confused over your loss, Mrs Searle,' he said, clearly embarrassed. 'I did mention it, but the Minister has rather a lot on his mind at the moment.'

Ruby dismissed his apology with a wave of her hand.

Mr Balentine was holding a folder. He opened it and took out some papers.

'You seemed to be expecting me,' said Ruby, 'but I can't think why. Until a week ago, I'd never even heard of Sir Hubert. Well, I passed the telephone to my husband one time when he called, but that's it.'

'Sir Hubert and I work with MI5,' said Mr Balentine. 'The British Secret Service. Your husband – your late husband – contacted us about some photographs he had taken. He explained that he couldn't get about too well and that he would send you over with them.'

389

'I have them with me,' said Ruby. 'Sir Hubert asked me to bring them, when I telephoned him. I didn't even know they existed until last week.'

'Was Jim working for you, then?' asked Imogen.

'No,' said Mr Balentine. 'He was concerned about some suspicious activity in Worthing and it was eventually referred to us.'

'Franz and Albrecht?' said Ruby.

'We believe they were not all that they appeared to be,' said Mr Balentine.

'That's exactly what Jim and I thought,' cried Ruby. 'For starters, they were so beefy.' She glanced over at Imogen. 'They were supposed to be schoolboys, but they were more like men.' She frowned and, looking back at Mr Balentine, she said, 'But hang on a minute. You were the one who brought them to us.'

'We had been alerted by our London office.'

'So is Miss Bullock . . .'

'Miss Bullock is a council employee.' He smiled. 'Her opinions are her own, but don't go seeing spies and secret agents lurking in every corner, Mrs Searle.'

Ruby blushed. 'I'm sorry. I'm getting carried away.'

'But we have the Munich Agreement now,' said Imogen. 'Surely there's no need to worry that we might go to war with Germany.'

'That's perfectly possible,' said Mr Balentine, 'but we would be failing in our duty if we didn't keep an open mind.'

'How do you know we're not spies,' said Imogen.

'Oh, believe me, Mrs Hayward,' said Mr Balentine,

with a mischievous grin on his face, 'we have checked your credentials very carefully. Now about these pictures.'

Ruby took them from her bag and handed them to him. Mr Balentine studied them for a moment or two, then rang a bell and shortly afterwards a woman came into the room. He handed them to her. 'Get these blown up, Elsie,' he said languidly.

'Look here,' said Imogen as she left the room, 'what's all this about?'

'I can't tell you everything,' said Mr Balentine, 'but I can tell you this. We believe there is a plot to flood Britain with forged five-pound and ten-pound notes. We have already found several in the Worthing area, which is enough to make us believe there is a contact in the town who is already passing them on.'

'But surely that would be a matter for the police, rather than MI5,' said Ruby.

'Not if the source of the plot is German,' said Mr Balentine, 'and the aim is to destabilize the whole country.'

'In one of those photographs . . .' Ruby began.

'Franz is handing something to a passenger in a car,' Mr Balentine finished. 'Is that what you were going to say? The photographs are very small. However, if you would be so good as to hang on, Mrs Searle, when we've made the pictures a lot bigger, you might be able to recognize that person.'

'I'll try,' said Ruby. She wondered if she should tell them about the other pictures she'd found, but in that split second she decided not to. They would most likely confiscate them, without showing her, and she had more right to know what they were than they did.

It was the smell of him that made the desk sergeant look up. The man standing on the other side of the desk was filthy dirty, but it wasn't ground-in dirt, like that of a long-term tramp. He looked more like a man who had fallen on hard times. He looked cold. He looked hungry. The desk sergeant was tempted to wave him away; to tell him to 'Clear orf'. Cleaning the man up – and he'd have to, if he didn't want the cells stinking like a sewer – would take time. He'd have to go through the lost-property box to find something for him to wear, and he wasn't sure they'd have much at this time of year.

'What do you want, son?' The desk sergeant noticed for the first time that the man's face was streaked with tears.

'I want to confess,' the man began.

The desk sergeant sighed. He'd heard it all before. They'd confess to anything, just to get a warm bed for the night, but this was three-thirty in the afternoon. He pulled the report book towards him and picked up his pen. What was it going to be? Theft? A bit of ABH? Murder? The desk sergeant dipped his pen into the inkwell. 'So . . . what have you done?'

'Passed counterfeit money.'

'What's your name, son?'

The man gave him a helpless look. 'Will I go to prison for that?'

'If you're guilty,' said the desk sergeant. 'So, what's your name?'

The man let out a sigh. 'Eric Farmer.'

CHAPTER 33

'Haven't you given the game away by telling us all this?' said Imogen.

Mr Balentine laughed. 'I think you have been reading a little too much John Buchan or maybe watching too many Alfred Hitchcock films, Mrs Hayward. I was undercover for a while, but that part of the investigation is over.'

'So you never did work for the council,' said Ruby.

'Only for a few days,' Mr Balentine admitted. 'By the way, we would like both of you to keep all this under your hats for a while.'

'Me? Keep a secret?' Imogen teased.

'I hope you can,' said Mr Balentine drily.

When the photographs were ready, Ruby, Imogen and Mr Balentine were called into the dining area where Sir Hubert was waiting for them. He had everything spread out on the table. Now that they were 16 x 12 inches, even though the pictures themselves were degraded, Ruby picked out a few things she'd not noticed before.

'What do you see?' asked Mr Balentine.

Ruby bent over the photograph again. 'It's a man at

the wheel and a woman taking the package,' she said. 'The passenger is definitely *taking* the package, rather than giving it. The driver has his head towards the boys, but the contour of the door frame has hidden his face. However, he is wearing a large, distinctive wristwatch.'

'I would never have noticed all that,' Imogen cried.

'That nail looks manicured,' said Ruby, pointing to the hand draped along the edge of the passenger door.

'Some men have manicures,' Sir Hubert remarked.

'She's right,' said Imogen. 'No man, unless he was playing a musical instrument, would have nails shaped like that.'

Above their heads, Mr Balentine and Sir Hubert exchanged a glance.

'That's an unusual ring she's got,' Imogen said. 'I'm sure I've seen someone with that ring, but I can't think where.'

'It looks a bit like a snake,' said Mr Balentine.

'Hmm, a snake eating its own tail,' said Sir Hubert. 'I must say, you two are both very observant.'

'I owe that to my husband,' said Ruby, looking away in case she began welling up. 'He was an excellent photographer. He taught me to look all around the frame.' She stepped back. 'The driver has a ring exactly like the one the passenger is wearing.'

The two men studied the photograph using a magnifying glass. 'By golly, she's right, Balentine.'

'So what happens now?'

'Nothing you need concern yourself with, my dear,'

said Sir Hubert. 'You have done more than enough. We are very grateful to you both.'

'You will catch these people?' said Imogen.

'Absolutely,' replied Mr Balentine.

'There's something else I think you should know,' Ruby began. 'Franz and Albrecht weren't all that they seemed. I can speak German, and I heard them talking. Why would two schoolboys be interested in taking a picture of the gasworks?'

'Why indeed?' said Mr Balentine.

Ruby went on to tell them about the suspicions that both she and Jim had about the Germans, and how Jim made sure none of their pictures went home. 'He gave them some postcards of Worthing,' Ruby went on. 'They were very old. Taken before the new pier was built, after the gales in 1913.'

'Your Jim sounds like an enterprising fellow,' said Mr Balentine, smiling sympathetically.

Ruby's throat tightened and she blinked as her eyes smarted.

'Leave it with us,' Sir Hubert assured them. 'Don't worry your pretty little head about it. You really need to get on with the rest of your life, my dear.'

Ruby cleared her throat. 'I think you should know, Sir Hubert,' she interrupted, 'I don't believe for one minute that my husband committed suicide.' Her voice had become thick with emotion.

'I'm sure you don't, my dear,' said Sir Hubert, patting her arm, 'but sometimes we have to accept the unpalatable truth.'

Ruby felt a twinge of irritation. How dare he say that! He could at least do her the courtesy of listening to what she had to say. Instead of pussy-footing around, why didn't they arrest somebody? This mild-mannered way of doing things made even the possibility of the ruination of the British currency sound like some sort of parlour game. As they were ushered from the room, Ruby wondered if she should tell them what she had done.

'I'll send Marshall round with the car,' said Sir Hubert as they gathered in the hall. 'I must let you get back to your little boy. Thank you so much for coming.'

Ten minutes later they were back in the luxurious seat of his chauffeur-driven car. Ruby was galled to be dismissed like an empty-headed feather-brain. The glass partition between the front and back seat was closed, so they talked freely.

'Oh, that wretched man was so horribly condescending,' she spat.

'Sir Hubert?'

'Well, I didn't mean Mr Balentine.'

'He was rather dishy, wasn't he?' said Imogen.

'Who?'

Imogen chuckled. 'Don't try and tell me you weren't looking.'

Ruby had been looking, but she wasn't about to tell Imogen. She hadn't been a married woman, in the biblical sense, for three years, but she had only just been widowed. It wasn't the right time to be looking at men. Besides, after the years she'd just endured, she didn't want a romance. Love, as far as she was concerned, was too costly; too painful. She didn't want it walking back into her life – certainly not yet, maybe not ever.

She began to think about the Germans' package. Could it have contained forged notes? She'd never ever seen one in her life – or at least she didn't think she had – and then she remembered the five-pound note in Jim's Post Office book. It was in her bag. She opened it and got it out.

'What's that?' Imogen asked.

Ruby held it up to the light. 'It was Jim's,' she said. 'I'm wondering if I should have told them about it.'

'Is it real?' Imogen asked.

'I don't know,' said Ruby. 'I need to put it next to a real one.'

Imogen opened her bag and pulled out her purse. When she took out a five-pound note, they compared the two.

'They're different,' Imogen whispered.

'So most likely this is a forgery too,' Ruby nodded. 'But where did Jim get it from?'

'From the schoolboys?'

'It's possible,' said Ruby, 'but why not do something about it then? Why wait all this time?' She frowned crossly. 'I bet Sir Hubert does nothing about it. Patronizing old goat.'

'Shh,' Imogen cautioned, and they both stared at the back of the driver's neck, but he showed no reaction. He seemed to be concentrating on the road ahead, and the glass partition between the front and back seat meant that he hadn't heard them. 'Anyway, what can he do?'

'Challenge them,' said Ruby. 'Make these people who want to wreck the country come out into the open.'

'Easier said than done,' said Imogen.

'Well, I've already done it,' said Ruby, looking rather smug.

'How?'

'I've written a letter to the *Surrey and Sussex Recorder*,' said Ruby. 'They're printing the picture of Jim receiving first prize for his article this week, so I told them my husband may be dead, but I shall champion his causes. From now on, I'm offering to be the voice of the people of Worthing.'

'But you don't know that the people Sir Hubert was talking about will even see the letter,' said Imogen. 'Why would they care about a small-time provincial paper and its readers, when they're aiming for world domination?'

Ruby was flummoxed. Put like that, Imogen was right. Had she allowed herself to get carried away on a wave of passion?

'Not only that,' said Imogen, 'but you do realize that you may have put yourself, and Michael, at risk?'

'How?'

'By giving out your details,' said Imogen. 'What if someone who disagrees with you comes knocking on your door?'

Ruby's face drained itself of colour. 'I'll ring them up

as soon as I get home,' she said. 'I'll ask them to withdraw the letter.'

Sir Hubert poured himself a whisky and soda. 'So what do you think of our Mrs Searle, Balentine?'

'I don't think she has any real idea of what's happening, but she's a bright woman, and right now she's probably putting two and two together.'

'I think you're right,' said Sir Hubert. 'Help yourself to a drink, and pour a sherry for Mrs Fosdyke while you're at it.'

The door opened and Freda Fosdyke came into the room. As she flopped into a chair, Balentine handed her a drink.

'Did she see you, Freda?'

Freda Fosdyke shook her head. 'Now that we've got the photographs, we can just about wrap this one up.'

'You've done an amazing job, Freda,' said Sir Hubert. Mrs Fosdyke had been gathering information on Nazi sympathizers for years, first as Head of House at Warnes Hotel and then as a trusted member of various clubs in the town. 'But,' Sir Hubert continued, 'we still have to get incontrovertible proof.'

Freda sighed. 'I shan't be sorry to see this lot behind bars.'

'We shall have to move you on, of course.'

'That's fine by me,' said Freda. 'It's uncomfortable spying on people I've known all my life, even if it is for the sake of public safety. They think I'm cold and aloof, but that's only because I have to be.'

'Well, we have something else in mind for you,' said Sir Hubert. 'And let me assure you, it won't go unnoticed, what you've already done for your country.'

'I should warn you,' said Freda, sipping her drink, 'don't underestimate Ruby Searle. It wouldn't surprise me if she took matters into her own hands. Once she senses something is wrong, she's like a terrier with a bone. She won't give up easily.'

Balentine smiled. 'What did I tell you, sir?'

Ruby dropped the telephone back onto the cradle. She felt sick. What an idiot she'd been. The secretary had been sympathetic. 'I'm sorry, Mrs Searle,' she said when Ruby explained, 'but there's no point in putting you through to the editor. The paper has already gone to print. We didn't put your name on the letter. It's just got "Name and address supplied" at the bottom. You needn't worry. No one will know it was you.'

Of course the people passing forged bank notes wouldn't know, and Imogen was right, they wouldn't care; but the people following Jim's old rants about Hitler, and the unfair treatment of migrants, might have their suspicions. To protect his identity, Jim had been deliberately vague in his letters. Ruby could see that now, but she had been angry when she wrote her letter. In the cold, hard light of day, she couldn't remember exactly what she'd said. Had she been vague enough? She was alone in the house, apart from Michael. Michael! What if she really had put him at risk? What a fool she'd been. What a stupid idiot.

After her phone call, Ruby went to her mother's place to fetch Michael. Apparently he had been as good as gold and had drunk her expressed breast milk from a bottle. The way he looked up at Bea as she chatted, Ruby could tell that the two of them already had a very strong bond. Bea handed her grandson back to his mother and he rewarded her with a wide toothless grin. Ruby sat cuddling him as she told Bea some of what had happened at Rustington.

'You still think Jim was killed?' said Bea.

'More than ever, Mum,' said Ruby. 'Why do away with yourself when you've just won a major prize, you have a column of your own in the paper and get paid for it, not to mention umpteen requests for crossword puzzles?'

'It could have something to do with the orphanage,' said Bea. 'You said he was upset about his parents.'

'I think he was coming to terms with that,' said Ruby. 'He'd been to see someone who worked in the orphanage office, and he was pretty sure he knew who his parents were.'

'Did he tell you who?'

Ruby shook her head. 'All I know is, he was writing letters.' She toyed with the idea of telling her mother about the letter she'd put in the paper, but thought better of it. Bea would only insist that she should stay at her place, and Ruby was anxious to be in her own home. So long as she kept Michael safe, everything would be fine.

Ruby stayed with her parents until around five o'clock, then walked back with Michael in his pram.

She was just pulling it over the threshold when Lena called over the fence, 'Eric's home.'

It was lovely seeing him again and Eric looked happy to be back with his family. The friends decided to share their evening meal together. Jean played with Michael, who was beginning to respond well. Ruby loved watching them together. Jean was so gentle and loving, and Michael had a real bond with her. He never stopped smiling when she was around and his eyes lit up when she came near.

'Ruby, I know people have said all sorts,' Eric began, 'but I want you to know that Jim was perfectly fine when I left him that day.'

'I believe you,' said Ruby, 'but I did hear that you two had a row.'

'We did,' Eric admitted. 'I'm not proud of it. He wanted to talk to me about Jean. I realize now that he wanted to tell me the police had decided not to pursue us any more, but I was so angry I didn't stop to hear that.' Putting his hand on his chest, he looked at Lena and said, 'I swear, on our baby's life, I never touched the man.'

'How did Jim seem to you?' Ruby asked. 'Was he depressed?'

'Far from it,' said Eric. 'When I went in, he said he was expecting someone. He was excited about it.'

'Did he say who it was?'

Eric shook his head. 'I never saw them. I was in the shed. I went in to punch a few flower pots and calm down.' He glanced at Lena again. 'It's the first time

I've lost my rag since I've been here. There was nobody around when I went back to work at a quarter to five.'

'I still don't understand why you cleared off,' said Ruby.

'I had a dud fiver and passed it on in the pub,' said Eric. 'I heard the landlord raising merry hell about it, and I knew it wouldn't be long before he worked out that it was me what gave it to him.'

'You could have explained,' said Ruby, 'or gone to the police.'

'I was scared,' said Eric sheepishly. 'I didn't want to go back inside.'

'But he did give himself up in the end,' said Lena. 'Didn't you, love?'

Eric grasped her hand. 'Only because I hadn't eaten for three days and I stank to high heaven,' he admitted. 'I couldn't come back home. I didn't want to get you into trouble.'

'But he's given a statement to the police,' said Lena. 'It's all right. He won't be arrested.'

It was at this moment that Ruby remembered the other set of photographs she'd taken to the shop. She glanced up at the clock. The shops closed at six. It was ten to now. If she ran all the way, she might make it in time to get them today.

'Take my bike,' said Eric, when she explained about her puncture, 'or, better yet, I'll get them for you.'

When he got back, Ruby couldn't wait to see what was on the photographs. She was confident the pictures would bring her a little closer to knowing what secrets Jim had unearthed, and would maybe even lead her to his killer. But when she opened the envelope she was sorely disappointed. Every frame was blank.

CHAPTER 34

It was the sound of running feet that woke him up. He must have nodded off. How long had he been asleep? Balentine cursed himself and struggled to sit up. It was cramped in the car, especially with his long legs. He must have slept with his mouth wide open too. A film of dried saliva crusted his chin and there was a wet area on the lapel of his coat. He was frozen to the marrow. He yawned and scratched his tousled hair.

It was lighter than he expected it to be. He struggled to focus his eyes and looked at his watch. Two-thirty. It was nearly Christmas, but it seemed as light as a summer's night. He turned stiffly to see who had been running by. At the end of the road a shady figure was climbing into a parked car. He watched as the engine revved into life and the car sped away. As he turned back to look at the house, his heart almost stopped. A plume of smoke rose in the cold early-morning air and there were livid flames around the front door. Sod it! He'd come to guard her and keep watch but, while he'd slept, someone had crept up the path and set fire to the house.

He leapt from the car and ran up the path. Whoever that man was, he had put accelerant through the letter box. He could smell it from here. Paraffin!

He'd been inside her house only twice, and that was more than a year ago, but he could remember the layout as if it were yesterday: front door, hallway, stairs. If the flammable liquid had spread far enough, she would be cut off, with no way of escape. If enough smoke filled the staircase, she and her baby might sleep on and never wake up. The thought filled him with a sense of panic. He couldn't get anywhere near the door to bang on it or ring the bell. The whole door and its frame had been doused and were already engulfed.

'Mrs Searle,' he shouted at the closed bedroom window. 'Ruby! Ruby, wake up.'

He bent down and picked up a small handful of gravel from the pathway and threw it up at the glass. It made several crisp ringing sounds, but there was no response. Where did she sleep? The front room was usually considered the best, but then he remembered that this was a guest house. She would most likely keep the better rooms for her visitors. He shouted one last time, before racing around the side of the house to the back door. He banged it with all his might. 'Ruby! Ruby, wake up!'

Eric stirred in his sleep. He was dreaming that he was back in the cold barn, hungry and wet, miserable and smelling worse than a pig. As he emerged from his dream, the wind was banging the barn door and he could hear someone shouting. All at once he was awake and scrambling out of bed.

Lena rolled over and murmured sleepily, 'You all right?'

Eric snapped on the light, and the single bulb in the middle of the ceiling seemed to bring the sound of a man's voice with its dull orange glow. Lena sat up. Eric was pulling on his trousers and a jumper. Lena climbed out of bed and pulled the curtain aside.

'Call the police,' Eric shouted as he made a dash for the stairs. 'Somebody's trying to get into Ruby's place.' Jean had woken up, but Lena didn't go to her. Instead she followed her husband downstairs and, while he unbolted the back door, she reached for the telephone.

Eric opened the door and the cold night air rushed in. He went outside and she heard him say, 'What the hell are you doing?'

Still shouting Ruby's name, the man had put his shoulder to the back door. Eric vaulted the low wall and the acrid smell of burning reached his nostrils. Now he understood.

'Help me,' the man cried. 'I've got to break down this door. She'll be burned alive.'

Other neighbours had gathered in the street. Two men were running with a long ladder. Eric hesitated for a second, then shouted for Lena again. His wife's white face appeared at the back door. 'Get the fire brigade. Ruby's place is on fire.'

The man threw himself at the back door again, but it wouldn't budge.

Eric put up his hands. 'No need to do that, mate,' he said. 'She's safe.'

Balentine was just about to fling himself against the wood again when Eric grabbed his arm. 'She's not in there,' he said. 'She and the nipper are sleeping in our place.'

Balentine stared at him for a second and then, spotting Ruby's pale face at the upstairs window of the house next door, sank to the ground and wept with relief.

CHAPTER 35

The damage to Sea View was devastating. Ruby stood on the threshold and looked around. It wasn't safe to go inside. The fire had roared up the hallway, stairs and landing. Fortunately Jim had always taught her to close every door at night, so although the fire had burned through the doors upstairs, they had acted as a deterrent until the fire brigade used their hoses inside. Fire wasn't the only damage. The whole place was doused in foam, waterlogged and dripping. The acrid smoky smell was still strong, and the blistered and burnt brown paintwork looked awful. Ruby wanted to cry again. It was a dreadful sight. Her home had gone. How would she ever manage to afford to repair it? Judging by the gaping hole in the roof, it might even be better to demolish it altogether.

It was tempting to feel sorry for herself. After all, she had lost her husband, her home and her livelihood in just a few short months; but, apart from the sense of despair, she also felt profound gratitude. If she and Michael had been asleep upstairs, if Rivka had been there on her day off, if she had had guests staying there . . . Ruby closed her eyes. It didn't bear thinking about. With the stairs alight, how would they have escaped? There wasn't even the low roof of an extension, which could have saved them. She shuddered. Thank God. Thank God!

The decision to stay at Lena's place for the night had been a spur-of-the-moment thing. They had eaten a good meal and talked until late. Michael was settled and sleeping in the same room as Jean. The adults were tired.

'Stay the night,' Lena had said.

Ruby had shaken her head. 'I don't want to be any trouble.'

'It's no trouble at all,' Lena had insisted. 'There's a bed already made up in the room next to Jean's. You'll be right next door to Michael. If you get him up now, you'll only disturb Jean. Stay the night.'

Those three words of invitation had saved their lives.

Her father came up behind her now. 'Looks a bit of a mess.'

Ruby nodded dully.

'Did you have insurance?'

She nodded again. 'But I'm not sure it will cover the cost of all this.'

Rex slipped his arm around her waist. 'You'll always have a home with your mother and me.'

She leaned against his shoulder. 'Thanks, Dad.'

Bea was coming up the path with May. 'Lena said you were here.' Mother and daughter hugged each other.

'Oh, darling, I'm so glad you're both safe.' Her voice was thick with emotion.

Ruby felt tears pricking her eyes. Letting her mother go, she hugged her sister. Moments like this were precious. If she had been in the house when the fire started, she might never have seen them again.

May wriggled to free herself. Ruby was holding her too tightly. 'I drew you a picture,' she said. Ruby thanked her rather absent-mindedly and, after glancing at it, slipped it into her coat pocket.

'Who would do such a thing?' said Bea.

'It was a good job he used paraffin rather than petrol,' said Rex.

'Why's that?' asked Ruby.

'Petrol would have gone up like a rocket,' said Rex. 'Paraffin burns more slowly. That's why the fire brigade had to put foam on it, to smother the flames.'

'Any chance of getting your clothes?' asked Bea.

'Even if we could get into the bedrooms,' said Rex, 'they wouldn't be much good. Everything is smoke-damaged.'

Ruby sighed. So she and Michael only had the clothes on their backs – and, she suddenly remembered, £130 in Jim's Post Office book, which by good fortune she had kept in her handbag along with the house keys.

The police asked a lot of questions, but Ruby had few answers. Remembering what Mr Balentine had said at Marama, she was reluctant to put forward any suggestions. Besides, she had no idea who would have wished

her any harm. Her letter to the paper had been so
heavily edited that it posed no threat at all:

> *My husband loved to champion people's causes.
> Although he is gone, it is my wish to continue
> what he started. I invite you to write to the Editor
> of this paper with anything that concerns you.*

It wasn't what she had actually written, and it was
hardly enough to warrant attempted murder, so who
had a grievance against her – and why?

In the end the police settled on the idea that it was
some disgruntled person who had objected to her
helping German refugees. Ruby didn't say anything, but
the idea seemed a bit far-fetched after all this time.

Mr Balentine tracked her down at her mother's and
came to see her in the late afternoon. 'I see they've
boarded up the house,' he said, after offering his sincere
commiserations.

Ruby nodded. Her mother, having shown him into
the sitting room, brought them a tray of tea and closed
the door quietly on the way out. Michael was in the
kitchen on a rug, playing with his toys. He could roll
now and, once he was on his tummy, he'd kick his legs
like a seasoned swimmer.

'You look rather pale,' Mr Balentine remarked as her
mother left. Ruby looked up in surprise. 'If you don't
mind me saying so,' he added quickly, as he lowered
his concerned gaze.

She gave him just the hint of a smile. It was kind of

413

him to show concern. 'No, I don't mind,' she said softly. 'And I have every reason to be grateful to you, for trying to save my life.'

'I didn't do a very good job,' he said apologetically. 'I had no idea you were with your next-door neighbour, although I am profoundly grateful that was the case. I set myself up as your protector, and then I nodded off in the car. It was only when I heard the arsonist running by that I woke up.'

She handed him a cup and saucer. 'You saw him?'

'Not exactly,' he said. 'I saw a running man, and then I saw the flames.'

'What did he look like – this running man?'

Mr Balentine shrugged slightly. 'I don't remember much.' He frowned thoughtfully. 'He wasn't a young man.'

'Why do you say that?'

'The way he was running, I suppose. He had a car with the engine running, waiting for him at the corner of Boundary Road.'

'So there were two of them,' said Ruby. She sipped her tea. 'There's something I need to tell you – something I should have mentioned when I was at Marama . . .'

He looked her straight in the eye. 'That you have a forged five-pound note in your handbag?'

Ruby's mouth gaped. 'How did you know?'

'On the way home the chauffeur heard you talking to your friend in the back of the car.'

'But the glass partition was closed,' Ruby said, with a puzzled expression.

'There's an intercom button in the back,' Mr Balentine explained, 'in case Sir Hubert wants to give the driver new instructions. One of you must have pushed it accidentally.'

Ruby's face coloured. 'So he heard every word we said?'

'Afraid so,' Mr Balentine grinned. 'Can I see the note? Do you still have it?' She rose to fetch it. When she returned to the sitting room, he was standing next to the mantelpiece. She handed him the note. 'Umm, definitely the same batch.'

Ruby returned to her seat. 'Is that why you thought I needed your protection?'

'Something like that,' he said, smiling. He drew a breath. 'Mrs Searle, who drew this picture?'

Ruby glanced up at the drawing May had given her outside the burnt-out shell that had once been her home. She had hardly looked at it at the time, but had given it pride of place on the mantelpiece at the earliest opportunity. May's drawings were improving all the time, and her mother had mentioned more than once that her new school had an art department. The hope was that May's talent would be nurtured and encouraged. The picture she had drawn for Ruby was a favourite theme: a princess (or bride) with a fabulous dress, standing next to her prince. They posed under a hoop of flowers (or heart shapes, or stars). At one side a pageboy held a ring-cushion, and a beautifully executed monkey sat on a cat's back on the other side. She was already beginning to understand perspective and the art of shading. Her figures had expressions and the drawing itself was quite adult.

'My sister,' said Ruby, in answer to Mr Balentine's question. 'She's very fond of drawing.'

Mr Balentine held her gaze. 'Look closely, Mrs Searle. What do you see?'

Ruby held the paper and studied the picture a bit more closely. It took several seconds, but then she caught her breath. 'Oh my goodness!' she whispered. 'She's drawn the snake ring.'

They were disturbed by the sound of a loud, anxious voice, and then Rivka burst into the room. She was obviously very distressed. 'I thought you were dead,' she blurted out. 'I thought you were dead.' She threw herself into Ruby's arms and sobbed.

Ruby was immediately seized by a sense of awful guilt. She had quite forgotten that today was Rivka's day off. As usual, Rivka would have caught the bus from Sompting as she always did. She would have come along the seafront and turned into Heene Road, eagerly expecting everything to be as normal, only to be met by a scene of utter devastation. Ruby could only imagine what was going on in her head. If losing her own family wasn't enough, and then being violated, Rivka had been such a wonderful friend and support when Jim died; at first sight of the house, it must have looked as if the one person whom Rivka had loved and trusted had been consumed by a terrible fire. What with one thing and another, Ruby had completely forgotten to telephone her.

'I'm so sorry,' was all she could say, 'I should have told you we were all right. I am so sorry.'

It took several minutes for Rivka to calm herself. Bea came in with some smelling salts, and Rex poured her a brandy. Rivka trembled on the sofa and clung to Ruby, who stroked her hair and spoke soothingly in her ear.

'How did you get out?' Rivka asked.

Ruby glanced at Mr Balentine, who had removed himself to the far side of the room and was staring out of the window at the garden. Ruby gave her a brief account. Rivka stood and went over to him with her hand extended. 'Thank you for helping my friend.'

Mr Balentine gave Ruby an embarrassed look, but nodded and shook Rivka's hand.

'Rivka, my dear, you must come and see the baby,' said Bea, drawing her from the room. 'He's on the floor in the kitchen, having a little stretch. My maid is keeping an eye on him, but she has to make the beds. Perhaps you wouldn't mind . . .' Bea's voice faded.

Ruby smiled. Good old Mum, the perfect diplomat. Alone again with Mr Balentine, she turned to him and whispered, 'What are we going to do about May?'

It had come as quite a shock to realize that May must have seen the man or woman who had taken the package from Franz and Albrecht. Ruby was quite sure her sister had never even met the German boys. May had never seen Jim's photographs of the incident, either; and, even if she had, the snake rings were not evident until the snapshots had been blown up to many times

417

their original size. So where and when had she seen the ring?

'I'd rather not draw too much attention to it,' said Mr Balentine. 'It's best not to frighten or alarm her.'

'I'm not sure my mother would want you to interrogate her,' said Ruby.

'Quite so,' said Mr Balentine, 'but if we can get her to say where she saw the ring . . .'

Ruby nodded and suggested that they join her mother in the kitchen. Bea stood at the kitchen table, cutting up vegetables for a stew. Michael gave Mr Balentine a gummy smile, but he was getting tired, so Ruby put him in his pram for a sleep. He'd probably manage half an hour or so and then he would want to be fed.

May came into the kitchen. 'Mummy, can I have a stamp?'

Bea put the finishing touches to a shopping list for the daily maid to take to Potter & Bailey's. With an extra mouth to feed, she needed to replenish her larder a little more often.

'Why do you want one?' asked Bea.

'I'm entering the Ovaltineys' competition,' said May. 'I've just drawn a picture and it needs to get to Uncle Monty by next Wednesday.'

'Allow me,' said Mr Balentine, taking a stamp from his wallet. Bea started to protest, but he waved his hand dismissively. 'You're very good at drawing, aren't you?' he said to May. 'I was admiring your picture in the sitting room.'

May blushed and thanked him for the stamp.

418

'Tell me,' said Mr Balentine. 'Where do you get your ideas from? It's very pretty.'

'I saw the princess in my drawing book,' said May. 'I've done it quite a few times, but I don't actually copy it.'

'And the monkey?' said Mr Balentine.

'Uncle Jim had a monkey,' said May, 'but it died. I used to draw it a lot. It's quite hard to do the fur so that it looks like fur.'

'I'm sure it is,' said Mr Balentine.

May was heading for the door.

'And the ring on the cushion?' said Mr Balentine. 'Where did you see that?'

'Oh,' said May, pulling open the door. 'Mr Rhodes has one of those. And Mrs Rhodes. She has one too.'

Ruby turned and looked at Mr Balentine. She put her hand to her throat as May left the room.

'What is it?' asked Bea. 'You've gone as white as a sheet.'

'Mum,' Ruby began, 'I can't tell you everything right now, but where does Mrs Rhodes live?'

'One of the Swiss Cottages in Park Crescent. Why?'

Ruby looked at Mr Balentine again.

'Where's your telephone?' he asked.

Ruby opened the kitchen door and indicated the hallway. He hurried to the receiver.

'Ruby,' said Bea crossly. 'What's going on? Why is he so interested in Effie?'

Ruby's eyes were swimming with tears. 'It's a long story, Mum,' she said.

'Tell me,' cried Bea.

'Her husband has been passing forged notes,' she said.

They could hear Mr Balentine on the telephone. 'Yes . . . Swiss Cottage, Park Crescent. Passing counterfeit money. Yes, that's right . . . Oh, and while you're there, take a look around for some paraffin containers. He may be linked to a fire as well – yes, attempted murder.'

Bea stared at her daughter helplessly. 'What's he saying?'

Ruby swallowed hard. She hadn't connected the two together, but now that Mr Balentine said it, it made sense. 'Jim photographed someone meeting Franz and Albrecht. Remember them? Well, apparently they were part of a plot to flood the country with counterfeit notes. Whoever took those notes wore a special ring. It was a snake, eating its own tail. May drew such a ring on her picture, and when we asked her who wore a ring like that . . .'

'She said it was Gus and Effie.'

Ruby nodded. 'I'm sorry, Mum.'

The back door squeaked shut.

'I can hardly believe it,' said her mother, 'and yet Effie can be a very nasty person. I haven't seen her for months.'

Mr Balentine came back. 'Sir Hubert has informed our people,' he said simply.

'May could have made a mistake,' Ruby cautioned. 'My sister has a very vivid imagination.'

'It's not very likely,' said Mr Balentine. 'She's a very bright child. Anyway, we'll soon find out.'

Michael stirred in his pram. Ruby turned round to tell Rivka that she could pick him up, but she wasn't there. 'Where's Rivka gone?'

Bea shrugged. 'She was here a minute ago.'

Ruby half-remembered something and drew in her breath. 'The ring,' she said. 'The night Rivka was attacked, the man damaged her ear with his ring.'

'What's that?' said Mr Balentine. 'What attack?'

'Surely she doesn't think it was Gus,' said Bea, her eyes wide with apprehension.

Ruby was pulling on her coat. 'Mum, that man ruined Rivka's life. After what he did to her, she can never have children. She told me once she wanted revenge.'

'Oh, Ruby, no . . .'

Mr Balentine looked from one to the other in frustration. 'Will someone please tell me what's happening?'

'The knife has gone,' said Bea.

'Knife? What knife?'

'The big meat knife. It was there on the table. I was just about to cut up some beef for a stew. It's gone.'

'Oh!' Ruby exclaimed and, turning to Mr Balentine, she said, 'Did you come in your car?'

'Yes, but . . .'

'Mum, look after Michael for me, please. I have to stop Rivka before she does something truly awful.' She glanced at Mr Balentine. 'For heaven's sake, come on! There's not a moment to lose.'

421

CHAPTER 36

They could easily have arrived at Effie's place at the same time as Rivka, except that Mr Balentine had parked his car outside Sea View and walked to Bea's house from there. Running back for the car was frustrating, but as they sped along Cowper Road, Ruby was sure they'd still be able to stop Rivka long before she arrived at Park Crescent. She was wrong.

To her horror, as they turned into the crescent, the gate to Swiss Cottage was wide open. Mr Balentine slewed to a halt and, although he took the keys from the ignition, neither of them stopped to close the car doors. At the windows of the beautiful terraced houses, several curtains twitched and curious eyes watched Ruby and Mr Balentine dash through the gate and up to the front door. Getting no answer, they ran around the back and found the door there open. As soon as they entered, they heard the sound of angry voices.

Rivka was in the hallway, holding Bea's kitchen knife out at arm's length in front of her. Mr Balentine pulled Ruby behind him and moved up cautiously behind her. Effie Rhodes stood on the stairs, clearly looking for an opportune moment to make a dash down the last six steps and grab the telephone. Gus had come out of his study. Absurdly, he still had his empty pipe between his teeth. Ruby guessed that, as Rivka came into the kitchen, the maid must have run into the hallway, screaming for her employer. When Gus came out of his study, coward that he was, he pulled the terrified maid between himself and the blade of the knife. Rivka was frustrated that she couldn't get close to him without harming his human shield.

'Let her go,' she was shouting.

The pipe fell from Gus's mouth. 'What do you want?'

'Who are you?' Effie demanded imperiously from the stairs. The hysterical maid screamed.

'You raped me,' said Rivka coldly. 'Now I kill you.'

'Don't be ridiculous,' Effie snapped. 'This is utter nonsense. I'm calling the police.' She came down two more steps, but Rivka swung the blade in her direction and Effie stopped. Mr Balentine inched forward.

'I never raped you,' said Gus contemptuously. 'I saw that look in your eye, you Jewish tart. You were gagging for it.'

'I was doing the washing up!' Rivka protested angrily. 'You violated my body. You ruined my life.'

Ruby decided that this was the moment to take matters into her own hands. The stand-off could last for some time and the whole situation was very volatile.

'Rivka,' she said softly, as she brushed passed Mr Balentine, 'this isn't the way. Don't do this. If you kill him, they'll hang you.'

Rivka half-turned to look at Ruby and, when she saw

Rivka's face, Ruby's heart went out to her. There was anger in her expression but, most of all, there was a look of hopelessness. Poor girl. If Ruby had lost everything, Rivka had lost even more.

'Rivka, give me the knife.'

As soon as she saw Ruby, Rivka relaxed a little. It looked as if she was about to hand her the knife, but then Effie shouted, 'Get this bloody slut out of my house.'

Rivka let out a howl of pent-up frustration and despair and made a lunge towards Gus. They heard Effie gasp as the hapless maid screamed again. Gus had pushed her towards the oncoming blade but, in the same split second, Mr Balentine reached out and snatched Rivka's arm from behind. The knife fell from her hand onto the parquet floor.

Outside they heard the bell of an approaching police car.

The maid, in floods of tears, ran from the hallway into the kitchen. Effie descended the stairs like some regal duchess, and Gus emerged cautiously from his study, where he had taken cover after pushing the maid into the line of fire.

Rivka was in Ruby's arms, sobbing her heart out. 'You should have let me kill him,' she said eventually. 'He deserves to die.'

'No, no, darling,' Ruby was saying. 'I know what he's done, but let the courts deal with him.'

Someone was banging on the front door, and the police arrived through the kitchen door.

'Nobody in this house is going to court,' said Effie haughtily. 'Except you, of course. Attempted murder carries a heavy prison sentence in this country.'

Ruby looked her straight in the eye. 'And you needn't stand there like some paragon of virtue,' she said coldly. 'You're not so lily-white yourself.'

Effie puffed out her chest. 'Well, really!' she exclaimed.

It was late evening by the time Mr Balentine arrived back at Bea's place. Ruby had been forced to return home fairly quickly after the police arrived at Park Crescent. Michael was due a feed, and she had to make her own way back on foot. Rivka had been arrested, and Mr Balentine informed Effie and Gus that they were to be interrogated about their role in the plan to flood the country with counterfeit bank notes and thus undermine the British government. They made a robust complaint, but nonetheless were taken into custody.

Back with her family, Ruby was left to try and make sense of it all. Having told her parents everything she knew, the afternoon had seemed endless. Bea phoned the police station several times, enquiring about Rivka's fate, but no one could – or would – talk to her. Rex went down in person at around four o'clock and, to Ruby's amazement and joy, arrived back home with Rivka. Pale and exhausted, she had been released without charge. Ruby and Bea put her to bed, and Rex gave her a strong sedative.

'Why didn't they charge her?' Ruby asked incredulously when she and her parents were back downstairs.

'My guess is that they had bigger fish to fry,' said Rex. 'Gus and Effie are in serious trouble.'

Mr Balentine turned up soon after Ruby had put Michael to bed.

He and Ruby sat in her mother's sitting room, he with a whisky and she with a sherry. 'So what happens now?' she asked.

'They're being taken to London for interview at ten o'clock tomorrow morning,' he said. 'One thing is for sure: they won't be coming back to Worthing for a long time.' He smiled. 'It looks as if my work is done.'

Ruby was surprised to realize she would be disappointed to see him go. There was something about him. He wasn't pushy, nor had he made any advances towards her. Why should he? She had only recently been widowed, and yet she felt a kind of connection with him, something she'd never felt with another man – not even Jim. When he was around she felt settled, content; and yet she knew, in her heart of hearts, that should he declare his affection for her, a passion of great magnitude would be unleashed. It was exciting and somehow terrifying at the same time. He had walked into her life when she least expected it, and now he was going to walk right out again.

'What about you?' he asked. 'Have you any idea about your future?'

She shook her head. 'My parents have offered me a home for the time being,' she said, 'but as for my future, your guess is as good as mine.'

'There's something I should like to ask you,' he began.

She looked up eagerly.

'The fact that you can speak fluent German has been a big plus in this case. It played no small part in flushing out these traitors.' He regarded her with a very serious expression. 'Would you consider using your talent for us?'

Ruby put her hand onto her chest. She felt a flutter of excitement and cautious fear. 'I am a widow and a mother,' she said quietly. 'My son needs at least one parent. I could never do anything to endanger my life. Does that sound cowardly?'

'No, not at all,' he said, shaking his head. 'With what I have in mind,' he went on, 'it wouldn't necessarily come to anything like that. I can't tell you more until after you have signed the Official Secrets Act, but might it interest you? You've already had a small taste of the things we'd like you to do.'

'Can I think about it?' said Ruby.

'Of course,' he smiled. 'Take your time.'

As he headed for his overcoat and the front door, he turned to her again. 'Putting aside my request,' he said softly, 'I wonder, on a more personal note, if you would consider having dinner with me one evening?'

'Oh, Mr Balentine,' she teased, 'you're surely not mixing business with pleasure, I hope.'

'Absolutely not,' he said with a very serious expression. For a second Ruby felt a stab of embarrassment, but then his eyes twinkled. 'The discussion we had in your mother's sitting room was business. Dinner would be purely pleasure.'

'In that case,' she smiled happily, 'it would be churlish of me to refuse.'

The morning post came early to this part of town. Ruby had only just picked up her father's post from the mat when there was a soft knock at the door. She opened it to find Eric standing in the porch. He handed her another envelope.

'The postman gave it to us,' he said apologetically. 'I said I'd bring it to you on my way to work.'

'Thanks, Eric,' she said, taking the envelope.

'You all right?' he asked cautiously.

'Fine.'

'Only Lena says if there's anything she can do . . .' He stared down at his feet.

'As soon as the insurance people come,' she said, 'I'll know more what to do.'

'She says to tell you she'll always put the kettle on any time you want to pop in.'

'Thanks, Eric,' said Ruby.

He smiled and reached for his bike. Ruby closed the door.

The letter was addressed to Jim. Even after all this time, it still made her heart lurch when she saw his name. She slid the paper knife from the hall table along the side of the envelope to open it. The letter inside was official-looking, but although it was beautifully typed, it had no logo or address for a reply:

Dear Mr Searle,

Mr Starling has told me that you are looking for your parents and that he foolishly suggested a name. I have to tell you that it is strictly against the policy of the Trustees to share such delicate information, and I am alarmed to discover that, despite my recent stipulation, you have attempted to make contact. I have to warn you that should the said parties make a formal complaint, there could be serious repercussions. I urge you, therefore, not to contact said persons or attempt to visit them.

Yours sincerely, H. Bloom

Ruby read the letter a second time and then let her breath out slowly.

Two identical police cars were already waiting outside Thurloe House in the High Street (known by the locals as 'the Gallows') when they arrived. Ruby wouldn't normally be in such a place, but Rivka wanted to make sure that Gus and Effie really were under arrest. She had come to terms with the fact that Gus wouldn't be charged with her rape. There was insufficient evidence, she'd been told, and it was her word against his; but she could at least see him in handcuffs.

They headed for the steps, only to be stopped by a policeman on the door. 'I'm afraid you can't go in for a minute, Miss,' he said politely. 'Important people are coming out shortly.'

'Could you tell Mr Balentine I have something

429

important to tell him, please? The name is Mrs Searle.'
He gave her an uncertain look. 'I'll wait here until you come back,' said Ruby, 'but it really is very important.'

A second or two later Mr Balentine came to the door and ushered them into the foyer. 'What's this all about?'

At the same moment she saw Gus and Effie coming along the corridor with their police escorts. Behind her, Rivka made a small noise.

'What's she doing here?' Gus demanded.

'It was you, wasn't it,' said Ruby. 'You killed Jim Searle.'

For a second there was a stunned silence, then Gus gave a contemptuous laugh. 'Whatever next, Mrs Searle? First you accuse me of rape, and now it's murder.'

'You came to see my husband about the counterfeit notes, didn't you?' she said, moving slightly towards him.

Mr Balentine put out an arm to stop her, but she batted him away. 'You knew he had one, because you gave the man who made your model train three of the notes,' Ruby went on. 'His wife gave one to my husband, so you came to demand it back. He wouldn't give it to you, so you killed him.'

'I didn't do it. It was Effie,' Gus whined. 'She did it.'

Effie tried to shake herself free from the policeman who held her arm. 'Be quiet, you fool,' she hissed. 'She's bluffing. She's got no proof.'

But Gus wasn't listening. 'She hit him over the head with the iron,' he said. 'He went down like a pack of cards.'

430

'Gus! Shut up, shut up!'

Balentine and the policeman looked at each other in stunned silence.

'So the pair of you put him in the gas oven,' said Ruby. She was trembling from head to toe, and was aware that Rivka had put her hand on her back to steady her. 'You killed him. You murdered my husband – and all because of a stupid forged five-pound note?'

Effie rounded on her. 'Serves him bloody well right,' she snarled. 'He should just have given us what we wanted, but oh no, he had to pontificate about honour and love and self-bloody-sacrifice . . . What would a useless cripple like that know about public duty? Well, we made him eat his own words, didn't we? How *dare* he preach to me!'

Ruby's mind darted back to the scene when Imogen and her mother were doing artificial respiration on the path. So that's why Jim had newspaper in his mouth. She could feel tears pricking the back of her eyes. She couldn't cry now. She swallowed hard and, looking at Effie, with her proud head tilted to one side and her jutting chin, she was filled with contempt. This woman was a monster.

'Come on,' said the policeman, tugging at Effie's arm.

'Get your hands off me,' she snapped. 'I'll have you know that I have important friends in high places.'

The man in charge of her ignored her. 'Time to go.' He cupped his hand over her elbow and they all headed for the door.

But Ruby wasn't finished yet.

'Just a minute,' she said, opening her handbag. Mr Balentine and another police officer lurched forward, but instead of producing the gun or the knife they expected, Ruby held up the letter. 'Jim probably didn't know you had anything to do with the bank notes when you came to the house,' she said. Effie turned to look at her. 'He did ask you to come, didn't he?'

'I told her not to bother going,' Gus protested, 'but of course she would have it her own way. We only meant to frighten him off.'

'Stupid idiot,' Effie glared. 'I knew his little game. Blackmail – that's what it was.'

'That's where you're wrong,' said Ruby. 'My husband was looking for his parents. That's what he was trying to tell you.'

'What's that got to do with us?' said Effie indignantly.

'You had a son,' said Ruby, 'and you kept him in an orphanage for the whole of his childhood.'

Effie turned her head sharply and glared at Gus. 'You kept it in the orphanage?'

'Couldn't do it, old thing,' he said meekly.

'You kept him there because you didn't want him getting in the way of your career,' said Ruby. Behind her, she heard Rivka draw in her breath.

Effie had a face like thunder. 'You were supposed to sort it out,' she growled at Gus. 'Get it adopted.'

'It?' cried Ruby. 'It? This is your child we're talking about.'

'I talked it over with old Stinky,' said Gus, hanging his head. 'Couldn't let him go, d'you see. He was my son.'

432

'Stinky?' said Ruby.

'Stinky Bloom,' said Gus. 'Howard Bloom, the headmaster. We went to school together. Of course, he was just one of the staff back then. I paid the fees directly to him.'

Ruby could hardly believe what she was hearing. 'How could you do that?'

Effie tapped her feet angrily. 'I don't see what it has to do with you, anyway.'

'He did well, old thing,' said Gus, trying to appease her. 'Became a photographer – according to Stinky, a prize-winning one at that.'

'That "useless cripple" you talked about was your boy,' said Ruby coldly.

Gus began to tremble. 'Jim Searle?'

Ruby nodded. 'I hope you can live with what you did, because now you both know that you killed your own son.'

Gus sank to the floor and began to weep. Effie stood defiantly with her head high. 'If you had done what I told you,' she snarled at her sobbing husband's back, 'none of this would have happened. All I wanted was to make a name for myself. Weak, that's what you are – weak.'

They hauled Gus to his feet and the pair of them were led away to the waiting cars.

Balentine touched Ruby's arm. 'Let me take you home.'

It was only then that Ruby realized she was crying.

CHAPTER 37

It seemed almost surreal. The day was warm and sunny. In the fields the harvest was ready to bring in. To the north of the town, cricket teams gathered on Broadwater Green and cricket-lovers settled in deckchairs or on rugs to enjoy a relaxing day. Being Sunday, Worthing itself was closed. The blue blinds in shop after shop were pulled right down over the windows to protect the goods inside from the bright sunlight. Strollers wandered along Marine Parade, determined to enjoy the last of the balmy days of summer. The Punch-and-Judy man set up his booth by the pier, and children frolicked at the water's edge. In the many churches of the town the faithful gathered to pray, while more athletic types were setting off on bicycle rides around the lanes and villages of Sussex. The few who had cars loaded up their boots and looked forward to a family joyride to Littlehampton or Bury Hill or Washington Woods. To all outward appearances, the only thought of every man, woman and child was to have a holiday from the pressures of the world; but in fact, that wasn't how it was. Everyone wanted to forget what was happening in the world. They wanted a normal day.

Ruby and her family had planned a trip to Shoreham Beach, where they would meet Percy, Rachel and Alma. The picnic hamper was almost ready. May was excitedly packing some tennis racquets and a couple of balls. Rex was loading up the car, and Bea was checking that everyone had everything they would need, like cardigans and sunhats, cream to ward off insect bites and cream to soothe them. As for Ruby, she was totally distracted as she scoured Heene Road looking for the first sight of Gregory Balentine's car.

They had been going out together ever since Gus and Effie were taken to London by MI5. Their relationship was very different from that which she had enjoyed with Jim, and nothing like the frantic romp she'd had with Bob Knight. This was slow-burning, but every bit as thrilling and wonderful as it should be. She hadn't yet slept with Gregory, but that wasn't for the want of it. Ruby knew that she already loved him with all her heart. He was kind and funny and he loved her son as well. As for Michael, he adored Gregory.

Ruby had thought long and hard about Gregory's proposal to join the Secret Service, but for the moment she held back. It wasn't so much because of fear of where they might send her, but she was concerned about her son. How could she leave Michael? She knew her mother would happily take care of him, but Ruby couldn't bear the thought of being parted from him, not yet.

The guest house had been repaired and Ruby had promised that she would take in some evacuees. As it turned out, the lion's share of the organization of that went to the WI rather than the WVS. Bea and Imogen had been disappointed, but not for long. The women's organizations put the men to shame, by working together as a team. Thus, on September 1st, 1939, lone children, siblings and sometimes mothers with their children poured into Worthing, but Sea View itself was requisitioned. Ruby had half-expected it to happen.

For several months the country had been moving inexorably towards war. Gas masks had already been issued, and Identity Cards and Ration Books were on their way. The government said it was still working for peace, but it was increasingly obvious that Hitler was only paying lip service to it. During the month of August he bombed Warsaw and Danzig, with the result that Neville Chamberlain issued an ultimatum.

Ruby looked up as a car came down Heene Road, with its horn blaring and Gregory Balentine at the wheel. He pulled up sharply and jumped out.

'You'll get us arrested, making all that racket on a Sunday,' she laughed.

He swept her into his arms and kissed her hungrily. 'Marry me,' he said as he let her go.

Ruby gave him a quizzical look. 'What's brought this on?'

'Marry me,' he said again.

Her father pulled down the sash window and called out, 'The Prime Minister is on the radio in a minute.'

Ruby gave him a wave, then turned back to Gregory's earnest face. 'It's bad, isn't it?'

He nodded. 'I can't bear to go through this without you, Ruby. Marry me.'

She reached up and touched his dear face. 'Will they send you away?'

'I don't know,' he said. 'Honestly, I don't. All I know is I want a bit of happiness before it's too late. I love you, Ruby. And I love Michael. I think I could make you both happy. Marry me, please.'

She stood on tiptoe and brushed his lips with a kiss. 'It's about flippin' time you asked me, Gregory Balentine,' she teased. 'Yes, I will.'

He enveloped her in his arms and swung her off her feet. They kissed eagerly and then walked into Bea's place, arm-in-arm.

Now, two days after the official evacuation had begun, Neville Chamberlain's dulcet tones filled the sitting room again as they walked in. Nobody looked up. They were all glued to the radio. Ruby gazed around at them fondly. Her mother, vibrant and healthy, a rock to them all; Rex, her father, kind and gentle, and still so very much in love with her mother; Rivka, a good friend who Ruby knew would move heaven and earth to help her any time she called. She seemed more relaxed, now that Gus and Effie had got their just deserts. Ruby sighed. They'd both been hanged by Albert Pierrepoint: Effie in Holloway and Gus in Pentonville. Jim could rest in peace now.

May sat at the table doing another life drawing as everyone listened to the radio. She probably had no real understanding of how life would change, from here on in. Ruby could only hope that she would have some sort of happy childhood, despite the events to come. And pulling himself up by her chair was Michael. She smiled as she watched him struggle to get upright, a rush of passion flooding through her chest. She loved Gregory so very much, but she knew that, if she had to, she would willingly die for her child. As she and Gregory walked into the room, her little son beamed from ear to ear and pushed himself back down to the floor. He could crawl at lightning speed now and wasted no time heading in their direction. Gregory reached down and picked him up. In his clumsy way, Michael tried to show his affection, first by slapping Gregory's face and then by trying to chew his nose. When he heard his mother's soft laugh, he turned his head and reached out his chubby arms to go to her.

Chamberlain was saying, 'I have to tell you now that no such undertaking has been received, and consequently this country is at war with Germany . . .'

Taking her baby in her arms, Ruby locked eyes with Gregory. So this was it. War. They would all have to fight for their very existence. She looked around the room again, her emotions surging. She loved these people. This was family. Her family. She knew then that whatever it took, like millions of others, she would fight tooth and nail to keep them safe in England's green and pleasant land.

Her eyes filled with tears as she glanced up at her new fiancé's face and smiled. He was right. They should snatch at every bit of happiness they could.

AUTHOR'S NOTE

For the purposes of the story, I have taken a slight
liberty. Mrs Rose Wilmot was the founder member of
the Worthing Townswomen's Guild when it began in
1933. She moved to Worthing in 1925 and, although her
contemporaries say she was a tiny woman (just five feet
two inches) and of a quiet disposition, she was at the
forefront of just about every organization in the town.
A member of the West Tarring Residents' Association,
a Friend of Fairfield House (a home for the elderly), a
governor of Worthing High School for Girls, president of
the West Sussex Battalion of the Girls' Life Brigade, an
active Guider and a member of the Education Committee
of Worthing Borough Council, she could apparently
remember the name of every young person in the town,
and even which youth club or school they attended.

When a youth centre was established near Durrington
High School in the early 1960s, they named it the Rose
Wilmot Centre. Renamed 'The Rosie' some thirty years
later, it still offers a range of activities for young people
aged twelve and over, although I wonder if today's youth
have any idea who Rose Wilmot was.

$\mathcal{A}$CKNOWLEDGEMENTS

I would like to thank the staff of Worthing Library for their invaluable help and for going the extra mile for me many times. I am also deeply indebted to Worthing's local historian Chris Hare, who first ignited my love of the town's history, as well as to my lovely editor Victoria Hughes-Williams and my agent Juliet Burton. The pages of this book wouldn't be room enough to thank the members of my family and the myriad of friends who have encouraged me over the years.